THE COURSE
OF HONOUR

Lindsey Davis has written over twenty historical novels, beginning with *The Course of Honour*. Her bestselling mystery series features laid-back First Century detective Marcus Didius Falco and his partner Helena Justina, plus friends, relations, pets and bitter enemy the Chief Spy.

After an English degree at Oxford University Lindsey joined the Civil Service, but became a professional author in 1989. Her books are translated into many languages and have been dramatized on BBC Radio 4. Her many prizes include the Premio Colosseo, awarded by the Mayor of Rome 'for enhancing the image of Rome', the Sherlock award for Falco as Best Comic Detective and the Crimewriters' Association Cartier Diamond Dagger for lifetime achievement. She was born in Birmingham but now lives in Greenwich, London.

THE COURSE OF HONOUR

LINDSEY DAVIS

arrow books

Reissued by Arrow Books 2013

1 3 5 7 9 10 8 6 4 2

First published in Great Britain in 1997 by Century

Arrow Books
Random House, 20 Vauxhall Bridge Road,
London SW1V 2SA

www.randomhouse.co.uk

Addresses for companies within The Random House Group Limited can be found at:
www.randomhouse.co.uk/offices.htm

The Random House Group Limited Reg. No. 954009

A CIP catalogue record for this book
is available from the British Library

ISBN 9780099515258

The Random House Group Limited supports The Forest Stewardship
Council® (FSC®), the leading international forest-certification organisation.
Our books carrying the FSC label are printed on FSC®-certified paper.
FSC is the only forest-certification scheme supported by the leading
environmental organisations, including Greenpeace. Our
paper procurement policy can be found at
www.randomhouse.co.uk/environment

MIX
Paper from
responsible sources
FSC® C016897

Typeset in Bembo by SX Composing DTP, Rayleigh, Essex
Printed and bound in Great Britain by Clays Ltd, St Ives plc

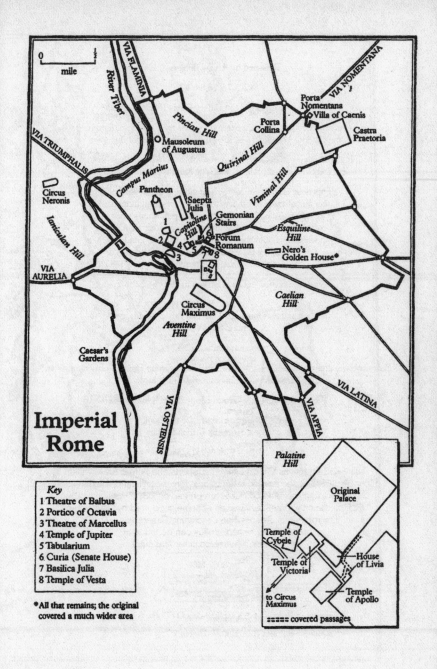

Imperial Rome

VIA FLAMINIA

VIA NOMENTANA

River Tiber

Pincian Hill

VIA TRIUMPHALIS

Porta Nomentana

○ Villa of Caenis

Porta Collina

Castra Praetoria

○ Mausoleum of Augustus

Quirinal Hill

Campus Martius

○ Circus Neronis

Pantheon

Saepta Julia

Viminal Hill

Janiculum Hill

Capitoline Hill

Gemonian Stairs

Esquiline Hill

1

Nero's Golden House ●

2

6

4

Forum Romanum

VIA AURELIA

3

5

7 8

Caelian Hill

Circus Maximus

Aventine Hill

Caesar's Gardens

VIA LATINA

VIA OSTIENSIS

VIA APPIA

Key
1 Theatre of Balbus
2 Portico of Octavia
3 Theatre of Marcellus
4 Temple of Jupiter
5 Tabularium
6 Curia (Senate House)
7 Basilica Julia
8 Temple of Vesta

● All that remains; the original
covered a much wider area

Palatine Hill

Original Palace

Temple of Cybele

Temple of Victoria

House of Livia

to Circus Maximus

Temple of Apollo

═════ covered passages

0   ½   mile

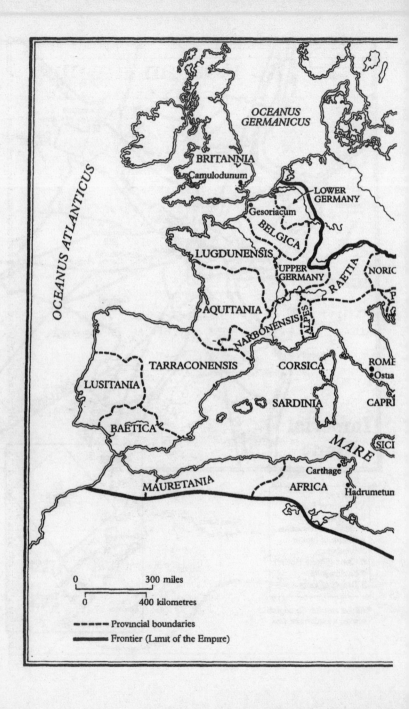

The Roman Empire AD41

PART ONE:
A BAD-TEMPERED SLAVEY

Commencing in the autumn of AD 31,
when the Caesar was Tiberius

I

Whatever was *that*?

The young man arrested his stride. He halted. At his shoulder his brother drew up equally amazed. An incongruous scent was beckoning them. They both sniffed the air.

Incredible! *That* was a pig's-meat sausage, vigorously frying.

Everywhere lay silent. The echoes of their own footfalls had whispered and died. No other sign of occupation disturbed the chill, tall, marble-veneered corridors of the staterooms on the Palatine Hill from which the Roman Empire was administered. Under the long-absent Emperor Tiberius these had never offered much of a homely welcome to strangers. Today was worse than ever. Arches that were meant to be guarded stood framed only by forbidding drapes whose heavy pleats had not been disturbed since they were first hung. No one else was here. Only that rich odour of hot meat and spices continued its ravishing assault.

The younger man set off walking faster. He wheeled around corners and brushed along passages as if he had just discovered the proper route to take until, after a fractional hesitation, he whipped open a small door. Before his brother caught up with him he ducked his head and strode through.

A furious female slave exploded, 'Skip over the Styx; you're not allowed in here!'

Her hair hung in a lank, sorry string. Her face was pasty, a sad contrast to the tinctured ladies at court. Yet despite her grubbiness, she wore her dull frieze dress with courageous style, and although he knew better he threw back at her drily, 'Thanks! *What an interesting girl!*'

Afterwards Caenis could never quite remember which festival it had been. The time of year was certain. Autumn.

Autumn, six years before Tiberius died. The year of the fall of Aelius Sejanus, the commander of the Praetorian Guard. Sejanus, who allegedly kept a pack of pet hounds he fed with human blood. Sejanus, who had ruled Rome with a grip of iron for nearly two decades and who wanted to be Emperor.

It could have been the great ten-day series of Games in honour of Augustus. The Augustales, which had been established as a memorial to Rome's first Emperor and were now conducted in honour of the whole Imperial House, would have been an occasion which explained why Antonia had given most of her slaves and freedmen a holiday, including her Chief Secretary, Diadumenus. Even more likely would have been the actual birthday of Augustus, by then a long-established celebration, a week before October began. Thinking of Augustus, the founder of the Empire, could well have stirred Antonia to what she was about to do.

Foolish, at any rate, for anyone to attempt business at the Palace on such a day. On any state holiday the priests of the imperial cult led the city in the duties of religion while senators, citizens, freedmen and even slaves, from the most privileged librarians to the glistening bathhouse stokers, seized their chance and piled into the temples too. Here on the Palatine the slop-carriers and step-sweepers, the polishers of silver cups and jewel-encrusted bowls, the accountants and secretaries, the chamberlains who vetted visitors, the major-domos who announced their names, the lifters of door curtains and carriers of cushions, had all disappeared hours ago. Sejanus would be lording it at the ceremonies; the Praetorians, who ought to be guarding the Emperor, would be guarding him. Caesar's palace complex, which even during Caesar's long absence from Rome thrummed with occupation every day and rustled with innumerable murmurs of life into the dead of night, for once lay hushed.

So the door flew open. Someone strode in. Caenis looked up. She scowled; the man frowned.

'Here's somebody – Sabinus!' he called back over his great shoulder, as he loomed in the low doorway. The fat spattered dangerously beneath the girl's spoon.

'Juno and Minerva –' coughed Caenis, as she was forced back from her pan while the flame lapped sideways across the charcoal brazier in a palely whickering sheet. 'We'll all go up in smoke; will you shut that door!'

A second man, presumably Sabinus, came in. This one wore a senator's broad purple stripe on his toga's edge. 'What have you found for us?'

The fat went wild again. 'Oh for the gods' sake!' Caenis swore at them, forgetting their rank as she was nearly set alight.

'A bad-tempered slavey with a pan of sausages.'

He had the sense at last to close the door.

They were lost. Caenis guessed it at once. Even the open spaces and temples among the homes of imperial family members above the Circus Maximus were deserted. The public offices on the Forum side of the Palatine were closed. Stupid to come today. With no guards to cross spears in their faces these two had blundered down a wrong passageway and ended up bemused. Only people who wanted to indulge in sad habits alone were lurking in corners with their furtive pursuits. Only eccentrics and deviants, misers and malcontents: and Caenis.

She was one of the group of girls who worked with Diadumenus, copying correspondence for the lady Antonia. Today he had ordered her to remain quietly out of trouble; later she must go to the House of Livia, where their mistress lived, and ask whether any work was required. Caenis was junior but capable; besides, Diadumenus had really not anticipated that anything significant would occur. In most respects Caenis was, like everyone else, on holiday.

Hence the sausage. She had been enjoying both her solitude – rare for a slave – and the food too. She had scraped together the price by writing letters for other people and picking up lost coins from corridor floors. She had crept in here, sliced the meat evenly and was cooking it in a pan intended for emulsifying face creams before she ate her treat deliberately, on her own. She craved her sausage with good reason: her starved frame needed the meat and fat, her deprived senses hankered after nuts, spices and the luxury of food fiercely hot from a pan. She hated being interrupted.

'Excuse me, sirs, you are not allowed in here.'

Warily she tried to camouflage her annoyance. In Rome it was wise to be diplomatic. That applied to everyone. Men who thought they possessed the Emperor's confidence today might be exiled or murdered tomorrow. Men who wanted to survive had to inveigle themselves into the clique surrounding Sejanus. Making friends had been unsafe for years, for the wrong association clung like onion juice under a chef's fingernails. Yet so many promising careers were ending in disaster that today's nobodies might just survive to ride in tomorrow's triumph beneath the laurels and ribbons of the golden Etruscan crown.

For a slavegirl it was always best to appear polite: 'Lords, if you are wanting Veronica –'

'Oh, do cheer up!' chaffed the first man abruptly. 'We might prefer you.'

Caenis gave her pan a rapid shimmy, agitating the spatula. She chortled derisively. 'Rich, I hope?' The two men glanced at one another, then with a similar slow regretful grin both shook their heads. 'No use to me then!'

She saw their veiled embarrassment: traditionalists with good family morals – in public, anyway. Veronica would shake them. Veronica was the one to astonish a stiff-necked senator. She believed that a slavegirl who was vivacious and pretty could do as well for herself as she pleased.

Caenis was too single-minded and intense; she would have to make a life for herself some other way.

'We seem to be lost,' explained the cautious man, Sabinus.

'Your footman let you down?' Caenis queried, nodding at his companion.

'My brother,' stated the senator; very straight, this senator.

'What's his name?'

'Vespasianus.'

'Why no broad stripes too?' she challenged the brother directly. 'Not old enough?' Entry to the Senate was at

6

twenty-five; he was probably not long past twenty.

'You sound like my mother: not clever!' he quipped.

Citizens never normally joked with slavegirls about their noble mothers; Caenis stared at him. He had a broad chest, heavy shoulders, a strong neck. A pleasant face, full'of character. His chin jutted up; his nose beaked down; his mouth compressed fiercely, though he seemed good-humoured. He had steady eyes. She looked away. As a slave, she preferred not to meet such a gaze.

'Not ready for it,' he added, glaring at his brother as if it were a matter of family argument.

Against her better judgement she replied, 'Or is the Senate not ready for you?' She had already noticed his obstinate roughness, a deliberate refusal to hide his country background and accent; she admired it, though plenty in Rome would call it coarse.

He sensed her interest. If he wanted it (and she reckoned he did), women probably liked him. Caenis resisted the urge.

'You have lost yourselves in Livia's pantry, sir,' she informed the other man, Sabinus.

There was a sudden stillness, which she secretly enjoyed. Though the cubbyhole looked like a perfumery, the two men would be wondering whether this was where the famous Empress had mixed up the poisons with which, allegedly, she removed those who stood in her way. Livia was dead now, but the rumours had acquired their own momentum and even grew worse.

The two men were nervously surveying the cosmetic jars. Some were empty, their contents evaporated years before; some had leaked so they sat embedded in a tarry pool. Others remained good: glass flasks of almond oil, soapstone boxes of fine wax and fat, amethystine flagons of pomade, stoppered phials of antimony and extract of seaweed, alabaster pots of red ochre, ash and chalk. No place for a cook; rather an apothecary. Veronica would give three fingers to discover this little cave of treasures.

There were other containers, which Caenis had considered but carefully left untouched upon the shelves. Some ingredients could have no possible benign use and had convinced her it was true that Livia must have been in league with the famous poisoner Lucusta. She would keep that to herself.

'And what are *you* doing here?' asked Sabinus, in fascination.

'Cataloguing the cosmetics, sir,' Caenis answered demurely, implying otherwise.

'For whom?' growled Vespasianus, with a glint that said he would like to know who had replaced Livia as dangerous.

'Antonia.'

He raised an eyebrow. Perhaps he was ambitious after all.

Her elderly mistress was the most admired woman in Rome. The first lesson Diadumenus had drummed into Caenis was that she must avoid speaking to men who might be trying to manoeuvre themselves into a connection with Antonia. Daughter of Mark Antony and Octavia; Augustus' niece and sister-in-law of Tiberius; mother of the renowned Germanicus; (mother too of the peculiar Claudius and the scandalous Livilla); grandmother of Caligula and Gemellus, who were to share the Empire one day . . . If a woman must be defined by her male relations, the lady Antonia had gathered some plums, even though Caenis privately found them a specked and mildewed crop. Afflicted with these famous men, Antonia was wise, courageous, and not quite worn out by the indignities she had seen. Even the Emperor took her seriously. Even her slavegirls might wield influence.

'I rarely see my mistress,' Caenis stated quietly, lest there be any misunderstanding. 'I live in the imperial complex here. Her house is too small.'

This was true, yet being appointed to work as a copyist for Antonia had been a magical opportunity.

Though born a slave, Caenis was no skivvy. She had been singled out as bright, then given an education in office skills: reading, writing, ciphers and shorthand, discretion, deportment, graceful conversation in a pleasant voice. She had first-class Latin, and better than average Greek. She understood arithmetic and cheerfully grappled with accounts. She could even think, though she kept that to herself, since she did not choose to embarrass other people by showing she was superior. Only her morose adolescence had prevented her being placed in one of the imperial bureaux before this. They did not allow you into a bureau until they were sure you could deal firmly with senators.

She moved the pan off the brazier and stood up straight to deal with these men now. She had been thoroughly trained. Caenis could melt into backgrounds yet radiate efficiency. She always sat well, to help her handwriting. She stood without slouching; she walked with confidence; she spoke up clearly: she knew how to show uninvited senators to the door with relentless charm.

Whether this applied to pantry doors remained to be seen.

'Antonia's cook?' Sabinus asked curiously as she moved the pan. Men had no idea.

'Antonia's secretary,' she boasted.

'Why the sausage, Antonia's secretary?' asked the brother, still regarding her with that long, frowning stare. 'Don't they feed you here?'

The way they were hanging around near her food seemed endearingly hopeful. Caenis grinned, though looking down at her pannikin. 'Oh the daily slave ration: nothing good, and never enough.'

Sabinus winced. 'Sounds like a middle-class lunch!'

She liked this senator more than she expected. He seemed honest and well-intentioned. She let herself exclaim, 'Well, everything's relative, lord! A rich knight is more cheerful than a poor senator. To be poor but middle class is still better than being a commoner who hardly has the right to pick his nose in the public street. A slave at the Imperial Palace leads a softer life than the free boatman who lives in a flooded shack on the Tiber's bank –' Since they did not pull her up, she went on rashly, 'The power of the Senate has become a delusion; Rome is ruled by the commander of the Praetorian Guard –'

She should never have said that aloud.

To distract them, she rushed on, 'As for me, I was born in a palace; I have warmth and music, easy work and opportunity to progress. Perhaps more freedom than a high-born

Roman girl with a garnet in each ear who lives penned in her father's house with nothing to do but be married off to some wealthy halfwit who spends all his time trying to escape her for intelligent conversation and unforced sexual favours – even perhaps if he's not an *absolute* halfwit, some genuine affection – with the likes of Veronica and me!'

She stopped, breathless. A political statement had escaped her; worse, she had betrayed something of herself: she shifted from foot to foot with unease.

The younger man's serious gaze was disturbing her. That was why she muttered, 'Oh do stop leering at my sausage! Want a piece?'

There was a shocked pause.

It was unthinkable.

'No; thank you!' said Sabinus hastily, trying to override his brother – no easy task.

Caenis was gruff but generous. Giving up the struggle for privacy, she offered the young knight a slice on the point of her knife; he nipped it off between his fingers at once.

'Mmm! This is good!' Laughing now, he watched her while he munched. His grim face lost all its trouble suddenly. She had assumed anyone in a decent white toga dined daily on peacocks aswim in double sauces, yet he ate with the appetite of any starving scullion she knew. Perhaps all their ready money went on laundry bills for togas. 'Give that fool a bit; he wants it really.'

Caenis eyed the senator. Once again she offered her knife; Sabinus gingerly lifted the food. His brother clapped his shoulder heavily so she caught the gleam of his gold equestrian ring. Then he admitted to Caenis, 'His footman, as you say! I clear a path in the street, chase off bailiffs and unattractive women, guard his clothes like a dog at the baths – and I see he gets enough to eat.'

She could not tell how much of this was a joke.

By now she found in his face the bright signal that he liked her. She knew the look; she had seen it in men who danced attendance on Veronica. Caenis shrank from it. She found life a burden already. The last thing she needed was fending off some overfriendly hopeful with a broad country accent and no money. 'Let me give you directions, lords.'

'We'll get the girl into trouble,' Sabinus warned.

For the first time his brother smiled at her. It was the tight, rueful smile of a man who understood constraints. She was too wise to smile back. Still chewing, he refused to move. Studying the floor, Caenis ate her own sausage from the knife point, slowly. It was decent pork forcemeat, flavoured with myrtle berries, peppercorns and pine nuts; she had tossed it on the heat in oil strewn with the good end of a leek.

Only two slices remained in the pan. The younger brother, Vespasian, reached for one, then stopped and reproached her kindly, 'You're letting us steal your dinner, lass.'

'Oh go on!' she urged him, suddenly shy and cross. It had been giving her pleasure to offer something other than a slavegirl's usual trade.

He looked serious. 'I shall repay the debt.'

'Perhaps!'

So they had eaten together, she and that big young man with the cheery chin. They ate, while the brother waited; then both licked their fingers and both rapturously sighed. They all laughed.

'Let me show you the way, lords,' Caenis murmured, newly subdued as the sunlight of a different world filtered into the bleakness of her own. She led them into the corridor; they walked either side of her while she basked in their presence as she took them towards the public rooms.

'Thanks,' they both said, in the off-hand way of their rank.

Without answer she spun swiftly on the ball of her loosely slippered foot. She walked away as she had been taught: head up, spine straight, movement unhurried and disciplined. The grime and desolation imposed by her birth became irrelevant; she ignored her grey condition and was herself. She sensed that they had halted, expecting her to look back from the corner; she was afraid to turn, in case she saw them laugh at her.

Neither did. The senator, Flavius Sabinus, accepted their

odd adventure quietly enough. As for his brother, he smiled faintly, but he did not mock.

He knew he should not attempt to see her again. Caenis had missed the significance, but he realised at once. It was like him; a swift assessment of the situation followed by his private decision long before any public act. He was due to leave Rome again, due to leave Italy in fact. But all through his long journey back to Thrace, and afterwards, Flavius Vespasianus still thought, *What an interesting girl!*

II

At dusk that same day, Caenis obeyed her instructions from Diadumenus, and went to check whether their mistress required her services. Washed and with her hair combed, she walked quietly, carrying a bound note tablet and her wooden stylus box.

The House of Livia lay adjacent to the Palace, convenient, yet still private when social distance was required. This was – in theory – the famous modest home which Augustus had ensured he kept. It had helped maintain the myth that despite the honours heaped upon him when he accepted the title of Emperor, he had remained an ordinary citizen: the first among equals, as a phrase wryly had it. In this house, it was said, his wife and daughter had worked at their looms to weave the Emperor's garments as Roman women were traditionally supposed to do for their male relatives. Perhaps sometimes, when other matters did not detain them, Livia and Julia really did devote themselves to weaving. Not often enough, in Julia's case. She had still found time to lead a life so debauched it earned her exile and infamy, then finally death by the sword.

Livia's House, for the past two years since the venerable Empress died Antonia's house alone, stood on the south-east corner of the Palatine Hill in an area where notable republicans had once owned houses. Augustus, who was born there, had bought out the other families and made this an exclusive domain of his own. His original private house had been demolished to make way for his great new Temple of Apollo in the Portico of the Danaids, so the Senate had presented him with a replacement next to the temple with magnificent rooms for entertaining. His wife, Livia, maintained her own modest (though exquisite) house behind the temple. So in effect they had the benefits of a private palace, while still pretending to live in a classically simple Roman home.

13

Antonia had lived here after she married Livia's popular and heroic son Drusus. When she was widowed at only twenty-seven, she elected to remain in her mother-in-law's house, keeping the room and the bed she had shared with her husband. By then the mother of three children herself, she had the right to avoid being placed in the charge of a guardian; living with Livia preserved her independence while avoiding scandal. It had also enabled her to refuse, for the rest of her life, to remarry. Rare among Roman women, Antonia made her independence permanent.

Livia's House was set against the side of the hill. Means had been provided for secluded access from the administrative palace complex via underground tunnels. Caenis automatically took the covered route. That way she was unlikely to run into the Praetorian Guards. Their job was to protect the Emperor, but with Tiberius away and their commander, Sejanus, usurping all authority, they had become unendurable. Luckily few were on duty today and none in the underground passages.

She passed the two side branches, then darted down the final stretch, feeling safe. Not even the Guards would normally interfere with Antonia's visitors. But if the mood took them, or if they had been drinking more than usual, they could still be dangerous to a slave. They were the arrogant élite, protected by the mere name of Sejanus, thugs who molested anyone they chose.

As for Sejanus, nobody could touch him. He had risen from the middle rank, a soldier whose ambition was notorious. A man of some charm, he had made himself the friend of the Emperor, who had few close associates otherwise. It was known, though never openly stated, that Sejanus had then become the lover of Livilla, Antonia's daughter, while she was married to the Emperor's son. It was even whispered that he and Livilla had conspired to murder her husband. Worse plots were almost certainly afoot. It was safest not to wonder what they were.

Shivering slightly, Caenis clanged the bell and waited for admittance, knowing the porter would probably be in holiday mood and slow to respond. Coming via the covered way had brought her to the back entrance near the garden, where the porter would be even lazier than at the main entrance near the Temple of Victory. She hated to stand outside a closed door expecting to be spied on by someone unseen and unheard within. Feeling exposed, she turned her back.

When Antonia's steward had purchased Caenis from the main imperial training school, the process was so discreet it seemed more like an adoption than a business in which title transferred and money changed hands. Antonia herself probably knew nothing about it. The opportunity to work in this high position had not come easily and once achieved it did not automatically lead to full trust. Caenis easily outstripped the competition in basic secretarial tasks, but Antonia was wary of granting access to her private papers, and rightly so. The girl had remained on probation, little more than a copyist. Her first sign of acceptance was when Diadumenus left her on duty alone today. It marked a vital step forward, Caenis knew that. She was desperate to do well.

A muttering porter finally answered her summons and admitted her. Patiently enduring the delay, she was still revelling in her luck. Through the discreet portals of this comparatively modest house came Roman statesmen and foreign potentates, the scions of satellite countries – Judaea, Commagene, Thrace, Mauretania, Armenia, Parthia – and the eccentric or notorious members of Antonia's own family. Influential Romans, those with a long-term eye on the future, enjoyed Antonia's patronage. Since today was a festival, visitors might have been here this evening, though for once Caenis found the house unusually quiet.

Passing through the peristyle garden and down a short internal corridor she reached a roofed atrium with a black and white tiled floor at the centre of the formal suite. Opposite, a long flight of steps led down from the main door. To either side of her lay public rooms, a reception area and a dining room, both exquisitely decorated with high-quality wall paintings. The private suites and bedrooms lay beyond them and on upper floors, all much smaller rooms.

Her role was to present herself to the usher Maritimus, then if required for dictation she would attend on her mistress in one of the cubicles attached to the receiving room. Tonight Maritimus, who seemed flustered, left her in the receiving room; then for some reason she had to wait. She studied the fine fresco of Io, guarded by Argus, and apprehensively eyeing Mercury as he crept around a large rock to rescue her; he looked like the kind of curly-haired lad-about-town Io's mother had probably warned her about.

Trying to calm herself, Caenis arranged her waxed note tablet and took out a stylus. Normally Diadumenus, as Chief Secretary, would be here to prevent her feeling so exposed. Still, she was familiar with the kind of correspondence required. Antonia owned and organised a vast array of personal property, including estates in Egypt and the East inherited from her father, Mark Antony. At her court she had brought up the princes from far-flung provinces who had been sent to Rome by shrewd royal fathers or simply carried off by the Romans as hostages, and many letters were still written to those who had since returned home. They held no terrors for an able scribe, although this would be the first time Caenis had worked unsupervised with Antonia.

Maritimus the tetchy usher bustled in again. 'I'm supposed to find Diadumenus. Is there only you? Where's Diadumenus?'

'Given free time for the festival.'

'It won't do!' He was sweating.

'It will have to,' said Caenis cheerfully, refusing to acknowledge an emergency unless he explained.

Maritimus scowled at her. 'She wants to write a letter.'

'I can do that.' Caenis longed for authority. She enjoyed her new work. She took genuine pleasure in using her skills, and was fascinated by what she saw of Antonia's correspondence. She accepted that she did not yet see it all. Even so, this sense of not being acceptable tonight grated on her. 'Will you tell her I'm here?'

'No; she wants Diadumenus. I don't know what's going

16

on, but something's upset her. You can't do this; it's something about her family.'

Antonia never talked about her family. She bore that dreadful burden entirely alone.

'I am discreet!' Caenis blazed angrily.

'It's political!' hissed the usher.

'I know how to keep my mouth shut.' Any sensible slave did.

It was not enough. Maritimus clucked and bustled off again. Caenis resigned herself to frustration. She wondered what crisis had upset Antonia.

Now she was seeing the world and her own place within it through fresh eyes. Working in a private house felt wonderful. She had already witnessed at close hand how Roman government was conducted. Like most family matters, it was based on short-term loyalties and long-term bad temper, pursued in an atmosphere of spite, greed and indigestion. Caenis had never had a family; she watched with delight.

Whatever had disturbed her mistress this particular evening, the young secretary already appreciated the background: the Emperor Tiberius, whose famous brother, Drusus, had been Antonia's husband, spent the last years of his bitter reign in depraved exile on the island of Capri; it had come to be accepted in Rome that he would never return here again. He was already over seventy so the question of a successor was never far away.

Since Augustus had first based his political position upon his family ties with Julius Caesar, ruling Rome had become an inheritable right. Between genuine accidents and the grappling ambition of their fearsome womenfolk, most of the male heirs had gone to their graves. The Emperor's own son, married to Antonia's daughter Livilla, had died in rather odd circumstances eight years before. By default the choice now fell between Livilla's son, Gemellus, and his cousin Caligula. A fine pair: Caligula, who when barely into his teens had seduced his own sister here in Antonia's house, or Gemellus, who was deeply unpleasant and permanently sickly. But if Tiberius died in the near future Rome would be left to these two very young boys while immense power

17

was also being wielded by Sejanus. Maybe Sejanus would prefer another solution.

Quite quietly and without any warning, Antonia came into the room. Caenis sprang to her feet.

Antonia was nearly seventy, though she still had the round face, soft features, wide-set eyes and sweet mouth that had made her a famous beauty. Her hair, thinning now, was parted centrally and taken back above her ears to the nape of her neck in a neat, traditional style. Her gown and stole were unobtrusively rich, her earrings and pendants heavy antiques – attributes of extreme wealth and power to which she paid no regard.

'You are Caenis?' The slavegirl nodded. The effect of her mistress' assurance was to make her feel coarse and clumsy. 'You are on duty alone? Well, something important has to be done. This cannot wait. We shall have to make the best of it.' Her mistress gave her a hard look. A decision occurred. The slavegirl's life took a sudden twist; for indecipherable reasons she was admitted to Antonia's confidence.

Somehow Caenis detected from the first that whatever was to be written had already been thoroughly considered. She had often seen her mistress composing correspondence as she went along; this was different. Now Antonia led her briskly into one of the more private little side rooms then signalled her to a low stool, while she herself continued pacing about, barely able to wait until Caenis had her stylus poised. It was a strange reversal; in Rome the great were seated while their inferiors stood. Caenis had been trained to take shorthand normally while on her feet at the foot of a couch where the dictator reclined.

'This is a letter to the Emperor about Lucius Aelius Sejanus.'

Then Caenis understood. The brief formal announcement warned her – and it stunned her. Her mistress was about to expose the man.

Speaking with pain and deliberation, Antonia dictated for Tiberius facts which she hated to acknowledge and which he would hate to hear. She had uncovered a great conspiracy.

18

The sensational story would surprise few in Rome, although few would ever have voiced it, least of all to the Emperor. Here in this sheltered house Antonia's realisation of it had been desperately slow to emerge, but those close to her had revealed the plot. She had not taken their word; she made her own investigations. Because of her privileged position she possessed the courage to inform Tiberius, and she supported all her accusations with telling detail. She did not spare even the parts which convicted her own daughter.

She told the Emperor how his friend the Praetorian commander Sejanus had been plotting to gain complete power. His feared position had ensured the allegiance of many senators and many of the imperial freedmen who governed the Empire; leading figures in the army had been bribed. Recent honours had been heaped upon Sejanus, increasing his own ambition and the control he wielded throughout Rome. He had moved in on the Imperial House by marrying one of his relatives, Aelia Paetina, to Antonia's son Claudius, by betrothing his daughter to Claudius' son (though the boy had died), and now after several attempts by persuading the Emperor to agree that he himself might marry Antonia's daughter. But he had already seduced Livilla, then either poisoned her husband or persuaded her to do it, and schemed to ally himself by marriage to the Imperial House in order to legitimise his own position as a future emperor. His own ex-wife, recently divorced, was now prepared to speak as a witness against him.

Sejanus planned to eliminate Caligula, the more prominent of the Emperor's heirs. If the old man refused to die of his own accord the Guard commander clearly intended to destroy Tiberius himself.

The dictation completed, Caenis managed to keep her face expressionless. At a brusque nod from Antonia she fetched the necessary materials from her work basket and absorbed herself in the letter's careful transcription to a scroll.

Pallas, Antonia's most trusted slave, came into the room, dressed in a travelling cloak and clearly primed to collect the letter. Their mistress motioned him to wait in silence while

Caenis completed her task. Newly confident, she copied her notes without mistakes, writing calmly and steadily even though her mouth felt dry and her cheeks flushed. What she was committing to ink and parchment could be a death warrant for all of them.

Antonia read through and signed the letter. Caenis melted wax to seal the scroll. Pallas took charge of it.

'Do not let this fall into other hands,' Antonia reminded him, obviously repeating previous instructions. 'If you are stopped, say you are travelling to my estate at Bauli. Give the letter only into the Emperor's own hands, then wait in case he wishes to question you.'

The messenger left. Pallas was not a type Caenis cared for. He was a Greek from Arcadia, visibly ambitious, whose appeal to Antonia struck her as incongruous. He went on his way with a jaunty step which seemed out of place. But perhaps his carefree manner would disguise the importance of his mission from soldiers and spies.

The two women sat for a moment.

'Remove every trace from your note tablets, Caenis.'

Caenis held the tablets above the flame of a lamp to soften the wax a little, then methodically drew the flat end of her stylus through each line of shorthand. Staring at the newly smoothed surface, she said in a low voice, 'It is useless, madam. I would have erased the letter in any case, but every document you ever dictate to me remains in my mind.'

'Let us hope your loyalty matches your memory,' Antonia replied ruefully.

'You may have faith in both, madam.'

'That will be fortunate for Rome! You will remain in this house,' Antonia stated. 'You may speak to no one until these matters are resolved. It is for the safety of Rome and the Emperor, for *my* safety – and for your own.' Faint distaste coloured her voice: 'Do you have male followers who will look for you?'

'No, madam.' Only that morning Caenis had encountered a man who might have troubled her thoughts for many long hours, but tonight had obliterated that. 'I have one friend,' she went on, matter-of-factly contributing to the discussion.

'A garland–girl called Veronica. She may come asking about me, but if the door porter says I am working for you, madam, she will be satisfied.' Veronica had never taken any interest in Caenis' duties as a scribe.

'Well, I am sorry to have to imprison you here.' ,

'I shall try to endure it, madam,' Caenis replied, smiling. She might as well acknowledge what it would mean to be living in Livia's House.

There was nothing for them to do. It would be weeks, if not longer, before Pallas reached the Bay of Naples and the Emperor reacted. The messenger might never get there.

Even if Pallas did reach Capri, from all Caenis had heard there must be a good chance that Tiberius would choose to reject what Antonia was telling him. He was moody and unpredictable, and nobody likes to hear they have been betrayed. Even if Antonia's measured words convinced him, there might be nothing he could do: the Praetorian Guards held absolute power in Rome. Arresting their commander appeared to be impossible. They would defend Sejanus to the last.

His agents were everywhere. Only the unexpectedness of Antonia's action could possibly outwit him.

III

For Caenis this was in many ways the most significant period of her life. It all seemed too easy. Everyone looked too happy to welcome her. Caenis, who distrusted smiles, felt off balance for some time.

Living in a private house was wonderful. She had been allocated her own tiny sleeping-cubicle instead of sharing with Veronica. She liked both the sense of belonging and the privacy.

Born and bred in the Palace, Caenis could have no country and no relations of her own; she was one of 'Caesar's family' but that title just made her imperial property. In some ways it had been good luck. It had spared her the indignity of standing naked in the market-place shackled among Africans, Syrians and Gauls, with notes of her good character and health hung around her neck while casual eyes derided her and rough hands pinched her breasts or forced between her thighs. She had escaped long-term insecurity, real filth, savage cruelty, regular sexual abuse. She understood that; she was grateful up to a point.

Of her father she knew nothing; of her mother only that she must have been a slave too. Caenis had presumably stayed with her mother while she was very small; sometimes a smear of memory would catch her on that threshold between waking and shallow sleep. Before she was committed to the nursery where bright brats were taught to write, her mother had pierced her ears even though all she had to hang there were pebbles on rags of string. She must have supposed her daughter was then ready to receive orbs of gold from susceptible men. There was always that foolish presumption that a slavegirl must look pretty. Caenis never had been; she knew her cleverness was the better bargain, but it made her sad all the same.

She had been clever from the start. As a child frighteningly so. She learnt to disguise it, to escape spite in the infants' dormitory, then later to use it so a usefully vibrant girl like Veronica would want to be her friend. Though a solitary child, she understood that she needed other people. As she grew older her resentments had dulled, so she neither tormented herself nor worried the overseers by appearing rebellious. But she possessed a keen drive to achieve the best she could.

That was why working for Antonia was so important. Encouraged by the new confidence now placed in her, Caenis began to acquit herself outstandingly. Having once caught Antonia's notice, every opportunity was hers. Straight-backed and calm, she worked as if nothing significant had happened – winning further trust from her mistress for her restrained reaction to events.

Diadumenus, who must have been told what had happened, showed occasional signs of jealousy. He was still Chief Secretary, but Caenis had a special quality to offer. She was a woman, and Antonia at seventy was short of female companionship. Her lady wanted neither a chit she could bully nor a monster who would try to bully her. Antonia needed someone with good sense; someone she could talk to; someone she could trust absolutely. She had found all that, though she did not yet know Caenis well enough to admit it. But they had shared an act of bravado (and of tragedy too, for Antonia had condemned her own daughter). They were now locked in a secret, awaiting the outcome. And if Sejanus discovered that Antonia had denounced him, there would be fatal results for both mistress and slave.

Life went on. An appearance of normality was crucial. Visitors came and went. For secrecy's sake Caenis was forbidden to approach them, but since she was tied to the house she was volunteering for any work she could. This included keeping a diary of visitors. Caenis was a secretary who could remain virtually invisible – while thoroughly inspecting all the persons whose names featured on her lists.

Among Antonia's private friends were wealthy men of

consular rank such as Lucius Vitellius and Valerius Asiaticus, who sometimes brought clients of their own. Caenis soon spotted among the names of Vitellius' escort that of Flavius Sabinus, one of the two young men she had directed at the Palace. He currently held the civic post of aedile so he qualified for an introduction here, although actually gaining admittance had required the patronage of a much more senior senator. This unofficial court circle could be a good place for impoverished new men from the provincial middle class to acquire influence. Here they would be meeting Caligula and Gemellus, the heirs to the Empire. They would mingle with ambassadors. They could even, if they wanted to risk ridicule, make the acquaintance of Claudius, Antonia's surviving son, who because of various disabilities took no part in public life.

The brothers came from Reate; Caenis burrowed it out. Reate was a small town in the Sabine hills – a birthplace Roman snobs would mock. Their family arranged contracts for seasonal labour and had made their money in provincial tax collection. Their father had also been a banker. They would be notables in their own country, though in Rome, amongst senatorial pedigrees that trailed back to the Golden Age, they must be struggling. Since Sabinus had qualified for the Senate the family must own estates worth at least a million sesterces, but it was obviously new money and if it were all tied up in the land she could well believe their day-to-day budget was tight.

With some difficulty, since no one knew or wanted to know anything about him, she discovered from the usher that the younger brother, Vespasian, had returned to his military duties abroad.

On 17 October a letter came to Antonia, brought by Pallas from Capri. She read it in private, then stayed in her room. Pallas did not reappear.

By nightfall word had run through the household notwithstanding, and the next day the results of Antonia's action became known throughout Rome: to sidestep the Praetorian Guards, the Emperor had called into his confidence past and present commanders of the city police force. One, Macro, had been secretly appointed as the new commander of the Praetorians. He entered Rome incognito and laid plans with Laco, the current Prefect of the Vigiles. After taking elaborate precautions, Macro had persuaded Sejanus to enter the Temple of Apollo on the Palatine where the Senate were meeting – only a few yards from Antonia's house. A letter from the Emperor to the Senate was to be read. Sejanus let himself be persuaded that this would be offering even greater honours to himself.

Once Sejanus had gone inside the Temple, Macro dismissed the escort of Guards, ordering them back to their camp (which ironically Sejanus himself had built for them in the north part of the city). He replaced them with loyal members of the city Vigiles. Macro himself then went to the Praetorian camp to assume command, confine the Guards to barracks and prevent a riot. Sejanus meanwhile discovered that the letter from Tiberius was a bitter denunciation of himself. Striding from the Temple, he was arrested by Laco, the Prefect of the Vigiles, and hustled off to the state dungeon on the Capitol. The Guards did riot, but it was soon controlled.

Sejanus and his fellow conspirators were executed. The strangled body of Sejanus was dumped on the Gemonian Steps which led down from the Capitol, where it was abused by the public for three days before being dragged off with hooks and thrown like rubbish into the Tiber. His statues were torn down from the Forum and theatres. His children were killed too, the teenaged daughter being raped first, to spare the public executioner from the crime of killing a virgin. Rome had harsh rules, but they did exist.

Antonia was acclaimed as the saviour of Rome and of the Emperor. Praising her role in uncovering the conspiracy, Tiberius offered her the title Augusta, with the formal honours of an empress. This she declined with the modesty her admirers would expect.

From the middle of October until well into November no visitors were admitted to Livia's House. Some normal life continued. A certain amount of correspondence had to be written, and the correct procedures of daily life were grimly observed. Meanwhile Antonia's daughter, Livilla, had been brought to the house and consigned, with the Emperor's permission, to her mother's custody.

Unlike previous errant daughters of the Imperial House, those who merely led scandalous, adulterous lives for their own pleasure, but who had refrained from poisoning the sons of emperors or letting themselves be manipulated into damaging the stability of Rome, Livilla was not to be exiled to a remote island or executed by soldiers. She had shamed the rigorous principles of her mother, Antonia, and those of her even more famously strict grandmother Octavia. She had been stupidly deceived by Sejanus. She had defiled the house of Augustus and dishonoured her own children, the grandchildren and rightful heirs of the Emperor. Her position saved her from the public executioner, yet her fate was merciless.

Antonia took Livilla into her own house, locked her in a room alone, and left her there until she starved to death.

IV

Grief and rejoicing each have their moments, and then fade. The screams and pleas for help from Livilla were reduced to weakening groans, then silence. Those who had been shaken by having to overhear what happened recovered as much as they ever would.

Gradually the House of Livia relaxed, returning like Rome itself to what passed for normal domesticity. Certainly a shadow had been lifted from the Empire and the city was full of relief.

Years passed. Nightmares ended. Individual lives improved. That was why, when the younger brother of Flavius Sabinus opened the door to a certain office in the administration sector on the Palatine nearly two years later, Caenis was singing.

She was singing quite loudly because she thought there was nobody nearby. Besides, she liked to sing. Livia's House would hardly be the place for it.

She stopped abruptly.

'Hello!' cried Vespasian. 'You look very efficient!'

He shouldered himself in. Caenis put on an expression of pious surprise. She had been aware that his posting to Thrace must have ended. She had somehow expected him.

Men of his status were not supposed to saunter into the imperial suites looking for female scribes. Completely unabashed, Vespasian took a good look round.

Antonia had borrowed a large office for her copy clerks. She ran a frugal household and was more ruthless in seizing advantages than her sovereign reputation might suggest. Tiberius would once have been mean enough to demand rent even from a widowed relative, but no one had ever told him she was here; he suspected that people deceived him, so inevitably they did. Still, Antonia could act as she liked nowadays. She was the Mother of Rome.

The room had a depressed air. It was cold. It smelt of hibernating animals. The paintwork on the frescos was faded. In the Emperor's absence large areas of his palace were declining in neglect; unsupervised, the imperial stewards took a slack attitude to redecorating any quarters they did not wish to lounge in themselves. Caenis, a girl who could get things done, intended to make friends with the prefect of works.

Vespasian prodded at a patch of wall plaster which was effervescing oddly: 'Bit rough.'

'The whole of Rome is collapsing,' Caenis observed. 'Why should the Emperor's house be different?'

Tiberius had a desultory approach to public construction; he began a Temple of Augustus and restoring the Theatre of Pompey, but both remained unfinished. He had occupied the Palace only fitfully before retiring from Rome. Vespasian grumbled, 'He should build properly. He should build more, build better, encourage others, and set a decent standard.'

He turned his critical attention to Caenis.

She showed distinct signs of improvement. She looked clean and neat; Antonia's staff were allowed to attend the women's sessions at the public baths. Her dark hair was knotted at the nape of her neck and she had acquired a better quality dress. Although she worked at a rickety table with a fillet of wood to prop up one leg, she occupied her place with an air of grand possessiveness. She had been promoted to be in charge. None of her juniors was present; she stayed here late on purpose, adoring her authority as she read and corrected their work. Faced with somebody she knew, Caenis openly glowed.

The returning tribune absorbed everything; she was sure he had noticed the subtle change in her situation.

'A tyrant of the secretariats!' he teased as he approached. He seemed larger and even fitter than she remembered, deeply tanned by outdoor army life. 'That marvellously frightening glint in the eye . . .' Caenis ignored this.

He had wandered right up to her table. Perching on the edge, he went on gazing around as if even a run-down cubbyhole in the Palace were new to him. An oil lamp tilted alarmingly. Caenis leant down hard with her elbows so the table would not rock over and tip him on the floor. He knew she was doing it but made no attempt to shift his weight. She folded her hands atop the tablets which she had just finished sorting to prevent Vespasian (who was craning his head) from reading them.

'Good evening, lord.'

Flavius Vespasianus had a rare but wonderful grin. 'You're mellowing. Last time I was told to skip over the Styx!'

'The lady Antonia's secretariat respects the privilege of rank.' Caenis was now allowed to be as ironic as the person she was addressing would accept. Authority attached to her through the importance of her mistress and the responsibility of her post. Antonia's visitors treated her with deference. 'Are you rich yet, tribune?' she taunted.

'I shall never be rich; but I have brought you a present. Don't get excited; it's nothing to wear.' He had come completely unattended. There was a rather greasy parcel squashed under his arm.

'Can you eat it?' she giggled unexpectedly.

'I owe you a sausage.'

'And this is it? After *two years*, lord?'

'I had to go to Thrace,' he told her gravely. 'If I had missed the sea-crossing it would have been the end of my career.' He spoke as if he had seriously considered missing his ship anyway. Caenis felt an odd flutter. She ignored it stalwartly. He handed her the parcel. 'I presume you are a girl who likes pickled fish?' She loved pickled fish. 'Manage a stuffed egg?'

'Only one?'

'I ate the other on the way.'

Genuinely shocked, she exclaimed before she could stop herself, '*In the street*, lord?'

'In the street,' he returned placidly. For a moment she thought him a real country boy, innocent of his offence, then his gaze danced on her troubled face; he knew. Caenis frowned with a mixture of pleasure and puzzlement. She imagined him, shambling through Rome's clamorous streets. Probably he would carry it off. Probably no one even noticed: a knight, a tribune newly released from military service and qualified for the highest administrative posts, all on his own, carrying a parcel, munching a stuffed egg.

'Deplorable,' he agreed wickedly. 'So: here's a man who pays his debts.'

'Outside my experience!'

Her wry comment on the harshness of her moral world made him pause, then he continued, 'I've been trying to find you for days. I'm such a permanent fixture the sausage-maker thinks I must be spying on him for his wife. I would have arrived earlier today, but the stuff was wrapped in some second-rate poet's cast-off manuscript. You know how it is – you glimpse one half-good phrase then an hour goes by with you stood on the same street corner unravelling the paper trying to find the last appalling verse . . . Well, can we share this?'

Caenis was beginning to feel frightened. Every word he uttered snatched at her sympathy. Alone with her for the first time, he made no effort to be gallant; nor did he fuss. Perhaps he supposed knights and senators were always dropping in with picnics. Those brown eyes knew exactly what he was doing to her. Suddenly he tried to beg for information: 'There were some grand events in Rome after I went back to Thrace. Were you aware what lay in store for Sejanus?'

Caenis still regarded Antonia's letter as a matter of confidence. Besides, she was trained to deflect curiosity from strangers. She demanded sternly, 'I don't expect you thought to bring any bread?' Then before he had time to look crestfallen, she reached down and hooked out the flat circular loaf she had been intending to nibble later on her own. 'I think we should decamp to the pantry,' she said. 'I don't want to be caught using my lady's letter to the King of Judaea as a napkin for eating pickled fish!'

Caenis now owned a plate. 'Chipped but not cracked, rather like my heart . . .'

He did not laugh. He had a way of looking noncommittal while he listened, so she could hardly tell whether she amused or astonished him.

It was a different time of year. April. The Emperor still away on Capri. The days lengthening but the Palace lying silent again, lit by a myriad oil lamps for no one's benefit.

This time they had the sausage cold. Vespasian sliced it up himself. 'I don't like this as much as yours; I should have asked you what to get –' It was a smoked Lucanian salami, rather strong on the cumin, not enough savory and rue. Caenis did not complain. It was the only present she had ever received. Veronica would have mocked; Veronica's idea of a present was something sparkly and easy to pawn.

'When you have waited over a year for a debt,' Caenis commented benignly, 'you make the best of whatever turns up.'

After a while he demanded, still chewing, 'Are you allowed any free time on your own?'

This was what she wanted to avoid. Being stupidly straightforward, she told him the truth: 'Sometimes.'

'What do you do with yourself?'

'Tomorrow I am going to see a mime actor.'

He looked interested; she groaned inwardly. 'I heard you singing. And you like the dancers?'

'I like the flute music. You can lose yourself,' she muttered, not wanting to talk about it. She knew better than to entrust her soul to anyone of rank.

'You don't need losing,' he chivvied her. 'Going with someone nice?'

'Oh yes!' she snapped without thinking. 'With myself.' She crunched her teeth into a crisp curl of the loaf and pointedly did not look at him. There was a very slight pause.

'No man?'

Better prepared now, she was able to duck the question: 'Men are not nice, lord. Sometimes useful, occasionally amusing, hardly ever genuine, and never nice.'

'Women are worse; they cost a lot and still let you down.' He was teasing. She let it pass.

'Actually I go by myself because I seriously object when idiots talk to me through the music.'

31

He smiled, because he recognised that was just like her. She was as single-minded as himself. 'Who's doing the mime?'

'Blathyllos.'

'Any good? I might come too. I don't talk; I always go to sleep. Luckily I never snore.'

They could not go to the theatre as a couple. They would not be permitted to sit together; even women of his own rank must watch separately. Antonia's slave should not be seen alone with him in any case. But he asked, without hesitation, 'Would you meet me afterwards?' Absorbing herself in biting a peppercorn from the pickled fish, Caenis tried not to answer. He interpreted her silence his own way. 'Where shall I find you?'

Too late; she was committed. Her heart pounded. 'A young lord who does not know the theatre rendezvous?' she reproved, still foolishly attempting to slither out of this.

'Sheltered upbringing.'

'Bit old-fashioned?' There was no escape. The truth had to be stated. She reminded him baldly: 'I am somebody else's slave.'

'I appreciate that.'

Defiance overtook her. 'Well then, if you mean it, you could meet me here beforehand. Ask anyone; they will find me.'

For the first time the senator's brother seemed uncomfortable. 'Who shall I ask for?' His sources of information must be thinner than hers.

She took a deep breath. Giving her name seemed a step she could never revoke. 'Caenis,' she said awkwardly.

'Caenis?' He tested it out in his strong voice. It was Greek; that was only a convention of slavery. 'Caenis!' he exclaimed again, and his speaking her name made everything unbearably intimate.

'Just Caenis,' she muttered.

'Just nothing!' he retorted angrily. She guessed he meant she should not denigrate herself. 'And listen, Caenis: always ask a visitor who he is!' He was evidently wanting her to ask his own name. 'The most dismal words in the world are

"Someone called to see you; I don't know who it was . . ." Don't be put at a disadvantage. You can't afford to be pushed into assumptions about anybody's status; you need to know for sure. You have to judge whether a person rates refreshments or only your polished sneer.' He stood up. 'So in answer to your next question –'

He must have thought she would have forgotten. She interrupted calmly: 'Your name is Titus Flavius Vespasianus.' He began to grin with delight at once. She recited in her most efficient voice, 'Your father was Flavius Sabinus, a citizen of Reate, so your voting tribe is the Quirina; your mother is Vespasia Polla. You wear the gold ring of the knights. Your patron is the elevated Lucius Vitellius, who brings your brother to Antonia's house –'

'Do you speak to my brother?' he interrupted in surprise.

'No, certainly not.' She was determined to reach her joke: 'You are a second son with no reputation, but respectable so I need to be polite –' Vespasian clenched the corner of his mouth in anticipation; he possessed a rapidly developing sense of humour and liked what he had glimpsed of hers. So Caenis said, knowing how much he would enjoy it, 'As for your rating refreshments, lord – I worked out your status the first time we met!'

V

When Vespasian collected her he held out his hand and swiftly clasped hers. Nobody had ever done that before.

'Hello, Caenis.' With the greeting his voice dropped half a tone. Her breath tangled somewhere above her middle ribs as she withdrew her hand with care.

'Hello –' She did not know how to address him.

He gazed at her for a moment inscrutably. 'Titus,' he instructed.

Very few people ever used his personal name. In the off-hand Roman way his whole family were named Titus – grandfather, father, brothers and cousins all the same – so people called him Vespasian, even at home. This intimacy offered to Caenis was the measure of the mistake the man was letting himself make. Presumably he did not realise; Caenis did.

'You look nice.'

For once she smiled. Antonia had given her a new dress.

She had felt compelled to mention him to Antonia.

'Madam, when I go to the theatre this evening, I have made an arrangement to meet a gentleman.' The statement plunged her into visible difficulty. Doubt was transfiguring her mistress' face.

They had been in a room at Livia's House where the walls were decorated with elegant swags of greenery looped between columns, below a high golden frieze portraying tiny figures in dreamy cityscapes. Antonia reclined in a long sloping chair while Caenis perched on a low stool with a tablet on her knees. Antonia liked to work hard without distractions, but once they finished sometimes she kept back her secretary for a few moments of casual talk. It did her good to unbend. She tired more easily nowadays than she wanted to admit. She had lived twice as long as many people and survived more griefs than most.

The old lady stirred. Her well-attended skin had preserved its sweet suppleness until now, but her face had grown thinner and since Livilla's disgrace despair was beginning to show in the fine creases at the corners of her eyes.

The moment had become awkward.

'Why are you telling me?' Antonia demanded. 'Do you wish me to forbid it?'

Caenis was taking an enormous risk. When the Chief Secretary, Diadumenus, had first stipulated that Antonia must be told of any approaches from knights or senators he had meant approaches on business matters; there ought to be no other kind of commerce with their lady's slaves.

'I prefer to be open, madam.'

In other households it was usually understood that other commerce did occur . . . Not here. Or if here, it never happened openly.

Even after knowing Caenis for several years, Antonia immediately decided her slave had loose morals and would be easy prey for a political shark. It was unfair; Caenis had always been scrupulous.

'You ask me to condone the friendship? How long have you been dealing with this man?'

Caenis said tersely, 'I don't *deal* with him. I don't even know if he expects it.'

Antonia moved impatiently. 'Come; who is he?'

'Flavius Vespasianus, a knight from Reate. The family are not prominent though his brother, Sabinus, has been here as a client of Lucius Vitellius. Madam, you asked me long ago if I had male followers, and I told you no.'

There was some improvement in Antonia's expression. 'So what is this?'

'A slight friendship I struck up with a newcomer to Rome, nothing more.' How could it be? The sheer impossibility filled her with dread. 'He has been on service abroad and has few friends in Rome.'

'Yet he sought you out!'

'I believe that was coincidence.'

35

'You believe nothing of the sort! Is he seeking only your favours, or does he hope for influence?'

'That I do not know,' admitted Caenis. 'But if I find out what he thinks he is seeking, the sooner I can disillusion him.'

Antonia sighed with irritation. 'Are you deceiving yourself – or trying to deceive me?' Caenis wisely made no reply. 'Have you confided in anybody else? I thought you were friendly with that girl Veronica?'

With a pang of resentment, Caenis finally grasped how nearly her friendship with Veronica had jeopardised her post. She took the opportunity to speak up: 'Veronica has a good heart. I do like her, but that does not mean I admire her life. And she has never influenced mine, madam.' She smiled reassuringly. 'I have never even mentioned Vespasian to Veronica.'

'I will not have my staff used by ambitious young men,' declared Antonia, though she liked people who stood up to her; she could be weakening.

Caenis decided to show she was shrewd. 'I value my position too highly to risk it through foolishness. Besides, madam, if your court is seen as a desirable forum for young men who wish to advance in public life – as it must be – then he and his brother have obtained their entrée anyway. Somebody, their father perhaps, has ensured that they are taken up by Vitellius. Vespasian cannot believe knowing me will improve on that.'

Now her mistress seemed amused. 'Then, my dear, what does he want?'

'I suppose, what they all want,' Caenis decided, so as two women together they laughed and nodded distrustfully. 'He will be due for a disappointment! Madam, if he intends to pick my brains for your secrets, I shall certainly give him a sharp answer. I believe he knows that. No – as I told you, I suspect he is just a young man who lacks friends in Rome. I am under no delusions; once he finds his feet in society that will be the end of me.'

'You seem to have worked everything out.'

'I think a girl in my position has to,' Caenis said quietly.

Antonia, who favoured Caenis strongly, and who disliked having to involve herself in the private lives of her staff, seemed to tire of the conversation. 'Well, you were right to speak to me. I have no wish to deprive you of companion-ship. But rank must be respected –'

'I am a slave,' Caenis agreed quietly. 'If he wants a mistress, he has to look elsewhere.'

'So long as you accept it. So long as you make him accept it too! Don't let him ask questions.' Don't get pregnant, thought Antonia. Don't force me to discipline you; don't betray my trust. 'And don't let yourself be hurt.'

Squaring up the writing tablets on her knee, Caenis laughed unhappily. 'Thank you, madam.'

'Caenis, you undervalue yourself!'

In the girl before her Antonia saw what Vespasian must see – that fine, bright, interesting look that marked an intelligent woman; a look which in drawing the eye also lifted the heart. A man with the taste to admire such quality was more dangerous than any philanderer or hustler.

With an angry jerk at the cushions under her back, Antonia conceded, 'Ask Athenaïs to find you something decent to wear.'

Caenis felt startled. She had been intending to borrow Veronica's best blue gown, since she knew that Veronica had worked herself an invitation to a function which required only a silver anklet and a wisp of gauze.

'Something will be found for you,' Antonia brusquely said again.

Then, much as she distrusted other people's support, Caenis understood that in speaking out she had softened Antonia's strict principles. Her mistress would keep her, and indulge her. She had earned more than her lady's goodwill. She had become her favourite.

Something was found; something wonderful. Athenaïs, who mended Antonia's clothes, carried the garment to her cubicle. Her face split with a shy grin. 'Pamphila has screwed up her face and let you have this!' Pamphila was the wardrobe mistress. She always ensured that her own turnout was spectacular, but was not renowned for parting with good things to other slaves.

Caenis whistled, which made Athenaïs giggle. She was deeply in awe of the secretary for being able to read and write, even though Caenis had made it plain since she first entered Antonia's household that to anyone half sensible she was perfectly approachable. Athenaïs immediately made her try on the dress then squatted on the floor to alter the hem length, frowning with concentration as her nimble fingers flew. She seemed even more excited than Caenis was herself.

'I don't suppose you could persuade Pamphila to find me an undertunic too?'

Athenaïs scoffed. 'I don't suppose you would like to try being the person who asked her?'

'No; I know my limits, dear!'

So Caenis came to the pantomime in her own shift, but a gown that had once belonged to the daughter of Mark Antony. It was one that showed its pedigree, in a shade of amber-brown, as plain as it had once been expensive. Veronica would think it dull stuff, but Caenis recognised true elegance. It was linen woven through at Tyre with Chinese silk, a material so light she found it fabulous to wear. The dress moved as she moved; it lay soft against the skin, tenderly cool during the heat of the day then with the evening chill whisperingly warm.

'You look nice,' Vespasian remarked. No man had ever said that to Caenis before; none had ever thought he needed to. But he as usual was examining her. 'You look happy.'

For the first time Caenis glimpsed that although exquisite features and fine robes must help, real good looks depended on a glad heart. 'Happy?' she quipped. 'Well, strolling out with a bankrupt will soon settle that! Shall we walk?' she asked helpfully.

'I do have the price of a litter for my female companion.'

'Of course,' she murmured. No slave travelled in such style. Teasing him helped cover her unease. 'But I was afraid that if you spent your small change now, you might have to miss your interval honeycake.'

'Thanks!' he said, suddenly meeting her halfway. 'I do like

a girl who grasps the practicalities.'

Caenis stated quietly for the second time that week, 'I think a girl in my position has to.'

They walked.

VI

To walk through Rome was to bludgeon through one teeming city bazaar. The main time for trade was in the morning before the fabric of the buildings and the air in the streets heated up unbearably, but in Mediterranean tradition, after a long siesta – lunch, nap, a little light lovemaking – businesses gradually reopened for their second, more leisurely session in the afternoon. This was the time at which Caenis and Vespasian set out.

They were starting on the Palatine, where the imperial family and those wealthy enough to imitate them had established their pleasant detached residences along the lower flank, with fine views over the Forum. When they plunged down from the Hill it was to make their way to the Theatre of Balbus along the Triumphal Way; their passage was hectic. To the rest of the world the Empire was giving the elegance of planned public buildings in spacious piazzas, wide roads, and new towns built upon geometric street plans that were four-square as the military forts from which they derived. Rome itself remained an eight-hundred-year-old honeycomb, a traditional maze of tight-cornered streets which clambered up and down the Seven Hills, often no more than inadequate passageways, twisting alleys, aimless double-backs, and crumbling cul-de-sacs. All of these were packed to bursting point.

'I'm going to lose you,' Vespasian muttered. 'Better hold my hand.'

'Oh no!' In horror Caenis buried her hands under the light folds of her stole. He raised a dour eyebrow; she would not give way.

The press of people in the narrow streets did not deter a man of his sturdiness. Keeping close behind his shoulder she slipped after him as he moved unhurriedly; he forced a path more courteously than most men of his status ever managed.

He checked frequently, though she sensed he was sufficiently alive to her presence to know immediately if they did separate in the crush. Once a water-carrier with two wildly sloshing cauldrons slung on a bowed pole pushed impatiently between them on his way from a public fountain to the upper quarters of an apartment block; she caught at Vespasian's toga, but with one of his abrupt smiles he was already slowing up to wait for her.

Freckles of sunlight flickered on their faces as they reached the smaller streets; these were just wide enough to glimpse the sky far away between corners of the roofs on the six-storey blocks whose cramped apartments were piled one upon the other like towers of slipper-limpets on a rock. Everywhere taverns and workshops spilled out in front of them, for by day life was lived in the streets. The pillars of the arcades were garlanded with metalware – bronze flagons and copper jugs with chains through their handles like preposterous necklaces. They stepped around leaning stacks of pottery, then ducked under baskets hung on ropes above their heads. They squeezed past touts with trays of piping-hot meat-pies, pressed back under balconies as sedan chairs jostled by, paused to watch a game of draughts on a makeshift board scratched in the dust. Assailed by noise and smells and the shoving of a polyglot humanity which at times carried them along helpless on the tide, at length they reached their destination.

'Show me your ticket!' Caenis commanded. 'Then I can look out for you – but you mustn't wave.' Gravely he produced the ivory disc from which she memorised the number of his seat. 'If you still want to see me, I'll wait over there afterwards by the fortune-teller's booth. If I leave early I'll send down a message.'

'I'll be there,' he assented sombrely.

Women sat at the top of the third tier of seats in the theatre, after the various ranks of masculine citizens; Caenis had saved up for a ticket, to avoid having to stand on the upper terrace with foreigners and less thrifty slaves. Even from this high perch she soon picked out Vespasian; already the way

41

he moved seemed vividly familiar. Usually she followed a play almost ahead of the actor, but she constantly lost Blathyllos today. Her concentration kept skittering off to the fourteen rows in the first tier, reserved for knights.

The art of the tragic pantomime had developed nearly to its peak. Few new plays were written; those shown now comprised part of the communal memory. The mood of the story was conveyed by an orchestra of wind and percussion while the words, which the audience often knew by heart, were sung either by a small choir or a soloist. Nowadays there was only one actor, who portrayed all the parts; he honed himself for this with a strict regimen of diet and exercise. He presented the action through a combination of mime and dance, where each gesture, each glance, each delicate flexing of a muscle, each precise modulation of a nerve, caught the imagination and through the imagination the heart.

Blathyllos was good. At first he commanded his audience simply by standing still and drawing on their expectation. His slightest movement carried right to the back of the auditorium and as in all the best theatre it was apparently effortless. He used suspense, horror, confusion, sentiment, and joy. He brought them through heroism and pity, anger and desire, grief and triumph. By the end even Caenis felt wrung. The final applause discovered her blinking, dry-mouthed, momentarily bemused.

When she regained the street she thought for one wild moment that Vespasian would not come. She was waiting, sufficiently far from the main throng of people for him to pick her out yet near enough to the entrance not to feel threatened by pickpockets or pimps. She saw Vespasian heading in the opposite direction, she was sure. Still highly strung from the drama, she could not believe it. Distraught, she almost began to walk away alone.

He materialised from the dispersing crowd just in time.

'Hello, Caenis!' He must have gone to find two slaves, his own or more likely his brother's, who now followed behind him with cudgels through their belts. 'Sorry; have I kept you waiting?'

'It didn't matter,' she lied gallantly.

'Want your fortune told?' Vespasian was glancing at the booth; a man of evil Egyptian aspect, with a red pointed cap and no teeth, popped up like a puppet over the canvas half-door the moment he spoke: evidently able to prophesy customers. 'I'll pay for it – are you frightened?' Very little frightened Caenis. She said nothing and Vespasian egged her on. 'Don't you believe in horoscopes? You old sceptic!'

'I know my future: hard work, hard luck, and a hard death at a hard age!' Caenis told him grimly. 'I can't do it. You need to say when you were born.'

For a moment he did not understand.

Each freeborn Roman citizen, male or female, was registered with the Censor within eight or nine days of birth. A free citizen honoured his own birthday and those of his ancestors and family as his happiest private festivals when his household gods were wreathed with garlands while everyone who owed him respect gave thanks. Important men honoured the birthdays of political figures they admired. The birthday of the Emperor was a public festival.

Caenis was a slave: she did not know when her birthday was.

He was quick; no need now to explain.

Pride made her do so anyway; she could be brutal when she chose: 'Slavegirls' brats, sir, are not heralded by proud fathers in the *Daily Gazette*. The fact that I exist is marked only by my standing here before you, blood and bone decked out in a new dress. The modern philosophers may grant me a soul, but nobody – lord, *nobody* – burdens me with a fate to be foreseen!'

'*Ouch!*' he remarked. She felt better. He did not apologise; there was no point. Instead he turned to the astrologer in his down-to-earth way. 'Here's a challenge then; can we offer this lass any consolation?'

The man let his eyes glaze with practised guile. He was draped in unclean scarves which were intended to suggest oriental mystery, though to Caenis they were simply a reflection of the poor standards of hygiene that applied here in the

Ninth District. A tinsel zodiac twinkled sporadically on a string above his head. One of the Fish had lost its tail and the Twins were slowly drifting apart from their heavenly embrace.

'Her face can never be upon the coinage!' the astrologer intoned suddenly in a high-pitched voice. How subtly ambiguous, Caenis thought. The man managed to imply that some uninvited blast of truth had struck him in the midriff just above whatever he had for dinner. Caenis reckoned this could not be healthy if he did it every day. He wavered; Vespasian chinked some coppers into a grimy hand which shot out promptly despite the apparent trance. 'Her life is kindly; kindly her death. Bones light as charcoal, thin hair . . . she goes to the gods wrapped in purple; Caesar grieves; lost is his lady, his life's true reverse . . .'

He fell silent, then looked up abruptly, his eyes dark with shock.

Vespasian folded his arms. 'Steady on with the treason,' he tackled the man jovially, 'but if some character's after my turtledove I'd like to be ready for him! What Caesar is this? Not the old goat, I trust –' Meaning Tiberius. 'Did you manage to get a glimpse of the laundry label in his cloak?'

Edging away in confusion at having been called his turtledove, Caenis murmured, 'Emperors don't have name-tags. It's considered unnecessary on the purple, you know.'

The astrologer gave Vespasian a nicely judged crazy stare.

Caenis had fled.

'Shall we walk?' Vespasian offered, as he caught her up with a sniff.

Wanting to resist being disturbed by the fraudulent predictions of a soiled Egyptian in a dirty Greek blanket, Caenis growled amiably, 'As you see I am already walking. I presupposed you had squandered my fare home on fly-blown titbits and lukewarm wine from every tout.' She knew he had kept his seat throughout.

'No need to get tetchy,' he complained, catching her elbow to slow her down. Unexpectedly self-conscious, she diminished her cracking pace.

It felt strange to be escorted by other slaves. Caenis was interested to notice that after a natural stare to evaluate what their young master had picked up, Vespasian's bodyguards bore her no obvious grudge. She was a girl doing her best; so good luck to her.

'Did you enjoy the pantomime, lord?'

Although he knew how much she wanted him to share her fierce enjoyment, he made no concessions. 'Oh, not bad. I think I stayed awake.'

'Not all the time!' she retaliated hotly. Then she realised he was teasing again so she softened her tone: 'As far as I could tell from upstairs you nod alarmingly, but you don't snore. The aediles were going to prod you at one point, but you woke up anyway.'

'Hah!' He pretended to cuff her round the ears.

This was a serious social mistake. Caenis became acutely conscious of her position as a slave. She refused the game; she walked straight, staring stiffly ahead. Vespasian gave no sign, but as long as she knew him he never made such a gesture again. His voice was deliberately friendly as he asked, 'What about you? Glad you went?'

'Yes; thank you.'

'Good.'

By mutual agreement they strolled beside the Tiber, across the Agrippan Bridge and into Caesar's Gardens. At dusk the gardens were rather cold, faintly ominous, and clouded at head-height with scores of nipping midges. Undeterred they toured the whole length; there were not many respectable places where a gentleman and someone else's slavegirl could go. Then he walked her home to Livia's House.

On the Palatine there would be sufficient light from flares, but they had to reach it first; one of his slaves had become their lantern-bearer. Even so, the narrow streets were dim and Caenis began to be afraid Vespasian might risk public familiarity. All he ever did, when builders' wagons or wine merchants' delivery carts trundled dangerously near, was to move her into the shelter of a house portico or close against the shuttered frontage of a shop with a light touch on her

45

arm, at once lifted. She hoped he did not notice how even that raised goose-pricks.

He did notice. His question was typically abrupt: 'Caenis, will you go to bed with me?'

'Certainly not!' She rapped back her refusal then, with the issue broached, relief flooded over her.

'You don't like me?'

'I like you far too much!' she found herself explaining briskly.

Vespasian rounded on her, forcing her to stop. 'What's that supposed to mean?' He was a big man, extremely blunt, and far superior in rank. She experienced real alarm. His chin was up, his mouth furiously set.

She faced him with a pattering heart. 'It means, I cannot afford the risk. I told you; I told you right at the start – I am the property of my mistress, and her approval matters to me. Please come along; people are staring.'

He ignored that. He was standing in the road, refusing to move.

'You need to take care of yourself too,' Caenis muttered morosely. 'Find a rich senator with a decent daughter you can marry. You need a fat landed dowry and you must become respectable if you want a career.' This was true; he acknowledged her wise advice. Duty and propriety compelled a citizen to marry, marry a woman of good background and character, then produce children. The *cursus honorum*, the official career ladder for senators, depended on it. 'I am sorry if there has been a misunderstanding,' Caenis concluded in anxious apology.

'Straight question: straight answer. Perfectly understood!' He was not angry, but bitterly hurt. With an unusual flash of spite he demanded, 'Got some fellow slave lined up, then? Jealous, is he? Think I'll scare him off?'

'Don't be simple,' Caenis rebuked him. 'Though I imagine you would; you're frightening me . . . I will not have a companion even from among the other slaves. I want to be by myself.'

He was not yet ready to let her smooth his ruffled crest. 'You should have told me you were so scrupulous!'

This time she would not reply; it was up to him whether he chose to see her distress.

Around them began Rome's terrifying transformation into night. Goods had been whisked from pavements; leaves of folding doors were drawn across shop frontages; bolts thumped heavily into sockets and elaborate padlocks rattled on cold iron chains. Above their heads a woman's thin-wristed arms hooked a cat and a pot of flowers from a window-ledge then slammed the shutter on a shadowy interior. It was now extremely dark. There were no streetlamps and hardly a chink of light showed where the crowded lodging houses faced the unfriendly streets. The grimmest alleys were emptying. Soon the city would be given over to a lawlessness where even the vigiles who were supposed to police the various districts were likely to dive into a drinking-house rather than answer a call for help.

Vespasian's slaves began to shuffle restlessly.

'Please come,' Caenis cajoled, concerned for his two guards.

'Well!' he complained crossly. 'Why did you bother with me, girl?'

Then Caenis answered with plain honesty, 'Because I do like you.' In for an *as*, in for an *aureus*. 'I like you,' she admitted, stony-faced, 'more than anybody I have ever known.'

She could tell that although he stayed where he was, indignant and disappointed in the public thoroughfare, Vespasian was utterly disarmed. Other women may have felt attracted to him, but others were not so direct. Suddenly Caenis recognised his solid exterior concealed genuine sentiment. He would never be able to resist anyone who confessed to wanting him; she dared not contemplate how warmly he would respond.

That was not for her.

'I suppose,' she acknowledged, 'this means I shall not see you any more?'

It was darker; she could not properly make out his face, but she heard his short bitter laugh. 'What do you take me for?' She dropped her head, though his voice was already softening. 'Oh lass; don't be so feeble. You know when you

47

have some poor beggar on your hook!'

'Well, why do *you* bother with *me*?' she flung back.

'He said very quietly, 'You know that too.'

His stance relaxed; he began to saunter on in silence, pulling her after him with a curt gesture of his head.

He had brought her to Antonia's house. 'Here we are; your palace, lady!' he declaimed mockingly. His guards were loitering discreetly behind the Temple of Victory as he lowered his voice. 'Going to give me a kiss?'

'No, I'm not.'

She shrank back, but after a brief stare he merely banged on the main door for her. He was persistent, but never aggressive. The porter squinted through his grating then began the extended process of unfastening locks. In the tiny square of lamplight Caenis saw a gleam in Vespasian's eye as he murmured back at her, 'Well then; are you going to let me kiss you?' At once he mimicked her crazily, '"No, I'm not!" Well, don't expect me to tussle with you in front of other people. Good night, girl. Dream of me and wonder.'

Caenis swallowed. She had no doubt of the energy with which this strong, competent man would take his pleasures – nor his ability to give delight in return. 'Wonder what, lord?'

'Wonder – what you missed!'

Looking at him, while trying not to, she felt aware of that.

The house porter was starting to pay attention. She touched Vespasian's hand briefly and turned to go in. 'Good night, Caenis.' They were friends again. His voice dropped; once more she felt stricken by its private, benevolent note.

She looked back. Vespasian had started walking down the narrow alley between the house and the temple which would eventually take him back down into the Forum or to the Circus Maximus; then he also turned. Suddenly smiling, he raised his arm in farewell. She watched him retrace his steps, closely shadowed now by the two guards. Rome at night was dangerous, yet he had a knack of walking without haste so he seemed invulnerable. Lunging towards him from their dreadful alleyways, robbers and bullies would stay their intended ambush and wait for easier prey.

It was how he walked through life: steady and unperturbed, a man who knew his way and who would arrive unscathed.

VII

Veronica knew about the walk in Caesar's Gardens by next day. 'Well; you were seen, Caenis!'

People called Rome a place where everything was noticed, and Veronica made it her business to ensure that any snippets about anyone's indiscretions were certainly picked up by her.

'I can assure you,' Caenis commented bitterly, 'I have done nothing –'

'Glad to hear it,' Veronica interrupted. 'Make them wait. They enjoy it more if they're keyed up – and if *they* enjoy themselves there is always a slim chance you might too! He'll bring you a present next time, to make sure.'

About to protest that he already had done so, Caenis realised that her powers of rhetoric would not stretch to justifying a Lucanian salami and a parchment of pickled fish.

'He won't,' she declared in a tiny saddened voice. 'I have decided not to see him again.'

This was dismally true. She had wrestled with the problem all night. It was the most anguished decision she had ever engineered.

'Oh yes; I usually do that,' Veronica languidly returned. 'But when they turn up with their present, what can you say?'

Caenis and Veronica had met at the baths. Caenis went every afternoon now, to a women-only one that was open all day (the mixed ones held women's sessions only in the morning, which was useless). She had a general arrangement to meet Veronica, an arrangement which Veronica kept with surprising regularity. She would arrive laden with trinkets that she had collected from admirers, filling the changing room with wafts of cheap perfume, taking up too many pegs with her baskets and mantles and handkerchiefs and scarves. She gave the impression she led a scatterbrained life, blown hither and yon by chance meetings with her numerous pursuers. In fact, fitting so many men into a regular scheme where the paths of those who minded about the others never crossed had long ago taught Veronica to be supremely organised.

Caenis always spent her first fifteen minutes at the baths boot-faced with bad temper. There was a convention that public baths charged women an *as*, while men only had to pay half. Caenis did not see why. In her opinion women were cleaner. It was men who used the exercise yards and swimming baths most often; men who stayed longest clattering over court cases with their friends; men who indecently assaulted the bathhouse attendants; men, moreover, who pretended they had left their money at home and tried to sneak in without paying at all. Paying double always made her angry. Veronica liked to arrive after Caenis had been ensconced in the hot-air room in her rope-soled sandals long enough for torpor to set in.

They had nothing in common as bathhouse companions anyway. Caenis wanted value for money. She went through the suite of rooms from the hot steam to the cold plunge with a gritty intent to extract every possible ounce of sensation and stimulus; if she had time she even patted a ball around or swam, which few women other than those of sinister athleticism ever bothered to do. Veronica came to chat. She certainly would not swim at the moment because her hair had been blonded and the dye would run. In fact she could not even float; she relied on the fine truth that when women with heart's-ease baby faces fall into deep water there are always eager men on hand to pull them out. Caenis, who lacked this advantage, had taught herself to swim strongly years before.

Veronica looked well with yellow hair. She also looked well with glossy blue-black curls, auburn towers of Celtic plaits, or rolling chestnut waves. If ever she grew old (though it seemed unlikely she would last so long) Veronica would be utterly distinguished once she settled for a smart silvery bun. Of them all, the present yellow crimping perhaps best suited the daintiness of her face.

Her language had never been dainty. 'Caenis, don't be such a stupid pen-pushing cow!'

As Caenis had said to Antonia, her old friend had a good heart. 'Juno! I spy some terrible spots on your back, Veronica.'

A game try.

'Oh piddle! Give me a scrape down, love – but don't try to drive me off the racecourse. I said –'

'I heard what you said.'

'Yes, but do you *listen?*' Veronica bawled.

They had known each other since they were ten and as neither was in a position to bring a body-slave they had been scraping each other's back with one borrowed strigil or another ever since. Caenis helped Veronica obliterate her shoulder rash; Veronica, using similarly brutal techniques, helped Caenis shed unsatisfactory men. Most of the men who had ever approached Caenis were hopeless; strong-minded angry girls are curiously attractive to inadequate types. She had not even told Veronica about the very worst. Nor had Veronica, who was soft-hearted in some respects, ever mentioned that there were several perfectly decent men who regarded Caenis with secret fondness; Veronica thought accepting fondness would be a fatal mistake.

'Darling, this character is completely insignificant. It's taken me half a day even to find out his name.' It had taken Caenis herself three weeks of hard effort with the usher Maritimus to extract any information. 'Time you were fixed up with someone useful, girl. Why do you always frighten the good ones off? Oh, you don't even intend to look!'

Caenis writhed. 'I do; I do! I tell myself an Indian pearl earring or several are just what I need – then I look at the types who might offer, and I curl up. It's not just the thought of their podgy fingers paddling in your private places; most of them are so *lacking*, Veronica.'

'Keep away from men with talent,' Veronica barked. 'If he falls, you may follow. If he rises you'll be dropped. *Ouch!*'

'Sorry. Give me your oil flask. *Phew!*'

'Deposited as an offering on the altar of love,' Veronica muttered.

'It's disgusting.'

'It's very expensive.'

'It would be – I'll use mine.'

As her friend ministered, Veronica lifted her own flask and sniffed at it uncertainly; she had educated views on material items, yet sometimes Caenis managed to shake her confidence.

'It's a pretty bottle,' Caenis consoled kindly. It was pink Syrian glass, traced with fine spirals and so delicate it seemed ready to shatter from the very heat of any hand that held it up to admire its translucence. That did not excuse the oil within this fine Syrian product from smelling as if it were concocted from the reproductive glands of a camel.

Wriggling her shoulders Veronica demanded, 'Well, failing some old millionaire to tickle your fancy, why refuse your Sabine friend?' She used the term 'Sabine' as an insult.

Caenis knew the answer; she had spent all night thinking it up. 'Because my Sabine friend has intelligence and good humour; both of those are qualities I like far too much.'

Veronica recognised how serious this was. 'You're smitten!'

'Oh I can't risk that.'

'No; you can't. That's losing in every way. But if you don't take the poor one and you won't find a rich one, you'd better work damned hard, then pray that your noble lady notices! Antonia may give you your freedom one day – but yours will be a small pension, Caenis, and not even happy memories at this rate . . .'

She turned around, grabbing at the oil flask, though before she started to dribble the stuff down her friend's own immaculate back she kissed her on the top of her head; she was a demonstrative girl. It was another way in which they had nothing in common.

'Now the minute he turns up with his present, I want to hear what it is.'

Vespasian did not turn up with his present: he did not turn up at all.

*

53

As Caenis gradually realised that the aggravating bastard had reached the same decision as herself, she started to dodge Veronica by taking a swim. Veronica rarely permitted herself to be dodged.

In the end she appeared at the side of the swimming bath, slapped down her rope sandals on the marble rim in a way that indicated she was not intending to go away, then waited for Caenis to surge up to her reluctantly. Caenis stayed in the water, floating on her back. Veronica stretched a fine ankle and splished the surface with one beautiful toe. They gazed at one another for a moment beneath the echoing hollow vault. Women's voices chattered against the pouring of water from jugs in the washing rooms in the background.

'Your friend's bunked off to Reate,' Veronica shouted, at her most businesslike. 'He's run home to his mother!'

Reate, famous to all Italy as the source of the finest white edible snails, was the Flavian family home. Vespasian's grandfather had settled there and he himself had been born at Falacrina nearby. Reate was where his mother lived, where both he and his brother owned summer estates. Sixty miles east of Rome, no one travelled so far and to such a country area unless they meant to stay.

Veronica usually tried to be kind for she felt Caenis had never enjoyed much of a life. 'Some of them don't know the rules. When you say no, they think you mean it.'

Caenis bobbed away from the side of the swimming bath then paddled gently back. 'I did.'

'Darling, there's your answer then!'

Before she back-flipped like some overeager performing dolphin, Caenis added with rueful bitterness, 'It's my own fault. When he promised that he would see me again I forgot the free citizen's prerogative – not to bother to tell the truth to someone else's scabby slave!'

Then Veronica replied with the two things a girl needed her friend to say: 'You're not scabby, you're lovely – and your Sabine friend's a fool!'

Going home to his mother was not the ideal escape. His mother had plans for him.

Flavius Vespasianus had been brought up in a family where women had a voice. The men went about their business in a perfectly capable manner, but they owed their position in society to the women they had married, and those women refused to be ciphers. For instance, though his brother had the same cognomen as their father, Vespasian was named after his mother. Vespasia Polla was not unique in receiving this sign of respect, though many women were denied it.

Vespasian's grandfather had married money, then his father allied himself to social status. While his father was away making a useful fortune as a banker in Helvetia, Vespasian had been brought up by his grandmother Tertulla on her large estate at Cosa on the north-west coast of Italy. Nowadays, with the family established nearer to Rome, his mother had assumed the influence that his grandmother had wielded during his happy childhood in Etruria.

His brother was doing well, as their mother pointed out. Sabinus, who had held the civic post of aedile the year Sejanus fell, had then progressed without difficulty to being elected as a magistrate two years later. By the time he was forty Sabinus would be hoping for a consulship. Meanwhile Vespasian had reached twenty-five, the year he himself was eligible to stand as a senator, though so far he had done nothing about it. A second son, he had a more easy-going attitude than his brother. He did not want to follow Sabinus into a public career – though he had no clear idea what he hankered for instead. His mother was determined to overcome his restlessness.

She was winning. She could not make him stand in the Senate elections the year that he should have done, but soon afterwards Vespasian let himself agree to return to Rome. Lucius Vitellius was prevailed upon to introduce him to high circles. This brought him into a tight-knit group of four notable families, the Vitellii, the Petronii, the Plautii and the Pomponii, who all had long-standing ties of marriage and common interest and who were increasingly prominent in government. After Sejanus fell their importance had increased. Their members were awarded a flock of consulships and it was generally perceived that they owed at least some of their success to Antonia.

Only foolishness would have allowed a young man who had access to this powerful group to miss his opportunity. Unless he chose to run off to be a travelling lyre player, with a beard and battered sandals, Vespasian was bound to end up dancing attendance at the House of Livia.

'I could bar this upstart!' offered Tyrannus.

Tyrannus was the slave who screened Antonia's guests. It was a post she had virtually invented, for in most Roman homes free access to the householder for people wishing to pay their respects or to submit petitions was traditional: but most households were not headed by women. Modesty forbade such free access to the House of Livia.

'There is no reason to bar him.' Caenis felt embarrassed to discover that everyone knew Vespasian had sought an entanglement with her – and that it had not happened.

'I'm on your side, Caenis.'

'I do appreciate that. We need not punish him.'

'Oh well – if you put his nose out of joint!'

Hardly likely, thought Caenis, as she braced herself to keep calm during Vespasian's visits.

She refused to hide. He too had no intention of pretending they were strangers. In what amounted to a public situation they were able to find a wry formality for dealing with one another. So they would pass in corridors as if by accident (though it happened quite often). They would treat one another to exaggerated politeness, enquiring after each other's health. They even stood in the atrium discussing the weather as if there had never been that fierce tug of attraction between them.

Yet remembrance of their odd friendship never died either. Caenis liked to let Vespasian see important men respectfully seeking her advice about how to approach Antonia. In return, Vespasian would fold his strong arms in his toga and cheerfully wink at her.

When he was twenty-six his mother finally prevailed. He was elected to the Senate, assuming the title of quaestor, a junior finance official, then given a posting to Crete.

VIII

'Hello, Caenis.' Her Sabine friend.

The odd thing was, even after so long she felt no more surprise when he turned up again wanting to see her than when he had first stayed away.

It was November. Huddled in her cloak because the Palace was freezing, Caenis drove herself to continue writing until the next full stop. Even then she looked up only with her eyes, the picture of a secretary too intent to interrupt.

'*Senator!*' She was shocked. Here was Vespasian's familiar burly figure uneasily swaddled in formal clothes – brilliant white woollen cloth, with wide new purple bands.

She did know he had been elected to the Senate. Antonia sent her every day to copy the news from the *Daily Gazette* which was posted up for the public in the Forum. Caenis had recited the latest list of postings to quaestor while Antonia, who realised the young knight from Reate was no longer an issue, ignored his name with tact.

'Ludicrous, isn't it?' he smiled.

'Is your voting tribe short of candidates?' Caenis jibed with mild offensiveness. Senators elect were entitled to sit on special benches and listen in to the judgements to gain experience; most provincials felt this entitlement was one a prudent man should be seen keenly taking up. It was late morning; Vespasian had probably come here from the Curia. Bound for Crete, he could only have come to say goodbye.

He hovered just inside the door. This time he passed no comment on the decor, even though the damp plaster had been cleanly reinstated while the new paint on the dados and frescos still smelt fresh. (Caenis had succeeded in subverting the prefect in charge.)

'You're going to throw me out,' said Vespasian unhappily.

'I ought to,' she replied with controlled candour. 'I owe it to myself.'

'Of course you do.' At last she lifted her head. He said calmly, 'Please don't.'

Caenis retorted, 'Naturally, sir, I abase myself like an oriental ambassador – on my face, on the floor, at your feet!'

She stayed at her table.

Vespasian quietly crossed the room, accepting her sarcasm, then piled his toga in untidy folds on his knees as he took a low stool in front of her. He watched her with those frank brown eyes; she tilted her head watching him. She remembered the frown; the energy of his stare; his physical stillness: the dangerous feeling that this man was offering his confidence and she might without warning find she was sharing hers.

'What can I do for you, senator?' she enquired, honouring him again with his new title, her tone more subdued than the question required.

Vespasian leant his elbow on her table. The wobbly legs had been stabilised for her by a carpenter who then polished up the whole piece with beeswax. Caenis folded her hands on the farthermost gleaming edge.

He was making no attempt to explain. First he had decided against seeing her again: well, she didn't want to see him. And now he had decided to come back: *well!*

He said, 'I'm trying to get hold of some notes for a decent shorthand system. The ones in the libraries are not for taking away.' This ploy was at least novel. Mad humour danced in his face as Caenis tried to resist laughing too. 'When I go abroad if I'm just trailing round after some self-opinionated governor who doesn't trust me to do anything, I may at least manage to learn taking notes properly.'

His year as a quaestor would involve travelling out to one of the foreign provinces to be the governor's finance officer and deputy. Unless they happened to have worked together before and had built up a friendship, governors and their quaestors often despised each other. In any case, she imagined Vespasian might make a prickly subordinate.

Delving into the conical basket in which she carried her equipment to and fro, Caenis produced her own battered reference sheets. She had been taught shorthand and several

58

kinds of ciphering long ago. 'This is a list of symbols I once made for myself. If you can read my scribble take it, please.'

When taking notes for her own purposes she wrote so quickly her handwriting could be eccentric, but as he glanced through he nodded. 'Thanks.' He was just like her: set a document in his hand and he was instantly devouring it.

While he was still reading she forced herself to say, 'I see the Senate have published next year's postings.'

'I've drawn Cyrenaïca and Crete.'

'Crete will be pleasant . . . When do you leave?'

'Tomorrow.' Immediately he looked up. 'Sailing when the seas are closed is traditionally the first test in the job. Sorry. I should have come before this. Stupid!' he added tersely.

Caenis did not reply.

The awkward low seat finally got the better of him. He stood up, stretching, though not yet ready to go. He began to pace about the room.

'I see you had the place cleaned up.'

'How did you know it was me?' she demanded. Vespasian let out a little laugh. Caenis blushed. 'Well, I finally nudged the prefect of works.'

He had been inspecting the new fresco. The painters had wanted to do a gladiatorial scene; painters always did. Instead Caenis had insisted on a soothing panorama of gardens, like the one in Livia's House: cranky trellises laden with creepers in whose shade three-legged herons pecked fruit from funereal urns amidst unlikely combinations of flowers.

'What does *nudging* entail?' Vespasian cracked, looking back over his hefty shoulder with a contempt that startled her.

'Oh – the usual!' When caught off guard Caenis could be a belligerent tease. She glanced down, then up again through her eyelashes. Veronica imbued this gesture with resonant sexuality; Caenis got an eyelash in one eye. 'I just took an interest in his work.'

Vespasian stared.

To soothe him, while she fiddled with the eyelash she

commented that Antonia was unlikely to keep this office once Tiberius either died or came home to Rome. It was years since he decamped to Capri. There he now owned a dozen villas plus a series of grottoes and bowers which provided a pretty playground for acting out orgiastic fantasies – or so it was said. Some of the terrible stories were probably true.

Sometimes the Emperor did make journeys to mainland Italy and circled Rome like a wary crab, informing the Senate that he intended to visit and yet then fleeing back to his hideaway with the headlong panic of a haunted man. Astrologers had decided that the hour of his leaving Rome had been so inauspicious that returning might be fatal. Caenis scoffed at the idea, but Vespasian folded his arms over his glossy new toga and said, 'Not if he really believes the prophecy.'

'That I accept,' Caenis agreed. 'He'd be quite likely to collapse if he heard a rat in the hypocaust, or a spider ran over his foot. You know, Antonia believes that is what happened to her son in Syria.'

'Germanicus? I thought he was poisoned?'

'He was; but he might have withstood it better if witches had not filled his house with fossils, and feathery monsters, and dead babies under the floorboards until they frightened him to death.' She was philosophical about Tiberius. 'So long as the creatures who parade for the Emperor's perversions volunteer, let him stay on his island.'

'Is it all true?' Eyes bright, Vespasian had a respectable man's shameless curiosity about the Emperor's fusty sexual habits.

'Worse.'

Disturbed, he saw the dismal memories clouding Caenis' face.

She braced herself to cope. She had never expressed her views on Tiberius; it had never been safe. Yet in Vespasian she placed absolute trust. To him she could speak. 'I was a child when he last lived here, but those years were very dark. His household existed in dread. He was most intrigued by persuading the aristocracy to commit obscenities, but no slave carried him a cup of wine or was sent to fasten his shoe without the risk of being stripped and subjected to indecency – either by him or the men and women who surrounded him. No one could save you if you attracted attention. Childhood was no protection. Ordinary rape was a kindness compared with the alternatives.'

In the schoolroom she herself had been relatively safe. Even so, as a teenager she had always carried her stylus knife so if she ever met trouble she could stab herself and perhaps take one of the Emperor's catamites with her. One of her friends had died of suffocation and shock during an ugly ordeal in the Emperor's underground entertainment room. Caenis would not repeat the details.

Vespasian walked slowly back to where she sat. Leering curiosity had given way to middle-class distaste. His face remained neutral though Caenis sensed the concealed throb of anger. 'Not you, I hope?'

'No,' she reassured him sombrely, with all the colour bleached from her own voice. Simply talking to him had healed her bad memories. 'Not me.'

She noticed a small nerve jerk in his cheek.

He sat down again. They changed the subject.

They spoke of Crete. They discussed the problems of running a province that was divided between a Mediterranean island and a tract of North Africa; the main advantage for the quaestor was that he could always send his governor to bumble round the other half of the territory while he enjoyed himself.

They spoke of Vespasian's mother. 'Is she fabulously pleased with you now?'

'Afraid so!'

They had become confederates. They were talking like two outsiders from society. They talked for the months they had already missed and the period of Vespasian's coming tour; openly and easily, sharing rudeness and laughter, discovery and surprise; until lunchtime, through lunchtime, and into the afternoon. They talked until they were tired.

Then they sat, two friendly companions just leaning their chins on their hands.

There were no sounds of habitation. It was so quiet they could hear the creak of walls contracting in the winter chill and birdsong – a thrush perhaps – from a far-off deserted park.

'Oh gods, Caenis; this is no good –' He flung out his arm across her table, stretching his hand towards her. '*Come here!*'

'*No!*' Caenis exclaimed. She shrank back from him instinctively.

Their eyes locked. His hand dropped. He sighed; so did she.

'All right. I'm sorry.'

'You're going away!' she cried.

They sat in silence again, but their encounter had brought them so close Caenis suddenly confessed with desperate clarity, 'I am afraid of what I feel.'

She should never have done it. She saw his face set. Men hated any admission of emotion. Men were terrified of the truth.

Not this one.

'So am I,' he acknowledged. 'But there seems nothing to gain by ignoring it.' Fiddling with her sticks of sealing wax, his tone was deliberately level. 'Are you still asking me to leave you alone?'

'I should,' Caenis returned carefully as she too found herself staring at the edge of the table. 'You know I am not.'

Though he wanted to disguise it, his gratitude was unmistakable. They both looked up again. Nothing had happened, yet everything had changed. They both smiled a little at their shared sense of helplessness.

Flavius Vespasianus was not a man anyone would expect to hold this kind of conversation. To Caenis he seemed too mature, too good-humoured, too cynical to be touched by internal conflict or uncertainty. Yet he was stubbornly himself.

'Hmm! I'm going away,' he agreed with a murmur of regret. '*What a shame!*'

After another pause he threw back his heavy head, his eyes on her all the time. 'Oh lass; I ought to leave you!'

'You must. I need to do my work.'

'I don't want to.' Yet he was already standing. They persuaded one another into sense; they always would.

Caenis had to finish correcting the copyists' work. She clambered to her feet and came round politely to take her visitor to the door. It was the first time she felt easy standing so near to him. Before he lifted the latch he turned back to her, smiling as he warned, 'I'm going away – but I shall be coming back!'

Expecting him to make some more determined move, she was startled when he carefully clasped both her hands in his while he stood, looking at her; making her look at him; keeping her close. Any other man gazing at her so intently would have made some declaration. Not Vespasian. It was illegal and impossible; Caenis accepted that he never would.

Instead, just before he released her he leant forward and kissed her, very lightly, on the cheek. It was not a lover's kiss. Nor was this formal social statement something a slave-girl would ever expect to receive from a young man of senatorial rank. This was how he must salute his mother and grandmother, how a man of his class would greet a daughter, a sister, or a wife: it was the gesture, between equals, of genuine affection and respect.

PART TWO:
ANTONIA CAENIS

When the Caesars were Tiberius and Caligula

IX

A windswept day in July. A senator, not yet thirty, bronzed from provincial service but today swaddled against the unseasonable gusts in a long brown hooded cloak with a heavy nap, walked into the Imperial Palace. He left his meagre escort of slaves at the entrance then proceeded alone. His pace slowed, more with reminiscence than uncertainty.

Tiberius still lived on Capri. There was, however, an official correspondence bureau here where the young senator conducted some perfunctory business in connection with his end-of-tour report. The secretary in charge, a Greek freedman called Glaucus, dealt with him restlessly; he found quaestors' financial statements thin on detail, loosely written, lackadaisical in style.

'You've missed your date badly with this.'

'Sorry. The new man for Crete was held up by wind and weather. I had to wait out there. Not a lot I could do about that.' His mildness was even more upsetting than the usual insolence.

Bitterly the secretary unravelled the report. By the stylish standards of this bureau it would be only a draft; Glaucus would work it over furiously before it was copied for the Emperor and filed. Most of the bored young sprats with whom he was forced to deal would never dream of disappointing his lifetime sense of outrage by producing anything remotely adequate. They were intensely competitive yet had no idea of disciplined hard work.

This one seemed to have grasped the point. If anything it made Glaucus more venomous. He asked his trick question: where was the breakdown of expenditure on entertaining distinguished visitors?

'Appendix at the end.'

On rare occasions Glaucus was compelled to endure

67

the prospect of a sprat who looked certain to go far.

Once he was released from his debriefing, the ex-quaestor turned deeper into the Palace interior. Strolling through the poorly swept corridors he passed faded staterooms long commandeered as stores. He took time to reorientate himself, but was soon nosing at that measured pace along a familiar route. He found the door he remembered. He knocked slightly; listened; his face cleared in anticipation; he went in.

Caenis was not there.

Everything had subtly changed. He had expected improvements (more of her 'nudging') yet still felt bemused. The light was muffled by a fug from two charcoal braziers; at last her room was warm. Opposite the door there now reposed a respectable table on marble feet, empty except for a bronze candelabrum in the form of a slim nymph with a look of dishevelled surprise.

There were two places on one side of the room; at each sat a smart young female scribe. Their training must be tiptop and their supervisor obviously kept a strong grip even when she was out. These girls were polite, wary, helpful, nicely spoken little things. They asked his name, though he did not tell them, then they repeated the question, though he still pretended to be deaf. Caenis would be furious with them for letting him get away with it.

He had only just missed her. Her girls, who were called Phania and Melpomene, thought she was dropping in at the Library of Octavia on her way home for lunch with Antonia; afterwards her nap, of course (*Oh of course!*), then probably to the baths to meet her friend. Phania and Melpomene related all this, without giggling, even though they realised that this must be the man who wrote to Caenis from Crete. Hoping to discover secrets, they offered to take a message; they offered to let him leave a note. He thanked them, but declined both offers, and he was still frowning as he collected his escort and left.

*

Rome had its quiet places.

He stepped from the pushing turmoil of the street into one of the dusty gardens that were open to the public, where the street-traders' cries immediately dropped to a distant background hum as if a giant door curtain had just swung closed across the garden gate. Even in Rome a man could stand and think.

Then, forcing a path along the Via Triumphalis – the same way he had once strolled to the Theatre of Balbus with Caenis at his heels – he came to the great open spaces of the Ninth District where no one was allowed to live except the caretakers of the public buildings and the priests at the temples and monuments. Plenty of people came this way, but once past the elegant Theatre of Marcellus this was another area where the noise dimmed and the pace of daily life pleasantly slowed. On the Field of Mars returning armies traditionally rested and polished up their trophies before their triumphal entry into Rome. The princes of the Empire and their chief men had established their memorial buildings here: the Theatre of Pompey, the Baths of Agrippa, the Pantheon, and the Mausoleum of Augustus.

Here too, in a muted corner of the city between that curve in the river and the dominating double heights of Capitol Hill, stood a series of monumental enclosures, the Porticos. Cool marble colonnades surrounded squares containing temples or planted groves, their internal walls adorned with magnificent frescos and their quiet cloisters filled with two centuries of booty from Egypt, Asia Minor and Greece. First on the right was the Portico of Octavia, produced by Augustus in honour of his sister; within its Corinthian columns he had deposited half the workshop of the sculptors Pasiteles and Dionysius, plus some of the finest antiques a civilised collector ever managed to loot, including a Venus and a Cupid of Praxiteles. It contained temples to Jupiter and Juno, and schools. This Portico also boasted a superbly endowed public library.

The searcher rested, his feet upon crisply frosted grass, his face upturned to the open sky, creamy as papyrus with the faint threat of rain. He gazed absently at Lysippus' slender group of Alexander and his generals conferring before the Battle of Granicus. Then once again he left his slaves outside, some squatting on their haunches and others lounging out of the wind beside the mighty columns, staring at passers-by.

The reading room was huge: thousands of manuscript rolls set into the walls like doves in a columbarium, guarded by humourless busts of safely dead historians and poets. He noticed a roped-off area where a major reorganisation was in hand. Caenis could well be involved with this; she was the sort of girl anybody would ask to help.

He invented an excuse to potter about, enlisting advice from the custodian of maps. 'Granicus, sir? Is that somewhere near the Bosphorus? No, here we are – it's on the Sea of Marmora.'

'Thanks. Stupid of me. Must have plodded through Alexander's campaigns often enough at school.'

A familiar shape on a mapskin arrested him. Caenis had called the island a scrawny goose braised in a swordfish pot: 'Somebody interested in Crete?'

'Just been returned, sir.' The custodian looked sheepish. 'We don't normally loan out the maps.'

'Nudged into it, eh?' The custodian pretended not to understand him. 'What's that racket over there?'

'Overhauling the main catalogue, sir; quite a task. A lady who is helping reminded us about the two hundred thousand volumes Mark Antony lifted from the Library at Pergamum. Some poor dog must have recorded those! She said, did we realise that Cleopatra was just a girl who liked to curl up with a good read . . .' He subsided into giggles.

After a worrying pause the senator abruptly grinned too, transfiguring his face. 'Sounds like Caenis!' He could hear her voice in his head, deceptive and crisp, as she made the daft comment. 'Is she here?'

'Not now.'

'Ah.'

Another pause.

Eighteen months abroad was nothing to a man who had already lived away from home, doing his military service at a much younger, more impressionable age. Who could say what eighteen months might bring to an ambitious female slave?

He had expected Caenis to make her way. Yet there seemed an odd discrepancy today. He had marked her as a worker. Now she seemed to rely on others, while she merely went flitting from place to place never needing to lift her pen; for a slave she was taking horribly public risks.

'Speaking of Caenis – I have something of hers I borrowed.'

'You could drop in on her at Antonia's house, sir. You might be offered lunch!'

A much longer pause: Antonia's house? Drop in? *Lunch?*

On rare occasions elderly citizens grew so incapable of managing their own affairs that unscrupulous slaves took over their property and ruled like monarchs in their homes, while the senile patrons were locked away in little rooms and starved . . . Still Antonia had family to protect her interests. Her son Claudius, though kept from public life, was an author and antiquarian – perfectly fit to supervise if ever his mother's capacities failed. And not Caenis, surely? Caenis could not be capable of abusing an old woman.

'Thanks!' the senator contented himself with saying sternly in reply.

He went home. He had lunch by himself.

There were two hundred public bathhouses in Rome. Fortunately Phania and Melpomene had mentioned which one Caenis used.

He was struggling down the Clivus Tuscus from the main Roman Forum, dragging his tired train of attendants like a magpie's unwieldy tail, when Cornelius Capito came out of the bookshop on the corner, hailed him and tagged along. By then the baths were in sight, so he stopped to converse as a man was supposed to do. A detachment of Guards came tramping straight up the centre of the road, grinding down anyone who meandered in their path; as the grumbling crowds pressed back into the gutters, Vespasian and Capito moved under the awning of a wineshop. Vespasian propped himself on the counter with its inset jars of red and white beverages; he paid for warmed measures for his acquaintance and himself, then spun a coin to the captain of his slaves so they too organised a round, glancing at him sideways, unable to believe their luck.

Vespasian's slaves knew now that there was a woman on his mind. They were still not sure if it was any particular one.

Capito gossiped happily of libel actions, charioteers, trade, the elections, his mother-in-law, his gambling debts, his barber's new Gallic pomades. A companion rarely had to answer him; he just liked a body there to spare him the ignominy of talking to himself . . .

There were two young women standing on the bathhouse steps.

'What's up?' Capito demanded, when his companion's cursory attention dried up altogether. He bore no malice; he was only surprised that Vespasian had troubled himself to loiter so long. The man was affable, but not renowned for chat.

'Wonder if I know that girl?'

Capito came to his shoulder.

One was a blonde, flimsily wrapped in a riveting crimson robe, with parcels spilling around her feet. She was exquisite, and no doubt exquisitely expensive. Cataracts of silver tumbled from her ears, flashing like cymbals in an amphitheatre parade; filigree ropes wound over her dramatic chest. She remained bare-faced and bare-headed, ignoring passers-by while the bead-sellers, the augurs' bowl boys, the plasterers, pastry chefs and pensioned-off centurions all longingly stared at her.

'It's Veronica,' announced Capito. At once a number of necks craned dangerously amongst their slaves. 'Much sought after, and amenable to being sought! Want an introduction?'

The other debated the offer as long as was polite. His slaves watched him curiously, keen for him to try his luck. They knew that when he chose he never went short. They also knew that he reckoned never to pay.

72

'Not my type.' He stroked his chin. Capito laughed.

Even from halfway down the street, Veronica's companion looked wondrously dignified.

The second girl – hardly a girl now – was wound several times in modest layers of cloth, wrapped around her body and over her head until her shape was completely disguised and her face invisible. Even so, that fine way she stood was all her own. Capito had said nothing about her. Nor did Vespasian. 'Thanks, Capito.'

With a nod to his escort, he shed everyone and began to work nearer up the street.

He was waiting for the women to separate but despite the poor weather they were dawdling on the steps. He stopped, side-stepping under the portico of a butcher's shop, pretending to eye up a rack of Spanish hams.

At last: Veronica was being collected by a double sedan chair; behind its opaque talc windows lurked a shadowy figure, no doubt some well-gilded crab. She scrambled aboard. The other woman patiently helped hand in the parcels, then leant forwards to allow herself to be kissed goodbye. As she straightened, her mantle fell back from her head. It was definitely Caenis.

She looked different.

This Caenis had parted her hair in the middle, twisted back interesting loops above her ears with glinting combs, then pinned up all the rest in fantastic plaits. With a man's eccentricity he wondered first of all *why?* – before he realised from the smart, poised, elegant set of her head exactly why: that was how Caenis had been born to look. The real question was: *who paid for her hairdresser?*

There was something wrong with her face. The defiant, demon-haunted look had been sharpened up with cosmetics – he could soon get used to that – and there was something else. Caenis had a strong face with a clear expression. He remembered the expression perfectly: the painful mixture of striving and mistrust. It had gone. Something had happened to her. Somebody had changed her. This Caenis looked strangely serene.

She had kept her knack of standing perfectly straight and

still. She was trying to lift her mantle again, but blusters of wind constantly snatched the edge from her hand. Vespasian arrived near enough to glimpse coral beads in her ears. *What bastard gave her those?*

Then something astounding happened.

Caenis turned suddenly, calling to a wizened scrap who skipped out from a pillar with the thong of an oil flask wrapped around her wrist. It almost looked as if she had her own slave, though that should be impossible. A discreet litter drew up; Caenis and her companion hurried in and at once the steps were folded away, the half-door shut for them and curtains impenetrably pulled.

As Vespasian sprang forward to roar out her name, an unusually solid footman swung smack into his path.

'Now, sir!'

Rome had turned upside down.

'I want a word with that woman –' The chair was already moving off.

'Not *that* one, sir! Try the racetrack,' advised the footman frankly, 'or the Temple of Isis. Plenty of nice girls about.'

'Thanks!' Vespasian observed civilly, though the girls at the racetrack were definitely not nice and the delicate creatures at the Temple of Isis were quite often not even girls. He let his cloak fall open so it was obvious he was wearing full senatorial fig. 'Don't I recognise your passenger?'

'I doubt it!' scoffed the footman, perfectly indifferent to anything less than a consular commander strung around with medals from at least three triumphal campaigns. But he condescended to let a junior senator grease his palm with half a denarius. 'That's Caenis,' he admitted discreetly.

'Antonia's slave?'

'No, sir,' protested the footman, with a smirk that very clearly said, *Back off, laddio; she's out of your class!* 'Antonia's freedwoman!'

There was only one solution now: laddio backed off; scowled bleakly; and strode home to write Antonia's freedwoman a grovelling note.

X

Vespasian was brief:

> O Lady! A rogue from Crete would very much
> like to see you!
>
> *T. F. V.*

He had written to her before.

The letters Vespasian wrote to her from abroad had not been embarrassing effusions. Caenis knew a great deal about love letters, from scribing them for other people. She had been deeply relieved when her own correspondent did not eulogise her as the soul of his heart and the heart of his soul, nor describe her divine eyes as entirely the wrong colour, nor spend half a page announcing in gynaecological detail the intimacies she could expect upon his return. Juno be praised, he never exclaimed that she was just like his mother. Instead he possessed the gift of apt quotation and a fine eye for the absurd. He told her interesting facts about his province and rude anecdotes about the people with whom he dealt. Years later, when he had earned a wide reputation as a joker, Caenis still thought that none of Vespasian's reported wit was so wickedly funny as the letters that he had written to her as a young man from Crete.

She had expected him to practise his shorthand. In fact since she had given him her ciphering notes too, he used code. At the back of her reference sheets he had found a system the teenaged Caenis once invented herself: 'My Code: By Caenis' was excellent; without the key, it took Caenis herself three weeks to unravel Vespasian's first letter even though she had once been the star of her cipher class.

She took a long time to reply. Caenis had never written a letter for herself. Vespasian's second arrived before she had answered his first. Yet by the middle of his tour she too had found her style and her length; she settled into speaking directly with the candour that he obviously liked, and learned to enjoy herself. Enjoying herself was almost certainly a mistake, but she no longer cared.

For reasons she could not explain, Caenis had never mentioned to him that she had gained her freedom.

That year a sense of fatality had afflicted her mistress, Antonia. She was bound to feel the loneliness of a woman whose contemporaries had all gone, many in grim circumstances, which as an elderly lady she remembered more distinctly than her breakfast that morning. She was smitten by an urge to set things in order.

Discussing with Caenis the library which bore Octavia's name, for the first time she had reminisced about her mother. Abandoned by Mark Antony, Octavia had brought up single-handedly not only their own children, but first Antony's by his stormy marriage to Fulvia and, eventually, even his children with Cleopatra. 'Not an easy woman, my mother,' Antonia had admitted. 'Impossible not to admire her – I am sure even my father always did that – but she often seemed reproachful and difficult to like.'

This was an intriguing glimpse of the legendary, much-loved sister of Augustus, so famous for her goodness. Caenis ventured curiously, 'Do you think if your mother had been less formidable, Mark Antony might have come back from Egypt?'

'Oh no!' Antonia was definite. 'Losing a man to a woman is one thing – giving him up to politics is final.'

On her birthday Antonia had freed several of her slaves who deserved retirement. Pallas was among them, rewarded by freedom and a large estate in Egypt for his good service with the letter about Sejanus. Diadumenus, the Chief Secretary, took his deserved retirement; Caenis was to be promoted. Antonia had asked her to prepare the manumission documents, which at last gave her the opportunity to speak on her own behalf: 'Madam, you know I have been saving since before I came to you. I want to ask to buy my freedom.'

Immediately there was a sense of strain.

She had known Antonia would not like it. Her patroness expected to plan her slaves' lives for them; in the Palace there had been much less scope for advancement but at least matters of business could be broached without irritating anybody else. She watched the old lady trying to be tolerant.

'That will be unnecessary.' Reluctantly Antonia explained that Caenis was to be freed one day under her will.

'Madam, I am grateful, but I should hardly enjoy looking forwards to your death.'

'Oh, I don't enjoy it myself! Now be serious; I cannot let you waste your money.'

Caenis sat still. She would pay for her freedom if she had to, but it would take all her resources. She would have nothing at all to live on afterwards. She had a bitter grasp of financial needs. Yet she wanted to be free. She had saved what she knew to be a good secretary's price; she was desperate to realise her ambition now. So many disasters might intervene otherwise. A will could be altered; Antonia's heirs might not honour it; the Senate might change the law. Now that citizenship stood within her grasp through her own enterprise, Caenis could not bear to wait.

Antonia understood the situation. A secretary might not command the outrageous price of a handsome driver or a sloe-eyed dancing-girl but Caenis, trained in the imperial school and with such good Greek, was still a prize. The fact that she managed to save her worth indicated strong willpower. Even with the offer of acquiring her freedom for nothing eventually, she would still be prepared for hardship in order to gain it now.

'You have to be thirty years old.' Caenis felt younger, but since she did not know her age she bluffed it out. Antonia pursed her mouth yet let that issue drop. 'You are forcing my hand, Caenis!'

Caenis made no reply. There was a long, not entirely amicable silence.

Antonia asked stiffly, 'Do you want to get married?' Caenis shuddered. 'Do you wish to set up in some business?

Run a salon? Open a shop?' Caenis laughed. Antonia breathed; the rings on her gnarled fingers flashed restlessly. 'Would you leave me?'

'Not if you would let me stay.'

Antonia knew she was beaten.

She sighed. 'Don't expect too much,' she warned. 'A slave is sheltered; a free woman faces more responsibilities than you may realise.'

Although Caenis was too sensitive to argue, she lifted her head; she saw Antonia close her eyes momentarily, with a faint smile. They both knew Caenis would glide into responsibility fearlessly. She was ready to be her own woman. To hold her back would condemn her. Anyone who cared for her must sympathise.

'Perhaps you will be good enough,' the lady Antonia instructed her, with petulant formality, 'to prepare for me another of these documents.' Caenis knew her well enough to wait. 'You will not be asked to buy your citizenship. Caenis, you are stubborn and independent – but, my dear, this was to be my gift to you and I refuse to forgo that pleasure!'

So it was now to a distinguished imperial freedwoman that Vespasian had to dispatch his least ruffianly slave. Not only was Antonia's house the highest ranking private home in Rome, by virtue of their position close to the imperial family, her freedwoman possessed more clout than any tax collector's son. Vespasian would not consider visiting the House of Livia without his own patron, Lucius Vitellius, and he felt wary of making a personal approach to Caenis before he knew how she would react. He was not entirely certain his scab-kneed lad would be admitted.

He was right that here they had no 'Welcome' sign set into their scrubbed mosaic floor. However, letters addressed to Caenis were always promptly delivered and Vespasian's slave was permitted to wait for her reply. At ease in her long chair in one of the tasteful reception rooms, with her own slavegirl in attendance for decency's sake, Caenis smiled a little as she dictated it to a thin Greek scribe.

So pleasant to hear from you; so kind of you to remember me. You may visit me here at any time, tomorrow perhaps if you wish. *I* should very much like to see *you*!

A. C.

Vespasian decided not to wait until tomorrow.

XI

The House of Livia, Antonia's house, like any substantial residence in Rome turned inwards on courtyards full of quiet sunlight and the soothing splash of fountains. Blank walls faced outwards, even though this dwelling possessed the added seclusion of a position on the Palatine. Everything was designed to eliminate the bustle of exterior crowds and to provide, even within the capital, a family haven of strict privacy and peace. The architects had not reckoned with the havoc that the mad Julio–Claudian family could cause in any haven, but for once the defect was not the architects' fault.

There was one courtyard garden, shaded in summer by a fig tree and overhead roses, surrounded by a colonnade. Nobody went there much nowadays. The wicker chairs and folding tables were stored on one side, together with terracotta urns of tender bulbs which had been brought under the roof for shelter. Entranced by a neglected sprawl of jasmine, Caenis had made this her private domain. It was a faintly dusty, comfortable place, kept private from formal visitors. She liked to lounge there even late in the day when the palest sunshine lancing down low over the main pantiles soon made it surprisingly warm. Sometimes after dinner when Antonia retired early to bed, Caenis sat there in silence in the dark.

Her little slave, a child who lacked any susceptibility to the romance of private thought, usually brought her a bowl of pistachios and a proper table lamp.

'Hello, Caenis.'

There was a lamp being brought but no nuts, and it was not her little slave.

'Who is it?' she gurgled foolishly. Pointless: no one else spoke her name with the solemnity of a religious address. Vespasian's substantial shadow unravelled and shrank down and up the folding doors that led out from the house. 'Oh! I

80

had better call my girl.'

'You had better not,' he retorted calmly. 'I've just given her a copper to keep out of the way.'

Reaching her, he held aloft his pottery lamp: the same sunny disposition, the same frowning face. Gazing back, where she reclined amongst cushions wrapped in a deep blue robe, Caenis felt herself breaking into a slow, tranquil grin to welcome him.

'Antonia Caenis; Caenis Antonia!' He pronounced it in full as a deliberate compliment, acknowledging her new right to be named after her patroness: that bad-tempered slavey he had first met with the pan of hot sausage, for ever now allied to the noble families of Augustus Caesar and Mark Antony.

'Just Caenis,' she shrugged. He barked with mirth; she would never change.

He set his lamp on a plinth. 'An imperial freedwoman,' he marvelled. 'Smiling in a verandah under the stars.' He sat on the edge of a pillar base, holding his head ruefully between his hands. 'O elegant and influential young lady! Far, far above a poor provincial bumpkin's reach.'

'Never,' Caenis told him softly. The dim lamplight wavered on that wonderfully jovial face so the shadow of his nose hooked in a mad slant over one cheek while the outline of his chin lapped wildly down into the hollow of his throat.

'Never? Oh I think in many ways you always were . . .' She felt like a flattered queen. He said, shining with joy for her, 'You look as if your heart could burst with pride. You should have told me you had been made up – I suppose you know I've followed you about all day. I won't tell you the things I was starting to imagine when I saw how you were queening it. Fortunately the Saepta Julia shuts up shop quite late.'

The Saepta Julia was the market for jewellery and antiques; Caenis reckoned it was not one of Vespasian's customary haunts. 'I thought the Saepta was where a gentleman goes when he wants to waste a great deal of money?'

.'Spend a lot anyway,' remarked Vespasian lightly. 'There you are. With my congratulations. Don't get excited; you can't eat it.' Withdrawing his right hand from the fold of his toga, he dropped a small but heavy package into her lap. It was tied with the kind of sleek ribbon which stated that the contents had been purchased at hideous cost.

Deeply troubled, Caenis shook her head. 'My word, this does look like a bribe, senator!'

'Sadly for me, I know you can't be bought. Go on.'

'What is it?' She was as stubborn as ever.

'New shackles.' He waited for her to look. It was a good gold bangle, in strikingly elegant taste, and of first-quality gold. 'Since you like to sit in the dark,' he said, 'I shall have to tell you I had your name engraved inside – so you can't pawn it and neither can you take it back. Your name, and also,' he added bravely, 'mine.'

There was a very slight pause.

'It's lovely . . . You can't afford it,' she protested. 'You know you can't.'

'No. A polite girl,' Vespasian observed, 'would try it on.' Caenis obediently did so.

That pillar base was striking up cold through his clothes; he stood up. For a bad moment she thought he was already taking his leave.

'Titus, thank you!'

He was visibly surprised. 'You accept my gift?'

'Certainly.'

They both knew that with her obstinate streak she might not intend accepting anything else; she wondered if his spirits sank. Without exactly flirting, she found herself enjoying her sense of command.

As she admired the bangle, Caenis lifted her feet from the floor. She was sitting in a silly summer chair that hung like a cradle from a frame. Now she automatically stretched her toes and swung; when she slowed, Vespasian lent a helping hand.

'Welcome home!' she exclaimed belatedly, looking up. 'Thank you for writing to me; I enjoyed your letters.'

'Thank you too.'

'My last to you has probably gone astray.'

Nothing ruffled him. 'Probably lie in the Cretan quaestors' work box for the next forty years, filed under

"Too Difficult" . . . Glad to see me back?'

'Mmm!' The chair spun slightly, so her robe brushed against him before he steadied the basketwork then pushed the contraption straight again. Lulled by the methodical rhythm of the swing, Caenis murmured, 'I have heard that the girls in Crete are famously attractive.'

'The girls in Crete,' returned Vespasian gravely, 'are ravishing. But their fathers are famously fierce.'

'I expect people manage.'

'I believe people do.' He pushed her chair slightly harder than before. 'Of course you always get the odd romantic who prefers to save up his initiative for some clever brown eyes he left behind at home . . . Antonia Caenis,' he mused, perhaps changing the subject. 'Caenis, in the dark with her shoes off – lovely feet! – Caenis, in a hanging chair. Very rash, young lady, *some bad man may tip you out!*'

And Vespasian tipped her out himself.

Her heart stopped.

He caught her, as he meant to do, with one strong arm around her while the other held back the chair and saved it from banging into her. He brought her close against him, as she immediately realised he would. He turned her into the tiny pool of lamplight so he could search her face while she could see the determination lighting his. As she came into his arms it felt as natural and secure as she had always known it would.

She squealed once, then grew still. 'Titus –'

'Caenis –'

They both knew what was going to happen next. They knew Caenis wanted it as much as he.

In the second when she passed from the cold atmosphere of the terrace into the warmth of his embrace she shivered, because she was startled, yet there was never any doubt. She had long ago made her choice. Against his chest she was conscious of his struggle to control his breath; her back arched slightly under the pressure of his arm; she caught his face between both hands and they moved together into an unfaltering kiss. At her eager response she heard his groan of

83

relief, then afterwards as her cheek pressed his, he felt her own shuddering sigh.

'Come to bed with me, Caenis. Oh –' Unable even to wait for her reply he kissed her again, at demanding length. 'Convinced?'

Caenis, who even now did not smile easily, smiled at Vespasian. 'Convinced!'

Then he astonished her again; he suddenly held her, not in the great wrestler's hug she expected but as tenderly as some ceramic almost too delicate to touch, while he muttered against the complicated pleating of her hair, 'Oh Antonia Caenis . . . Welcome to freedom – and welcome to me!' Then she knew this was a truly sentimental man. She put it from her mind. 'Is there somewhere we can go?' He could have taken her then and there, in the dark, amongst the stored furniture and tubs of desiccated flowers; he was ready and her need was as urgent as his.

But Caenis possessed a modest comfortable room where, as a freedwoman, she was entitled to entertain her friends. She was proud of her achievements; she took him there.

It was as she had always expected. This man was her other half. The bungled conjunctions in her previous experience were swept from her memory. The unwelcome clutches which had once seemed to be her only future could be angrily rebuffed. She would never again fall prey to incongruous hangers-on. She need never be coerced by her own insecurity. Now she knew everything. She had found the joy she had tried so hard to believe in.

They were perfectly at ease. They had already established a companionship which ran deep and true. Each took, each gave with overwhelming honesty, openness and delight.

When at the end Vespasian rolled over and lay on his back, he covered with one great hand deep brown eyes that were no longer so steady. '*Oh lass!*'

Caenis was laughing as she rested her head upon his hammering heart, one arm outflung across his body to the edge of the bed. '*Oh yes!*'

She felt his breathing start to settle but he was not asleep, for after a time he drew the coverlet around her and gathered her close. When he spoke his voice sounded subdued, as if he had somehow been caught off guard. 'A fine pair, you and I.'

Caenis found and kissed his hand. After a moment she confessed, 'I wish you had not given me your present.'

'Mmm?'

'I did not want a bribe.'

By then he was shaking with laughter. 'You deserve a present. And you're well worth a bribe! . . . I was certain it would make you say no.' His arm tightened around her; his voice steadied. 'I won't be shaken off now.'

'What?'

'Don't try to send me away.'

He knew her at least as well as she knew herself, for that was of course what Caenis had intended to do.

'No,' she told him gently, and settled against his shoulder as if for sleep, so he probably assumed his challenge had persuaded her. 'While you want me, I shall never do that.'

Her intention had been overturned. Quite simply there was no longer any choice. She would not send Vespasian away because she could not.

Nor could she sleep. She lay with a throbbing brain as she buckled together her resources to cope with the commitment she had made. Impossible to tell whether Vespasian realised how she had withdrawn into herself; she hoped not, for she did not want him to wonder why. There was nothing to be done about it; nothing she even wanted to do. But Caenis recognised now, now when it was far too late, the mistake she had made: she had entered into a contract whose conditions were the exchange of friendship and pleasure on terms that should be utterly businesslike.

And she had given this terrible contract to a man with whom she was inescapably in love.

XII

There was a way around the difficulty. It was perfectly simple: Caenis would make sure Vespasian never knew.

She was his mistress for two years. To be attached to a young senator was useful to her and helpful to him. He took her where a woman without family could not otherwise go, while she introduced him to people a man so obscure might not otherwise meet. The situation never deteriorated into the one-sided disaster it could so easily become. Caenis made up her mind that she could either suffer – and suffer very deeply – or accept for however short a time what could be the most joyful experience of her life. So she tried to stay sweet-tempered, as no doubt he did too, and they were the firmest of friends.

They settled into a tranquil routine. Each was considerate of the other's private life; each gladly set aside time for them to be together. Neither was selfish or quarrelsome. Quiet conversation walking in a garden or sitting in some congenial room meant as much to them as the times they spent in bed. So far as possible they were open about their relationship, though discreet. Neither thought it clever to shock. Whenever they could they went to the theatre or listened to speeches; occasionally they dined with sympathetic friends. People liked them; they were an undemanding, easy-going pair. A world of casual couplings and cynical self-interest was perhaps intrigued by the warmth of their steady affection. It never became scandalous.

Caenis tried to explain to Veronica but with little success. Veronica dismissed Vespasian as a disastrous unknown. Although Caenis had tried to live by a strict code (men she liked were few enough; best not sleep with men she liked), Veronica's code was even stricter: best not to like men at all.

Quite soon after Vespasian came home from Crete Caenis

met her girlfriend, buying garlands on the Sacred Way. Veronica, who was still a slave, did have official duties though she somehow arranged they should be as light as possible. Some people manage to establish that their contribution at work is merely to move around being pleasant; it is understood that no more is to be expected of them and it would be pointless to chastise them for being as they are.

Veronica was not foolish. She never forgot she might one day be challenged. She was the slave who ordered the wreaths for the banquets the absent Emperor never gave. So she made sure she was seen from time to time with abundant armfuls of flowers.

It was early morning, the light already bright today as the florists set out their trolleys and trays, and refreshed their blooms in the public fountains. Men of all ranks were hurrying through the streets to visit their patrons and claim their daily dole – a basket of bread or a small gift of cash – in return for obsequiously paying their respects. There was a scent of new-baked loaves. Tired women draped bedclothes over balconies to air or swilled water across the lava pavements to wash away the rubbish and trickled stains that were the gifts of the previous lawless night.

'Caenis! Caenis, wait!'

Veronica's voice had rung effortlessly above the raucous cries of 'Garlands; garlands! Best on the Sacred Way!', 'Fine crowns of roses!', 'Myrtle wreaths; spikenard from India; garlands for your guests!' as the sellers plied their wares. Little boys in sweatshop basements, where the atmosphere swooned with the sickly reek of violets and rose petals, worked through the last hours of darkness, with damp tingling fingers bending stiff stalks into long strings which tonight would adorn fat necks and sagging bosoms. Veronica came early, while the blooms were fresh; she would keep them all day somewhere in deep shade, sprinkling the wreaths with water and standing the glorious bouquets in tubs. 'Help me carry these festoons.'

Caenis obediently let herself be weighed down under ropes of white and gold, with seven crowns of laurel plonked for convenience on her head; once your arms were full it was the best way to carry crowns. 'Come with me out of this racket. I want to step into the Temple of Cybele –'

They struggled to the temple on the Palatine. Caenis had no real objection, because it lay almost adjacent to Livia's House, so she could be close to home when it was time to attend on Antonia. Veronica laid out her flowers in the portico where they would not be crushed, curling the garlands on a grey stone floor like wriggling caterpillars frilled with crisp yellow stripes. Here the background was quiet, with languorous oriental music and intoning priests; occasional triangles and cymbals made them jump. Incense, subversive as a drug, prickled the nerves. It was a place of impersonal mystery; Caenis had always found it faintly seedy, not least because the steps of the Temple of Cybele were a famous pick-up point. The annual rites, led by male priests notorious for their frantic dancing, were an occasion for women's unbridled release; it was not to her taste.

Veronica urged with hushed excitement, 'Sit by this pillar. You did it then? The bangle!' Caenis wore Vespasian's bangle every day. Veronica twisted it about on her arm, testing the weight. Caenis resisted taking it off; she did not want Veronica's comments on the two names engraved together inside. 'You've done well there. It's a good one –'

Caenis said bluntly, 'I didn't want this. I wish he knew I took him for the joy of it.'

'You know better than to ever tell them that!' Veronica retorted. 'Watch yourself.'

'I know.'

Caenis really did know. She had always been eccentric. She understood what she had done.

Veronica despaired of the girl. She could not bear to witness that look of being quietly reconciled. To Veronica this deliberate facing-up to unpalatable facts, this stoic acceptance of pain even before it occurred, seemed unnecessary. She offered consolations Caenis did not want; she offered self-delusion; she offered dreams: 'Don't underestimate yourself, Caenis. You can hold on to that one if you want. Even if he marries –'

'*No!* When he marries, he goes.'

'Oh dear. I see. My poor girl . . . Oh help! We'd better salute the goddess. That priest with the watery eyes has spotted us.'

Veronica always knew what men were doing; he had. At once they saluted the lofty statue through the portals of the temple, making it plain to any slyly watching Corybantes that they required neither mystic intercession with the goddess nor whispered proposals for commerce of a more sensual kind.

Cybele, the oriental matriarch sacred to chastity, who had lured her lover Attis into self-inflicted castration, was not the obvious choice for Veronica's devotion. Perhaps the attraction was that she lacked the patrician smoothness of the Graeco-Roman gods. Cybele was blood, and earth, and the knife in the grove – a goddess of the ecstatically anguished scream. Her statue was within the sanctum, enthroned, guarded by lions, and bearing an oriental drum representing the world.

The two women made no attempt to breach protocol by entering the temple, but approached the outdoor altar. Veronica offered to this dark lady a small cluster of violets then prayed aloud with her own inimitable good cheer: 'O Cybele, Mother of the Gods, Lady of Salvation, accept these blossoms. Make me handsome at thirty, rich at forty, and please, lady, dead by fifty! Make me careful, make me cheerful and (if you must, O Cybele!) make me good.'

Caenis produced no offering. But she looked back, glimpsing through the portal the hard face of the goddess from the east who was supposedly friendly to women, and she prayed in her heart. *O Cybele, great Idaean Mother, let me not love him more than I can bear!* Adding, because she did love him and she recognised in him a man who would be genuinely concerned at her yearning pain, *And, O Cybele, don't let him love me!*

Two years was a long time to keep a secret from somebody so close. But she never said.

Well; once.

Once, at the end of a dinner party, when she was tired and

at her low time of the month, when she had perhaps in consequence drunk far too much, he muttered something under his breath to her, with his head against her head, something spectacularly rude about one of the other guests, which made her suddenly giggle so much that her tension slithered away like a runnel of sand until, weak with laughter, she let herself exclaim with the force of desperate truth, '*Oh, I love you!*'

Then she did not know how to cope.

People had probably heard. It was not what she had said that mattered, but what saying it aloud had done to her. The look on Vespasian's own face was so odd she was forced to apologise, sliding atilt to her feet: 'I've had too much wine; I'm embarrassing us. I'll go home – you don't need to come . . .'

But he came. He came, ambling after her like some great loyal mastiff, nuzzling the back of her neck while she tried to put on her outdoor shoes, towing along when she went for her chair, clambering in with her to the despair of the slaves who had to carry them both and then fondling her on the way home almost to the point of highway rape. He came into the house, nibbling her left ear, bribing the porter who did not normally expect to let him indoors so late; he came with her all through the elegant corridors, wrapping her around pillars with tipsy abandon then growling rumbustiously when she escaped. He came, mad as a clown in some rude Atellan farce, into her room.

Where in darkness and complete silence he seized her, every line of his body melting into hers; and kissed her, absolutely sober, absolutely serious, absolutely still. Terrified, she tried to close her brain to the fact that he understood. She was ashamed to speak; he would not let her. Elated by a passion that seemed to devastate them both, he undressed himself; he undressed her; he brought her to the bed, still without speaking a word as if what he wanted to say was inexplicable. Then he made love to her as even he never had, befuddled as she was, befuddled as she thought *he* was, drawing them to ecstasy over and over again. When Caenis slept, perhaps the deepest slumber of her life, for once he was there throughout the night, not even lying at her side, but encircling her with every limb, every inch of him flooding her with abundant companionship.

Vespasian awoke just before dawn; his lifelong habit. Caenis awoke with the change in his breathing which was, whenever she had the chance, a habit of hers. He kissed her lightly on the forehead.

'I enjoyed that!'

'So did I.'

His mouth tightened into the line that she recognised as his most personal smile. 'I thought you did!'

He left the house quietly. They never mentioned the incident afterwards. Sometimes she caught Vespasian's eye carefully upon her when she knew he thought her preoccupied and then, although Caenis was not normally given to frantic gaiety, she would turn on him and pelt him with mimosa blossoms, or snatch the cushions from under his elbow, or tickle his feet.

After they settled down, she always knew when he was watching her again.

XIII

The Emperor Tiberius died in his seventy-eighth year at Cape Misenum. He had been riding to Rome but turned back when his pet snake was discovered dead and half-devoured by ants. Caenis thought any pet doomed to be hand-fed daily by Tiberius would fling itself cheerily to the ants.

. Soothsayers decided that if the Emperor entered the city he would be torn apart by the mob. For once their interpretation seemed adept. Tiberius' last years had witnessed a reign of terror during which the appalling cruelties inflicted upon his own family and on members of the Senate were only equalled by the vile debaucheries to which the Emperor subjected himself. Show trials for alleged treason had become commonplace. His absence encouraged wild rumours about his personal habits. Rome viewed him with horror and his death was greeted with joy.

It was typical of Tiberius' malevolence that since he knew people wanted him to die he had struggled violently to disappoint them. He had tried to disguise his failing strength and clung so stubbornly to life and power that he even climbed out of bed calling for his dinner after being once pronounced dead. In the end his impatient young heir, Caligula, was widely believed to have assisted his adoptive grandfather into the underworld by applying a pillow to his face.

Caligula was a tall, pale, prematurely balding youth. Caenis had known him slightly when he lived with Antonia before being summoned by Tiberius to Capri, perhaps to be trained as a successor – or simply to let Tiberius gloat over the viper he would be bequeathing to Rome. The young man appeared to have a quicker intelligence than his coheir, Gemellus, was reputedly eager to learn, and had distinguished himself at an early age making formal public speeches, including the funeral oration for his great-grandmother Livia. Yet Tiberius had held reservations about him and uneasy stories circulated. He was certainly under the influence of Macro, Sejanus' even more brutal successor as chief of the Praetorians, the man who permitted his wife to have an affair with Caligula, and who probably helped him speed Tiberius' death.

Caesars who overstayed their welcome must expect to be hurried along. Even Augustus was supposed to have been poisoned at the end by his famously devoted wife. Of the nine Caesars who ruled Rome during Caenis' lifetime, only one would die of natural causes, quietly succeeded by his own elder son; only one sardonic soul would leave the world joking even at death: 'Dear me! I feel I must be turning into a god!'

If Caligula had a sense of humour it was to prove macabre, and he wanted his divinity in his lifetime. Yet he began discreetly. The Senate were too frightened of the army to protest when he asked to be awarded sole rights as Emperor; the army loved him because since a baby he had been their mascot, and while armies may change their minds or their loyalties they do not so readily change their mascots. No doubt encouraged by their commander, Macro, he had awarded each of the Praetorian Guards a thousand sesterces which ensured their loyalty. Two days after Tiberius died, Caligula supplanted his coheir, Gemellus, and assumed in a single decree of the Senate all the powers which Augustus and Tiberius had collected gradually and with modesty.

Rome first hailed his succession as a new golden age. He was the people's pet, their shining star. He was the son of their hero Germanicus and after twenty years of Tiberius, who terrified and appalled everyone, Rome badly wanted to find good in Germanicus' son. Gemellus was quickly sidelined. At twenty-five Caligula had become lord of the civilised world.

Caenis was to observe that the worst Emperors all began with sanctimoniously proper acts. Caligula, Nero, and also Domitian – though she never saw him rule in his own right – started public life with a show of youthful good behaviour. It was as if those whose balance of mind was most vulnerable to excess made a last effort to win real admiration before absolute power sent them off their heads.

People called Caligula deceitful. It was certainly said that when Tiberius had summoned him to Capri he willingly joined in the foul practices, and he turned himself into Tiberius' agent and spy; this hardly fitted the personable image he first tried to cultivate as Emperor. He had previously acquiesced in silence to the exile and death of his mother, Agrippina, and his two elder brothers. Yet perhaps if he had not done so he might have ended like his brother Nero Caesar, who was forced to commit suicide on a remote island, or his brother Drusus, who was starved in a cellar under the Palace until he choked to death on pieces of flock from his mattress. Perhaps an adolescence spent in such danger and an apprenticeship under Tiberius explained, if they did not excuse, Caligula's unhinged mind.

Under Macro's tutelage he cultivated a pious image at first. Among his first popular actions was a journey to fetch the ashes of his mother and brother from their island prisons for ceremonial interment in the Mausoleum of Augustus; at the same time he renamed the month of September after his father Germanicus. Even then there were signs of extravagance, for in honouring his sisters, particularly his favourite, Drusilla, he went to extraordinary lengths, giving them the privileges of the Vestal Virgins, allowing them, though women, to watch the Games from the imperial seats, featuring all three on the coinage, and including them in the vow of allegiance which the consuls swore.

He did banish all the painted androgynous perverts who had entertained Tiberius. For a time he set to with political will, reducing taxation, relieving censorship, reinstating the independence of the courts, compensating householders for losses through fire, purging scoundrels from the lists of senators and knights. But Rome was his plaything. There he could soak in baths scented with exotic oils, invent extravagant cuisine, dress in outlandish tunics and footwear, flood the Saepta for naval battles, build his own racetrack, gamble like a fanatic, and indulge in chariot races and theatrical shows to his heart's content. He was a man who had been an underprivileged child, now given a whole city as his personal toy.

His relationship with his grandmother became prickly right at the start. Shortly after his accession the new Emperor sponsored a decree in the Senate to confer upon Antonia all of the honours which had been awarded to the Empress Livia during her lifetime. Antonia had always taken a sour pride in refusing to emulate Livia. She had rejected every title offered by Tiberius, even after she informed him of the dangers of Sejanus. Now it made no difference. Respect for his noble grandmother would enhance Caligula's reputation: the honours were hers. It was as useless to refuse the gifts as to hope the respect was genuine.

Caenis noticed Antonia began to look physically grey. People wondered afterwards if Caligula tried to poison her. It was not so. He simply eroded her spirit. She had been responsible for him after Livia died, and she was aware of the danger in overloading him with honours – or even too much responsibility. Antonia felt bound to attempt to restrain him, which inevitably turned him against her.

Caenis found her one day with her face streaming with silent tears. 'Never have children!' she said bluntly. 'Never marry, and be thankful that you have no family!'

Caenis remained still, allowing Antonia the opportunity to speak. 'I have been to see the Emperor. He makes unfortunate friends; he is too easily influenced. But I am accused of interference, of course.'

During those first few weeks of his reign she was still the only real influence for good upon Caligula. She alone dared urge restraint. But when she requested a private interview, he offended against all decency by bringing Macro, his unsavoury commander of the Guards. It was an insult to his grandmother, and perhaps a threat too. If Caligula had been truly mature he would not have needed to do it. Still, it was now being said openly that Macro was grooming a protégé who would soon need no tutor.

Caenis was furious at the insult to Antonia. 'I would have come with you! I am not afraid.'

'Perhaps we should all be afraid, Caenis.'

95

Antonia was heavy with despair. Caenis lifted away the mantle she wore outdoors, helped her to her long chair, settled feather-filled cushions under her spine, pursed her mouth in warning to disperse the house slaves who were flitting about in uncertainty.

Antonia sighed wearily. 'My grandson Gaius Caligula informs me he can do whatever he likes to anybody. It is effrontery – but it is all too tragically true!' Caenis had never heard her speak with such bitterness. 'The fate of everyone in Rome and the Empire rests in his hands. He is not fit. Not even his father could control him – not even Germanicus. And the fools have given him unrestrained power!'

They were silent for some time, Caenis hoping that her patroness would share whatever had occurred; however, Antonia had regained her rigid self-discipline. When she did speak, it was to say in her normal abrupt tone, 'You are expecting your friend. Is he here?' When Caenis was with Antonia, Vespasian usually waited in another room. 'Call him in!' commanded her mistress, for once surprising her.

He entered quietly, a sturdy figure with all the well-tempered qualities the latest wild crop of Claudians completely lacked.

'Flavius Vespasianus, there is no point lurking in corners. Caenis has the sensitivity of a guardian goose on the Capitol; the girl can hear your footfall three streets away and I know she has heard your arrival by the way she jumps!'

For a moment the old lady's attention seemed to wander. She had become markedly frail lately, although six months earlier she had been still strong enough to have visited her villa at Bauli, where she had defiantly tackled Tiberius about his treatment of her rakish, debt-ridden protégé Herod Agrippa, walking alongside the Emperor's litter until he acquiesced to her demands for leniency. That spirit seemed to falter lately. Now when she gave Vespasian her hand Antonia held on to his much longer than he expected, gazing at him as if she had forgotten to let go. Her fingers were ridged like the bark of a carob tree. In the end she did release him; then he bent to kiss Caenis on the cheek, though he murmured, 'Excuse me –' politely to Antonia first.

96

'Well; I have not seen much of *you*!' Antonia scolded him; it was slightly unreasonable since she had always remained impatient of their friendship. 'Caenis tells me you are standing for aedile?' This post, as one of the curators of the city, was the next step in the *cursus honorum*, his upward progress through the various ranks of the Senate. 'Confident?'

'Not in the least!' Vespasian returned frankly. 'Too provincial and too poor.'

Antonia considered the point. 'Too much the bachelor.'

There was a complex array of legal discouragements to the single life, partly hitting a citizen where it hurt most, in his bank box, but also giving precedence to married men and fathers at elections. Not only were bachelors disreputable, they were disloyal to their ancestors and the State. Even so, Antonia seemed comparatively indulgent. 'Your day will come. Caenis believes in you. Take my word for it, that makes you exceptional!'

Vespasian was standing just behind Caenis' couch and although public gestures of affection were traditionally improper he set one hand on her shoulder and kept it there, his thumb moving fitfully against her neck. Old-fashioned as she was, Antonia seemed not to object. Caenis herself peacefully laid her hand upon Vespasian's to still his caress.

After one of the remote pauses which were becoming characteristic Antonia observed unpredictably to Caenis, 'Always favour a man who is tolerant of old ladies: you will be an old lady yourself one day.'

Caenis let her hand fall.

Vespasian said nothing. He must know, as Caenis did, that she would have to cope with old age by herself. They were both realistic people.

Antonia was surveying him, while he steadily returned her stare. They were in some subtle way vying with one another. Caenis felt troubled. These were the two people she allowed herself to love; their jealousy of her affection seemed ridiculous.

'I cannot require you to take care of her,' Antonia said to him. 'You are in no position to make promises.'

Despite the critical undertone, he humphed with amuse-

97

ment. 'Madam, we both know Caenis. She will insist on taking care of herself.'

'Oh she expects to get her own way,' Antonia scoffed. 'But sometimes even she will need a friend.'

'Caenis will always have more friends than she realises,' Vespasian declared in a low tone.

They were now speaking as if Caenis had left the room. Embarrassed for Vespasian, she wondered why women always imagined that caring for someone gave them the right to interfere.

Then her patroness turned to her with a swift and unusually intense smile. 'Forgive me, Caenis; I must leave one person at least who is prepared to overrule you!'

It was an odd scene, which left Caenis puzzled and disturbed.

Antonia's son Claudius was expected. His visits were rare. The butt of the court for his apparent feeble-mindedness, he had been deemed unsuitable for public life – a bitter contrast with his glorious brother, Germanicus. He had retreated into obscure branches of scholarship; he aggravated his mother and tried to keep out of her way.

Anticipating a visit had made Antonia restless. She told Caenis and Vespasian to take themselves off, but before they left the room she suddenly called Vespasian back. 'You invited Caenis to your grandmother's villa at Cosa?' He had; Caenis refused to go.

Annoyed that the subject had come up, Caenis stood glaring from the doorway. She had consistently avoided Vespasian's family, for while they probably did not object to his taking a mistress who was highly placed and obviously discreet, dealing with a freedwoman socially would be as difficult for them as for her. His grandmother, the formidable old lady who had brought him up, was dead, yet even now visiting her house seemed indelicate to Caenis.

'Madam –'

'I want you to go,' Antonia interrupted her. 'Go, and enjoy yourself.'

At that moment her son was announced; it would be

discourteous to let him find his mother quarrelling. Claudius came in, with that vivid shock of white hair and the strange halting gait; he made as if to kiss his mother, thought better of it, started to say something to Caenis, decided against that too, then seated himself, looking immediately more controlled and more at ease. Antonia visibly struggled to disguise her agitation. Their relationship was hopeless. Claudius was too close; with him her normal inflexible courtesy broke down. Then her tension communicated to him, so that in her presence his tic and his stammer grew far worse.

'Caenis is going to Cosa,' Antonia said gruffly. 'With her friend.' It was impossible to rebel against this public instruction. 'Do you know Flavius Vespasianus? My son —'

In this way it turned out that Vespasian was introduced to Claudius, and by Antonia herself. Although she thought her son ridiculous and ineffectual, he was the grandson of Augustus after all. The pretence had to be maintained politely that Tiberius Claudius Drusus Nero Germanicus was a useful person for an obscure young senator to know.

XIV

Caenis could not understand why people regarded travelling as a nuisance. Until she went to Cosa she had never been any distance outside Rome. She found the experience wonderful.

Admittedly it was an uncomfortable journey. First she made her way alone by chair, over the river at the Pons Sublicius, through the Fourteenth District where the street-sellers and other itinerants lived, to the outskirts of the city. Vespasian met her on the Via Aurelia with a two-wheeled conveyance drawn by a pair of unkempt mules.

'Bring cushions,' he had warned tersely. It was good advice.

Some people travelled in massive four-wheeled stage-coaches, big enough to take their beds yet effortlessly dashed along by two pairs of swift and shining steeds. Some owned carriages lined out with scarlet silk curtains, decorated with silver filigree, equipped with integral footrests, wicker food baskets and fold-down draughtsboards to keep them entertained. Even within the city most senators were carried about reclining in litters borne high on the shoulders of fearsomely tall slaves. The Flavian brothers shared a light fly with just room for two people and a wineskin; luggage was tied on the roof with a goat-hair rope. The Sabine territory was supposed to be famous for fine quality mules. One of theirs, Brimo, was notorious all along the old Salt Road to Reate for his snorting bad-temper. The other, though sweeter-natured, was susceptible to bald patches and missing an ear; Brimo had bitten it off.

Caenis discovered that the hazards of travelling made Vespasian unusually bad-tempered. Fortunately he spared her. Caenis was no trouble; Caenis only gazed about, uncomplaining and utterly enthralled.

The first time they stopped to rest she walked by herself a

little way into the open countryside where she simply stood, with her arms wide, soaking in the unimpeded spring sunlight and the peace. They were in Etruria. They had wanted to make the town of Caere for lunch, but Brimo decided to slack. Instead they had eaten salad and fruit amongst the soft round tumuli of the Etruscan houses of the dead. To the right were low hills; to the left newly ploughed fields stretched towards the distant twinkle of the sea.

Vespasian, calmer now, came up behind her. He tickled her neck with a great piece of grass; Caenis took no notice.

'Whatever are you doing?'

'Looking at the emptiness – so much sky!' She had never been out of the city before.

Vespasian scratched his ear, amazed.

Cosa was eighty miles north from Rome as the crow flies, more by road. An imperial courier could have covered the distance easily in two days with time to spare for a meal, a bath and a massage in the *mansio*; not so the Flavian mules. Trailing at a crawl through Tarquinii, Vespasian muttered they would all go home by sea.

Cape Cosa unfurled out into the ocean on a stout stem like a bullock's ear. The town lay just to the south, where the peninsula joined the land, with a strange lagoon filled with light as green as bottle-glass. Small boys, like Vespasian himself years before, jumped tirelessly into the clear water then raced back along the mole to jump in again. Cosa was a neat Greek-founded sea town with an unhurried atmosphere. Vespasian's grandmother's estate lay a little way to the east. It was perfectly obvious this would always be his favourite place.

Afterwards Caenis rarely spoke of the time she had spent at Cosa. She knew it was their one chance to live together in the same house. She glimpsed Vespasian as he was at home; watched the full span of his day in its regular rhythm from waking before dawn, through correspondence in the morning, lunch and a siesta in bed with her, then a bath and his cheerful dinner at night. She observed the good-humoured mistrust between him and his slaves – he expecting to be cheated, they grumbling at his miserliness – yet all somehow rubbing along together loyally for years; if he was mocked by other people, they knew he also mocked himself. People who dealt with him regularly all accepted the man as he was.

He showed Caenis the places that held memories of his childhood, the objects about the house that recalled his grandmother. He was preserving the villa as it had always been. It was his festival place. Here his face lightened; his intensity relaxed. He was visibly happy; and seeing him so made Caenis set aside her own doubts in order to be happy with him.

Most people, Caenis supposed, existed in their hopes for the future; she could never do that. She must live for the present. At least now she would never again be someone with no past. She too would have, if she could bear them, affectionate memories to carry forward to her old age.

They did go home by sea. Caenis liked sailing even more than travelling overland.

By the time they came into Rome from Ostia it was all she could do to disguise her gathering misery. This was not simply because she had been forced to view so closely all she could never possess. She thought she knew why Vespasian had wanted to take her to Cosa. It was his favourite place: he was arranging for his own memories to include one of Caenis there. With leaden foreboding, she guessed why: their time together would not last much longer.

She was too depressed even to be surprised when he made a detour with her chair to the apartment where his brother lived. Vespasian lived there too, though he was planning to take rooms of his own before the next elections in order to seem a more substantial candidate; no one would take seriously a man who only lodged in his brother's attic.

Caenis had never been there before. She waited outside in the chair while Vespasian went into the apartment block. The area was run-down but adequate; Caenis recognised the district, somewhere near the Esquiline on the less fashionable side. There was a wonderful parchment and papyrus warehouse nearby where she had been once or twice to order supplies.

He came back. 'Step indoors for a moment.'

He had opened the half-door and offered his arm for her to clamber out before she had any time to hesitate.

It appeared Sabinus was not at home. His wife stood waiting in the hall, a short girl about Caenis' age with a round pleasant face that looked understandably concerned. Theirs was a house rather bare of furniture and what they did have was all rather heavy and old-fashioned, though Caenis guessed that was just Sabinus' sombre taste. There were massive red curtains that looked difficult to draw. Though the atmosphere was initially so formal, all the legs of the sidetables and couches had been scuffed by children's toys.

She experienced a sensation that this visit had been pre-arranged. Afterwards she felt certain, though she never found out how Vespasian knew what had happened. They wanted to take her into a side room, but she was already demanding in agitation, 'What is it? *Titus!*'

Sabinus' wife reached for her hand. Caenis felt a sense of despair closing in.

He said, 'I wanted to tell you this myself.' She knew. He was leaving her. 'Lass, I didn't want you to get out of the chair and see the cypress trees standing at the door, the house dressed up in mourning –' She did not know after all. Sometimes the brain is stubbornly slow. She put up one hand, foolishly smoothing her hair. He had to tell her, for even then she did not understand. 'Your lady Antonia is dead.'

She refused to accept it. She did not move; she could not speak.

'Caenis! Oh my dear –'

Caenis closed her eyes. Vespasian was holding open his arms, but although she desperately wanted to bury her face in his shoulder she had to blot him out. She could not afford his comfort. If she gave way now, she would never be brave again – and, Caenis knew, she would certainly have to be brave.

She said, with brutal clarity, to Sabinus' anxious, well-scrubbed wife, 'I am alone. That lady was all I ever had!'

Vespasian's arms dropped to his side. It was too late to take the words back.

Sabinus' wife – Caenis had been introduced, but she found she could not now remember the young woman's name – had taken her somewhere, some room, a library perhaps.

'What happened? Was this Caligula?' Caenis asked her.

'We don't think so. Not directly. It appears to have been natural; she was an old lady, after all. But people are not sure. It may have been her own choice.' Suicide. 'These things are not given out.'

'No,' Caenis responded dully. 'No. They are not.'

'Cry if you want to.'

But Caenis could not cry.

And then the young woman said, 'Don't go home yet; stay and have some lunch. There's nothing to be done. You may as well go home braced.'

Caenis almost felt amused. She protested grimly, 'Your brother-in-law has no right to ask that of you!'

Sabinus' wife looked at her levelly. 'He didn't,' she said. In that moment Caenis recognised that the wife of Flavius Sabinus was the friend she could never have.

Although eating was almost impossible, she stayed to lunch.

When she was ready to leave she refused to let Vespasian go with her. She and Sabinus' wife exchanged weak smiles. They had surprised him; they had even perhaps startled themselves. They were enjoying their small revolt against the order inflicted upon women by men. They had weighed one another up; then sharing that small sad smile they gave way to the social rules. However, it was his brother's wife, not Vespasian, who hugged Caenis at the door.

By then Caenis was impatient to reach home. Her balance had to some extent stabilised but she felt as if she would not entirely accept Antonia's loss until she returned to the house. She needed to be alone in her own room there before she could even begin to assess her feelings.

Vespasian looked disturbed, but she had no spare concentration for soothing him. 'Caenis, she wanted you to go to Cosa. It was deliberate.'

104

'I should have been with her. Why didn't she know that?'

'You had a special place with your lady. She knew.' His hands were heavy on her shoulders; she could not easily escape. His own face was white. 'I imagine she could not bear to see you upset.'

He could not bear it either; Caenis understood. She finally wrenched free and stood off from him. Grimly she took upon herself the duty of the bereaved to reassure those around them. 'I'm sorry for what I said. I have you; of course; I know.'

Impassive, he said nothing at first, then dismissed it with, 'This is not the time.'

Being a man he had failed to see that it was only now, now when she was too deep in some other trouble, that she could ever speak of what she felt for him. Yet he had never flinched from reality so Caenis told him tersely, 'Never lie to me. Tell me the truth, as soon as you must. Don't just hope I will work things out for myself; Titus, don't leave it to me –' She stopped.

'No,' he said.

Then as she turned to climb aboard her chair, he suddenly spoke out too. 'Your idea of other people's loyalty is as empty as your view of a country landscape. But, Caenis, in the country, just when you think you have the whole world to yourself, you wander into an olive grove and find some old shepherd squatting on his haunches in the shade.' He paused. His voice rasped. 'Smiling at you, lass.'

'The country is your world not mine,' Caenis returned, managing to find a shred of humour for him. 'And even a city girl, if she reads any poets at all, knows a shepherd is the last person to trust!'

Despite her pleas, Vespasian insisted on going with her as far as Antonia's house. There was nothing she could do; he marched along with the footman in front of the chair.

Bluntly undeterred, when he left her at the door he said, 'Send to me when you need me.' Then, since he was a brave man, he cupped her stricken face in his large hands. 'Lass; I am here. You know that.'

She could not risk flinging her arms around him as she

wanted to do, for she must be alone when she started to cry.

'Caenis –'

She had to stop him. She knew that whatever he was going to say would be more than she could bear. 'Yes. I know. As my lady said to us, Titus, "Sometimes even Caenis will need a friend." And when I do, you are here. Yes; I know.'

XV

Flavius Vespasianus was now eligible for the next rank in the senate. He stood for election – and came nowhere.

Caenis was in a mood to feel guilty over anything; she convinced herself that her position in his life had contributed to his defeat. Some years one bad blow follows another until it becomes impossible to tell how far each has been caused by the depletion of spirits resulting from the rest. Losing Antonia had buffeted her badly; she was physically tired and emotionally drained. However her need to grieve had really made her so abstracted it left Vespasian free to canvass support. He did all he could. When he failed, his brother told him his approach had been too diffident; he remained a stranger to many in the Senate. He would have to establish himself more strongly and try again next year.

He started to organise straight away. Caenis watched with reviving fascination as he and Sabinus worked through the entire senatorial list, analysing the voting then discussing whom they might sway. They could only use verbal persuasion; they had no money for bribes.

She realised Vespasian was by no means as politically half-hearted as his initial reluctance had implied. She noticed his incisive mind, his thoroughness, his ability both to plan ahead and then to carry the plan through. Not many men could claim such talents. Of the two brothers it was he who possessed the steadier resolution. Once Vespasian did decide to act his energy was fiercer and his imagination more acute.

So he sat with Sabinus, lists covering a low table, both leaning forward on their stools, endlessly turning over names. Although they had courted patrons, it was always his brother Vespasian really worked with. Men from the Sabine territory had a tradition of public service and the Flavians were particularly clannish. They kept their political trust within the family.

Caenis was a frequent visitor at the tiny apartment Vespasian now rented; without Antonia she had little to keep her at home. While the men worked, their voices at one constant, thoughtful pitch, she sent away the hesitant skivvy. She served them wine herself, moving about the ill-furnished room in her silent way, drawing the mothy door curtain to deaden the racket from the copper-beater's workshop downstairs, opening the rickety shutters slightly to let in a breeze, which if no less malodorous and hot in such a decrepit neighbourhood was at least different air. Then she would curl up by herself on a battered couch, with an old cloak of Vespasian's over her feet, glad of an opportunity in this low period of her life to lose herself in her own thoughts.

It was taking her a long time to recover from Antonia's death. Caenis, who had respected and loved her as a friend, continued to churn with anger that her last weeks had been marred by discord with the new Emperor. She never found out whether Antonia's death had been by her own hand. Other people in the household assumed she had heard the full details; in fact she preferred not to know.

Claudius had had to speak to her about the will; Antonia had left modest bequests to all her freedwomen and as her primary heir it fell to her son to distribute the money. He said he would do what he could – but it depended on the Emperor. The House of Livia remained imperial property, and so far there was no suggestion that Antonia's freed clients needed to move on; later it was bound to become convenient that they did so – one more problem that Caenis would need to address.

Though they never discussed his mother, she found herself more at ease with Claudius nowadays. For one thing she had noticed that ever since she was known to be Vespasian's mistress other men had ceased to make unwelcome advances. She could not tell whether this was due to some masculine code, or whether she had herself ceased to signal that she was vulnerable. Perhaps she simply looked older nowadays.

In time it was confirmed that because of its position on the Palatine, the House of Livia would not be sold and neither did any of the imperial family want to claim a right to live there. Caenis was able to stay, preparing inventories of the furniture and household goods. This was not for the normal purpose of a sale at the Saepta Julia. Although Caligula had inherited a bulging treasury from the cautious Tiberius he was running through his funds at an astonishing rate as he delighted the populace with an almost daily programme of theatrical extravagances, public games and wild beast spectaculars, presents thrown from the roof of the main courthouse and gift vouchers left on theatre seats. Already there seemed a good chance that if the thought struck he would overturn his grandmother's will and himself carry off her treasures to replenish the Privy Purse.

Caligula had not attended Antonia's funeral. He watched the burning pyre through his dining-room window, joking about it with Macro, the commander of the Guards. Antonia's ashes were placed in the Mausoleum of Augustus but with minimal ceremony.

'Caenis!' Flavius Sabinus usually took his leave with a word for her. 'My wife sends you kind regards.'

Caenis had not seen his wife again, nor did she honestly expect to; still the girl took trouble to send her compliments, often accompanied by flowers or some other gift. Her warmth appeared quite genuine.

'This young lady's looking tired!' Sabinus then chided his brother.

Vespasian tucked a solid arm around her waist. 'She'll be all right. I've bought her a slab of must-cake – great restorative powers!'

Sabinus smiled at her sadly. He was hard-working and affable; he suspected Caenis needed more than sweetmeats. Once he had put aside his basic disapproval, he felt that his younger brother treated his mistress too casually. It was useless to try to explain that Vespasian's small but careful present meant far more to her than a string of beads snatched from a jeweller's tray with no real thought behind the gift.

'Mmm – come to bed!' murmured Vespasian, kissing her after his brother had gone.

Caenis pierced him with a steely eye. 'What about my cake?'

'Well, bring it of course.'

'You'll have crumbs in the covers –'

'I have noticed,' Vespasian commented, 'that when you and I eat anything there are rarely any crumbs.'

The must-cake was splendid, and he was absolutely right: there were no crumbs. Caenis responded with an enthusiasm that in Veronica's scale of values would equate to repaying a pair of Etruscan earrings or a silver collar.

Afterwards Vespasian exclaimed, with his wild, wide grin, 'Well, lady! That was an occasion to treasure when we are old and incapable!'

He was strong and endlessly healthy; even after making love with the fervour of a man who regarded this as the most natural and enjoyable way of taking exercise, his ribcage soon rose and fell again in its normal regular rhythm.

Caenis, gasping, thumped his chest. 'Oh I'm speechless!'

'What a change.'

'You great ox; you'll never be incapable. You'll still be sending for some girl – or a whole troupe – to liven your afternoons when you're seventy!'

Chortling, he flung back his great head, and for some minutes they lay together in silence before talking more reflectively.

'Wonder if we'll know each other then?'

It was an unfair question: men could be such pigs. Caenis responded drily, 'I imagine I shall have died of drudgery long before.'

He croaked, mimicking the astrologer at the Theatre of Balbus, '*Her life is kindly; kindly her death . . .*' He knew well enough that Caenis rejected omens. She had told him, whatever either of them were to become must lie in themselves. Neither had any advantages, nor anyone to help. Life would be only what they chose to make it, grappling within the straitjacket of society. 'You were quiet tonight,' he suddenly observed. She was less startled that he noticed than that he commented. 'What were you thinking about?'

She did not answer.

He usually knew anyway. 'Has your lady's house been reoccupied yet? What about Claudius?'

To his own surprise as much as anyone's, Claudius had been selected by Caligula for the honour of sharing the Consulship with his Emperor. Claudius had never held public office of any kind before, since both Augustus and Tiberius openly judged him unsuitable. As Caligula's colleague as well as his uncle, he had been compelled to go to live at the Palace. He was bound to be looking for a way to escape, and his mother's house might partially provide one.

'You are quite right,' agreed Caenis, though Vespasian had not said it. 'I shall need somewhere of my own to live.'

Without any hesitation he asked her, 'Want to come here?'

She was dumbfounded.

Caenis wanted to live with Vespasian more than anything. 'No, Titus. No thank you. No.'

It was unbelievable even a man could be so crass. Dammit, she had thought Vespasian relatively humane. She sat up abruptly, hugging her knees. She could not bear this.

'Why not?' he demanded stubbornly.

Caenis resisted the temptation to wrench away from him, to walk out and never come back. She compressed her anger, though she had no inhibitions about letting it show: 'Dear heart, I'll never catch a rich senator if they all know I'm living with you! And how, in Juno's name, am I expected to get you sensibly married off? Besides, if I come here while you are single, what is to happen to me afterwards? Oh you bastard, you absolute bastard; you know all this!' He had an aggravating habit of merely looking intrigued when somebody completely lost control. 'I do hope you have noticed,' Caenis went on coolly, fighting down her temper as she spoke, 'how rare it is for me to call you names.'

He said nothing. There was no doubt: he had noticed. He knew he had punished her beyond reasonable limits.

Still he persisted, as if it were in some way relevant, 'Caenis – do you think my career will ever come to anything?'

More tolerant with the apparent change of subject, she answered at once: 'Certainly. You know I do.'

He sighed slowly. 'If I thought not . . .' Perhaps fortunately he did not finish. 'Once, when I was a lad, my father took an augury that his second son would be something really special. This was a long time ago – and I won't tell you what I'm supposed to become! My grandmother burst her girdle laughing. Told my father he was going dreamy. Said he should be ashamed to act the dunce in front of his own mother.'

Caenis laughed. 'I like the sound of your old granny!'

'My old granny,' Vespasian chuckled, 'would not have liked the sound of you! She would have known you were after my cash.'

Giggling, because he was so poor it was ludicrous, she turned round to him slightly, as she did so feeling his mighty hand spread companionably on her back. His eyes seemed unusually still. 'Titus, you don't need superstitious permission. You won't fail. You can be whatever you want.'

His palm moved methodically along her spine. She tried to ignore the goosepimples. He was doing it on purpose, to tease her, and to calm her down. 'Hah! Going to encourage me? Live out your ambitions through me like the crazed crows of the imperial family? Are you a schemer, lass? A palace puppeteer?'

Hurt again, she dropped her head on to her knees. 'You are not mine to manipulate! Oh you'll take your aedileship next time around and everything will be easier for you after that. But I hope –'

He had scrambled up close, wrapping his arms round her, knees and all. Eagerly he demanded, 'What? What do you hope? Caenis, tell me your hope!'

'That when you are grizzled and famous,' she mumbled against his shoulder, 'you may still sometimes remember munching a sausage in a pantry with a bad-tempered slave.'

'Oh my dear lass!'

When someone touched him on a nerve, he was utterly soft. If Caenis had owned the confidence of a Veronica, she would have realised she could easily bring him to tears. Instead he pretended to be smiling, then drew her back down with him; a man of his build needed exercise, and making love to women was an easy way to take it.

Besides, he wanted to make another memory for their old age.

It was not long afterwards he made his next trip to Reate. His mother still lived there at the family home. He was a good son; Caenis was used to him visiting his mother. She never went with him; she knew that she and his mother would never meet.

A woman of both force and tact, Vespasia Polla probably did not like the sound of Caenis either; she would never waste her breath saying so. She was one of the few people who knew how, and when, to persuade her stubborn younger son to settle into something he really did not want to do. He had loved his grandmother Tertulla; he liked to please his mother. Throughout his life he would be a man who nursed a serious regard for the women who were close to him.

He was affectionate with his mistress. And, Caenis knew, one day he would be loyal to his wife.

XVI

As soon as she saw his face she understood everything.

He had come to her at home in Antonia's house, unexpected and unannounced, while she thought him still at
Reate. She went through the motions; Caenis after all was a
first-class secretary. She had been trained to behave with
aplomb in any social emergency.

'Titus! You're back in Rome.'

'I'm back,' he stated sombrely. '*Oh Caenis!*'

It was all perfectly obvious from his face.

The scene fixed itself in her memory as if she were some
hapless insect being slowly trapped in the bark of a stone
pine, transfixed under a sluggish ooze of amber for the next
two thousand years. There it all was: the woven rug in faded
shades of crimson and blue at her feet, folded under at one
far corner; the Greek black-figure vases displayed on the
sideboard; the list she had been checking which fell from her
hand as she rose at his entrance; the pin on the shoulder of
her dress that worked loose and scratched her if she moved
but which she could not spare concentration to refasten. The
chandelier had creaked on its ceiling-chain as he carefully
closed the door.

There was nothing unusual in his expression itself. He
always frowned in that grim way; people laughed at him but
there was nothing he could do to change it. She recognised
the horror only because every plane of that face had set rigid
in misery.

Her voice sounded remarkably ordinary. 'Whatever's the
matter? Tell me.'

He came right up to her. Apparently it felt inappropriate
to kiss her. She did not want to be kissed – then she wanted
it desperately. For a moment he placed both hands on her
shoulders; meeting her stare, he let his arms drop.

'You guess. A suitable woman has agreed to be my wife.'

Caenis wanted to fight. She could never win. There was no enemy. She heard herself saying in a low respectable voice, 'Quite right. Dear me; what took so long? Yes. You must. Well! . . . Rich, I hope?'

Vespasian was drawing her to a couch where he made her sit, taking a place beside her, holding her hand – not so much to console her, for he would realise from her resistance that she could hardly bear to be touched, but as if he himself needed to grip some part of her in order to go on. 'The rich ones,' he confided greyly, 'seemed curiously slow to take me up. She is not. Do you really want to hear?'

Caenis closed her eyes. For some quaint reason she seemed to nod her head. 'Other people are bound to tell me. I would rather have it from you.'

'Well. Someone from Ferentium. Father in the financial service; not quite a provincial but she should understand my difficulties. Her father had to appear before a Board of Arbitration to establish her right to the full citizenship but I think it went through on the nod –' He was using the tone which on other subjects had been his vehicle for asking her advice. He fell silent.

'Good character?' Caenis encouraged drily.

He answered like a man under examination in the Senate on some imperial informer's wild charge of impropriety: 'Oh; all right!' He relented. He sighed. He forced himself to be less offhand. 'No; let's be fair – a decent woman.'

'You've seen her?'

'Yes.'

'Slept with her?' Caenis demanded.

'No,' Vespasian answered patiently. Really it could not matter any more, yet Caenis was glad of that. 'I had better tell you; she has been someone's mistress – Statilius Capella, a senator from Africa –'

Gods, she was nothing! Caenis snapped, 'Excellent! A senator? Decent of you both to leave one free for the rest of us . . .' She took back her hand and stood up, pacing the room.

'Caenis, don't.'

He followed her, as she ought to have known that he would. She wanted to crouch in some dark place like a hurt beast. There was this dreadful need to be civilised. There was this appalling obligation: not to hurt him. She had no escape.

'Caenis, I'm desperately sorry. Don't be brave and bitter. Scream at me if you like, rant, rave, beat my chest with your fists, cry; cry all you want and I'll probably join in –' It was hideous; he was frantic.

Caenis let him take her into his arms.

'Titus, hush. It was brave of you to come. I appreciate your honesty. You don't have to dread a scene.'

She stood there, not responding, but leaning patiently up against him until, helpless, he let her go. 'Shall I leave you now?'

It was over. Everything was over.

'Wait a moment; please.' Her numb brain reminded her to make everything absolutely clear. 'You know I shall not see you again.'

'No.'

He would not create difficulties. Nor would she, come to that. There was only one kind of discipline for either of them now.

'Not even acknowledge you; it's best . . . What are your plans?' she asked more gently.

'Oh – aedile, praetor, then start angling for an army post.' His tone was more harsh than she had ever heard it. 'The *cursus honorum* stretches idyllically away!'

'Titus? Oh love, what is it?' Caenis had to ask.

It was Vespasian's turn to move away. He stood rigid, that face still as drained of colour as it was of permitted emotion. He was quite obviously deeply upset.

For the first and only time he said curtly, 'You were right all along. We should never have done this.'

There was nothing she could safely reply.

She held him; what else could she do?

'Stupidity.'

'Never say that. Don't devalue it.' She folded her arms around him, rocking slightly, with her face against his, though safely turned away.

She was surprised to hear anyone else so bitter: 'Was it worth this?'

And, '*Yes!*' Caenis bellowed gloriously: Vespasian winced.

By then they were laughing together, painfully verging on tears.

'Oh Titus, Titus; don't. I am supposed to make the fuss, not you. Ah you great soft-hearted wretch, how dare you be upset? Be a monster, damn you – be a man – be typical!'

Ruefully he laid his forehead against hers. 'I'm doing my best.'

'Not good enough. Are you short of cash?'

He was thunderstruck. 'Oh Jupiter! What a ludicrous question –' He had drawn back; she had steadied him; he had lost his temper; it would be all right. 'In the first place, I'm always running short and in the second, lass, spare yourself that. You are not obliged to worry any more about me and my filthy bank account.'

Caenis decided she would worry about just whomsoever in Hades she chose. 'Never mind that. Listen. I have ten thousand sesterces; Antonia's legacy. I can't spend it, it's my insurance, and I don't want to trust it to a strong box in the Forum to be fiddled away by some obnoxious Eastern banker who smarms around his abacus trying for a kiss when all I want is a decent rate of interest –' She was running out of breath.

'No, Caenis. Caenis; not your savings –'

'*Yes!* Borrow it; use it for your good. Enhance your state; buy some support. It won't achieve much but it's a gesture: somebody believes in you.'

'It's a wicked gamble,' he scoffed.

'A shrewd investment,' Caenis quipped back. 'I want you to have it; no one else in Rome is worth it. If I can't have you, then by the Good Goddess I'll help to make you – you owe me that!'

He buried his face in his hands. His voice was very quiet. 'I will send you the interest – and I will pay you back.'

'Perhaps!' Caenis barked, more like herself.

'If you need it just ask me.'

Since she was never intending to speak to him that would be difficult. 'Titus – I must return this to you.'

The bangle he had given her to celebrate her freedom was on her arm now; he had bought her occasional trinkets since – pins, a shell necklace, an ivory comb – but her only other good pieces were gifts from Antonia. Antonia's presents had been of impressive antique workmanship, set with garnets, opals, tourmalines. Caenis' gold bangle was to her still the most beautiful thing she had ever owned.

Vespasian was furious at her offer. 'No dammit!'

'Is it paid for?' she insisted. He never answered that.

'Caenis, that's yours; yours from me; yours to keep. If you don't want it, all right get rid of it, but don't tell me and don't try to antagonise me by handing it back!'

She assumed he had forgotten how both their names were engraved inside. Doggedly she pulled off the bangle and gestured to the lettering: 'Don't you mind?'

'No.'

'You may do one day.'

He folded his arms grimly. 'Shall I really?'

Caenis slowly replaced her gift, with a feeling of relief. He laid his hand there briefly where the gold burnt on the fine skin of her arm. Their eyes met. She whispered, 'I'd like you to go now.'

'Are you all right?'

'Don't worry. Are *you* all right?'

Another question he refused to answer. So he was not all right: she was learning this language. She had after all been the star of her cipher class.

People were supposed to quarrel. Quarrelling made it bearable. Here they were, nursing one another through; something would have to be done: she, of course, would have to be the one who did it. 'Just go – go *now*!'

Men so liked to drag things out. 'I'll never forget you.'

'Men always say that.' How touching, thought Caenis, forced beyond the bounds of charity again, to be the romantic blossom a man chooses to remember from his youth.

Vespasian argued anxiously, 'Women say they'll never

forgive.'

She was brisk. 'Not me.'

'No. Thanks, Caenis.'

'Titus.'

She stood quietly, with the humility a woman was expected to show, while Vespasian gently kissed her cheek to say goodbye.

But at that, in her one gesture of absolute defiance, Antonia Caenis blazed with the love she was never permitted to acknowledge, as she seized him and kissed him back: fiercely and furiously, full on the mouth, intending that the man should know *exactly* how she felt.

All things considered, he took it very well. She thought the bastard smiled at her in fact. So, with a regretful little smile from him, Caenis was left.

And even then, she did not cry.

The woman was called Flavia Domitilla. Veronica told her.

'Capella's mistress,' she announced angrily. Caenis had been right; people did so want her to have to know. 'Capella's nothing; I don't know why she bothered. Come to that, she's nobody herself. Her father actually had to appear before a tribunal to disprove some claim that she was born a slave –'

'She won't be a slave,' Caenis commented quietly.

'I thought your high and mighty Flavians like to parade themselves as a respectable family?'

Veronica fell silent. She finally realised that even where a mistress had always known disaster would be unavoidable, she might prefer to be abandoned for a person who was somebody.

Once or twice in Rome Caenis saw Vespasian's wife. She was neither beautiful nor fashionable; rather too dark, and bony-looking (thought Caenis, who was in that respect quite well made). Flavia Domitilla seemed neither happy nor unhappy. Still, she became the mother of a daughter and two sons; the elder boy was a charmer, people said. As far as Caenis knew, the woman's husband treated her with good humour and respect. Perhaps he loved her; possibly she loved him. These were things that in Roman society remained private between a man and his wife.

Marriage certainly helped his career. Flavius Vespasianus stood again for aedile; though he only scraped into sixth place on the list that did not matter since there were six vacancies. Two years later at the age of thirty he became eligible for the rank of praetor. At those elections Caenis almost missed finding his name in the *Gazette*: he had romped home, the first time he stood, right at the head of the list.

PART THREE:
THE HERO OF BRITAIN

When the Caesars were Caligula and Claudius

XVII

Almost three-quarters of a century afterwards in the reign of the Emperor Hadrian, the historian Suetonius had to mention Antonia Caenis in one of his essays on the Caesars. The Emperor Domitian had once been rude to her, which illustrated perfectly Domitian's defective character for it was accepted that being rude to Caenis was the act of a charmless boor. In another way too, the freedwoman and secretary of Antonia the Younger was impossible for a historian to overlook.

Caenis would have liked to know, during the next fifteen or twenty years, that she was working her way into the end of a paragraph in the work of a chronicler whose titles included not just *The Lives of the Caesars* but *Famous Prostitutes*, and as a particular highlight the slim volume *Greek Terms of Abuse*. She would have liked to own a dictionary of Terms of Abuse herself – in order, for one thing, to express more fluently her views upon historians.

What were twenty years to a literary biographer? The period from one mad emperor, through another who was merely inconsistent and undignified, and on to yet another madman: undisciplined men with monstrous wives, a handful of territorial adventures, a lively set of poisonings and stabbings on stairways, a financial scandal here and a legal outrage there, ambition, greed, corruption, lust – just technical ingredients. Useless to rise up booming like a cow over its lost calf because a historian, who needs to move on his narrative slickly to the next cogent point (or the next racy scandal), has slid over in the second half of a sentence the whole dismal, humdrum, suffering course of the best years of some woman's life.

Caenis knew better than to hope her story would become the triumph of the obscure. She did not suppose it would even be told.

*

So, once Vespasian had left her, she sat and listened to the silence of Antonia's slowly dying house. No one here even knew of her devastating blow.

This silence seemed to stretch ahead for the rest of her life. She might die young. Plenty did. Or she might last another forty years. There was nothing. Absolutely nothing. Nothing expected of her; nothing for her to expect. All her duties to Antonia were done. There was nothing else.

She considered the alternatives. She could set herself up in a pretty salon for the gentry – music and good conversation, raffish elegance and fairly clean sheets. She could live chastely in single state, being sour and strict with her own slaves. She could pool resources to buy a lock-up shop with some skinny freedman: marry him, and snap at him, and struggle. She could in fact marry anyone in the Empire she liked, except the six hundred men who were members of the Senate. Augustus had debarred those from marrying freedwomen; he decently allowed the senators anybody else, though he obviously preferred them to stick at one another's sisters, daughters and aunts. (Caenis had always reckoned that otherwise there was not much chance for some of the senatorial sisters, daughters and aunts.) Vespasian had not even managed that: his new wife's father was only a knight.

She could jump off a bridge. Useless; she swam too well.

She could simply go on, as she had always known she must.

So she went on. Her patroness would have expected it. More importantly she expected it of herself.

Afterwards she was proud of her tenacity, and glad. Glad because having lived her own life she could value all the more the rewards she eventually did win; glad too because it made her braver when she realised that she had to give them back.

Her first action now was to find somewhere new to live. Born in a palace, she went to live in a slum. Caenis, who had spent her happiest years in the most select private house in Rome, exchanged it for two rooms and a scullery on the squalling fifth floor of an unspeakable tenement. She remained perfectly calm about it. This was her own choice: she was short of ready cash; she avoided obligations; it was her own. She could have done better; she had endured worse. She remained calm even though for the privilege of living here on her own she was paying an unbelievable rent. As a ploy to forget a lost lover, the irritation this flagrant rent caused her was ideal.

She lived among the gruelling goat-paths that bordered the Via Appia in the Twelfth District. It was a dense plebeian settlement, added to the ancient city environs by Augustus. Her own block had been destroyed by fire then rebuilt by landlords with an eye to future compensation when it all collapsed again. They had invested little in the fabric, and there was even less chance they would pay for improvement or simple maintenance.

To find her apartment she turned off the narrow hubbub of the Via Appia, down a pitted sideroad just wide enough for two wheeled vehicles to sidle past one another in the night, and into a lane where a single handcart might squeeze; there she lived high above a yard bordered by flaking tenements. All the blocks looked the same and all the apartments inside them were arranged identically. The first week she forgot her way home three times; no point asking directions: in this rabbit warren street names were unknown. Panic-stricken, she chose markers: the fountain with three conch shells where in due course she recognised the women washing one end or another of their recalcitrant children, the corner where the sharp smell from the tannery caught the back of her throat, the midden, the tired walnut tree, the local market.

Life held its compensations; in Rome there would always be mullet and oysters. There were cold meats and hot pies. She could bathe every day. She could escape to the theatre. She could sink her teeth into the sweet golden flesh of a luxurious nectarine . . .

The ground floor of her tenement was leased to a wineshop and a furrier, and used also by a morning nursery school. Whenever she came in or went out the vintner winked at her, the furrier whistled, but the schoolmaster only stared. For some time Caenis foolishly supposed the schoolmaster's nature was more refined than the others'.

Everybody hated the landlord. Not simply because of his outrageous rents. He was a seedy, leery capitalist who preyed on the lower levels of society while pretending to render favours in providing desperate folk with a roof over their heads; all his roofs leaked. He lived on the first floor. Although in subletting her apartment he had made great play to Caenis of the fact that her rent would include the provision of stair-sweepers, porters and water-carriers, these functions were in fact all delegated to one African slave called Musa, who had a bad leg. The landlord's name was Eumolpus. In Roman tradition he was almost certainly not the owner of the ground lease for the building, nor even the principal mortgagee.

On the second floor lived a retired ex-centurion, whom nobody ever saw, and his middle-aged mistress, who fluffed about her balcony like a peachy powder-sponge. Caenis won her confidence and found her a lonely woman who lived in terror that the centurion would die and leave her penniless. In the end she worried herself to death first; the centurion was heart-broken and Caenis had to help him with the funeral.

On the third floor lived two separate families of equestrian rank who were enduring temporary shortages of funds. These good people felt no necessity to pass the time of day.

On the fourth floor lived four brothers all engaged in running a second-rate gymnasium for third-rate gladiators. They constantly quarrelled with various strangers who rushed up from the street to complain when slops were sluiced from their windows on to clothes and heads. The law took a strong line on flinging down slops; however, in the Twelfth District, law took second place to huge men with brutal tempers who trained gladiators.

On the fifth floor at the front lived Caenis.

At the back were several other ladies on their own. Eumolpus said he liked female tenants because they were quiet, and keen to pay their rent. Caenis soon worked out that Eumolpus was disappointed if they paid up in minted

126

coin rather than by taking him to bed: she herself stoically paid him in coin, to his visible distress. The other ladies who shared her landing kept households that constantly ran out of flour or oil or salt. One or two could be abusive but on the whole they were a feckless, bleary, harmless group. Most were caring for infants of the tousled, gravy-faced sort who were put out for long periods on the stairways playing with surprisingly expensive toys while their mothers, who did a lot of entertaining, entertained.

On the sixth and seventh floors above lived innumerable groups of people in several sad generations, crowded many to a room. To these belonged swarthy men with set faces who broke roads, stoked furnaces, and unbunged the sewers. With them lived weary, bowed, meticulously clean women, who looked sixty but were probably not yet thirty, women who embroidered marvellous scarves, threaded cheap beads, and stood at street corners silently offering penny packets of sesame seeds for sale. Some of these families disappeared abruptly sometimes; others seemed to have existed in that place for many decades. They spoke strange languages, when they spoke at all, and occasionally burst into wondrous song. With them, more than anyone, Caenis felt a dark affinity.

One of the painters from the Palace decorated her apartment with purloined paint. 'I've sealed up the walls with new plaster as best I could,' he told her cheerfully. 'Hardly soundproof, but it might hold back the bugs.' Caenis swallowed. 'I take it you're familiar with the mouse?' She had seen the mouse.

There had been much mention locally of Doris, the previous tenant of her rooms. Apparently this Doris had been a very peculiar girl. Caenis made no comment; she was peculiar herself – and probably proud of it. The oddest thing Doris appeared to have done was to rush screaming from the apartment when she first saw the mouse, threatening to take Eumolpus to court. Foolish people sometimes did that. It was very expensive; landlords learn the art of litigation with their mothers' milk.

When Caenis first saw the mouse she walked quietly on to her balcony until it went away. She stopped up its hole with depilatory wax, then watched in horrified fascination as it chewed its way straight out. Burrius, the painter, brought her some poison, which he said came from the private cabinet of the late Empress Livia; the mouse dropped dead before it had time to jump back from the saucer where Caenis had laid the bait.

She had her few rooms painted the colour of mature honeysuckle flowers, a thin dry gold through which the pale plaster beneath seemed to gleam.

'Want an erotic fresco in the bedroom?' offered Burrius. 'Satyrs with gigantic phalluses? Get your men in the mood? Nice?'

'Nice; but no thanks,' returned Caenis drily. 'I'm having a rest from moody men.'

'That's very sad!' commiserated Burrius. Like everyone, he knew her history.

Caenis laughed. She bore no grudges against men. She regarded her past as fortunate. 'The saddest part about it is the fact I do agree with you it's sad.'

Burrius thought about that. Any casual painter tries his luck. 'I don't suppose –'

'Quite right,' agreed Caenis mildly. 'Don't suppose!'

Despite her own occasional depression and the constant amazement of her friends, Antonia Caenis lived in the Twelfth District for over three years. She was surrounded by life at its most varied, life at a level to which she dismally believed she belonged. Luckily she had never been afraid to be alone.

She was sometimes afraid of going mad.

'People who see the risk,' Veronica assured her, 'never manage to go mad, however hard they try.'

Caenis simply recognised that she thought now, as she always had thought: life was hard; life was foul; but if you were too poor and too unimportant to have hopes of a heroic eternity in the Elysian fields, you must make the bitter best of it, for life was all there was.

It was towards the end of the first year, when madness still seemed a vague possibility, that something happened which could well have tipped a less robust person into that long slide down into the desolate pit. She was walking in her self-contained way along the Via Appia towards home. She had been to see Claudia Antonia, the daughter of Antonia's son Claudius by one of his enforced marriages. As his mother's freedwoman, a client of the Claudian family, Caenis was helping informally with the young girl's education.

Returning home, her slaveboy ambled with her. Veronica had taken on the wistful little girl Caenis had owned in Antonia's house, whose regret at the loss of Vespasian's bribing coppers had grown too much to bear. So now Caenis had instead this boy, Jason, a dim but cheerful child, constantly ravenous, who carried up her water, carried down her rubbish, and on trips out loafed along behind her with a meat-pie in one hand and a truncheon slipping through his belt. He was supposed to be her bodyguard. Looking after Jason occupied much of her mind.

It was a wild day at the end of spring. After a long spell of wet weather the streets were choked with mire. Picking her way to try to avoid taking in squelchy sandalfuls of mud, Caenis soon noticed irritably that the hem of her dress and mantle had been heavily splashed by less careful passers-by. At the crossroads where she would turn off the main highway she found herself in the middle of a curious crowd. The source of the commotion was not the normal dog fight or stall-holders' argument.

The Twelfth District was being visited by the Emperor.

By this time Caligula had developed the startling mania for which he would become a legend. The previous year he had suffered a devastating illness. Rumours ran riot about what form this took – epilepsy, perhaps, or some inflammation of the brain brought on by stress. Whatever it was, once he recovered he had changed fully into the monster that had been merely foreshadowed before. He was ready to test his power to the limit – and there was no limit.

He killed his rival, Gemellus. Son of Livilla, Antonia's

disgraced daughter and according to scandalmongers son of Sejanus too, Gemellus had been pushed aside by the Senate in the euphoria which greeted Caligula's accession. Although Caligula had formally adopted him as a gesture assuring the family succession, his generosity soon gave way to suspicion and contempt. His own illness caused him to accuse Gemellus of plotting to seize power. He complained that Gemellus was afraid of being poisoned – a wise enough fear –and that he constantly stank of antidotes (Gemellus was a hypochondriac, who regularly took linctus for a cough).

Caligula had Gemellus executed. A military tribune sliced off his head with a sword. There was no antidote for that, as Caligula remarked.

Shortly afterwards Macro, the commander of the Guards, was impeached for pandering his wife to Caligula, then forced to commit suicide. He had possibly conspired with Gemellus while the Emperor was ill – and had certainly reminded his protégé once too often of services rendered.

The Emperor then declared himself a living god. Caenis thought privately that Caligula's claim to be Capitoline Jove did founder on the fact that it was reported he regularly slept with his own three sisters. Caligula's sisters were a frightful trio. The real Capitoline Jove would have better taste.

Even before Caenis saw him on the Via Appia, she realised it was Caligula from the sneering presence of the Praetorian Guard, strutting like spurred fighting cocks in their glittering breastplates and stiff red helmet sprouts. The tradespeople craning their necks were suitably wary, more of the Guards' dismal reputation than the man at their centre who was so incongruously dressed up as Jupiter. Caenis instantly recognised his high forehead and balding head. Hard to tell what the people made of that false curling beard, the bracelets, the face-paint and the stage thunderbolt; it was an insult to their intelligence, yet they seemed to respond with good-humoured sympathy. They stared at Caligula not because he was demented, but simply because he was the Emperor. Apparently they accepted his mania as matter-of-factly as they accepted the local cooper's spastic child and the pastrycook who saw cockatrices biting his legs when he was drunk.

Jupiter was enough in command of his senses to have noticed that conditions in the Twelfth District were scruffy. He was now enjoying himself, having a divine rant. The gracious god had been struck by the filth in the road and pavements, and to the delight of the populace, he was venting his fury on the officer who held public responsibility for cleaning the streets. Berating this man at Olympian length, Jove paused long enough to restick a corner of his beard that had in the heat of the moment come unglued, then ordered his soldiers, 'Fill up the folds of his toga with this mud!'

Caenis stood appalled. It was a terrible humiliation for an aedile – and she immediately recognised this one: Vespasian.

Evil with malice, the Praetorians set to. Gleefully seizing potsherds from the clogged gutters, they began to scoop up mud and load it into the heavy folds of the aedile's toga. He knew what he had done – and he knew the risks of offending a mad emperor. He stood meekly enough, arms outspread and head bowed before the rattling of the tinsel thunderbolt. It was a disgrace, but a light punishment. In a different moment of Caligula's caprice he could as easily have called for an executioner.

The crowd cheered. Caligula acknowledged the applause and passed on. The Praetorians reluctantly abandoned their sport and followed him.

Left behind, Vespasian folded his arms to support the strange weight of his filthy garments. The crowd stilled. He made no attempt to shake free the clods.

'Well, citizens –' His voice carried grimly; people began to shuffle amidst their mirth – 'we all know the system. Shovels out!'

They all knew the system. In the ten days it would take him to arrange official contractors to do the work at their expense, each piece of pavement would be transformed by its frontager, rather than face a fine to pay the contractors; then the aedile would move on to harry the next district; in another two weeks all the mud and debris and donkey droppings would be back. The problem was not entirely his fault;

131

the hallowed system had a great deal to do with it. Faced with their own responsibilities, the crowd diplomatically melted away.

It had begun to rain. Jason started to dart across the road, but Caenis trapped him with a firm grip on the scruff of his neck. 'Wait, sunshine!' Absently he began to pick at the loaf she intended for lunch.

Caenis stood absolutely still. Nonetheless she had been found by the aedile's temperate stare. He was shaking off his personal slaves as they fussed around his ruined clothes. Across the five-yard width of the Via Appia her quiet eyes locked on to his. Vespasian had the grace to blush.

And then, allowing his muck-encumbered toga to be plucked away by his dithering slaves, he broke into what she knew was his rarest and richest grin. He made no move to cross the street; neither did she. Very slowly, in disapproval of his public disgrace, Caenis shook her head. Then she spun neatly on the ball of her foot. Slim and straight, with one hand gripping the elbow of her youthful bodyguard, she slipped across the highway and disappeared into the impenetrable warren of streets on the other side.

Flavius Vespasianus made no attempt to follow her.

XVIII

She had tried to forget. She had tried to stabilise her life. Now she was plunged once again into turmoil and loss. The worst part was how, even while the familiar wash of panic set her heart banging, she recognised that simply to see Vespasian had lit her life. All her being sang with happiness.

Yet Caenis refused to feed on tragic foolishness. She knew she must reject such stupid joy at the mere glimpse of some man smiling at her in the street.

Watching Vespasian take his native soil so curiously to his bosom had delayed her beyond the time when she usually reached home. Midday: the tiny children who sat on cut-down benches under the street-awning and chanted their lessons so automatically while their great eyes wandered from their master to any distraction, had now finished their sad torture and scampered home. Their desultory master was starting to furl the leather awning on a pole.

The furrier had drawn and bolted his shutters, then retreated up the ladder to the backbreaking loft above his workshop where he lived with his family. The wineshop was still open; wineshops rarely closed. However, the three old men who habitually sat there had decided to drain the earthenware tumblers over which they had been dreaming for the previous two hours, and go home to whichever bent little wife or brawling, sprawling daughter normally provided them with lunch.

Jason set off at once up the five flights of stone stairs. Caenis stayed behind, for somebody was waiting in the wineshop wanting her to write a letter about a will. Since she had her stylus case with her, she sat down at a stained table. The task was swiftly done.

Caenis looked ruefully at the handful of coppers she had earned. 'Just enough for a jug of my new Campanian!' consoled the vintner. 'Steel yourself for the stairs!'

Campanian his brutal red ink never was, but for once she agreed cheerfully to being bamboozled. The vintner took a tumbler himself; he liked any excuse. The schoolmaster had now come in for what was obviously his regular midday tipple so with blissful expansiveness she offered him a drink too. Caenis had never lost her slave's habit of sharing whatever she might have with those she regarded as her equals in low fortune. The vintner carried off his tot into the curtained nook behind the counter, leaving customers to plunder an amphora for themselves and deposit the money in a dish.

Caenis and the schoolmaster sat for a while in silence. Caenis was lost in her thoughts. The schoolmaster leant forwards, twisting his winecup between both hands. He was obviously shy. He did not on this occasion feel able to stare at her.

A well-trained secretary does not gaze silently into the distance for long. Caenis roused herself and dutifully asked the man how he enjoyed his work. He replied in gruff monosyllables. He looked about forty but that was because he had badly thinning hair; he grew the rest longer to compensate, but instead of appearing intellectual as he may have hoped, he merely looked badly groomed. He seemed unhappy and unhealthy – someone who regularly drank too much and ate too little, and who paid no attention to personal hygiene, exercise or sleep. It was well known that immediately after parents paid their fees he spent heavily, then towards the end of each term he ran out of cash. How he kept discipline remained a mystery for he seemed too indolent to use his staff and too dull to hold the attention otherwise.

'Personally,' suggested Caenis, who had been wanting to tackle this subject ever since she arrived, 'I believe it is time traditional schoolroom methods were challenged. Don't you agree?'

She knew the traditional method was how he taught: the children recited their letters and numbers over and over, without illustration, without variety, a dreary daily singsong through one or another alphabet. 'I was educated at the

Palace; they wanted quick results. I have to say that when the Palace needs good secretaries its methods of obtaining them are excellent.'

She herself had been blessed with inspired teachers. Every time she went by the nursery here, the sad, bored, patient eyes of these children caused her distress.

Caenis had the rare gift of remembering what it was like to be a child. She wanted to explain to the schoolteacher how half his class were aimlessly repeating by rote what they had learned long before, though they did not understand it, while the rest knew nothing at all but had the knack of joining in a second after the others spoke. None of them ever progressed. She wanted to encourage the man to devise some rapport with his charges. She wanted to convince him that he must be interested in what he was doing, so the children would be interested too . . .

Most men are not keen to hear they are bad at their work. The schoolmaster changed the subject. He lifted her hand and placed it under his grubby tunic upon his private parts.

Caenis could not immediately accept what was happening.

Shock transfixed her. She could not bear it. She sprang up; the wine jug flew from the bench; she was furious.

Partly, she was furious with herself. She had forgotten people were not neighbourly. Her time with Vespasian had made her too safe. Once so sensitive, she had just issued an invitation without a thought of how it could be misinterpreted.

She felt ill with dismay. She was imaginative enough to realise her response would damage a soul that was already inadequate, but really there were times when an intelligent woman, with burdens of her own, needed to think of herself. Without a word spoken on either side the schoolmaster got to his feet and blundered from the shop. She saw the scorn in his eyes. She realised he had now brutally defined her – for himself, and probably half the neighbourhood: tense, teasing, frigid, mentally odd.

She was more angry then, because she saw how easily men might deprive a woman in her circumstances of her self-esteem and her public confidence. It was true she carried within her a great pain. Even so, she knew she lived her life more vividly and with greater good humour than most people around her.

Thanks to that, she was able to put aside all thought of this schoolmaster, his solitary world, his misplaced contempt, before she gained the third flight of stairs to her room. By then she was remembering only a face that was alive with sardonic intelligence. She was exulting in the frank, straightforward, enduring friendliness of a man who had been her lover, a man she had once loved.

Caenis would always have the courage to be true to herself; at her lowest ebb, she now possessed the gift of a joyous past.

Sanely, she went on with her life.

XIX

When the Emperor's uncle Claudius married Valeria
Messalina – this sad jest was entirely a whim of Caligula's –
Caenis was privileged to attend. Messalina came of impeccable family, she was wealthy, she was exquisite – and she
looked about nineteen. Claudius was forty-seven.

Teenage brides were common in patrician society; it gave
a man the chance to train up the child in his own house his
own way, which is what men sometimes imagine they want.
For a person so susceptible to women as Claudius though,
this girl was a disaster. He fell head over heels in love, before
he had spoken to her twice. The sly cat would run rings
round him. Still, that too is what some men want.

'I should be grateful if you felt able to come, Caenis,' he
had faltered. 'A man at his wedding needs the support of his
family and friends. Of course, I will have the Emperor . . .'

Caenis gave him one of her looks. 'Sir, your nephew the
Emperor may stand as your family, though I doubt whether
in this matter he has acted as one of your friends!'

She always spoke to Claudius firmly and extremely
frankly. He permitted it. In all other respects Caenis treated
him as her patron, a courtesy which few members of his late
mother's household would ever emulate.

When he had realised, many months after everybody else
had noticed, that Caenis was no longer Vespasian's mistress,
Tiberius Claudius had enquired tentatively whether she
would like to become one of his mistresses instead, but
Caenis had dealt frankly and firmly with that too.

'I shall come to your wedding, sir,' she promised. 'For
your daughter's sake, for your mother's – and as one of your
good friends.'

They both knew, there were not many of those.

*

Going to a wedding attended also by the Emperor won Caenis a certain amount of prestige in the Twelfth District. Another event at about the same time lent even more crazy colour to her reputation. This was a visit to her apartment by Veronica. That girl surely knew how to make herself useful. Every man in the block now treated Caenis with awe. The vintner and furrier became positively chummy, longing for another glimpse of her dazzling friend. Caenis did not point out that Veronica had no energy to spare for walking up five flights of stairs so was unlikely to repeat their treat.

She never understood why Caenis did it. Least of all for a steep rent. Paying money to a man for anything was a concept Veronica found ridiculous.

Veronica herself had decided with the advent of Caligula that sharing the Palace with an emperor was not for her. For one thing, she was disgusted by the imperial bordello he devised. Having finely decorated a suite of rooms at the Palace he threw them open to all comers, offering loans to the men who visited and shamelessly listing the income as donations to the imperial treasury. With such competition, how was a simple girl expected to make her way?

Veronica had acted with alacrity. She understood that senators did not want compulsory brothels at the Palace, where Caligula's idea of adding insult to the Senate – whom he now passionately hated – was that they should be forced to bring their wives. A man enjoying off-side relaxation wanted a different face than the one at home. Veronica purchased her freedom, skipped the Palace, and began to offer an establishment that was equally expensive without the political disadvantages and the risks. At Veronica's there were no wives.

She did not, of course, pay rent. She occupied a prestigious mansion which she looked after for an octogenarian ex-consul who never visited Rome. The consul paid all the bills and when he died he left Veronica the house. Meanwhile her success was assured. She let it be known that no one need apply who commanded less than a hundred million sesterces; rather than be thought too poor to attend her salon, clients flocked in.

Veronica repeatedly asked Caenis to live with her. Caenis always refused. She did however go there sometimes in the evening. She liked Veronica's house for the same reasons as the elderly gentlemen of conservative opinions who treated it like a military dining club: the place was warm, the cooks were excellent, the women were civilised, and the sanitation worked.

Caenis came to be regarded as a kind of inky-fingered duenna. Her connections were respectable and when she felt like it (not invariably) she made people laugh. She never slept with men, though for three years Veronica tenaciously shovelled men her way. If necessary, Caenis slid them off elsewhere. It was not always necessary. Many were grateful that she made no demands. Some men who patronise exclusive salons are frightened they cannot live up to expectations (Veronica agreed tartly that most could not). For them, talking to Caenis was polite and safe.

Caenis herself did not altogether appreciate the arrangement. The men Veronica thought suitable for her all fell into a certain type: recent widowers with far too much to say now about their previously neglected wives, or bachelors so trying that their loneliness was all too understandable. The other thing they had in common, Caenis soon noticed, was that none of them was a man whom Veronica wanted to have to entertain herself. Being a convenience sometimes rankled.

She put up with the situation. Caenis never lost her sense of humour entirely.

Sometimes there was political talk. Veronica discouraged this. Treason could lead to trouble, and if things became too heated men lost their tempers and stormed off without wanting a girl, which reduced her income. Caenis, who only went there for something to eat and companionship, rather enjoyed the politics.

On one occasion she thought Veronica would have a seizure: someone openly raised the question of disposing of the Emperor.

Caenis noted that there was not the shocked silence that anyone who lived outside Rome would expect. By now Caligula had worn the purple for four years; he had also dressed up in silken robes encrusted with gemstones, theatrical costumes, elaborate military uniforms (usually with the breastplate of Alexander which he claimed he had stolen from the hero's tomb), and rather common women's dresses in colours which did not suit his pasty face. His behaviour had been odd, baffling, and exorbitantly expensive. While staying at Antonia's villa at Bauli, he dreamt up a plan to defy the old prophecy that he could as soon become Emperor as ride dry-shod over the sea at Baiae: he built a three-mile bridge of galleys, turfed it over and for two days trundled in a chariot to and fro across the Gulf; several people cheering his entourage were knocked into the sea and drowned. He had bankrupted the Treasury with his constant Games and circuses; he brought business to a standstill and even cancelled the rites of mourning so no one had an excuse not to attend his shows. His cruelties extended from the execution of his own cousin King Ptolomy of Mauretania (who had offended him at a gladiatorial display by winning the crowd's applause for a smart purple cloak), to dispatching common criminals in batches, without even a glance at the charge-sheet, in order to feed their carcasses to his panthers and lions. He blighted trade with fierce taxation. He chained up the granaries when the populace were starving. No one forgot how he had worried his grandmother to death.

People were now looking back fondly to the golden age of Augustus, a man who in retrospect had genuinely seemed to want to do right. People remembered that even under Tiberius the city and the provinces were efficiently run. After four years there was a slow groundswell of understanding in Rome that Caligula must be removed. He was still not yet thirty. People felt tired just thinking how long they might have to endure him if nothing was done. Needless to say, most people hoped somebody else would volunteer to risk doing it.

There had been one plot, apparently brewed by his sister Agrippina. Drusilla, to whom he was most deeply attached, had died suddenly; her death caused a florid outburst of grief in the Emperor, who proclaimed Drusilla a goddess, established a cult for her, ordered public mourning on a scale that was disaster for small traders, and then fled to the country to soak himself in misery (mitigated by occasional gambling bouts).

Afterwards the position of the surviving sisters, Agrippina and Livilla, had declined. While accompanying their brother on a visit to Germany they found themselves accused – probably rightly – of plotting with Lepidus, Drusilla's widower. He was executed and they were exiled, but first Agrippina was compelled to bring the cremated remains of Lepidus, who was allegedly her lover, back to Rome in a casket – a grim parody of her mother returning from Syria with the relics of the dead hero Germanicus. The Senate had had to frame its reaction cautiously, and since the plot had been put down, there was only one tactful course: one of the praetors issued congratulations to the Emperor on his expedition, then denounced Lepidus and suggested that his ashes should be denied the family mausoleum and cast out unburied.

The praetor concerned was Flavius Vespasianus.

When plotting came up in conversation it was Caenis herself who said quietly, 'There will always be the convention that the Senate creates the Emperor – then cannot be seen doing away with him.'

There were senators in the room. Mostly they followed the pattern of slow, sombre, self-opinionated men in late middle age. Now, after feeding on swan cunningly presented as porpoise, turbot in aspic, and suckling-pig served with two wine sauces reduced to a delicate glaze, they were lying on their couches holding back belches whilst pontificating bitterly on the world's decline. They thought this was daring enough.

Caenis felt disinclined to let them get away with it. 'It will be,' she suggested, 'some disgusted individual who dares to plunge in the knife.' Veronica closed her eyes, gleaming silver with mercury. Caenis refused to take the hint. 'Then the Senate, to excuse its own cowardice, will execute that individual for his courage.'

She fell silent, having noticed with more interest than usual that her leg was touching the leg of the man to her left.

141

It had been an accident, but she ignored what had happened and so did he. He was Lucius Anicius, a knight who had made a fortune in charioteers: not her type at all. He spent a lot of time with the Praetorian Guards and was, Caenis realised afterwards, probably the one person present who was fully aware of the burning hatred felt for Caligula by their current commander, Cassius Chaerea. Caligula was always giving obscene watchwords to Chaerea, a decent, proper man who had to pass them on straight-faced to the rest of the Guard.

Anicius said, seeming to take her part, 'The question seems to be, not whether a plot will succeed – but which one it will be.' Agreeing, people laughed and listed some of them: Aemilius Regulus, an unknown from Spain; a senator called Vinicianus who had been friendly with the dead Lepidus; Chaerea, the much-humiliated commander of the Praetorian Guard; members of the Emperor's own household, particularly his freedman Callistus . . . Those were the acknowledged plotters. Any moment someone here would be revealing the secret ones.

Caenis saw Veronica signal to her waitresses to bring in towering platters of fruit. In a crisis she always ordered the dessert. Peeling it kept troublemakers quiet.

'Personally,' mused Veronica to lighten the atmosphere, 'I think Incitatus is the only one who comes out of this reign at all well.'

Incitatus was Caligula's racehorse. He lived in his own house with a marble stable, purple horse blankets, jewelled saddlery and troops of slaves to attend to his every need. There was a rumour that Caligula intended to award Incitatus a consulship.

Caenis, who held there was no reason to believe Incitatus would do any worse than some of the legitimate candidates for consul, now relented and helped Veronica out. 'Io! Incitatus is modest, hospitable, kind to his slaves – and rises above the glamour to run his heart out on the track. Have a pomegranate and don't worry!' As she called cheerfully across the table, she finally shifted her leg. Lucius Anicius plundered the cornucopia, nodding for more wine. The

142

wine at Veronica's was tolerable, and her stewards had a knack of warming it pleasantly with herbs, but for good professional reasons she discouraged too much drink. While he waited for the rather slow service, Anicius helped Caenis to a hand of grapes.

People were now talking about the Emperor's military deeds in Germany. This was simple scandal, so Caenis saw Veronica relax. Caligula had rattled about Europe in spectacular battledress, fleecing the good burghers of Lugdunum in Gaul at compulsory auctions of Palace furniture, throwing his uncle Claudius fully clad into the Rhine, taking hostages from a primary school, then chasing them like fugitives up a road, and finally marching home with a bunch of 'German' prisoners of war who turned out to be just tall bemused Gauls with their hair and beards dyed red.

'I do feel,' Caenis observed in an undertone to Anicius, 'that a man who owes his position to the adoration of the army was unwise to take the field unless he could live up to the gallantry the army expects!'

'Oh yes; he's a bully – but also a complete coward.' Anicius poured wine for her from the flagon he had captured. He had not bothered to grab the water-jug so they tilted their cups together and like hardened drinkers took it neat. They drank in silence, cynically observing the rest with hooded eyes.

By now the older men were lathering themselves into fine indignation over the Emperor's Ovation, a kind of secondary triumph which he had been awarded for the British affair. After showing himself in Germany, Caligula had assembled a huge invasion force and fleet, announcing his intention of seizing the island which Julius Caesar had failed to keep. He accepted homage from a British princeling who had been exiled for arguing with his Celtic papa, and then announced Britain's surrender without even setting foot in the place.

Returning home, the Emperor abused the Senate roundly for omitting to vote him a full triumph. It was a vicious circle; his express orders had been that they must not.

'Antonia Caenis, I'll tell you an amusing story about Britain,' muttered Anicius. 'In a minute.'

A praetor had smoothed things over by suggesting that special Games be held to celebrate the Emperor's German campaign. This was all the more creditable to the praetor since as holder of that office he would be expected to help pay for the Games himself. He had no money, Caenis knew; it was Vespasian. He then gratified the Emperor by thanking him before the full Senate for his graciousness, simply because Caligula had invited him to dine at the Palace.

Caenis heard this praetor's name being scoffed at without a pang. 'Poor lad!' she commented drily. 'Dinner is going to test him a bit. He tends to nod off; Olympian Jove won't like it if he dozes over the ambrosia.'

Everyone laughed.

Veronica, who was not a sentimentalist, remarked briskly, 'I dare say if his eyes start to droop, his wife will give him a kick!' And without looking again at Caenis, she signalled to her waitresses to start clearing the tables and let in the Spanish dancing girls.

Caenis hated Spanish dancers. She groaned in disgust, 'Oh Juno! Not the tambourines and castanets!'

It was a cliché to have girls from Gades to entertain your dinner guests. That never prevented their popularity, sweeping the floor with their handsome hair, while furiously clicking and clattering.

She knew what would happen next. Veronica was already bestowing her charm on the man at her side; he was faintly pink, thrilled at being singled out, but forgetting the premium he would have to pay. Soon there would be other pairings and disappearings, with or without the dancers whose moral reputation ranked only slightly above Syrian flute-girls (who at least could play). Then Caenis would be left here to preside over noncombatants, taking charge in Veronica's place while tiresome men tirelessly talked.

For once a surge of resentment swept her. 'Lucius Anicius, your funny story would be kind.'

Assenting suavely, he stabbed his knife into a peach. 'They are trying to keep this dark. Apparently the conquest of Britain involved much more than giving houseroom to some British king's delinquent boy. God-on-earth conquered the Ocean.'

Caenis gazed at him over the rim of her cup. 'I heard God-on-earth built a lighthouse,' she offered.

'True.' Anicius was leering at the dancing girls. 'Very public-spirited in that wild part of the world – No; I think you'll like this: I'm told he paraded all his soldiers on the beach, and commanded them to gather seashells in their helmets and tunic skirts. He's brought it all back to the Capitol in chests, and presented it to the Senate as the tribute of the sea.'

Caenis flashed her teeth against the cup. 'Cowries and cuttlefish, winkles and whelks? Imagine the smell! Oh yes,' she agreed slowly. 'Oh I like that very much.'

'Good!' responded Anicius, returning his attention lazily to her. He was the sort of man who spent a great deal of time wrestling and playing handball at the baths; he was built like a barrack wall. 'This must be the first time I've seduced a woman by talking politics.'

Caenis, who had enjoyed dressing for this evening more than she had done for a long time, tidied the folds of her gown with a well-manicured fingernail; for a moment she dipped her ochred eyes – then raised them and held his look. 'Is that what you are doing?'

'Am I not?'

'Oh yes, I think so,' she murmured, though he was not her type at all. 'Lord, why me?' she asked.

She had wondered if he had instructions from Veronica, though if so his next reply was far too blunt. He laughed. 'Lady, why not?'

She laid her hand formally upon his iron fist as he helped her rise and led her from the room.

She had chosen well. She knew a disaster would end her confidence for good, but there was no danger of that. Anicius used his women with a vigour that bordered on force; Caenis, in wild mood, took and was taken with a spirit that matched his. It was over very quickly; she was glad of that.

She conducted herself irreproachably. She avoided disgrace; she was free. No stranger would realise how detached

145

she wanted to remain. Only when she thought herself awake alone afterwards did she creep against a wall and give way to the relief of deep, convulsing, almost silent sobs.

After she was still Lucius Anicius moved. It hardly mattered. She had no desire to see the man again; nor would he expect to seek her out. 'Too much wine?' He was curt, but not rude.

In a moment Caenis said quietly, 'No. Sorry.'

'Feeling all right?'

'Wonderful, lord!'

'What is the lady thinking then?'

Drained of all feeling, Caenis spoke candidly with her head against the wall. 'That the saddest sight of this stupid reign must be a decent man reduced to flattering a political grotesque.' The name of the praetor Vespasianus remained unsaid.

She heard Anicius move again. Not without instinct, he asked wryly, 'Do I take it we have just crossed your Rubicon?' Then when she did not answer, he proved she had chosen someone more generous than she had thought; he whistled softly. 'Why me?'

Allowing her to fling it back to him – '*Why not?*'

After four mad years the Emperor Gaius, nick-named Caligula, was to die during the Augustan Games in the Portico of the Danaids on the Palatine. The plot was so open, conspirators called out and wished each other luck as they took their seats. A mime was produced, which involved the death of a king and his daughter, with the use of much stage blood. Retiring for lunch, the Emperor declined to follow his uncle Claudius down the alley lined with imperial slaves, but paused to greet a group of young boys practising to sing for him later, then took a short cut down one of the covered passages. There Cassius Chaerea, the Guards commander, came to ask for the day's password, and was given the usual obscene answer. Chaerea drew his sword and stabbed Caligula, at which the group he had organised rushed in to finish off their victim before his special cohort of German bodyguards, shut out from the corridor, could burst in to

146

save him. The conspirators then fled through the nearby House of Livia.

Chaos broke out. The German bodyguard ran amok and killed three senators. A group of Praetorian Guards invaded the imperial quarters, discovered Caesonia, the Emperor's wife, murdered her and dashed out the brains of Drusilla, her infant child. The Senate gathered on the Capitol, which was defensible, having had the forethought to take with them the State and Military Treasuries so they could pay their way out of trouble. The mob milled about in the Forum below, where they were harangued by men from noble families who wanted to claim they had not been involved in the plot.

The Senate briefly fancied that the Republic might be restored, though individual members were acutely aware that would threaten their personal power. But then an odd accident intervened. Some soldiers, cheerily looting the Palace, found the last remaining adult male of the imperial family hiding behind a curtain and for a joke proclaimed him Emperor.

The poor soul they seized on was Claudius, the son whom Antonia had always called ridiculous.

XX

The imperial freedman Narcissus could not remember who this woman was.

'Well,' she cried, with more irony than most people were using nowadays. 'A new emperor; a new Chief Secretary!' He was the most important man on Claudius' staff; he was expected to recognise everyone.

She had probably touched thirty. She had neither the flounces nor the necklaces of some citizen's matronly wife, yet despite all the spear-carriers, cloak and footwear attendants, name-takers and door-keepers, she had got into his office, brushing off the paraphernalia of delay as carelessly as a naiad paddling through foam; she knew palaces. He wondered: *one of us?*

'Narcissus.' *Yes. And she knew she had floored him.* 'Little did I imagine that one day I should find you in an office as big as a wrestling hall, with a desk like Aphrodite's bedstead and a ruby signet ring. Come to that, which of us foresaw clownish Claudius being shouldered through the streets by the Praetorian Guards? Did somebody in the Praetorians get up with a headache, or did they only get the headache after they realised what they had done?'

Narcissus, who had shared some interesting conversations in the last few weeks, made no answer while he went on sizing her up. Quality clothes – sage-green linen, evenly dyed and belted in with simple cords; a modest stole; gold at her arm; a pair of shoulder brooches, with very good garnets in antique metalwork. A stately walk; a gloss of hair folded back neatly from a vividly reminiscent face; that rapid gaze. He was certain he knew her. He knew those searching eyes.

Since he had not asked her to sit, she stood. His stern act rebounded; the freedman felt himself rebuked. He cleared his throat and signalled her to a stool.

148

Dammit; he definitely knew that air of haughty rebellion as she declined.

'It has been a long time,' she derided him gently. 'I used to think you were wonderful.' Her eyes had a teasing gleam that must be new. 'Easily the most intelligent man that I had ever known ... So this elevation of yours is not, *O my master*, entirely unexpected –' She had excellent manners; she was graciously helping him out now. 'You always said I was the quickest child you ever taught – but I should never get anywhere until my handwriting was neat.'

Of course!

Twenty years ago. He remembered now; he had a meticulous brain with a long reach. Thin as a strip of wind, and that morose, wounded stare that ripped into you like teasel hooks. Oh, he remembered this one: he used to start explaining something difficult, but before he was halfway through the logic, she would be up and asking questions on a point he hadn't intended to cover for another hour. The only thing that ever really held her back was that she understood the end of the lesson before her leaping brain had properly learned the steps along the way.

The others all hated her. Because she found everything so effortless – but most of all because, in a dull world, that ferocious scrap was bound to be any teacher's favourite.

'*Caenis!* exclaimed the freedman Narcissus.

Then all the whifflers and fly-swotters who cluttered up his office leant back in alarm from the roar as the Emperor's Chief Secretary laughed.

She would never be a beauty but working for Antonia had turned her out immaculate. Fastidious, austere, sinfully clever – and probably still furious underneath.

They surveyed one another, smiling; neither was giving anything away.

'Want a favour, miss?'

'Do you one, sir.'

These days that was a pleasant change.

Caenis had worked out that an emperor whose popularity amongst the establishment was so shaky must be looking for

149

new men. To cope, Claudius was setting up an organisation at the Palace from the trusted ex-slaves of his own household: his mother's freedman Pallas at the Treasury, Caligula's man Callistus as Secretary of Petitions, and this fellow who had once been her own teacher, Narcissus, as the overall head of administration. Putting the Empire in the hands of his freedmen would never be approved by the patricians, but it would work. The Emperor's freedmen had a vested interest in keeping their patron on the throne.

With a new emperor the convention was that every senior post in provincial government and the army would be looked at afresh. Many officials would be changed. Narcissus was now in charge of that. So Caenis knew, Narcissus would be recruiting the new men.

He was magnificently able. Wary to the point of seeming sinister, he would certainly use his grand position to his own advantage, but he could be relied on to enjoy organising the Empire. He had dedication and flair. Quite likely a Greek in origin, he spoke with the extremely cultured voice of a foreigner who had the ear to overcome his oiliness; his Latin was better than that of most senators, and his Greek impeccable. He must be hated too.

'What favour, and why?' he demanded. He had always been testy.

'You sound just like a woman, Chief Secretary!'

'It's the job, dear. Organising fools all day. Don't mess me about,' he commanded. 'What's his name?'

They were speaking now in low, familiar voices, people who had once worked together as slaves. No point in further delay. 'Flavius Vespasianus,' she said crisply. 'His brother is a commanding legate in the army on the Rhine.' There was a slight pause. 'This one's brighter and more thorough,' Caenis claimed. She still remembered the criteria Narcissus applied when judging people.

The Emperor's freedman pursed his lips and stared up at the ceiling high above his head. It was decorated with rotund cherubs and fauns surrounded by exquisite bouquets of flowers. Caligula had extended the Palace to take in the Temple of Castor and Pollux as his vestibule. At the same time some superb redecoration had been done. The Chief Secretary had allocated himself a showpiece suite. Well; he had an excuse. This was where ambassadors would soon be homing in from all over the world.

'Lover?' grilled the freedman nastily. .

'No,' Caenis replied, keeping her tone level. She had come prepared for his direct methods. '*Was* my lover, I admit. It's not at all relevant; you will find out when you check.'

He laughed. So far there were not many people who gave him credit for cautiousness. And there would never again be many who dared stand up to him. 'She wants him back!' Narcissus tried her, with that terrible grisly grin.

'No. Married. Haven't seen him for years.'

'Years! You owe him money, girl?'

'Freedman, you taught me better than that!' Careful herself, she declined to confess that the debt owed was from Vespasian to her. He had never managed to repay the loan (although he kept his word and sent her interest via an embarrassed accountant once a year).

Narcissus hauled himself upright and moved to a carved chest behind his chair; she noticed that the padded braid on his tunic was a good handspan deep, stiffening out the neck and hem. As he turned away she recognised the signs: he wanted one of his special lists. Here it came, and he was running his split pen-nib down the names with a secretive air that told her he already knew his way about these characters much better than he wanted to reveal. He glanced up sharply as she craned her neck, searching for tell-tale notches besides the names. 'You haven't seen this!'

'No, sir,' she simpered, enjoying herself hugely.

'Flavius Vespasianus . . . Titus, would that be?'

'Titus,' she agreed, more awkwardly than she had hoped.

'Titus,' he repeated; he had always been an aggravating man. 'Hmm. Military service in Thrace, kept his nose clean –'

'He liked the army,' Caenis interrupted quickly.

'And how did the army like him?' Narcissus barked. 'Quaestor in Cyrenaïca and Crete; produced a good report. Must be *bloody* good, if they acknowledged it! Aedile –' It was all there. He stared for a moment then scoffed; evidently he had a record of that business with the mud. 'Praetor at first attempt. What's this – it was he who made that speech when Caligula sent his sister home with the ashes of her lover? For plotting against the Emperor Lepidus should be denied public burial? I could call that crawling! I don't want him if his judgement is flawed –'

'No choice,' Caenis defended Vespasian.

'It looks inept.'

'Expedient. Caligula had taken command of the situation. The Senate had to support him or go down with the conspirators. Besides, who would want that wretch Agrippina to succeed in a plot?'

'Who would want Agrippina as an enemy, Caenis?' After the sharp retort Narcissus let it go. 'Brother of Sabinus . . . I know the brother; he waffles, but he's all right.' He laid down the list abruptly and looked at her. 'Difficult.'

'Narcissus, the man is good.'

'It's not his turn.'

'He has no money, no reputation and no famous ancestors. You condemn him, Narcissus; it will never be his turn!'

Narcissus gave her his vile laugh. 'Keep your wig on! I'll look at him. There's plenty for a good man to do.' That was interesting. 'Come and see me this evening; ask them in the outer office for the map to find my house.'

Caenis chuckled. How like the old fusspot to organise a map. 'Your house? Don't you want a suite here, three steps from the Emperor?'

To her, since they knew one another well and from a different time, Narcissus made the admission in a low voice, 'Of course! And only two steps from his interfering bloody wife. But sometimes I shall want to be unavailable. Besides, woman,' said the Emperor's Chief Secretary, 'I prefer to keep a private corner to entertain my own friends.'

His idea of a private corner boded well for his friends.

Narcissus, who was to make himself the master of four million sesterces, the richest man in Rome, lived even at that stage in a house of distinctive opulence. Deft slaves silently slipped about. Caenis permitted a houseboy to lift off her outdoor shoes. She eased herself into a sleekly tasselled mound of swansdown cushions, accepted a sweetmeat, toyed with honeyed wine.

'*Nice!*' she teased Narcissus sceptically.

He gave her a look. Even before he spoke she guessed he had made enquiries where and how she lived herself. 'Better than your frowsty eggcup off the Via Appia. Do you know that Claudius never sold his mother's house? I pointed out that you've been polishing his daughter's shorthand without a salary.' Claudia Antonia was now to be married, so any education she needed would be of a different kind. 'He agrees; I've earmarked you half a wing.'

She had forgotten how hard he worked. Nor had she reckoned on his establishing his kitchen cabinet so speedily.

'I can't go back to Antonia's house. It would break my heart. Besides, who gets the other half of the wing?'

'Agrippina; she's being allowed back from exile.' As Caenis exploded with disgust, Narcissus rushed on, 'We'll find you some cash then and you can sort out your own place.'

'I want a nice apartment with a fig tree and a female landlady who's too embarrassed to ask for a high rent.'

'I interviewed your man.'

Their eyes clashed. Caenis snapped, 'Not mine!'

'Sorry; I forgot! He wasn't what I expected; we had an interesting chat. Has an infant son, did you know? Poor little sprat came into the world in a back bedroom not much better than the flea-trap you lurk in yourself: Titus.'

Caenis wondered what sort of chat. 'What?'

'Vespasian's son.' As a family the Flavians still lacked inspiration when it came to naming their boys. 'You might have mentioned the son, Caenis.'

'Why? So what have you offered his obviously virile papa?'

'Nothing yet. It's up to my man.'

Caenis made herself more comfortable among the swansdown and to assist her task of trying out all his sweetmeats she commandeered their little silver plate. In such matters

Narcissus had excellent Greek taste. The honeyed balls were packed all over with sesame seeds: twice the fun – eating them first, then hours of extra pleasure picking your teeth. 'What we may offer him,' Narcissus said carefully, 'would hardly be a hammock in the sun.'

'Something going on?' Caenis rapped back at once.

The Empire stretched from Africa to Gaul, from Farther Spain to Syria. Decades ago, when Varus lost three legions in the traumatic massacre in Germany, Augustus had decreed this far was enough. For thirty-five years now the policy had been to contain military effort within Rome's existing boundaries. Trying to expand would involve vast tracts of territory, small profit for a large outlay and no particular prestige. There remained only one possibility that might be tempting for an emperor who needed a mad rapid exploit to confirm his position at a time when the legions were not even sure who he was and the Senate were tolerating him only until they thought of somebody to hoist up in his place.

Narcissus watched her working it out; he was proud of her.

'You're not serious, freedman! Not another crack at Britain?'

The island beyond the edge of the known world. It hummed with mystery; there was talk of deposits of silver and gold; Julius Caesar had been there, though he had had the sense to back off hastily; the great British King Conubelinus, who for years had preserved stability in the south and was tolerant of trade with Rome, had recently died leaving a nest of ambitious, more hostile sons.

And the stores were already in the warehouses in Gaul; the plans worked up and filed; the triremes built.

Narcissus shrugged. 'Thanks to Caligula all the logistical work has been done. There's even a glorious new lighthouse to beacon the way. Does he shrink in the wet, your Sabine friend? Will he frighten at blue men and druids' spells?'

'He can cope. Especially if there's a salary.'

'Oh, I do like an army full of men who need the money! So reliable and keen.' The freedman's voice suddenly dropped.

154

After all, she had once been his favourite. 'What do you want, miss? Shall I tell him you spoke to me?'

'No!' Caenis was horrified.

'Want to hear that he's happy and well?'

'No.'

'I see. Sulking? Wants him miserable and off-colour instead.'

She lost her temper. 'I just want him to be given his chance! I want a man who has real talent, and energy, and the will to serve, to stop being hampered by the snobberies of the system –'

'*Caenis!* You predicate a society in which a man rises through merit!' Narcissus broke in with a shocked voice. She was still wondering whether to deflate him for 'predicate' when he gave her an evil grin: bad teeth – a poor diet in infancy exaggerated lately by luxuries for which his constitution was ill-prepared. He held out a warning hand. 'Excuse me; I have another guest.' For one dreadful moment she thought it would be Vespasian himself.

It was not. Shuffling apologetically, it was the Emperor.

The slave who had showed him in was asking whether to light the lamps. Narcissus declined. 'Leave them there for the moment. It's good to sit quietly at dusk among friends.'

Caenis wondered whether she should leave. It seemed easier to sit tight. She noticed that here in his own house, even for the Emperor Narcissus did not rise. Claudius, that white hair and the limp instantly recognisable despite the half-light that had fallen while she and Narcissus talked, found himself a couch with touching informality.

'Antonia Caenis, let me introduce you to my patron –'

'I know your patron,' she interrupted quickly. Despite everything, Claudius might possibly not remember her; he drank heavily and his recollection for faces was notoriously bad. 'I am his mother's freedwoman; he is my patron too.'

The Emperor nodded to her with that helpless quirk of the head.

They all sat, as Narcissus had suggested, quietly in the twilight. It was then for the first time that Caenis realised she was part of something new. Some strain which she had always known was lifting from Rome. By chance she belonged to the private household that was so unexpectedly governing the world. Narcissus, who approved of her, would bring her into this Emperor's tight-knit circle to watch, and if she wanted, to help.

Narcissus was saying openly to the Emperor, as if Caenis were already acknowledged as a colleague, 'I left you the list to consider for army legates. You might give thought to Vespasianus. He could suit the Second Augusta. They're at Argentoratum now; ideal candidates for your British scheme.'

Argentoratum was one of the big military bases on the Rhine. Caenis knew the legions there had been fractious for years. It would be useful to pull them out of their secure pitch where they fraternised too closely with the locals and were apt to forget they owed allegiance to Rome. In other respects the legions in Germany were first class. It would be a good command.

Claudius had turned to her. 'I know Vespasianus, don't I?'

She reminded him quietly, 'You met him, sir; at your mother's house.'

'Yes . . . oh yes.' He had taken on his wandering air. Oddly, it seemed to be settled at that. The freedman winked at her.

'If you take to him,' Narcissus mentioned to Claudius after a time, 'he has a boy we may educate with your own.' Suddenly Caenis understood why he had been so interested in Vespasian's son.

Messalina had crowned the Emperor's astonishing rise to power by presenting Claudius with a male heir just twenty-two days after he accepted the throne. It would be seven years before the little prince went formally to school; Narcissus must be making long-term plans. With one Caesar barely pinned into his gown of woven gold, he was already plotting the school curriculum to produce a dynasty.

Narcissus himself handed wine. Caenis had withdrawn into herself, winded by a vision of Vespasian with a baby on his arm. She was also having some difficulty hanging on to the dish of sweetmeats; Claudius was addicted to food.

'To the Emperor!' murmured Narcissus, the civil servant at his most wickedly urbane. Claudius ducked his head, not fooled by it.

'To good government!' Caenis staunchly returned. She grinned at Narcissus, aware that she had for once embarrassed him. 'Sorry. I forgot to tell you; I'm a secret republican.'

'Forgot to tell you, Narcissus,' mused Tiberius Claudius Drusus Nero Germanicus, with the slight melancholy of a man sitting quietly at dusk among his friends. 'I am a secret republican myself!'

And as they all sat eating Greek sweetmeats, they laughed.

It was a new world, a new order, staffed by people with like minds: Caenis could hardly believe it; she was part of this.

She had an interview with her landlord later that week. Eumolpus came into her room without knocking, as she knew he did when he thought she was out.

'Ah!' exclaimed Caenis quietly, and had the satisfaction of seeing the slimy bastard jump.

He stared at her so the tendons set in the back of her neck. His provocative eyes lingered on her skin and on the subtle folds of her dark red dress. The dress had loosely draped sleeves, fastened to the elbow five times along each arm. 'Always so smart! I do like that dress, Caenis. Those with the little buttons are the most seductive kind; a man always imagines them being very slowly unfastened one by one for him . . .'

'Actually,' Caenis crushed him, 'these are purely decoration – permanently sewn up.' She could hardly bear to be in the same room. 'So glad you called; I can serve you my notice. I shall not charge you,' smiled Caenis gently, 'for all the painting and shoring up of your walls and woodwork I have had done – though I may suggest to the incoming tenant that she changes the lock!'

And in answer to the gratifying curiosity she had caused,

'I am fortunate,' she said modestly. 'The new Emperor has offered me a suite in his mother's house.'

It was a lie, because she would never accept the offer of returning to the House of Livia. And this was the only time Caenis, who was no snob, ever used her connections so publicly.

She did it on behalf of all the struggling women down the years who endured invasions of their privacy and acts against their person from men whose only advantage was the possession of property. She did it for them, and she did it for the bitter, barefoot slavey she had once been herself.

She was fortunate now. Emperors would come and go. But as Narcissus so shrewdly deduced, Antonia Caenis would in many ways be bitter and barefoot all her life.

XXI

Narcissus went to Britain himself.

In fact he almost went to Britain *by* himself: all the more ludicrous since according to his plan he should have been nursing things along in Rome.

The plan was: the troops would sail over, establish a foothold, batter the heads of a few southern tribesmen, then invite the Emperor to join them for finishing off the by-now groggy tribes; afterwards he would push off home as *Claudius Britannicus*, leaving the army to pin down as much territory as they could without serious expense, loss of face or loss of life.

It was a perfectly sound plan. Once Narcissus wound the machinery into action, like some solemn donkey toiling at a plod around his eternally creaking water-screw, the plan worked pretty well. Once, that is, he got himself to Gaul and shifted the invasion force.

The troops refused to go.

'*That* was not in the *Daily Gazette*!' Caenis exclaimed, when she saw Narcissus after he returned to Rome. She had found him at his house, which had been redecorated meanwhile with a great deal of Carrara marble and flagrant use of gold leaf: all rather wearing on the eyes.

'It seemed to us,' returned the freedman, meaning it seemed to him but he possessed a shrewd degree of modesty, 'that it would be ill-advised to let it be known too widely how four of the Emperor's best legions, forty thousand of the finest, in the peak of condition, all flush with their recent bonus for the Emperor's accession and looking up to a general (Aulus Plautius) against whom no troops could possibly hold a grievance – utterly decent all-round sort of chap – as I say, four spanking legions had trudged their way through Gaul, to camp at Gesoriacum (pig of a hole; just a

159

dot on the map), only to sit on their beds looking out of their tents, staring boot-faced at the sea.'

'I understand,' suggested Caenis gently, 'that the Gallic Strait is very rough.'

Narcissus, who had been across in both directions, shuddered wordlessly. It was accepted by cultivated people that the thirty-odd miles between Britain and Gaul formed the wildest stretch of water in the world. That was the main reason, as the legionaries had advised their general frankly, why they did not want to go.

'I told them,' said Narcissus, 'I thought they had a point.'

Caenis slowly sucked a red-rimmed peach between her teeth. '*You told them!*' she repeated thoughtfully, imagining the scene.

Fortunately Aulus Plautius was a rare specimen: a general who never panicked. Faced with a polite though stubborn mutiny, he had written to the Emperor for advice. The Emperor sent the head of his secretariat to represent his views. So Narcissus had dragged himself seven hundred miles overland across Europe from Massilia, which was itself five hundred miles from Rome by sea.

'You told them – oh, *of course!*'

Caenis rolled on to her back on the healthily plump crimson quilting that covered the visitors' couches in Narcissus' grand reception room. 'Now let me be quite sure I understand this: you, my fellow-freedman, have no remit in the army. Soldiers, let's be honest, despise you as a stylus-pushing bureaucrat. So you climb on a military rostrum – the tribunal, that's the word? – in a huge new transit base at the far edge of the world. In the poker-faced presence of this exemplary general Plautius, his four legionary commanders –' including Sabinus and Vespasian – 'and all their stiff-necked officers – who presumably had already been trying very hard for weeks to make the soldiers go? – you address forty thousand hard-bitten, foul-mouthed, filthy-tempered rankers, some of them bearing the scars of twenty years and all of them trained to the teeth? – Tell me, Narcissus; was this well-received? *Didn't they laugh?*'

Narcissus smiled. 'They laughed,' he agreed. Caenis

160

removed the peach stone, now clean as a whistle, from her needle-sharp front teeth and smiled at him. 'It reminded them of the Saturnalia,' he admitted, rather sheepishly.

Caenis thought of the jolly winter carnival when in good-humoured households the slaves and their masters all changed places for a day. She tried to draw favourable comparisons but instead she heard in her head forty thousand ribald voices as they cried, '*Io Saturnalia!*' like the terrifying roar in unison of the crowd at the races in the Circus Maximus; it was her turn to grimace. 'Yes; I see. And then they went?'

'And then,' boasted Narcissus, 'they were so surprised, they went.'

Caenis scrambled round on to her front with her chin in her hands as she listened like an eager child. 'And was that when you went yourself?'

'It was blowing a gale, Caenis; credit me with sense! I waited in Gesoriacum for my man.'

Still he could describe it: the wind so ominously cold; the heavy sky; the sails that snapped to and fro overhead unpredictably; the rowers anxious; the soldiers huddling on the verge of panic and the commanders trying pallidly to look calm. As the transports moved out from the shelter of the Gallic coast, a force of truly bleak water had rolled under them, sinister as pewter, with a nasty yellow tinge. Then the storm rose. Energy surged through the channel from one bloated ocean to another as it never did in the land-locked seas at home, while the gale blew them back upon themselves as if the great god Oceanus were calmly clearing his domain with the flat of a mighty hand.

'Then they saw the great green light.'

'Dear gods! What was *that*?'

'We have no idea. It was tactfully passed off to the troops as a meteor heading east – Jupiter's sign that he had countermanded Oceanus and blessed our enterprise. At any rate, the wind completely changed. The boats made headway, then were dragged by the tow of the tide and reached the other side. It all added to the pantomime.'

The army had landed unopposed. The months of delay

during the mutiny had caused the British tribes to pack up away from the cliff-tops and go home. There was no need to hack ashore. The legions beached at a new harbour where, since Caesar's day, the sea had burst a channel to create the Isle of Thanet. The whole fleet anchored safely in a sandy creek where they found the oysters that were to become famous throughout the Roman world. They named the place Rutupiae. They dug in; the invasion was under way.

Caenis realised it would be no sinecure. No one knew what to expect. That difficult coastline just out of sight from Gaul was by now fairly well known to traders, but traders for their own reasons gave nothing away. Little of the interior had ever been explored. Even Julius Caesar, a century before, had thought Britain was no place for a wise general to delay. He had created what was supposed to be a client kingdom paying tribute to Rome, but no one ever put the theory to the test. Britain remained hopelessly mysterious, shrouded in bad weather, an implausible shape on an old Phoenician map. It was a refuge for druids who had been dispossessed from Gaul with their secrecy, their political intrigue, their shocking rites of human sacrifice. Now the powerful princes in the south-east hated the recognised Roman threat; in the south-west were dark tribes living in spectacular hilltop fortresses who had alliances of trade, kinship, and common interest with the Celts in western Gaul, who had themselves been brutally defeated by Rome in Julius Caesar's time. One thing was certain: there would be fierce hostility.

Yet Narcissus argued the odds must be favourable. The four legions he was sending had the Emperor's personal interest and support. Their commander was experienced. The Roman army was one of the best supplied and organised ever in the world. This was a professional army, with its own colonies, contractors, burial clubs, savings banks. The men were magnificently organised, equipped and exercised, trained to run, ride, swim, leap, fence, wrestle, even trained to use their heads. They owned a time-tested book of tactics; in any situation every one knew what he was expected to do. In a wilderness like Britain the legions were prepared to build their own roads as they marched, to dig ditches and canals, to throw up frontier walls and fortresses, to dredge rivers and harbours, to colonise towns. Once they found the precious metals, they would run the mines. Men in the ranks were trained for every kind of specialised work. Whatever they might possibly want they either carried with them or could make once they arrived. They had javelins, swords, daggers, laminated shields, field artillery of many sorts. They wore bronze-tipped leather stomach-guards, articulated plate armour or chain mail, shoulder-plates, leg-protectors, heavy-duty helmets and the most efficient boots in the world. Against them stood brave but disorganised tribesmen, naked, almost barefoot, armed with stones and a few unwieldy swords.

Caenis suggested in a dry voice, 'So it was easy?'

'No.' Narcissus sighed. 'Caratacus and Togodumnus, two shaggy British princes, nearly beat three crack Roman legions in their first fight.'

He went back to the beginning.

'They got there; sick but safe. Landed in the east. Found the natives – a stiff fight – overnight. I hope a girl so well read as I tried to make you realises that not many Roman battles take more than one day. The hero of the hour was . . .'

Caenis sat up. 'Who?'

'Hosidius Geta.'

'*Who?*'

'One of the legionary legates. Brilliant chap.'

'Well done, Hosidius!' Caenis said mockingly.

Narcissus released a tetchy laugh. 'Oh, your lad did well enough.'

From Rutupiae three legions had moved out westwards, thousands of horny feet in studded boots tamping down the chalk of an ancient Downland track. Eventually from a high ridge above the River Medway they had glimpsed the grey skein of the River Tamesis and beyond it, the marshes that guarded the heartland of their main opposition, the Catuvellauni tribe. Skirmishers began to harry the legions but were beaten off. At the Medway, Togodumnus and

163

Caratacus stood. The ford was too narrow, the ground too spongy to cross under attack. Any bridge there had ever been had disappeared.

Aulus Plautius prepared to cross the river.

On the far bank the warriors in checkered trousers and bare chests watched. Roman standard-bearers marched meaningfully to the approach, where they planted their eagles firmly on a knoll. Ranks of infantry moved from the ridge, then stood guard while men with poles tested the softness of the ground. Cavalry wheeled towards the ford then circled back abortively, plashing through the shallows to the general's command point. Sometimes a horse, sucked in to the hocks amongst the silt, reared in panic as it tried to regain firmer ground.

Behind the Britons sprawled a careless jumble of camp sites where levies from different tribes had parked just as they arrived, confident that their attackers would be caught fast in a bottleneck. Further off still were their horses and chariots. Not until they heard the first screams from the ham-strung horses did they realise that the Romans' Batavian auxiliaries had already come across.

Silently and without fuss, almost unnoticed even by their own army, the Batavians had slipped down the north side of the escarpment, entered deep water far away to the right, and swum to the western bank. They were attached to the Fourteenth Gemina; they were one of the many groups of native specialists who were taken into the Roman legions to give them a chance of achieving citizenship and to let the army exploit their unique skills. These Batavians came from the area around the estuary of the Rhine; they were famous boatmen and pilots – and this detachment had been trained to swim, with their horses alongside, in their full weight of kit.

They went straight for the chariot park and put the British horses out of action. At the roar when the tribesmen realised what was happening, the Batavians melted away.

On the Roman bank it was the two legions commanded by the Flavian brothers, Sabinus and Vespasian, who then made the move. Order materialised from the diversionary exercise. Screened by mounted auxiliaries – a line of cavalry upstream to break the force of the water and another lower down to catch any baggage that floated off – the soldiers began to swarm across the marsh while the Britons were unscrambling their chariots. The Britons hurled themselves upon this bridgehead. Vespasian and Sabinus held them off until dusk.

The third legion under Hosidius Geta went across in the dark.

The battle continued almost all the next day. In the end, Hosidius Geta's legion forced a wedge into the crammed ranks of half-naked warriors. Geta himself was surrounded but cut a swathe free and broke out. His legion wheeled round to encircle the enemy, and the day and the province were won. The British forces broke and galloped north. Picking off stragglers and gathering up their own casualties, the Romans made after them. But the Britons had crossed the river where it widened; by the time pursuit arrived the tide had turned and flooded back up the estuary to form an impassable brackish lake.

Some Batavians swam the river, but they grew careless, lost their way amongst the marshes, and were cut apart by Caratacus. The general Aulus Plautius pitched camp on the south bank of the Tamesis while pontoons were towed from Rutupiae to build a temporary bridge. The legions waited two months for the Emperor and the elephants to come from Rome.

'*That* was when you went?' demanded Caenis triumphantly.

Narcissus confirmed at last, 'That was when I went across.'

'What was it like?'

'Densely populated farmland with some forest in between. Wattle huts, mostly round, surrounded by tiny square fields with built-up boundary banks. Cattle, dogs everywhere, the best corn outside Africa.'

'And the blue men?'

'Extraordinary!' Narcissus exclaimed.

'Are the women blue?'

'No. And really, not many of the men. The women,' Narcissus thought it appropriate to tell her, 'were very tall, tawny as lions, and apparently more outspoken and single-minded even than you. Thank the gods we couldn't understand them! The ones we met were of course mostly princesses and queens.'

'I suppose,' Caenis glowered, 'commanding officers abroad may have to have a lot of dealings with fierce barbarian queens?'

'Not,' commented Narcissus, 'if they have any sense!'

From what he had been telling her she gathered that the eastern sector of the country was by now subdued. One of the chieftains was believed to have died of wounds after the Battle of the Medway, though his brother Caratacus escaped into the west. Claudius had entered the Catuvellaunian citadel at Camulodunum, which he inaugurated as the Roman provincial capital.

'Useless,' Narcissus moaned. 'Too far east. Have to change it when we can. Still, he enjoyed himself.'

'How long did you stay?'

'Sixteen days.'

'What happened then?'

'Various kings surrendered and were laden with loans and gifts. Aulus Plautius was named first provincial governor. We sailed home. I left my man pottering round Gaul on his own.'

'And that's it?'

'No, woman,' Narcissus rebuked her. 'That is by no means it.'

He reckoned it would take them fifty years. Aulus Plautius would start now, planting a network of military forts, gravelling roads, opening the ironworks in the south-east. Wine, oil, glass, perishable goods, would all go north in massive quantities; hides, hunting dogs, jet, oysters, grain, start trickling south. The legions – the Twentieth, Ninth and Fourteenth – would establish bases in the east, the north, the middle west. But so far they had barely scratched a toehold, that was clear. In the south the Second Legion faced a major task.

Narcissus asked dourly, 'I suppose you want to hear about your man?'

'Is there,' Caenis enquired innocently, 'anything to hear?'

She must know, since she knew Vespasian, there would be.

'With that one –' Narcissus stretched – 'it is entirely up to him.'

She said baldly, 'I always told him that.'

'This is between the two of us.' Narcissus loved his secrecy. It usually meant what he had to say would be astounding half the world within a week. 'My man really takes to him. Sent him into the south on his own – a free hand. He reports to the governor but his orders come direct from Claudius. There's an odd friendly king, Togidubnus, on the coast, who for some reason has offered the Second Augusta a safe base. From there they can have the run of the south-west: the most ferocious tribes; dozens of hillforts bristling with nasty-tempered settlers slinging stones; some of the most fabulous defensive earthworks in the world. Somewhere in all that lot is more iron, plus the silver, the copper, the tin, and possibly the gold. The south-west, you realise, is where Rome really wants to be. The Second Augusta, in the command of your man, will be there for three years. I think we can assume that if he manages this, Vespasian will be made.'

'Will he manage?'

'What do you think?'

'I hope he does,' taunted Caenis, with her occasional abrupt habit of not thinking before she spoke. 'The old skin-flint owes me ten thousand sesterces!'

It was Narcissus who blushed now. Vespasian was notorious for never having any money, but this glimpse of his bedroom habits was too startling to be believed.

'I had hoped,' returned the freedman tartly, 'I had taught you never to lend!' He was looking faintly worried as he tried to make her out. Since he had known her as a girl, someone, perhaps even Vespasian himself, had turned this one into a tease. 'I should have found him myself in the end, you know, Caenis; he was always on my list.'

'Does that mean you agree with me?'

'Oh, he's outstanding,' said Narcissus tersely. Then, unable to resist his nagging anxiety, 'I'll give you ten thousand; it seems fair, and that tight-fisted miser will never pay you back.' Curious, when she did not answer he felt compelled to insist, 'You'll laugh if he does.'

Caenis laughed now. '"Never lend if you need repayment; never give where you want a return." Now who told me that? Oh Narcissus, believe me, if ever he does repay me there is no question about it – I shall cry!'

XXII

By the time the last squadrons of auxiliary soldiers had left the Field of Mars, the magistrates were just approaching the Capitol. The long procession snaked through the Flaminian Circus, and entered the city through the Triumphal Gate, which was opened especially for the day. Following the Via Triumphalis, it wound past the theatres in the Ninth District to give as many folk as possible a decent view, made a complete circuit to the right around the Palatine, included the Circus Maximus, turned left at the Caelian Hill, took the Sacred Way into the Forum, passed along the southern side, then ascended Capitol Hill by the steep approach of the Clivus Capitolinus, up to the Temple of Jupiter at the heart of the Citadel. So Rome saw the army; the army saw most of Rome.

Everything moved at a dismal crawl. The whole city was at a standstill. The noise was incredible. The spectacle took the best part of a day.

Vespasian said, years afterwards in the procession he shared with Titus for the capture of Jerusalem, that asking for a Triumph (it was customary to ask) was the act of an old fool.

There had already been the expected Triumph for Britain, when Claudius came home. The Senate could only vote one Triumph for any campaign. Strictly speaking, this later event was an Ovation for his returning commander-in-chief: a secondary thing. No one cared; everyone called it a Triumph just the same.

Earlier, in the real Triumph, the Emperor had done himself proud. He adopted the name Britannicus for himself and for his infant son. The senators who had gone with him to Britain were honoured in suitable ways, while collars and crowns and headless spears for valour were handed out

169

among the army like beechnuts at a wedding; Messalina rode in a special covered carriage right into the Citadel; there was all the pomp and racket that a conqueror might expect. All the provincial governors had been invited home to witness their new Emperor's status and power.

So Caenis had seen Antonia's ridiculous son received by Senate and people in triumph. His appearance was the high spot of a memorable day. Claudius came, in his circular chariot drawn by pure white steeds, as the military victor to beg the city's welcome home, and as a religious representative interceding for that city with its gods as chief priest for the day. He wore a flowered tunic and toga all of purple, richly decorated with patterns and deep borders of gold. In one hand the staff of Jupiter, an ivory sceptre with a gold eagle at its head; in the other a symbolic laurel bough. Upon his head a laurel wreath; held above him by a public slave, the solid weight of the Etruscan chaplet of oak leaves and ribbons in pure gold, brought to him from the statue of Capitoline Jove, the Crown of Triumph that was too heavy for a mortal man to wear. In the chariot rode his infant children, Octavia and Britannicus.

But that was all three years ago. Everyone had said at the time how disappointing it was that most of the army needed to stay behind in the new province to contain the dangerous British tribes, and that although Hosidius Geta came home for the Triumph, it was the general, and some of the other commanders, that they really wanted to see.

Well; the great names were here today.

Rome could take another holiday. Claudius, who was a fair man, wanted this to be his general's day. Aulus Plautius would have in his own right the procession, the acclaim, the sacred ceremonies at the fulfilment of his vows, all the honours and all the feasts. The Emperor trotted out in person to congratulate him and as they rode back into Rome together, Claudius surrendered to Aulus Plautius the place of honour on the right. The name of that dignified, diffident, subsequently scarce-remembered man was hailed by his soldiers and by the populace all along the route, acclaimed over and over to the skies.

But even before the street-sweepers had sluiced the pavements clean at dawn, while the shopkeepers were still garlanding their porticos with flowers, another name resounded through Rome.

'*Io Triumphe!*' cried the people and the soldiers. 'Hail Claudius! Hail Plautius!' and '*Hail Vespasian!*'

Veronica had managed to hire a balcony that overlooked the processional route. It cost so much Caenis felt churlish for wanting to refuse her invitation. So she went, and took the picnic: some cold Lucanian salami, bread, stuffed eggs and pickled fish. She was not sure whether this choice made her a sentimentalist, or stupid, or ludicrously brave.

It was bound to be a long hot day. There were eight of them to a balcony that would comfortably seat three. Elbows kept knocking the plant pots down into the crowd below. Veronica regimented everyone endlessly. She had allocated them all broad-brimmed hats against the sun, and parsleycrowns for when they grew tired of keeping on their hats. She had brought deep baskets of rosebuds for hurling at the parade, and to complete the chaos vast quantities of jugs of wine. 'Just be grateful,' cried Veronica, who was a hostess of the most considerate kind, 'the price for the balcony includes the lavatory downstairs!'

The city was in turmoil long before there was anything to see. People had to arrive early in order to squeeze through the streets. This meant standing or sitting about getting sillier and louder, while far away Aulus Plautius was still reviewing his troops. The pickpockets were putting in gallant work.

At the Field of Mars further honours were announced, this time by Plautius himself. There were batons for the legionary commanders, more headless spears for soldiers who were valiant in battle, coronets for every man who saved a colleague's life, harness-medals for the cavalry, armlets for some and a bounty in cash for everyone. The legions and their individual cohorts all adopted commemorative standard-discs. And then there was a special award, one which Hosidius Geta had already won (most unusual since neither

171

man had been a consul yet): the granting of full triumphal honours – the right to wear his triumphal wreath at festivals and to have his statue in bronze erected in the Forum of Augustus – to Flavius Vespasianus for his masterly campaign in the south-west.

All this delayed the march off for hours.

The procession marshalled in traditional form. This saved the need to issue programmes and helped the sculptors to record things accurately after the event. Caenis knew the procedure by heart; the order of a Triumph had always been a favourite subject for dictation tests. It was:

First: *The Civic Escort*

Caenis popularly pointed out this was a good time to eat the picnic, while everyone was bored. With reasonable tolerance for sickness, bad manners and the distant funerals of rich provincial aunts, most of the knights and many representatives of the people turned up: it took some time getting them all past.

Second: *Flutes*

Very pleasant. In the first Triumph there had been trumpets at this point; some of the trumpets had gone out of tune in the heat. It needed a good ear to notice, but Caenis had winced. Flutes were much more amenable.

Third: *The Spoils of War*

While this lengthy part of the parade was going by people in the crowd had a chance to give sticky melon slices to their children and soothe the babies who were suffering from heatstroke.

Born aloft by stout lads in laurel wreaths came yet more trophies seized in battle: armour, weapons, dragonesque embossed shields, wonderful light wicker chariots – followed by treasure: huge twisted golden torques and enamelled harnesses and gear – then representations of places where the army had fought: models and pictures of fortresses, towns and islands, living statues of weed-

172

shrouded river gods, all with their outlandish names painted on boards: *Camulodunum, Caesaromagus, Durnovaria, Vectis Insula,* and the warlike tribes too: The *Catuvellauni,* the *Trinovantes,* and Vespasian's wild opponents in the west: the *Dubonni, Durotriges, Belgae* and *Dumnonii,* against whom he fought his thirty battles and from whom he wrested twenty savage hilltop settlements.

This strange stuff left people so confused and argumentative that Veronica made them all change stools.

Fourth: *The White Ram Prepared for Sacrifice*

With gilded horns, trailing garlands and scarlet ribbons, the magnificent beast was escorted by a string of priests all bearing implements and sacred vessels, with strong wafts of incense, and accompanied by cymbals, triangles and flutes. Veronica's party had by then drunk most of their wine, but the lull while the religious throng intoned its way past provided a good opportunity to open up what remained.

Fifth: *The Principal Captives*

No one knew the names of these British captives since Togodumnus was dead and Caratacus still remained at large. Still, captives there were, and some were duly tattooed with vigorous patterns in blue woad. They had long limbs, white skin, light hair, and pale eyes in blue or grey. Among the sky-scraping buildings, the forests of statues and the roar of thousands of Romans in raucous holiday mood, they looked apprehensive and bemused. Veronica threw them a few stuffed dates, but they only shied away.

Sixth: *The Commander-in-Chief's Escort of Lictors*

Smarter than ever, though today without the axes they normally carried among their official bundles of staves. All in red. A splendid show.

Seventh: *Lyre Players and Dancers*

Exulting over the vanquished enemy. Extremely tiring to do, but fun to watch.

Eighth: *The Victorious General*

Aulus Plautius, a surprisingly small man, looking worried by the capering of his huge white horse; he wore magisterial robes and a heavy myrtle wreath. He was extremely popular. At his side:

Ninth: *The Emperor Claudius Britannicus*

Caenis by now had a splitting headache.

Tenth: –

'I'm terribly sorry,' Caenis murmured in apology, as she clambered over knees and baskets with the embarrassment and relief a woman feels after she has brought herself to the point of saying what she has been too shy to mention for three-quarters of an hour. 'I just can't wait any longer. It must be the excitement. Tell me what I miss. Veronica, where's this famous lavatory of yours?'

Tenth: *The Chief Officers of the Conquering Legions*

Caenis took her time.

Even so, she badly misjudged it.

When she finally returned the noise was at its height. The spectators, swaying fearlessly on scaffolds, could hardly contain themselves as before the legions in full dress parade filled the streets, one by one drawn in chariots at their head they came: the four famous legates who commanded them.

The cheers had become frantic. People were scrambling up pillars to try to find a better view. The air was thick with flung flowers. Everyone was on their feet. Veronica, scarlet-faced with exertion, was jumping up and down in hysteria. She was clapping her hands and flinging violets and roses, then olives from the picnic, as every new legate passed.

Caenis, returning, was manhandled joyously by the others in their group back over wine-jars and fallen chairs to her previous place at the front. Veronica mouthed something; Caenis grappled in the picnic case for tasty morsels to calm everybody down. While she was away the legates of the *legio XIV Gemina*, the *legio IX Hispana*, and the *legio XX*

Valeria, had all come by at a snail-pace crawl. Now away at the Capitol, Aulus Plautius, supported by the Emperor, began the last long climb up the Gemonian Steps, which by tradition he had to do on his knees; behind them the whole tail of the procession suddenly clogged up, faltered, swayed, and juddered temporarily to a halt.

A standard-bearer in his fanged bearskin who was forced to stop, planted the tripod feet of a legionary eagle on the tufa pavement where they skidded awkwardly; the silver-winged eagle lurched as he adjusted his aching fingers on the handle grip. Attached to the pole, which was garlanded with greenery, were two triangular emblem plates: Pegasus and Capricorn, which had been the symbol of the Emperor Augustus; above them was displayed the legion's number and name. Behind the standard that must always mark his position for his men, the legate of the *legio II Augusta* came to a standstill, rocking gently on his heels as he rested his hands on the front rim of his ceremonial chariot.

'*Vespasian!*' the crowds roared, bursting their lungs at this marvellous stroke of luck. The Hero of Britain, Flavius Vespasianus, folded his arms while he waited, and nodded absently to the crowd. The Hero of Britain: twelve feet away from Caenis, immediately below.

Hoarse with anguished adulation, Veronica clutched her throat.

'*Io Triumphe!* My darling, will you look at him – the Hero! Your lovely Sabine friend!'

Caenis had never seen her Sabine friend in uniform before.

He gleamed with bronze and glittered with buckles and medals in chased enamelware. Four honorary batons were tucked under one great arm. Much of him was hidden beneath breastplate and boots and the heavy scarlet swirls of his commanding officer's cloak. His hair looked thinner and the strong distinctive neck was invisible beneath the knotted wisp of a regulation scarf, but nothing could disguise the crank of that nose or the glorious upward angle of his chin. The wreath that he should have been wearing with such pride had dipped casually over one ear.

Someone had thrown a froth of rose petals that were clinging to his shoulder-clasp. He was brushing them off; they
drifted languidly as far as the hem of his woollen cloak. All
around him was ecstasy; trumpet blasts; cheers and screams.
He stayed utterly himself. He glanced back at his officers,
turning up his eyes to heaven at the delay while he gave the
young men behind, who were grinning back, an amiable
frown. He thrust out his lower lip. He reached for his chin
with the back of his hand as if he wanted to stifle a yawn.
Caenis smiled. Anyone who knew him could recognise that
the Hero of Britain was seriously bored.

Veronica was squealing with despair. 'Oh Juno! There's
nothing left to throw –'

Snatching it off, she tossed down her limp parsley crown;
Caenis leant a little over the balustrade, laughing, as she
watched the dark sorry skein twist slightly before it bumped
past his tunic skirt and landed on the tip of the legate's orna-
mented boot, like something slightly unpleasant marring
the silver gilt below his sturdy knee. Vespasian flexed one leg
to flick it off. He glanced down.

Then he looked up.

Caenis realised the world was very sad.

She supposed he saw a balcony like all the others he had
passed, crammed with vulgar people screeching and waving
stupid hats. She could tell at once that he had noticed her,
standing silent at the front, for his face automatically
cleared. A woman in a white dress. He used to say, white
made her seem invisible; he liked her best in blue.

It was six years since Caligula was assassinated by
Chaerea. The man below had spent a year and a half in
Germany while Narcissus organised the landing force, then
nearly four in Britain, and almost twelve months handing
over the Second to his successor before making his way back
to Rome. He would be thirty-eight on 17 November. Caenis
was – whatever age she was. She had a fair idea: the same as
he. Even a little older perhaps. Yet she looked down at
Vespasian with a clear, unashamed gaze, for she kept the
comfortable habit of still thinking herself a girl, standing at

the eager threshold of life. (Sometimes Caenis made herself wonder how long this habit could go on.)

Everything passes.

Feeling nothing so much as mournful regret, Caenis could see that Vespasian felt touched by a similar moment himself. He looked thoughtful, and a little melancholy.

He had everything now. It would be easy to feel jealous — yet so much less tiring at her age to be conventionally tolerant instead! She had always known he would be famous. She had once asked him to remember her, when he was. It did not seem important any more. Yet she knew he did remember. The quiet recollection flickered in his face; she permitted a pale acknowledgement to answer in her own. She was glad that she had known the man; glad too that she had seen him come to this.

Old friends. Two people who knew nothing now of each other's lives, nor ever would, nor even wanted to. Two people merely happy, amidst a clamour that was disturbing to them both, to recognise some stillness and calm in an old familiar face.

He was still looking up.

'Do something!' squeaked Veronica. Then in horror, 'Caenis, *don't do that*!' Caenis had something from the picnic ready to hand.

His face lit.

'*Caenis — no!*'

Vespasian, expectant, lifted his chin. Caenis leant out, held his eye for a second and a half, then lobbed her gift. '*Io Vespasiane!*'

She had thrown it straight at him: he trapped it against his brilliant armour with one wrist. It was half a Lucanian salami. Veronica collapsed.

Somebody pulled Caenis back before she fell. Laughing, laughing with him, she struggled to keep her feet so she could see.

The procession jerked. The chariot moved. The crowd were acclaiming him; his business was with the crowd.

'*Io Vespasiane! Triumphe Io!*'

After him his officers stiffly marched past. Then after

177

them the whole street became dappled with the reflected light that flashed off the armour of Vespasian's marching troops.

Veronica whimpered, 'O Juno, Caenis. Oh my heart! What did he do?'

Caenis, though she realised she must be white as theatrical chalk, managed to speak complaisantly enough. 'Tucked it under his elbow, in a bundle with his batons – saving it for later, I dare say!'

'Did he smile? Did he wave? *Did you see what he did with my crown?*'

'Always was a surly bastard,' Caenis said.

'Turn round here!' commanded Veronica, above a new wave of commotion from the crowd. '*What else?*'

'He saluted,' Caenis said, in a faint voice that her friend could hardly catch above the row. 'Actually, I think he saluted me.'

There was nothing for it: Caenis turned around.

Then Veronica could see that all the kohl with which Caenis had earlier that morning outlined those great cynical eyes was now streaking down her face. Caenis was by nature incompetent with cosmetics, but Veronica had done her best to train her, so she was not as bad as that. She was crying.

Veronica still thought Caenis had never enjoyed much of a life. Which was why, since she understood these things, she spoke quite gently, explaining to her friend in simple terms the sterner points of military etiquette: 'Darling, be fair. What choice did he have? You can't expect Vespasian, the Hero of Britain, to salute *a Lucanian sausage*!' Veronica said.

PART FOUR:
BRITANNICUS

When the Caesars were Claudius and Nero
But not Britannicus

XXIII

They had fourteen years, almost, of the new order under Claudius.

It was a long time for any government; long enough, at any rate, for people to forget what things were like before. As long as it took for the child Britannicus, who had been born at the moment when his father was propelled so quaintly to the throne, to arrive within sight of his coming-of-age.

Fourteen years. Then Claudius ate a dish of mushrooms which disagreed with him so violently he died. But what happened to Britannicus had begun some years before. It started with his mother.

By the time Narcissus called the secret conference about Valeria Messalina, Britannicus was seven. He had been familiar with crowds all his life; while he was small Claudius loved to hold him up in the amphitheatre and cry, 'Good luck to you, my boy!' The audience always roared it back with enthusiasm; Britannicus was popular. He became tall for his age, showing character and quick wits. The Claudians were in general a good-looking family (Caenis believed a few more snub noses and squints might have produced more sensible Claudians). Even the Emperor himself, in repose, stopped slobbering and twitching and looked a handsome man. His wife, Messalina, possessed captivating looks: their son became an attractive child. Good luck he never possessed, however.

If Messalina had not captivated Callistus, Pallas or Narcissus it was only because she never tried. She preferred Mnester, the ballet dancer, for a time; afterwards a parade of young knights, senators, gladiators, soldiers, ambassadors even, then finally Gaius Silius, a consul elect at an impressively youthful age who was, as Veronica said, the best-looking man in Rome.

Caenis reflected, 'I suppose she feels there is no point

181

being an empress unless you can pick and choose.'

Veronica winced and peered at her sideways, not sure how much Caenis knew. 'Darling, Messalina is not choosy at all!'

Caenis nodded; she knew.

Whether, as people besotted by her crimes wanted afterwards to recall, Messalina really did leave the Palace at night disguised in a blonde wig to offer her fine body to all comers at a common brothel was to some extent irrelevant. Her behaviour was bad enough to make people believe it. Her bored trifling with noblemen, then her infatuation with Silius and the dangerous farce to which it led were true, and enough to bring about her fall. If satirical poets and salacious biographers wanted to be bawdy about an empress, it would be good news for booksellers. It was not so good for Octavia and Britannicus. But they were Antonia's grandchildren; in their family tradition unless they became monsters themselves, life would deal monstrously with them.

Messalina's affair with Gaius Silius was too dangerous. Lovers alone might have been overlooked; revolution could not be. When the Empress actually persuaded Silius to divorce his noble wife – at which he with logic and some spirit responded by asking the Empress to divorce her husband in return – Narcissus had little choice but to act. He summoned the Emperor's committed friends to a meeting at his own house. Caenis now realised the full value of this house: it was wonderfully comfortable, packed with pleasing works of art, he had Alexandrian flautists, there were flatfish in marble pools, the kitchen never closed and the water was always warm. It was an ideal place to plot.

'As a woman am I invited on the principle of setting a thief to catch a thief?' Caenis demanded of Narcissus scathingly. He did not deny it. He knew she was truculent and outspoken, but blisteringly loyal to Antonia's family. He knew too that she despised Messalina but probably understood her.

It was Narcissus himself, still with his old pinched oriental nose but nowadays distinctly fleshy otherwise, who set out the situation for the rest: 'It's quite clear Messalina has been waiting for our man's visit to Ostia. He's gone off to inaugurate his new harbour. This evening, while Claudius is safely out of Rome, she will marry Silius. You can't blame him – tangling with the Empress is dangerous enough; he may as well risk everything on the throw. So he marries Messalina, in full form; he adopts Britannicus, and they grapple for the throne.'

Callistus, who as Secretary of Petitions spent his whole life stating the obvious to people who did not want to hear it, said at once, 'That's the end of us!'

No one answered. For some, that was not entirely the point. It would be the end of them, and their man – and all their work.

Pallas, Antonia's old messenger, shifted suddenly on his couch, exclaiming in exasperation, 'I still can't believe it can go so far and poor besotted Claudius has not the slightest idea.'

After a moment Narcissus murmured, almost in embarrassment for their man, 'You know Claudius.' And when no one answered that either, 'Well; he has a great deal on his mind.'

It was true. Claudius as Emperor had produced the energy and concentration that only a true eccentric ever shows. In the year his wife tried to divorce him (Romans were always divorcing their wives; it struck Caenis irreverently that while it was discourteous of Messalina not to mention to her husband her plans for that afternoon, at least taking the initiative herself made a change) – in that year, Claudius was preoccupied with his administrative duties as Censor, easing the penalties for debt, issuing edicts about snakebites and against unruly behaviour in the theatre, then finishing construction of his splendid aqueducts which brought the clear water of the Caerulean springs fifty miles from the mountains across the Campagna on arches that were in some places a hundred feet high. He had continued to write scholarly histories. He involved himself in the internal affairs of Armenia and Germany, then in a speech whose political diplomacy would have astonished those who had judged him inadequate in his youth, he persuaded the Senate to open their ranks to some long-standing allies from Gaul. He survived an assassination attempt without losing his nerve. He gave time to his pet schemes: he revived the College of Soothsayers and introduced three new letters into the official alphabet.

It was the eighth centenary of the traditional founding of Rome. Claudius inaugurated the *Ludi Saecularii*, the ancient commemorative Games. They were supposed to be held only once every hundred years so no one would attend who had ever seen them before; in fact Augustus had held them too, but that was a mere technicality. This time there was a Trojan Pageant in the Circus at which young boys from leading families performed intricate feats of horsemanship while their parents and grandparents chewed off their nails expecting tantrums, broken legs and trampled heads. On this occasion Britannicus led one of the dressage teams. The other was taken by Domitius Ahenobarbus, the son of Claudius' niece Agrippina. He was three years older and far more confident so of course he came off best; although Britannicus conducted himself with the gravity of a tiny Aeneas in the field, as soon as the dimple-kneed imperial infant reached home it ended in tears.

Claudius did all this, and no one had ever suggested he was too busy to pay attention to his wife. Everyone else knew, she was too busy for him.

Caenis spoke, since no one else would risk it: 'Claudius believes his pretty darling is matchless in bed and a perfect mother – faithful, devoted, clever, helpful and sweet. Whatever you do, remember he believes that *because it is what he wants to believe.*'

Various freedmen wriggled and scratched themselves, sensing some general criticism of their sex.

She leant forwards with her elbows on her knees. She addressed herself to Narcissus, partly because she knew and understood him best, and partly because his colleagues were arguing for caution, frightened that interference would have unpleasant results for themselves. 'Show him that they are stealing his throne – he believes himself the best man to hold it now. Perhaps he is. His ignorance of Messalina's antics makes it easier; the truth will be devastating, and he is a vain man. She can work him; ensure that she never gets the chance. Work him yourselves –' She used the plural, though she guessed that this would be one man's work. 'What will affect Claudius most will be the fact that she has thrown up their marriage in his face.'

It struck Narcissus that Caenis was not, as it had turned out, telling them the woman's point of view but the man's. He glanced at Callistus and Pallas for support, failed to find it, then rehearsed what he could say: 'Yes . . . *"Sir, do you know you are divorced?"*' He ended with a gesture, open-palmed like an acrobat. The effect was sinister.

'That poor besotted bastard!' Callistus commented.

Going home afterwards, Caenis reflected privately how Claudius had a graceful knack of choosing whom to trust as his friends. His wives were disasters and though all four of those, including Messalina, had been chosen for him by his relatives, Caenis doubted he would do better for himself. In marriage a man looked for a boost to his bank account, adornment for his home, and a submissive sexual partner. It would be a man of rare intelligence who realised he might so much more wisely share his household with a friend.

That was a long night.

The sharp clear morning with its indigo sky had become the blazing autumn afternoon when Narcissus came to Caenis at Antonia's house. She had never seen anyone so completely exhausted. He owned a home that ran with peaceful decorum, yet she saw on this one occasion that to return to his good-tempered battalions of servants would be to remain unbearably alone. He had passed beyond his private strength. His competence was all used up.

'Freedman, rest. I will send word; I will watch.'

She dismissed all her own slaves. Then she herself attended to the shutters, poured water for him to wash his hands and face, mixed wine with honey which he proved too tired to drink, took his shoes, set the cushions around him and laid the rug over him while he slept.

Caenis stayed in the room.

'Thank you,' he said briefly when he woke.

185

He lay on his back for a long while, the rug flung aside now so she could see his hands interlaced limply on his chest. Narcissus' hands were unusually small. She had noticed that when she was fourteen and secretly in love with him in a frightening physical way, as a girl will be with a teacher who concentrates her mind. They had come a long way since then.

He was thinking. From a nearby reclining chair Caenis silently watched; it was an intimacy few would ever share with him. The olive-skinned face was hollow-cheeked in rare relaxation, although he knew she was there. His eyes were frantic with thought and dark with melancholy; their gaze fluttered about the ceiling, from bead-and-dart cornice to the plaster moulding that had been smoked to an oily gloss by lamps, and on to the solid ball from which hung the delicate bronze swansnecks of an unlit chandelier. He saw nothing.

People blamed the man for personal ambition. Yet his gratitude to Claudius would always come from a full heart. He regretted his patron's weaknesses, but appreciated the man's strengths and did so completely without cynicism. There was love there. He would be glad that he had saved the day (Caenis recognised from his stillness how he must have done that) but Narcissus would not really exult. He would feel for his man's tragedy as Claudius himself, understandably, could not bear to feel.

Sensing some shift in the focus of his reverie, Caenis asked gently, 'Well?'

'I have watched a heart break.' He closed his eyes.

Finally he spoke again. 'How does a man react? While returning from a journey in all innocence, he meets the stark news that his wife has taken a lover – many lovers – there is incontrovertible proof. Now she has left him without a word and been married, in front of witnesses: banquet, bridal regalia, sacrifices, new marital bed. All this is common knowledge in the city from the Senate and the army down to the sleaziest barbershops and waterfront booths. His clean white pearl has been rolled in a night-soil cart. His betrayal is a barrack-room byword. Caenis, what should he do?'

186

He turned on his elbow and stared at her.

'What happened?' she asked again in her calm, quiet way.

'He said very little. I don't suppose he ever will. The story was so fantastic he realised it must be true. As we approached Rome on his return from Ostia, Messalina was celebrating the marriage with a mock grape harvest at the Gardens of Lucullus. Hair flowing in the breeze, treading vats, waving Bacchic wands – everyone disgustingly drunk. You can imagine the scene.'

There was a fastidious pause. The gardens had once belonged to Asinius Gallus; Messalina accused him of adultery with a woman of whom she was jealous, then compelled him to judicial suicide; it was the easiest way to wrest away the man from his gardens, which he had refused to sell. 'Her party vanished; most of them were picked up later by the Guards. She walked – walked! – the whole length of the city almost alone, then started out towards Ostia in a garden-rubbish cart. She took the Chief Vestal Virgin to help argue her case, and sent for the children to soften his heart.'

'Poor mites!'

Caenis imagined them brought by panic-stricken maids, presented to a silent father more or less in the public street, glimpsing their mother distraught, terrified by wild faces and the charged atmosphere – then taken home to an empty palace with no one to explain. Britannicus was seven, Octavia not much more than a year older. Caenis would go and see them when she could.

Narcissus went on in that terrible dull tone, 'Vitellius was there, but he couldn't bring himself to say much.' That was Lucius Vitellius, Vespasian's old patron. He was the Emperor's closest adviser, almost his only friend.

'So who had to tell him?'

'I stuck with him wherever he went. Rode in his carriage, talked to him constantly. My instinct was to remain in the background –' Caenis violently shook her head. Narcissus agreed: 'No. Wrong. So; when she found us – which frankly I wasn't expecting – I managed to outface her temporarily with the plain fact of the wedding and a charge-sheet of her crimes. She decided to cry a lot – bad mistake; no chance to speak to him. As soon as I could, I sent the Vestal packing, had the children removed, opened up Silius' house. I showed Claudius how it was stuffed with his own things – his household slaves, the masks of the Caesars, his family heirlooms; oh he was angry then. So I got him to the Praetorian Camp –' By now his voice was dragging with suppressed reluctance to relive that sorry night. 'For a time I seem to have taken command of the Guards myself. Sometimes, Caenis, I think we live in an old wives' tale! The Guards rallied; I believe I made some sort of speech. By the time we had him sat down to his dinner in the Palace the situation was stable, with most of the conspirators tried and hanged.'

'And the woman?'

'The woman executed. Run through with a tribune's sword.'

Caenis swallowed, saw his face, then for his sake asked in a neutral tone, 'On whose orders?'

'On the Emperor's orders,' said Narcissus. He sighed. 'Or so I had to say.'

After a silence, Narcissus confided, as if he could hardly bear it but had to share this with someone, 'You know, he called for her at dinner. Truly, I had told him she was dead. He never asked me how. Then later he wondered aloud where she was. He was drunk.' That was not unusual. Claudius was also extremely forgetful, whether for convenience or not. '"That poor unfortunate woman," he called her.'

'So she was,' Caenis said. Knowing her strict good sense Narcissus looked surprised. 'They have too much,' Caenis decreed savagely. 'These ladies. Taking risks, shocking society, is the only challenge left for them. Yet compared with us they know nothing: nobody has taught them self-respect or self-discipline. So I do pity her. Besides; I am a party to this. I must take the responsibility of a witness, you know: I went to the poor woman's wedding!'

The events of the night were so wrapped up in his thoughts that it took Narcissus a moment to remember that apart from the wedding to Silius there had once been another grim farce with Messalina wearing her saffron shoes and vermilion veil in front of witnesses.

He was ready to go.

'Thanks, Caenis.' On his feet he was staring at her in an odd way. 'There is something I want to ask you.' He rubbed his eyes, so shy of making the request that Caenis was embarrassed by the fact that she thought she had guessed what it was.

Narcissus was not effeminate. She believed he had mistresses, though they flitted in and out of his life leaving no substantial mark. He was too serious now to be offering such a liaison to her. He needed her to confide in; he would not surrender that for some fleeting dalliance.

He was thinking how to put it.

'I can look after the Empire,' Narcissus said in that flat, tired voice. 'I need somebody to look after the Emperor.'

Caenis breathed. It was not what she had prepared herself to hear. Those sharp wits of her childhood still betrayed her into difficulty.

In her surprise she became more vicious than she liked. 'I always knew a state servant resembled a pimp! All that pestering and being pestered; all that soiled money changing hands on the backstairs!'

'You are quite right; if I could save him by fixing him up I would!' Narcissus replied patiently, though he was still so weary he could hardly stand. 'He told the Guards, he had been so unfortunate with his wives he was determined to live single all his life; they could kill him if he changed his mind. Well, the Guards may, or they may not – but he has already demanded a shortlist from Pallas, Callistus and me, so unless I can call up some generous and discreet alternative, we can reckon the next matrimonial disaster is well on its way.'

They were not exactly quarrelling so an answer was required. For once he had astonished her. He assumed that Caenis would want to do this for Rome – not at the expense of her personal interests; rather, he did not realise she might have hopes or ambitions otherwise.

'Oh I am grateful for your flattery; a girl needs a bit of that!

But looking after an emperor,' declared Caenis, comparatively mildly for her, 'is something for which I am unqualified.'

'An emperor could do a lot worse.'

'Oh he will!' she returned drably. 'We both know that.'

She would not shift. It was his own fault: he had taught her to reach rapid judgements, then bravely stick to them.

So Narcissus braced himself for the burdens of the Empire, the Emperor, and the Emperor's new wife, whoever she turned out to be. He did wonder (Caenis had not entirely lost her sensitivity) whether if he ever needed it Caenis would look after him. On the whole he preferred not to ask. He knew he sank too much of himself into his work for the question to be fair. Besides, he also knew his capabilities. Taking care of an empire was straightforward enough, but taking responsibility for Caenis required a special kind of man.

She had always been his favourite, and he wanted the best for her. He still thought, even an emperor could do worse.

XXIV

The search for a new wife for Claudius was conducted on brisk official lines. His Chief Ministers each selected a candidate, whose merits they set out in elaborate position-papers which were debated at a formal meeting with the Emperor in the chair. This system seemed no worse than granting free rein to the ludicrous eccentricities of personal taste.

Narcissus supported: *Candidate A, Aelia Paetina*; married to Claudius once before, she was the mother of his daughter Claudia Antonia – the sound, no-nonsense, known-quantity candidate.

Callistus supported: *Candidate B, Lollia Paulina*; an extremely beautiful woman, she had married Caligula briefly, though under duress – the brilliant and popular candidate. She was fabulously wealthy too. Lest anyone doubt it, when she went to a dinner party covered in jewels she took the bills of sale to prove what her gemstones had cost.

Pallas supported: *Candidate C, Agrippina*; Claudius' niece. She was Caligula's sister, one of the famous three – the underhand, dangerous, dark-horse candidate. She had a son, Domitius Ahenobarbus, so she had proved her fertility. Her ambitions for that son were likely to be ferocious – but then Claudius had a son of his own, Britannicus.

It was illegal for an uncle to marry his niece, so Claudius did just that.

'That's the trouble with formal meetings,' Narcissus sighed despondently. 'Either no decision at all, or the worst choice on the Chairman's casting vote.'

It was when Agrippina married Claudius, as a sense of impending doom depressed her, that Caenis deliberately took a decision which surprised some of her friends. There was a knight she knew privately, Marius Pomponius Gallus, a well-tempered, decent, thoroughly amusing man. Narcissus had introduced them. For several years past Marius had been asking her to marry him. Quite suddenly, Caenis agreed. He had in fact asked her the first time they went to bed. This burst of initial enthusiasm later faded to a good-mannered routine; he was more startled than anyone when she did say yes. But he received the news stoically, and they began to look for dinnerbowls and napkin sets.

A couple of years later, luckily before Agrippina really made her presence felt, Flavius Vespasianus was elected to a consulship. That same year, still intending to marry Caenis, Marius Pomponius Gallus unexpectedly died.

It all seemed sadly unimportant. Caenis knew she could have organised Marius into a bridegroom – quite a keen one – if she had wanted; she realised that what she had really been looking forward to most was a home of her own instead of the inelegant apartments where she had lived ever since Antonia died. She wanted peace and permanence, and on a long lease. So with the help of Narcissus, who was generous with money and time, she found a site and had built for herself a substantial, tasteful house which she would own until she died.

Her new home lay just outside the north-east city boundary, on the Via Nomentana. The site was not well chosen, since it was right beside the huge Praetorian Camp, built for the Guards by Sejanus. The location caused her constant teasing from her friends. Still, she was spared from enduring neighbours. And there would never be burglaries or riots.

Narcissus had given her a steward: Aglaus. Caenis first inspected Aglaus in the wild garden at Narcissus' own private house. She knew better than to accept a gift from a minister of state sight unseen.

Narcissus' gardens, though enclosed on all sides by the wings of his mansion, were as spacious and well-designed as any public park. The noise of the city was muffled by trees. Songbirds clustered in the bushes and bounced about the gutters of the house; there were white doves basking on the pantiles of the roof. The wild garden was full of water: rectangular pools where stone nymphs with calm, regular faces

192

looked down into the reeds amongst whose wiry clumps moved contemplative fish; fountains everywhere; and streams that wriggled through casual arrangements of shrub to splash into shell-shaped porphyry bowls. Sometimes at night little candles were set afloat like stars in these bowls. At every turn stood a bench or seat; every bench had a pleasing view.

There was another more conventional garden, with neat borders set with hedges of trimmed rosemary, grave statues of the Imperial family that studded formal acanthus beds, and cypress trees bristling at intervals like a military guard along the fine-grained gravel paths. That was a place to take foreign ambassadors. This was for friends.

Caenis and Narcissus relaxed on a stone seat amongst the arching fronds of an abutilon, with their feet on the edge of a pond. It was late in the year. Caenis was still in mourning. She wrapped her head in a dignified white mantle and hoped to impress her new slave. They watched him approach: not quite in his twenties, short as all Palace slaves were and slightly rickety, a lean face with a blue chin. He had a way of looking at people too directly which Caenis recognised; he was brave to the verge of revolt. If he chose, he would do his work well in a defiant, off-hand way; handled wrongly he was at an age where he could soon be written off as insubordinate and sold to a lupin-seller.

Narcissus let him stand.

'This is Antonia Caenis, an important freedwoman of the imperial family.'

No sign of recognition; he was definitely surly. She let him see her weighing him up then spoke in her calm, trained voice. 'Aglaus, isn't it? What's his work like, Narcissus?'

'He's lazy, sly, and insolent,' Narcissus replied cheerfully. 'They all are nowadays. Don't expect our standards any more.' He was well aware Caenis would think the belligerent lad worth saving: so like herself at the same age.

'Tell me, Aglaus; are you ambitious?'

'Yes, madam.' He spoke with the weary indifference of someone giving the answers he knows to be correct.

Caenis pinched her mouth. 'Then you have a rare choice.

I need a steward. Your chance to be in charge.'

Now the lad put his shoulders back and began to act on his own behalf. Obviously he had thought this through. 'The penalty, I suppose, is a mistress who knows all the dodges herself? Safe enough if I know before I start! I suppose madam will have a front door with a bronze seahorse knocker, and closed shutters shading all her rooms?'

This was rather twee for Caenis but she understood what he meant. 'Naturally! Dried flowers, tiny portions at table, all the servants creeping around in soft felt shoes.'

Narcissus gave vent to his awful laugh.

'Men visiting?' interrogated the slave. He certainly had a cheek.

'Not often,' she returned placidly, retreating from the thought of Marius.

'Women then?'

'Not if I can help it. And unless you ask my permission, neither will you! Nor do I want smooth-faced altar boys from the Temple of Ganymede loitering around my kitchen door.'

His impertinence, far from enraging her, was winning her interest. She could not bear people in her home who lacked character. He was deliberately trying out how far he could go, his lip curling into a sneer that would do well for suppressing butchers who overcharged. 'Keep leaky lapdogs? Tame ducks? *Crocodiles?*'

'No,' Caenis responded briefly. 'Whose interview is this?'

'Mine, I hope.' Aglaus was forthright. 'You can sell me; I'll be stuck.'

Caenis turned to Narcissus dispassionately. 'No harm in spirit, but will he be polite to my friends?'

'*Yes, madam!*' smirked the slave. She guessed he did not want to work for a woman; she did not blame him for that since with the rare exception of Antonia, neither would she.

The chance of responsibility was tantalising him. He declared, 'I'll risk it. I'll take the post.'

'Will you, by Jupiter!' Narcissus exclaimed.

Caenis shushed him. 'Oh I'll give him a trial. Thank you, Aglaus.'

He saluted her politely enough now. 'Antonia Caenis.'

'Caenis will do. Just Caenis.' She would never change.

'Well; Lady Caenis then.'

Narcissus nodded tetchily to dismiss him.

Both Caenis and Narcissus smiled, suddenly remembering old times.

'Seems ideal to me,' the freedman told her. 'You'll squabble, but the fellow will adore you.'

Caenis said drily, 'I'm not sure adoration is a commodity I recognise, or even want.'

There was a small silence. She needed to ask Narcissus about Marius' will; he was giving her time to start.

It was at that point she became aware, and Narcissus must have noticed too, that hasty footsteps were approaching from the house. Someone had clattered down the informal stone steps behind them, skidded under a small palm tree which leant across one of the paved areas, and was now striding through the long arch of trellis where in summer the honeysuckle formed a sweet approach to this nook where Narcissus liked to sit. Someone who knew Narcissus well enough to come straight out here unannounced. Someone thoroughly agitated. A man whose heavy step Caenis had instantly recognised.

She settled her mantle more closely around her face. The man arrived. Narcissus looked up. His visitor flung himself on to a second bench. He began to speak; saw someone there; recognised her; checked himself quietly. 'Sorry. No one told me I was disturbing you. I'll come back.' He was already on his feet.

It was Flavius Vespasianus, minus his troop of ceremonial lictors but otherwise in full consular robes.

Normally everything gave way for a city magistrate. Even the Chief Secretary became faultlessly polite. 'Consul! I know this lady has something to discuss with me but she will not object to waiting; shall I ask her to withdraw?'

Vespasian muttered in his abrupt way, 'Thanks. No need.'

'Is this private?' Narcissus worried.

Vespasian flopped down again on the other bench. That old frown bit deeply into his brow. Now that he had accustomed himself to the situation, he resented its disturbing anyone else. 'No. Stop flapping, Narcissus. If the lady wants me to go she'll tell me to skip over the Styx, and if she wants to leave herself she'll up and disappear.'

So true! Caenis looked at the pool.

Narcissus was sufficiently shy of private relationships to be embarrassed by this meeting; until now he had somehow prevented any such confrontation with what he thought was exquisite tact. He was feeling far more uncomfortable than either of the other two. Blushing, he asked the Consul whatever was wrong. Vespasian wrenched off a branch from a nearby shrub which he began tearing to shreds.

'Oh these accursed imperial women! First we come home from the back of beyond to find Messalina picking off every friend or colleague Claudius owns, then you and Pallas set him up with another scheming, suspicious, incestuous Julian cow who decides to make it her business to run the Empire —' This description of the Augusta, as Agrippina now styled herself, exactly fitted Narcissus' own opinion, Caenis knew.

He murmured fussily, 'Consul, you are under stress.'

'*Stress!* Narcissus, the woman's impossible. I have to deal with her so long as Claudius leaves her loose. Oh I'll stick out my term, but she must know what I think.'

'She knows what you said when Caligula accused her of adultery and conspiracy!' Narcissus reprimanded him.

'So we're permanent enemies! When my time's up as Consul I'll have to leave the court.'

'Sounds wise!'

'Sounds unjust!'

Narcissus shrugged in that slightly oriental way. 'Yes. Still, serenity and leisure on your country estate: it's a Roman ideal. You'll be balloted soon for a provincial governorship. Enjoy yourself meanwhile. Weed your vines, or whatever you have; keep your head down and keep your temper. A good man – best out of the way.'

The Consul was still furious. 'I'll have nothing!'

Narcissus suddenly sat up. 'No, sir! On my list you have

an honest wife and three healthy children, the army's acclaim, the Senate's respect and the liking of a great many private citizens. Your funds may be low –'

This was not the best way to calm Vespasian down. He hurled what was left of the branch into the pond, slightly splashing the edge of her white funereal dress so Caenis pulled back her feet to protect it. She only ever owned one. There were few people Caenis thought worth wearing mourning for.

'Low? Low? Listen,' Vespasian raged. 'I've thought about this! She's going to block my appointment; I know it. Anyway, if I do get a province, I'll need to mortgage my estate just to be able to live in the proper style, even abroad. Is this right? My children were born into beggary; we have no family silver on the table and Domitian's just made his poor little entrance in an attic over Pomegranate Street.' He was well into his stride. Domitian was his second son, born at the end of October. There was a daughter too. 'I shall be a governor who runs mule-trains and dabbles in franchises for fish – a trader in tuna, a fiddler with flounders, a man permanently after his percentage on cuttlefish and cubes of cod! Your lady-friend can stop twitching and laugh if she likes.'

Caenis, who had been sinking deeper into herself, realised abruptly that she was the audience for whom his last flamboyant outburst had been played.

Vespasian had at first been ignoring her as deliberately as she was ignoring him; suddenly he turned and addressed her directly with that disconcerting drop in his tone: 'Hello, Caenis!'

'Hello,' she said.

It was the first time they had spoken for nearly thirteen years.

The Chief Secretary, whose very inexperience made him a sentimentalist, noticed at once that the Consul stopped frowning. Vespasian's mood had clarified like a wax tablet melting for reuse. Even so it seemed that these two wanted nothing more to say to one another.

Sucking his lower lip, the Consul challenged the freedman again, 'Well! If you're so sure it's going to be all right, which province will I get?'

'Africa,' replied Narcissus. Vespasian whistled; Caenis stirred: Africa was the prize.

'Thought it was supposed to be a lottery?'

'Oh it is, Consul! Never let anybody tell you otherwise.' Repenting his frankness, Narcissus told him carefully, 'You must keep up your state.'

'Oh thanks!' Vespasian was scathing, but looked preoccupied; Caenis knew he would be trying to work out just how the lottery was fiddled. So was she. 'Ask your gloomy visitor if she needs her savings yet?'

Narcissus merely looked demure but when Caenis continued to stare into the pool in silence he felt obliged to clear his throat and ask, 'Do you, Caenis?'

Caenis replied quietly, to Narcissus, 'No.'

'Generous friends!' rapped Narcissus to Vespasian.

He commented tersely, to Narcissus, 'Yes.' Then he burst out at Caenis herself. 'Always in white these days! You look terrible in white.' Caenis was damned if at this time of her life she was going to start letting men tell her what she ought to wear. He detected the thought. 'Sorry. Impertinent. You'll have to forgive me; I've known you a long time.'

'No, Consul.' He was startled. So was she, yet she continued without mercy: 'You knew me,' Caenis told him bluntly, 'for a *short* while, *a very long time ago!*'

She shot to her feet, tight-lipped, and walked away to another part of the garden by herself.

There was a tense silence. Narcissus had no idea what he ought to do. 'Shall I –'

'Leave her!' Vespasian whipped towards him. 'So long as she gets angry,' he explained clearly, as if it were important that in future Narcissus understood this, 'she's all right.' There was another pause. Vespasian was staring the way Caenis had gone.

Narcissus muttered, 'I'll –'

'No. I'll go.'

'Then I had better explain why she's –'

'No need,' said Vespasian. 'I know. Of course I know.'

Her feelings had nothing to do with Vespasian being there.

She sat on a seat beside the dripping fronds of a monumental fern, breathing hard, with one hand to her head. It was all too much. Marius dead, and now his stupid will . . . He had left her precisely half as much again as he had left to each of his freedmen: enough to embarrass his family, yet a harshly unequal gesture for a woman who had been prepared to become his wife. She wanted to refuse the legacy, as any heir was entitled to do. His cautiousness was so insulting.

She sat, thinking about this, and thinking too about Marius. She still knew he was a comparatively decent man. He had not understood what he had done.

Someone was coming for her. She heard the footsteps, while trying to ignore them.

'Caenis?' Her Sabine friend.

He waited, the other side of the fern, to let her readjust. Probably afraid she had been crying. Left to herself she probably would have been. People never knew when to leave you to yourself.

'Your old Greek nanny panicked.'

'I'll come.' Caenis sat forwards intending to rise, but Vespasian was on the narrow path, sticky with fallen leaves. He was blocking her way.

'Don't get up.' He stayed there; so she stayed on the seat. 'You're wanting advice?'

Caenis said nothing. Obviously Narcissus had told him everything. Politicians were so arrogant about other people's private affairs.

Vespasian risked it: 'Share your troubles with a friendly magistrate. I won't charge,' he chivvied, as she still sat stony-faced. He was more heavily built and a great deal more pompous nowadays. 'Though you might consider a drop in the interest on my loan.' She still said nothing. He went on, with the natural complaisant assumption that no one in good society would ever be deliberately rude, 'Tell me to mind my own business if you like –'

'*Mind your own business, Consul!*' Caenis roared.

She turned away bitterly.

But all he said was, 'Don't be daft, lass!' then came and sat beside her on the bench. Caenis was probably forty. Even in the country, nobody was ever going to call her 'lass' again.

'Don't fight.'

'Don't interfere!'

'Look; Caenis –'

'Leave me alone!'

'I can't; I promised your lady a long time ago – I had heard you were planning to get married. I'm so sorry.' Caenis once again spun to her feet. He snapped: 'Oh, sit down, you short-tempered shrike, and listen to me!'

Marius would never have called her names. Nor, she knew, would she ever in fact have married him. This stranger knew her better than Marius would ever have done.

'Come on; come back.'

Although she did not storm off she huddled away, shrouding herself in the white robe he so hated. He sighed. Then, speaking formally as a magistrate he told her, 'Listen then. It's quite simple. Legally the choice is yours. But unless you feel very strongly, my advice is to keep quiet. The man is dead; you can't get back at him. Taking a stand is fine in principle, but you'll be the one who ends up feeling wretched. If you reject his miserable legacy, you'll stir up more bad feeling than if you meekly accept and spend it all on a new hat.' Caenis had the grace to nod. His voice softened. 'There's a knee here you can sit on if you want to have a cry.' She ignored that. After a moment he demanded sourly, 'Whatever did you want to get married for anyway?'

'Oh the usual reasons!' Caenis flared. 'Bed, board, someone to bully – and a half-decent companion for my old age!'

Vespasian laughed.

She whirled back towards him so at last he could see just how colourless she was, and her despair. He was truly appalled. Whatever she was intending to hurl at him died on the instant.

In fact they had frightened one another.

Yet he was not Rome's Consul for nothing. His face went blank. He turned the situation at once. He stood up. 'Yes;

quite right. Better go back. That oily-chinned old woman of a freedman will think something's going on.'

So they went back.

'Get your advice?' Narcissus fluffed.

'Yes.'

'Will you take it?'

'Probably.'

'*There!*' Narcissus exclaimed, like the nanny Vespasian had called him; Vespasian to his credit openly winced.

Unable to bear any more of this, Caenis was determined to go home. Narcissus embraced her as he usually did when she left. He said to Vespasian (so Caenis began to wonder just how many conversations about her these two had held), 'I'll have to fix her up with a nice tolerant widower; somebody brave, someone the Empire owes a favour to –'

Caenis broke free. 'Oh you brass-necked cretin! Being saddled with a half-baked widower is *not* what I require at all.'

Even Vespasian crackled, 'Great gods, Narcissus – leave the poor girl alone!'

For a second she felt they were haggling over her, as Vespasian had once done with Antonia. They talked across her, about her, at her, with men's knowing air. They liked to flatter themselves they could help in her business affairs. They liked to fidget when she showed distress. Because they were men they were competitive. Neither wanted her. Neither wanted to know anything of her private aches. But neither wanted the other to show he knew her best.

Vespasian held out his hand. In front of Narcissus, she really had no choice; Caenis gave him her own. A Consul probably shook hands with hundreds of people every day. But not crushing most of them in such a deliberate grip. 'Antonia Caenis.'

When he spoke her name she had to look away.

After she had gone, Narcissus agitated primly, 'Thanks. Anything happen?'

'We had a brief but bloody fight.' Vespasian was staring at him. 'Nothing unusual.'

'Actually, I was afraid that seeing you might upset her.'

Some grim jest twitched at one corner of the Consul's mouth.

'She's all right,' he said. Helpless, Narcissus realised the full extent of the mistake he had made. 'She's used to it,' Vespasian stated drably. Then, after the faintest pause, 'No doubt one day I'll get used to it myself.'

XXV

Claudius had married Agrippina on the New Year's Day immediately following Messalina's death. On that occasion Caenis made an excuse not to attend the wedding. She could not in conscience offer her support.

On the day Claudius was married, Lucius Silanus, who had been betrothed for years to the Emperor's infant daughter Octavia, accepted the inevitable and committed suicide (a heavy hint that he was in disgrace had been dropped when he was struck off as praetor with only one day of the magistracy left to serve). Agrippina's son by her previous marriage, Lucius Domitius Ahenobarbus, was betrothed to Octavia instead.

At Agrippina's urging, Ahenobarbus was soon also adopted by Claudius. This raised some eyebrows. No outsider had ever been adopted into the patrician Claudian house, and besides, the Emperor had a son of his own; the adoption unnecessarily supplanted Britannicus. As a newcomer to the family Ahenobarbus took a Claudian surname; now he was called Nero.

One of the arguments used by Pallas to secure Nero's adoption was that Claudius ought to arrange a protector for his own boy. Ironically, from then on even during his father's lifetime, Britannicus was treated at the Palace as an unwelcome guest of doubtful parentage; any slaves or freedmen loyal to him were gradually removed and officers in the army who gave him their allegiance were encouraged to transfer abroad or promoted out of the way. His new brother gave him no support, entirely the opposite.

Next, Claudius agreed that Nero should be declared of age early and start his public career. He became a consul designate without holding other positions, and was styled Prince of Youth. There was a difficult scene when Britannicus refused to address him by his adopted name.

Britannicus was disciplined, his best tutors were dismissed, and he lost even more of his slaves.

At the age of sixteen Nero married Octavia. This made Octavia his sister, his cousin and his wife; Claudius was both his father and father-in-law. Even by the contorted standards of the Julio-Claudian house it was unusual. Nero arranged celebratory Games in honour of the Emperor, appearing himself in full triumphal robes while Britannicus wore the usual narrow-striped tunic of a boy at school. People in the audience exchanged old-fashioned looks.

There was now a most unfortunate change: Britannicus briefly became popular again. Claudius, who for a long time after Messalina's death had viewed Britannicus with painful reserve, seemed to rediscover his original dislike of Nero, who was indeed regarded as highly unpleasant by all people of style and taste. Instead the Emperor took to flinging his arms round Britannicus whenever they met, quoting darkly in Greek and exclaiming, 'Grow up quickly, my boy, and your father will tell you his plan!'

Britannicus had become a stoical child. He took all this in apparent good part. He had two sensible allies throughout: one was Narcissus. The other, who held no official post so she could never be dismissed, was his grandmother's freed-woman Antonia Caenis.

Caenis and Britannicus became good friends. Caenis was well-presented enough to carry a sniff of danger for an adolescent boy, yet ancient enough to be safe; she said she refused to mother him, though when he needed it she always did. Britannicus had been brought up rather primly; she discussed politics with him in a way that sounded treasonous and told him stories that were definitely rude. They played a private game of challenging each other in any situation to find a song from the drama to fit. He had an excellent voice. It was natural that Caenis should be drawn to a child growing up in the Palace so starved of affection yet so good-humoured and sane.

She was giving Britannicus secret shorthand coaching so he could catch up with one of the other boys who shared his education. It was while they were practising, ready to surprise the Other Boy that the door flung open and someone shot into the room. There was no doubt who it was. It had to be the competitive rival, because Britannicus with great presence of mind slipped his notebook down the back of his reading couch and adjusted a vase to hide the water clock by which he had been timing himself. Then he winked at Caenis.

She had never seen him before, but she recognised the Other Boy at once.

Her protégé, Britannicus, was by now as tall as many men, with the same gaunt neck and prominent ears as his father; at thirteen he was going through a gangly, self-conscious phase. Since their mother's death both he and his sister Octavia were understandably solemn and withdrawn. This boy was quite different. Britannicus' friend – they were obviously friends – was a short, square, dynamic tugboat of a boy. He was built with the graceful solidity of an obelisk. He had a thick thatch of tightly curling hair, and though his nose was straighter than his father's, an identical upjerking chin and rectangular brow.

'Aha! New ladylove?' he cried, stopping in surprise. Britannicus blushed; he was old enough to be interested yet young enough to be terrified of women.

Caenis tried to adopt the air of a sophisticated, extremely expensive witch. 'You must be Titus!' she divined coolly. 'Titus Flavius Vespasianus, son of Titus, voting tribe Quirina, citizen of Reate.'

Both children were deeply impressed.

'This is the face-detector?' Titus demanded of Britannicus eagerly.

Britannicus replied with a nicely suave, secretive smile. He was learning fast; it was wonderful to watch. 'Just a friend,' he tormented the other, who was bursting with curiosity. 'Going to give me a second opinion, I hope.'

Caenis endured the odd experience of being eyed up appraisingly by Vespasian's teenaged son.

It turned out that Narcissus was still worrying over his dynasty, pointless though that was beginning to appear. He

205

had called in a physiognomist: someone who would tell Britannicus' fortune from his face. Since Narcissus entered the room almost immediately with this character, Caenis had no opportunity to say to the boys just what she thought of that.

The seer was an overweight greasy Chaldean in a shiny emerald overshirt, his knuckles carbuncled with mysterious scarab rings. He wore bright green laced-up pointed shoes; Caenis had made it her lifelong rule never to trust a man with peculiar footwear.

Narcissus, who knew just what she would think about this business, avoided meeting her eye; he was obviously hoping Caenis would go away. She crossed her ankles calmly, looked dignified and stayed. When Britannicus noticed how Narcissus was flapping he winked at Caenis again. She had taught him to wink. His upbringing had been first at the hands of slaves hand-picked by Messalina as easy to manipulate, then seedy nominees chosen by Agrippina out of spite; it had been uninspiring and totally neglected useful social accomplishments. Still, he could sing, and he did; no one would ever be a complete failure while they could sing.

Britannicus was poignantly nervous of having his face read. Narcissus and the physiognomist at last finished fiddling about setting a stool in the best light. Caenis placed herself behind their reluctant subject, resting her light protective hands on his shoulders and staring belligerently at the Chaldean over the top of the prince's head. Young Titus scrambled over and knelt beside the stool to get a good view of what went on. As Caenis said to them afterwards, it was sensible to be nervous of someone who smelt of such a strange mixture of patchouli and onions.

The physiognomist stood in silence, looking at Britannicus from directly in front. He came close, giving the Emperor's son a full blast of his onions, then lifted Britannicus' chin on one finger. At a younger age Britannicus would certainly have bitten him. At thirteen he was, thank the gods, too proud.

The physiognomist stepped back. Caenis and Britannicus stopped holding their breath. The Chaldean turned to

Narcissus. 'No,' he said off-handedly, and prepared to leave. Even Narcissus seemed nonplussed.

Titus who was lively as a monkey in a warehouse of soft fruit, was bursting to ask a question but he was forestalled. Narcissus had not been a bureaucrat for thirty years in order to be baffled by the mysteries of Ur. '*No?*' he challenged briskly. The pained monosyllable indicated that this verdict was too short, too vague, and much too expensive for the Privy Purse.

'No,' repeated the Chaldean. Sensing a proposed abatement in his fee, he condescended to explain: 'He will never succeed his father. I presume that is what you wish to know?'

It seemed to Caenis that anyone with the smallest knowledge of Claudian family life – or as much awareness of recent history as could be gleaned from skimming lightly through the obituaries in the *Daily Gazette* – would be able to make that prophecy.

'Are you sure?' Narcissus was bound to be disappointed.

'Certainly!' The man brushed him aside with an irritation that Caenis quite enjoyed.

He was heading for the door, but Narcissus liked to get his money's worth from specialists. 'So what do you expect to happen to him instead?'

A prince learns to put up with impertinence; Britannicus did not move.

The physiognomist gave Narcissus a pitying look. 'He will live out his span, sir, as we all must, then as we all must he will die.'

'How long is the span?' urged the Chief Secretary harshly.

This time Caenis felt the long-limbed boy tense beneath her hands. At once she stated curtly, 'Britannicus prefers not to know!'

The physiognomist seemed to like her firmness; he nodded to the boy. Some things were confidential to the victim, apparently, even when the Privy Purse was footing the bill. Narcissus had to subside.

Only when he reached the door did the man turn back. 'Of course,' he said, 'the other will.'

There was a small pause. He had hardly glanced at Titus

207

the whole time. No one liked to risk offending the man again, but when the attendant started to lift the door curtain so she thought they were going to lose him Caenis demanded patiently, 'Titus will what?'

The Chaldean did not hesitate. 'He will succeed his father.'

'As what?'

'As whatever his father is or becomes!' Even Caenis was making his hackles rise. 'I cannot tell you that, lady, without seeing the father's face.'

Caenis laughed. She pointed to her Sabine friend's son, then told the man in ringing tones, '*There!* Is there no imagination in the Chaldees? Add a nose like a boxer on the brink of retirement and you have it.'

For the first time the man showed that he too could smile. 'Ah *that* face!' he mocked. (He was not being paid for Titus, let alone his Sabine papa.) 'That would be the face of a nobody.'

Then at once Caenis wished she had not asked, because although she was certain Vespasian himself would have roared with delight, the poor child kneeling beside Britannicus was bitterly upset. She was so concerned about Titus it caught her off guard when the Chaldean asked quietly, 'And your own face, my lady? Will you not ask?'

Yet she found an answer for him: 'Oh, that has been prophesied,' said Caenis, with a slight smile. 'Of my face one has said, "It can never be upon the coinage."'

'He spoke well!' observed the Chaldean, who obviously appreciated a pointless remark.

XXVI

The face-detector was quite right: Britannicus did not succeed his father.

The light that had cheered the early years of Claudius' reign went out with Messalina's death. He allowed Agrippina, who was a strong, strong-willed woman in the single-minded political mould of her family, to govern the Empire. She did it as ruthlessly as she governed Claudius himself. And when Britannicus was in sight of his coming-of-age, Claudius died.

The Emperor's death was not immediately announced. Not until Agrippina, pretending to suffer inconsolable grief, had gathered into her grim clutch all of her husband's natural children – Claudia Antonia, Octavia, and of course Britannicus. Once they had been secured at the Palace, her own son Nero was wheeled out in a carriage and presented to the Praetorians as their new Caesar.

Claudius had left a will but it was never read in public.

When his father died, the young prince Britannicus was thirteen years and eight months old. He ranked as a child – though not for much longer. That was significant. It was a principle of Roman law that between the ages of seven and fourteen a boy obtained limited legal rights, those at least which were plainly for his benefit and not restricted to needing the approval of his guardian. At fourteen he reached a more specific maturity: then he could marry, vote in local assemblies, become liable for military service, and manage his own property. The milestone of entering public affairs normally came at twenty-five, but by fourteen he was a person of account. Until then, a mere child.

Britannicus' adopted elder brother, his stepmother's son, Nero, had been declared of age before he became Emperor. In Rome the difference was crucial. For four critical months

Britannicus was bound to take second place: the natural son, publicly superseded. But once he came of age, enemies of Agrippina and her son would naturally gravitate to his support. Narcissus, who loved Britannicus as his own, and Caenis, who originally knew his sisters better but had always liked the lad, never discussed what might happen to him. For anyone who had lived under Tiberius and Caligula the possibilities were obvious and grim.

Narcissus had problems of his own. Even before Claudius died he had been ill. In a left-over minister from the previous reign an indisposition was clearly convenient; Narcissus' illness was strongly encouraged by Agrippina and her son. He had never expected a quiet retirement. He withdrew to 'convalesce' at Sinuessa on the Bay of Naples. But death was his only tactful course.

Caenis, as the Chief Secretary's most discreet associate, escaped such drastic obligations. Before he left Rome Narcissus gave to her a handsome gift of cash, probably more than she could have expected to receive under his will, if the will of the Chief Secretary of the previous Emperor had ever stood a chance of being honoured by the new one. She never saw him again. Within weeks Narcissus had been flung into prison, badly treated, and hastened to his death. It was said to be suicide, but who could tell? And what difference did it make in any case? Caenis missed him even more than she expected.

She tried to keep an eye on Britannicus. She was pleased with the way he was holding his own. At the Festival of Saturnalia in December, two months before his birthday, the young men at court played dice to be King-for-the-Day. Nero won. To a degree this spoilt the point, which was that someone unused to honours, a slave even, should wear the spangled winter crown. But it avoided unpleasantness; Nero had no concept of allowing himself to lose.

At the evening banquet the King-for-the-Day gave out forfeits, most of them innocuous enough. When it came to Britannicus, who was shy in noisy company and also quite unused to heavy drinking bouts, Nero called him to the centre of the great dining hall – an ordeal in itself – then commanded him to sing. Undeterred, Britannicus piped up at once with a stalwart rendering of a theatrical lament: "I am cast out from the King my father's house . . ." He sang well; he possessed a much better voice than Nero, who was so vain of his own talent. Britannicus had the satisfaction of silencing the room.

A few days later something made him dramatically ill.

Caenis went to see him. 'Was it something you ate?'

'No,' replied Britannicus, who was developing a taut sense of humour. '*Something I sang!*'

Without Narcissus they had nowhere to turn for help. Callistus had always been pitifully cautious, and there were clear signs that Nero was on the verge of dismissing him from his post. Pallas was the only one of the senior freedmen who retained any vestige of power, but only because when she thought it might be useful he had been Agrippina's lover; for that very reason Pallas could not be asked to protect Britannicus.

Caenis felt helpless. She would have brought herself to beg advice from Vespasian, but he was sixty miles away, living quietly at home in Reate with his wife.

She was positive that somebody had tried to poison the prince. The nearer Britannicus came to fourteen the more danger threatened him. The first attempt might have been amateur, but next time his enemy might realise a violent laxative was hardly the best medium to choose. Whoever it was would try something different.

Then she found out that the famous poisoner Lucusta, who had been in league with the Empress Livia, had been glimpsed visiting the Palace. Caenis made her way to the old stillroom where she and Vespasian had met. As well as ingredients for cosmetics there had been plenty of more sinister vials there then. It had been said that when Claudius became Emperor he found and destroyed quantities of poisons collected by Caligula. He threw one great chest into the sea; thousands of dead fish were washed ashore.

But even after Caligula had remodelled the Palace area, the little room still existed. Caenis felt no surprise to discover that its low door now refused to open, held fast by an

211

obviously brand-new lock. She told Britannicus. They shared the information with nobody. There was no point.

'Nero's in love,' Britannicus explained. 'He's flexing his muscles away from his mama.'

'Dear me,' Caenis responded as lightly as she could. 'He needs lots to eat, much more sleep, no poetry, and private chats with poisoners should definitely be banned. I take it your sister Octavia is not the favoured recipient?'

'Well hardly; Octavia is his wife. He would think it improper. Actë – one of her maids. She's very beautiful.'

Caenis knew Actë and thought her a pallid little thing, but she did not want to disillusion an adolescent with her own cynicism. Octavia would not take this kindly. She was that rare bloom an aristocratic girl who was virtuous; in the way of virtuous people she had no idea of standing up for herself.

'But how does the fair Actë affect you?'

'When Agrippina tried to stop the business, she was shut out from Nero's confidence. So guess who suddenly became her protégé instead?'

'Not you?'

'Isn't it horrible? She threatened to plead with the Guards, as Germanicus' daughter, to give the throne to me as my father's natural heir. There was a great deal of screaming domestically, and my popularity with her lad in purple –' Britannicus still never called Nero by his adopted name – 'dived in a way that has only been equalled by the speed with which my dinners get thrown up if I eat with him. If I got you an invitation,' Britannicus offered shyly, 'Caenis, could you bear to come to the Palace tonight?'

'It's your birthday tomorrow, isn't it?'

He blushed that she should have remembered, though in her concern for him she had it engraved on her memory. 'Come tonight; tomorrow may be hopelessly formal –' In fact there was little chance of his being given ceremonial for his special day. 'Titus will be with me, of course, but I should like to be able to wave at another friendly face.'

And that was why Caenis, in a headache and a brand-new pair of sandals, attended a state banquet as the guest of the

212

grandson of her patroness. As a boy still, Britannicus was not allowed to have female guests at his own couch. So Caenis found herself a place at the far end of the room where she could at least watch what happened higher up.

The first thing that would strike any stranger was the noise. Anyone who paused to think about it would become dizzy as the buzz of innumerable different conversations rose all around the hall against a constant background clatter of heavy gold and silver tableware, and the busy chinking of spoons on bowls and jugs on cups. The heat, too, quickly became incredible; many people changed into floating chiffon robes. There was soon a fug of perfumed, sweaty bodies vying with the pungent aromas of simmering wine and waxen flowers.

Caenis had brought her own slave, Demetrius, a treasure Aglaus had found for her, an impassive Thracian who doubled quite competently as table attendant and bodyguard. She took off her sandals, then Demetrius washed and dried her feet; he handed her her napkin while, with a fleeting smile, she took her place amongst her neighbours. As a compliment to her young host she had spent the afternoon being manicured and pedicured at the baths. She was decked in her best finery – her formal violet-coloured dress embroidered at its edges with heavy borders of Etruscan meadow flowers, her hair trapped under a fine gold net, all Antonia's brooches, Vespasian's bangle, and some earrings she had borrowed from Veronica, the size of cavalry harness discs: a girl could do no more.

Nero dominated the top table: that unpleasant neck, the chubby jowls, the beardless blond good looks that appeared washed out and grey. His mother, Agrippina, was there, of course, queening it in a tiara and gold silk; and Octavia, the out-of-place teenaged Empress, who hardly spoke. Caenis recognised also Nero's two tutors, such markedly different men: Seneca, who made a decent stab at writing the speeches Nero so woodenly declaimed, and Burrus, the blunt soldier who commanded the Guard. There was no sign of Actë, though people spoke of her. Someone said, 'A common girl who bears no grudges – she's ideal!'

Britannicus and various other young sprigs of nobility

were consigned to a less luxurious table to one side, in what passed for the old-fashioned, austere way. It was probably a deliberate insult. At other low tables around the arc of the room were all the sycophants, time-servers and snobs a palace dining room expects.

Everything seemed fairly routine. There were the usual incidents of slaves dropping overloaded dishes so pints of sticky brown liquid sprayed across the central serving-floor. A woman fainted in the heat from the lamps and food-warmers and was carried out head first. Caenis made the mistake of accepting an hors-d'oeuvre which looked like eggs in fish-pickle relish – fairly safe, she surmised – but which turned out to be anonymous crustaceans, boiled to a fibrous mush and floating in sadly coral-coloured grease. On the whole all the food was overcooked, overspiced and oversalted, then it had stood too long before serving so none of it was warm. Demetrius did manage to commandeer her a decent artichoke in hot-herb sauce; the calf's tongue in fennel cream was genuinely tasty and the white bread rolls were not unbearably hard. Yet in the strict tradition of large-scale catering, all the meat was carved too thinly and all the vegetables were limp.

Caenis began to long for a plain honey omelette in a bowl she knew was clean.

Most of the time she could not quite see Britannicus. However, she was able to watch the slave who tasted his food. Standing behind Britannicus' couch this man appeared to be doing a thorough job. He took proper mouthfuls, and chewed them down well before he gave Britannicus anything to eat. The mushrooms which had dispatched the boy's father appeared to have been deleted from the chefs' repertoire.

Nero looked in ghastly good form. He was seventeen, an uncouth age at which most Romans were kept decently out of sight by the parents they oppressed. He did try to demonstrate the rudiments of culture – sculpture, singing, writing poetry, recitation, the harp – but it all turned out too laboured. He had no natural artistry. Caenis, who so loved music, was hoping that he would not sing tonight.

The slaves had carried out the serving-tables once; they now brought in others with the fruit and the dessert. She risked a dish of custard, mainly because she was attracted by the pretty green glass in which it came; she regretted it at the first curdled mouthful, then listlessly nibbled a pear. She still had a headache and she wanted to go home.

By this time she was feeling the melancholy irritation of a woman on her own at a party who has realised she is twice the age of most of her fellow guests. This was a young man's court. She had strayed into a world she found shallow and loud. Foolish laughter surrounded her – shrieking girls in off-the-shoulder necklines and youths who were almost too drunk to finish a sentence trying to tell long-winded pointless jokes. One of Veronica's huge earrings was pinching her ear. She even experienced a faint trace of hostility towards her young host.

The attendants, by now red-faced and too harassed even to try to be polite, were carrying out the half-demolished pastry towers; others were sweeping up the litter of stalks and peel and pips. Standards amongst both diners and attendants were definitely starting to relax.

Nero had poured a formal libation at the start of the meal; there had been wine mixed with honey between each course; now the heavy drinking would start. Short-legged boys, puffing with exertion, struggled in with giant decorated cauldrons of steaming wine infused with cinnamon and herbs. Trays of cups, flagons of cold water, honey to mix – all the apparatus of preparing toasts to the niceties of personal taste, had already appeared. There were amphorae, sooty with age, leaning in rows behind the imperial couch. One or two people took advantage of the lull to leave the room to attend to personal needs. Caenis stayed where she was for the time being; as soon as she could she intended to slip away for home.

There was a pause. Following ancient Roman custom slaves paraded round the room with the imperial family's household gods. The small bronze statues of dancing *lares* held up their horns of plenty as gracefully as those in any ordinary home. They were left on the low table immediately in front of the group of youngsters amongst whom Britannicus dined. Now that the room had cleared somewhat, Caenis could just make him out.

A ruffle of movement, a wave of anticipation, started at the top table then rolled along each arm of the room, as the flagon-bearers served the first wine. The noise, which was by then making her head throb at every movement, dimmed slightly as people stopped their animated chatter to watch the mixing of their drinks. Skilful slaves poured the hot crimson liquor through funnel-shaped strainers in a hiss of aromatic steam; others followed with the cold water in a practised routine, providing whatever was required by each diner almost without bothering to listen for the request; sometimes they got it wrong and caused a spat of indignation. There was a certain amount of extraneous activity as people summoned rosewater and napkins to wash the final stickiness of the dinner from their hands. One or two women idly poked at ringlets unwinding from their padded towers of hair.

While his taster was occupied with his goblet of wine, Britannicus rose from his couch to wave to Caenis as he had promised, down the length of the room. He looked happier; she smiled. He accepted the goblet, then stayed on his feet – a tall, slight figure with rather too big ears like his father, but that sweet-natured grin. As the young prince raised his cup to her, she felt her heart warm. She was glad she had come, for his sake.

She noticed Nero pause in his conversation, critical perhaps that the young man should openly salute his grandmother's ex-slave. She shook her head at Britannicus, but he only glanced at his adoptive brother and deliberately rebelled.

The wine was too hot for him. Before he drank, he held out the cup to be topped up with cold water by a waiting slave. At once he took it back, tipped it casually to the watching Emperor, then raised it – formally, between both his long hands – to his lady guest. She had been kind to him, and Britannicus did not forget. Then he drank.

There was nothing she could do. Caenis realised at once.

The taster had made no attempt to try it; he would have been warned not to. The poison must be in the cold water.

If she had called out, Britannicus would never have heard her above the din. It was too late anyway. She saw Nero's triumphant half-shadowed glance. She watched the young Octavia notice what was happening, whiten, then grow expressionless as she knew she must. Even Agrippina for an instant showed by her consternation that she had been no party to this.

Britannicus drank.

At the first mouthful he dropped the cup. His whole body convulsed. He stopped breathing. He fell. Britannicus crashed full length across the low table in front of his couch where the bearers had placed his family's household gods, so when the diners' cacophony stilled in amazement, the dreadful hush was broken by a slowly settling scrape on the tiny marble tiles as the Claudian god of the larder skittered in ever diminishing half-circles over the floor, then finally came to rest.

Everyone stopped talking. Everyone looked at the Emperor.

Slaves had scattered in terror; Britannicus' friends were transfixed. Nero signalled for people to carry his imperial brother from the room. Caenis was already fastening her sandal straps.

Nero said – announced it perfectly coolly – made the claim without a stammer – uttered it without a blush – that Britannicus was epileptic: he had been epileptic all his life; he would soon recover his senses and his sight. Nero ordered the banquet to recommence, which after a short silence it did.

Caenis was already halfway from the room.

As she went she turned back once, to glance at Octavia. The girl sat motionless. There was no lack of courage there. Her brother had been killed by her husband in front of her, and she had to endure it. Nobody would support her if she tried to protest.

Caenis turned away; but before she did she had spotted Vespasian's son, Titus. She noticed the young idiot pick up his friend's skittled winecup, and taste what remained of the dregs.

By the time she found the right anteroom, Britannicus was dead.

218

XXVII

Britannicus was dead.

There were people everywhere, none of them with the slightest sense. They had carried him into a salon where one or two slaves of his own and some dilatory Palace attendants were milling about. Caenis felt her new sandals skid on the glistening tessellated floor as she barged through a knot of waiters to come to him. They had him on a couch, his head lolling awkwardly over the edge, arms and legs all akimbo as he had been dropped. Pulling his tunic straight for decency Caenis took him in her arms.

There was nothing she could do.

So many murders; it had become a way of life. Apart from Antonia, who was close to her heart at this moment, Britannicus was the first Caenis had really known and loved. She realised something now: she had always believed she lived by expecting the worst. That was quite wrong. She had lived in hope. It was the only way she could bear continuing. She and Britannicus had come here tonight in that spirit, because they knew they had no other choice.

Hope is such a foolish thing: Britannicus was dead.

Ignoring all the others she pulled up his eyelids, listened for breathing, massaged him, called to him, pounded several times hard on his chest in a helpless attempt to restart his heart or clear any blockage if he had simply choked. She knew something of what to do; it was part of the lumber of useful information she had been collecting all her life. Now someone who seemed to be a Greek doctor was standing nearby, but he let her act as she wanted and made no effort to correct or encourage her. It was always up to you. Other fools just stood around.

There was nothing to be done but she worked on, even knowing it was pointless, to avoid having to think. She did her best for Antonia; for Claudius; for Narcissus; for the sweet-natured boy himself. She did it for herself too. In the end she abandoned the attempt and sat, still nursing Britannicus in her arms, her tender fingers smoothing the death-throe grimace from his elfin face. There was nothing to be done.

People fled: Nero had come.

The young Emperor, swaying slightly, had appeared on the threshold. Everyone except Caenis was terrified. She remembered saying to Antonia that emperors saw too many faces full of fear.

Nero knew he was dead. Oh Nero knew. He himself must have stood over the poisoner Lucusta after the first bungled attempt, beating her and bullying her to boil down her black ooze until it would work. In his own bedroom Nero had seen the poison instantly kill a pig. He knew. Nobody bothered to say, and, of course, he did not need to ask.

Caenis had never been so angry in her life. She had nothing left; nothing to lose. She was about to fling at him the words that needed saying, however swiftly they condemned her. Once, once if never again, she would tell the ruler of the world that it was not for him to abuse the power of life and death purely to gratify his ambition and cruelty . . . But then she became aware of someone else: Titus. That boy Titus. Vespasian's son.

He too must have come in, and was half-lying on another couch. At the Emperor's entrance he started to haul himself upright, although he could hardly move. Gods, he was like his father when he set his jaw! He was about to lose his temper. He had to be stopped.

Caenis flung back her head and addressed the Emperor across the width of the room in the iced voice of a trained secretary whose work has been regrettably disturbed by some untidy break in office routine. 'An unfortunate occurrence, lord! Please don't disturb yourself. It seems there is no more we can do. Your brother,' she stated crisply, using the word 'brother' with a whiplash of malice, 'is cured of his epilepsy now!'

The lad Titus had become brick-red with defiance, bursting with the indiscretion of youth. One leg was bent beneath him on the couch; he was struggling to break free. With any luck he would collapse.

'With permission, lord,' Caenis asked the Emperor though she did not care whether he gave permission or not, 'as a client of your family I will attend to the funeral.'

'Tonight,' Nero said, in his brash voice. 'Hasty deaths should be hastily removed.'

Titus gagged. The Emperor turned upon him his bloodless gaze.

'Too much wine!' Caenis uttered with contempt. 'The young fool's drunk.'

Moving with that disgusting cormorant strut, Nero then left his family's female client to tidy up death and drunkenness together.

Caenis sprang to life. 'Demetrius, close the door!' She was already setting down her pointless burden gently and squirming to her feet. 'Hot water and salt!' she barked to her slave. 'Not from the dining room; be quick but be discreet. Demetrius, run!'

As she reached him Titus began to slither towards the floor. She caught him under one armpit – this was the moment where all her future nightmares would begin: that painfully familiar Flavian face slipping past her knee, with chaos all around them, while she heard her own voice appealing to him not to die. He was a well-made chunky young man, gripping his stomach in obvious agony. He was too heavy; she had to let him slide to the ground, where she knelt, gathering him against her knees with one hand supporting his warm head.

'I drank –'

'I know.'

He was flopping semiconscious; in a moment he would be gone. She began to shake him like a maid plumping a pillow; she slapped him; she shouted his name. 'Titus! Come along now; this won't do. Wake up; Titus!'

Demetrius was at her side. Thankfully Aglaus chose his

221

subordinates for their quick response in a crisis. Caenis herself mixed a strong emetic while Demetrius began the desperate process of hauling Titus upright again. Seating him on the couch seemed to revive him to some degree. He was white-knuckled with pain. His eyes looked opaque. 'Come along; drink. Titus, you know you must!'

She held his head, gripping the curly hair at the back of his neck, forcing him to swallow the warm brine. He drank it all. He wanted to live; he was a fighter in the stubborn Flavian mould, and he trusted her instinctively.

'Demetrius, find my litter; bring it in here. Say I'm ill if needs be. Nothing to do here until I get him to vomit the poison.'

Titus was changing colour even as she spoke, from his hectic flush to a dreadful doughy grey. Demetrius met her eyes. She nodded; her slave slipped away.

'Britannicus –'

'Britannicus is gone. I'm so sorry. I know you were his friend. Save your energy; Titus, do try to throw up.' He would not need much trying; he had that worried look. 'One day,' Caenis promised him grimly, 'all this will be stopped. One day, Titus; you and I will see a better world.'

Then Vespasian's son was violently sick all over her feet.

He was mortified. 'Oh lady, I'm so sorry –'

Her new sandals! But he looked better. 'Thanks, sweetheart. Come on; try again. I don't think I liked them anyway, and I certainly don't like them now.'

Behind her, she suddenly heard the wailing of the slaves who attended a death to clamour in case there was a hope that the victim might after all wake. People had no sense of discretion. This was the ritual, so they performed it mindlessly. Nobody murdered in this palace was required to be revived. People had no sense.

No one paid any attention to Titus and herself. Just as well. Too close an association with this poisoning would do the Flavians no good.

She had been prepared to thrust chicken-feathers down the boy's throat but by now he was being helplessly ill. Caenis talked to him, willing him through, holding him more kindly now. He no longer seemed conscious of his surroundings, but she tried to make her voice reach his brain and drag him back. She was losing him; she could see that.

'*Titus!* Titus, come on, my Flavian; you can do better than this.'

He groaned. Still talking, she massaged his limp, sweating hands. 'What a truly awful banquet; I don't know why I came. Abandoned by my host — Titus, make an effort, please! — the floor show was deplorable, and I had to leave before the decent drinking got under way . . .' He had nothing more to bring back. Wiping his face, she let him rest with his poor fevered head against her upper arm. Tears splashed on to his cheek; her own tears. 'Oh my darling; don't die, Titus! I can never tell Vespasian that I let him lose his son.'

Demetrius was back with her litter and its two frightened bearers. She gave them quiet instructions. They were to take the boy to his father's empty apartment; Demetrius would go to explain, or if there were no servants there he would fetch Aglaus instead to look after the boy.

Titus was wrestling against unconsciousness as they lifted him inside the chair. Just before she closed the half-door Caenis leant in to tuck her shawl around him. He was shivering uncontrollably; she had never seen anyone so white.

He opened his eyes in a moment of puzzled lucidity. 'Do you know my father well?'

'Not any more,' stated Caenis tersely. 'And you can tell him from me, I can manage without his off-spring being sick in my best new shoes!'

Yet she kissed him, before the bearers began to move off — that old social gesture of affection, the light touch on the cheek. So once again, Titus felt the lady's tears.

Perhaps he had glimpsed that a little of the love she once gave to Britannicus had transferred in that dreadful hour to him. Perhaps too, he recognised the shadow of another kind of feeling. Within the soft folds of that lady's shawl he shuddered, for as he was carried away from the Palace to the safety of his father's house he understood that he had trespassed among the secrets of a grown-up world. Unimagined aspects of his own existence faced him. With the heart-rending clarity of someone who was dangerously ill he was viewing not merely his father, with whom he had always been on the best of terms, and his mother, whom he loved as he should, but also this lady with whom he was sharing the loss of his friend. Love of Britannicus seemed their special interest, a bond even more private than the fact she had just saved his life.

But there was something else between them too. She had called him her darling. Then, with a flood of sensation as intense as biting on an unexpected clove, Titus Vespasianus understood her warning and her plea. He realised exactly why, when they spoke about tonight to other people, they would have to make such a joke about him ruining her shoes.

XXVIII

They buried Britannicus in the pouring rain.

Someone with enormous forethought had provided a pyre. Slaves must have been building it before the banquet even began. So a small group of friends cremated the son of Claudius on the Palatine that same night, while Nero watched from his dining room much as Caligula had once watched Antonia's funeral. It was raining from the start, but when they brought the boy's ashes to the Mausoleum of Augustus in the north of the city, all the heavens opened and this was taken for a sign of the gods' wrath. For Caenis, the filthy weather merely matched the filthiness of life.

It was a pitiful group that trailed out to the Field of Mars then through the sodden public walks to the Mausoleum. As they approached, the weather was so bad they could barely make out the exterior, mounded with earth in the Etruscan style, though massively terraced and planted with cypress trees. The bronze statue of Augustus which surmounted the great circular tomb was quite invisible in the murk.

The wind keened eerily in the trees. It was night; the company sparse and deeply depressed. When lightning flashed off the obelisks which guarded the entrance to that dark place, those who had been brave enough to attend the cremation understood that all the new optimistic order was now quite lost. Their unexpected Emperor Claudius had been decreed a god; as they brought his murdered son to the family tomb, that was the final irony.

The mourners descended by the flaring light of torches to deposit the urn in the white marble basement. It took place without eulogy or ceremony. Nero had forbidden a procession. There was no time to bring out the masks of Britannicus' ancestors. People came hurriedly; muttered their farewells; departed into the storm. So they buried the last of the Claudians, the son of a deified emperor, yet murdered in boyhood as so many were, with nobody willing or able to raise a hand in his defence. So they buried Britannicus, in the pouring rain.

Caenis went home.

She was shaking. She was sneezing. She had no shoes and no shawl; she was drenched. She was entering a state of shock. She had been wet for a long time, since before the cremation when she washed her feet and the hem of her dress in a fountain, leaving her ruined sandals on the rim. Noticing she had lost her litter, Pallas took her in his own. They did not like one another but as clients of the same family, decency demanded he did not let her walk across the north of the city weeping and barefoot, in the dark, alone. Caenis was past knowing what had happened to her, and had she known she would not have cared. By next day she was seriously ill.

Caenis was so ill, for so long, that she reached a point of not even understanding who or where she was. Aglaus must have coped. She never really knew. Doctors came, though not often; Aglaus told her afterwards that despite any delirium, at the first sniff of poppyseed and cabbage-water she had managed to be magnificently rude. Even when she started to recover she could barely find the energy to lie in bed hoping there would be nothing to decide or do.

Eventually she passed into a stage of being bored yet unable to concentrate, so once again she could only drowse, while occasional tears whimpered down the line of her cheekbone and chin. Even her flute-girl was more than she could bear; after a few minutes of the softest music her head hurt. People sent fruit, which she did not eat. People came; she begged not to have to see them because she realised she was too miserable to cope – then when she knew they had gone she became desolate with loneliness.

Every night, when the delirium returned, there was the dream: young Titus falling to the floor at her feet while she begged him not to die. That dream at least grew so familiar it seemed almost comforting.

*

At last the day arrived when she woke and knew she was much better than the day before.

'You have a visitor,' Chloe, her maid, offered, at which for the first time Caenis looked keen to know who.

Then a familiar scathing voice burbled, 'Don't worry; it's only me! And don't try to turn me out.' It was Veronica. To see her was glorious. 'Juno, Caenis; look at you! The rumour's true then, that you had pneumonia?'

'That rumour's not true; I have not had pneumonia, I've still got it!'

Veronica dismissed the maid herself. At first she sat beside the bed, so wonderfully sane, with that well-groomed inquisitive face. It was a tall bed, so she soon gave up the wicker chair which made her crane her slender neck; instead she perched up on the edge of the coverlet with one slim foot on the step at the side.

Caenis drifted back to the real shore of the world. Her room, which had for so long been a hall of leaping ghosts, assumed its familiar shape: smaller, and even on a wintry afternoon full of light. Once again it became her special place – the great screw-down clothes-press in one corner smoothing her own tunics and cloaks, the long Egyptian chest, the wicker chair, her dressing table which was set with her jumble of knick-knack boxes, half-empty cream pots, pin trays, combs and perfume jars. Though she had lived among them for many days and nights, she greeted her own things now like a traveller returning from a long journey: her silver scarf-case, her sandalwood trinket drawers, her pottery lamps, that ancient rug in warm stripes of cinnabar red and umber, which clashed with the cushions and the crimson counterpane but was so cosy and comforting under her feet while she dressed that she never managed to change it for a newer, harsher one . . .

'I have brought you some nice barley broth, Caenis; I left it with your cook. Don't for one moment imagine I made it myself, though I did give it a poke with a spoon so my woman would think I know what kitchens are about.'

Veronica had wonderful taste in clothes. She had come in a purple so deep-dyed it was certainly illegal; her presence filled the room with vibrant colour even before she began to speak in that familiar racy style. They looked at one another, and were at once as they had always been, two women who spoke one language, two women who shared a conspiracy against life.

Veronica said softly, 'Love, I met your Sabine friend. He was in the Saepta Julia of all places. I gathered there had been an amount of feeble family debate, and the upshot was they felt a polite Flavian ambassador should call on you. Well; I soon stopped that.'

Caenis managed to smile.

'Your old friend the Hero,' Veronica went on. She stopped. She was usually so candid her obvious reluctance felt odd. 'Vespasian apologises. He has had a bereavement –'

'Oh – not the boy?' Caenis could hardly bear to ask.

Veronica patted her hand. 'No. No; not the boy. I saw the boy too. A heart-breaker if ever I met one! He has been dangerously poorly – but will live, though he's a disgusting saffron colour at the moment.'

'He seemed a tough little shoot. Is he yellow? I was terrified,' Caenis worried, 'that his liver might be damaged.'

'Yes. His father was fretting but their doctor says he will recover. He looks strong. You will have to brace yourself: I found them buying an antique Greek vase painted with a whole ocean including a hideous octopus – just your type of thing! The object will come by night on an ox-cart and you'll need to build a viewing gallery to hold it. It will have cost the child his life-savings, though I dare say the loss will be replenished by discreet paternal hands – assuming Vespasian ever has any money . . . I mention it so you can have your smile of gracious pleasure ready.'

Caenis practised her gracious smile. Her brain worked only slowly nowadays: 'What bereavement?'

Finally Veronica told her, still looking at the counterpane, 'I believe, his wife. Flavia Domitilla had for a long while not been in the best of health.' Caenis schooled her face. 'I deduced that if you wanted, I could arrange for you to meet him,' Veronica confessed abruptly, after which she was at last able to look up.

'No thanks.'

Caenis hardly paused for consideration. She could not bear it.

Veronica smiled. She was in her way an eccentric woman. 'Well!'

'Did he ask you to ask me, Veronica?'

'Yes.'

Caenis took a deep breath. 'Do you blame me for refusing?'

'I certainly do not. You know my views. The man was a liability from the start. Incidentally, he still has no money. And good gods, it must be nearly twenty years.'

'Probably is,' Caenis marvelled wryly. 'See him again? Juno –' Veronica let her maunder on. 'I filled my life. I had to; it was too long to waste. I was never the docile Penelope type – what, twenty years with nothing to show but a nicely stitched sampler and ruined eyes? Then some raddled old traveller turns up expecting you to have fed his dog and kept his favourite winecup dusted on the sideboard, and be ready to rub liniment on his scars and listen to his dreadful stories until he drops? Oh Veronica! Whatever does the silly man expect?'

Veronica thought about it. 'Who's Penelope? Do I know her?'

'Oh in a story. She waited for a hero for twenty years.'

'A man wrote that!' Veronica guessed acutely.

Vespasian would be forty-six next November. On the seventeenth: Caenis still remembered his birthday date.

It was indeed nearly twenty years. That dark corridor between rage and simple disappointment, where a bright young girl's uneasy hopes dulled into resignation; her long, tired decline into just another elderly, dowdy, ordinary woman.

It was all far too late. They could never go back. And Caenis would not like to see a man she had once loved so dearly on any lesser understanding now.

Veronica broke into her reverie to say quietly, 'It's an insult. If it makes you feel any better, I told him exactly what I think.'

'I'm not insulted.'

Caenis imagined that Vespasian would treat Veronica warily. She was not his type, though he would admire her as an artefact. He would not, however, want her to tell him what she thought.

'Credit where credit is due,' Veronica admitted, 'I do believe he badly wants to thank you for saving his son.'

Caenis spread her hands with a watery smile. 'Tell him I am thanked. But he knows what I feel about being asked to console widowers.'

'I'll soon settle him!' Veronica became brisk. She stood up, shaking her jewelled skirts. 'And now, if you can face it, I want to smother you with rugs and take you in my litter to a shoemaker few people can afford, who will measure you for the prettiest and most comfortable pair of new sandals in Rome.'

Caenis began to climb shakily out of bed. 'That I can face!' She paused, with one bare foot feeling for the step.

Veronica paused too. 'This is a gift from me, Caenis.'

Caenis did not so easily give up. 'And whose was the idea?'

'Ah that,' conceded the friend she had known since she was ten, 'I am not supposed to say.'

Caenis worked out for herself that Vespasian had made the suggestion, but left Veronica to pay for the shoes.

So, cheered at least by comfortable feet (which any sensible woman valued highly – most of all if she had once been a barefoot slave) Caenis gradually came back into society. There did not seem a lot to come back for.

Veronica had obviously assumed Caenis would behave exactly as she did herself. Next time she came she cried, 'Right! Have you seen him yet?'

'No,' Caenis answered.

'You are intending to?'

'No.'

'Hasn't he asked you again?'

'No. I mean, yes.'

'Well, that seems clear!'

'Titus sent the octopus vase with a note from his father saying he'd like to hear my opinion of it. I thanked Titus

230

formally by letter but didn't answer his father's note. Satisfied?'

'He must make new arrangements, Caenis. He strikes me as the dozy, loyal type. The minute he comes to visit you, I want to hear.'

Caenis, who was feeling better, quietly quartered herself a pear which a kind friend had sent her from the storeroom of his country estate north of Rome.

Vespasian had gone back to Reate, taking his son.

'He's having a terrible time lately,' Veronica told her, persisting doggedly. 'He lost his daughter too.' Then Caenis was genuinely distressed, for she imagined that Vespasian was a man who would make his daughter a favourite. 'Childbirth, I imagine. Teenaged bride; poor little shrimp. She left a baby,' warbled Veronica. 'Little girl, I believe: yet another Flavia.'

Vespasian was a grandfather! The ridiculous old devil was courting her through a third party like a bashful teenage boy. Caenis could accept he was the type of man to reminisce fondly over his youth, but she had assumed anyone so hard-headed would realise the past should now lie undisturbed.

The fool kept sending her fruit. Sometimes Caenis felt she was the only person in Rome with any tact or sense. And a grandfather: at this news, for the first time since she was ill, she actually began to laugh out loud. Veronica shrieked for a servant; she could tell the poor woman still needed rest.

As Caenis expected, Vespasian never came. Fruit kept arriving in unmarked Sabine baskets for the next six months. She ate the fruit, but never responded. In the end he gave up.

After all, it was nearly twenty years. A woman learns to cope. A woman knows she must.

Until one day, when she has grown accustomed to life's centrifugal drag, suddenly the earth tilts. And an elderly, dowdy, ordinary woman may find herself quite unexpectedly thrown off among the stars.

231

PART FIVE:
A HALF-DECENT
COMPANION

When the Caesar was Nero

XXIX

The Via Nomentana: sunlit on a lunchtime in September.

A man walked steadily up one side of the road from the city, crossed at the Nomentana Gate, then walked slowly away again. In the main thoroughfare were baths and a public lavatory, and the local streetmarket, its stalls lively with poultry and singing birds. The pale round cheeses looked excellent and the fish were displayed on moist mats of dark green leaves in patterns of circles and stars; pilchards in basketfuls glittered like well-polished cutlery, crayfish peered out of wicker cages still alive, and gleaming blue-black mussels lay in buckets under the shade of the trestle tables. The man counted three sausage shops.

This was a quiet little nook in the suburbs, cleaner and neater than many parts of Rome. All the shop porticos carried climbing plants, while window boxes frilled the balconies overhead with carnations and ivy, scillas, rosy balsam and hot-orange marigolds. Houseproud owners had swept any litter from the street; the gutters ran free; some of the pavements still shone wet where they had recently been washed. A pert brown dog sat outside a chandler's looking interested, but made no move to investigate as the man passed again, once more heading for the gate.

Outside the Porta Nomentana no one was about.

This was better than where he lived himself in the Sixth District, the *Alta Semita*, the high quarter on the slopes of the Quirinal full of people who would like something better. Here there was the Praetorian Camp, to be sure, ringing with its aggressive racket by night and day, but apart from the occasional mausoleum along the main road there were only isolated market gardens, making the atmosphere open and airy. The man strolling up and down had lived not far away for years though he had not, until now, ever allowed his steady footsteps to bring him here.

235

He attracted the attention of a fat woman who thought he was up to no good; he was clad in senatorial robes though for some reason he had turned up here with no escorting slaves. He looked out of place and shifty. The fat woman was pretending to hang rugs over her balcony while she made up her mind whether to send a slave running to summon the Vigiles. She did not know this was just the stubbornly eccentric ex-Consul Vespasian.

Passing the chandler's shop for the third or fourth time he quickened his step abruptly as if he had made up his mind, and dived out through the gate. A short walk brought him to a mansion which was obviously owned by somebody with money, although unlike his own peeling portal the stepped entrance was not crowned with triumphal insignia. In fact there was nothing to indicate who lived here.

This house had blank walls facing the Nomentana Road, though their formidable air was relieved by the visible tops of trees in the internal courtyards. Reaching those peristyles and colonnades might not be easy; visitors were greeted by a solid, studded, massive black door. A fierce iron inspection-grille took the central position amidst much well-oiled furniture – workmanly hinges with massive pinions, lantern-hooks and locks. A tiled fingerplate warned of a crusty watchdog, though no barking began. Two stone tubs of nodding ferns flanked the white marble step, and the knocker took the form of a well-fed bronze dolphin with an encouraging curly grin.

He knocked.

Nothing happened. Indoors no one stirred. There was silence. This must be the time of day when door-porters around the Porta Nomentana ate their lunch and sorted out their gambling debts.

He banged again, patiently. On a lattice beside the door there was a nasturtium which suffered badly from blackfly, still dripping where someone had sluiced it down to discourage them. In the distance above the market gardens a skylark was singing its heart out.

Abruptly the porter, with his napkin under his chin, opened the door. He had not bothered to peer through the grille first. Coincidentally he was followed by a steward with an empty shopping basket, who took over as stewards like to do. The visitor watched them note his senatorial toga and then wonder why he seemed to own no slaves. Nobody owned no slaves at all; they put him down as a careless type who had lost his escort in the Forum crush.

They all three held an interesting conversation in which the unattended senator claimed to be a friend of the lady of the house but refused to give his name, while the steward satirically pretended she was not at home. When they grew bored, the steward admitted she was there, asleep, then threatened to wake her up.

'*Mars Ultor!*' exclaimed this man who claimed to know her. 'Don't do that. Her temper's poisonous if anyone breaks her nap!'

The steward and the porter gazed at each other in surprise, then both agreed that the stranger could be invited in. He knew her; there was no doubt of that.

Everywhere was spotless. There was a light hall, with a half-length bust of Antonia when young, surrounded by flower petals. Somewhere in the distance a musician was playing a flute. The steward led the visitor across an expensive mosaic floor, around the marbled atrium pool and past several doors opened to allow any breeze to cool the house, then into a feminine sitting room painted in panels of a soft honey-beige with delicate borders of crimson ribboning. Here, apparently, he could wait.

There was a couch, strewn with casual cushions, or two sloping women's chairs. He took the couch but sat, so he could watch the door. At his elbow appeared a bronze tripod table with the latest *Gazette* and a glossy ceramic bowl of fruit. He declined other refreshment but was shown a silver gong to ring if he changed his mind. Once he had gained admittance everything was done with unfussed efficiency. This seemed a comfortable, cheery sort of house: nothing too brash or too opulent, though all chosen with a good eye. The lampstands were rare Etruscan antiques. The slaves were content; their manners businesslike.

237

Hé ate two of the apples because they smelled so fresh and good, then after a moment's hesitation stowed the stalks on the rim of a lamp. He deduced this was a house where no one would mind if a stranger put his fruit-cores in the wrong place.

It was wonderfully restful. He felt liable to doze. With an effort he managed to stay the right side of sleep to hear any movement outside. So, when the sunlight finally moved around until it fell through the slatted shutters of a bedroom in another part of the house, he did catch the distant tinkle of a light bell and knew she must be awake.

Very soon afterwards came swift footsteps in the corridor outside.

The door began to open. Outside a familiar voice spoke tersely. He folded his arms. The lady of the house walked in.

She was a middle-aged woman with lucid eyes set in a calm expression. It was deceptive; she was trained to appear tranquil in public. Not tall, not beautiful, she moved with self-contained assurance though her rig was far from ornate: a green-grape gown and a bangle she had owned for years. Her hair, still dark but with fine silver wings above the ears, was rolled simply for an afternoon at home, then speared in place with a couple of wooden combs. A whisk of some clear, pleasant perfume enlivened the room as she entered. Behind her shoulder the steward ogled anxiously.

She had recovered from her illness but seemed quieter than ever before. After the first few seconds Vespasian really did not register that she was older, and heavier, and perhaps her spirit was more tired. She was herself. For him, nothing about her that mattered would ever change. His breathing quickened; his brows knit.

She had obviously guessed who it must be. For old times' sake he rather hoped she would exclaim, 'Skip over the Styx; you're not allowed in here!' But age and polite manners overtake everyone.

'Hello, Caenis.'

'Good afternoon, Consul.' Caenis insulted him with the title she must know had expired. 'Please don't get up.'

238

She could probably tell it had not until that moment struck him that he ought to rise. She was a freedwoman, one of some standing and in her own house; her house, to which she had stubbornly declined to invite him. Her voice sounded steady. It was only in the set of her mouth that an old acquaintance could identify irritation and distaste.

'Aglaus, you should have recognised this gentleman; his stature is in the Forum of Augustus – though perhaps when you're scuttling to and fro you never glance above their noble marble feet. This one is Flavius Vespasianus – the Hero of Britain.'

The Hero of Britain twitched his living feet and decided that everything was going to be a great deal more difficult than he had hoped.

There were fairly decent women, Vespasian knew since they had already made the situation plain to him, who would readily tolerate a man of forty-six if his statue stood in the Forum of Augustus and he was entitled to wear a triumphal wreath at public festivals. They would expect him to give them money (he had learnt this too from experience) and he believed it unlikely that any of them would want to stay friends – if that was the correct designation for such types – for as long as twenty years.

It never once occurred to him that Antonia Caenis might no longer be his friend.

Nor after twenty years was he surprised to find her angry; she had been angry all her life, Narcissus had told him that. Resting his chin on one hand, watching her while she briskly dismissed her servant, he noticed changes – particularly in the assured way she moved, here in her home, and the low tenor of her voice as she spoke familiarly to the steward. He noticed too, with an internal burn of excitement, what had *not* changed about this woman: that her scowl made him smile; that her hard edge made him soft; that merely to sit in her presence for a few moments had brought him peace, and a sense of wellbeing he had not known for years.

That was when he knew he still thought, *What an interesting girl!*

XXX

Caenis had been furious when they told her he was here.

After her nap she was as usual well-tempered, joking with Chloe as the girl massaged her throat: 'Rub the oil well in, girl; if the neck's half decent I may get away with an antique face – strong cheese: intriguingly mature!'

Then Aglaus appeared, looking oddly smug. 'Madam, someone came to see you. I don't know his name.' She had told him before, he would make a poor secretary.

'A man,' Chloe informed her. 'He says, a *friend*!'

People liked Caenis, but she had always limited her friends. Her standards were too high; her patience and her temper both too short. She scoffed, 'A *brave* man then!'

When she had asked what this brave friend of hers was doing, they said he appeared to be asleep. So then she knew. She tried to stop herself wondering what he must want.

Now Vespasian was fixing her with that long grim stare of his; Caenis ignored it, finding herself a chair.

Aglaus did his best. 'The Hero of Britain! *Yes, madam!* Another time I'll demand a boot inspection on the step so I can match the feet . . . Will you want refreshments?'

'Later perhaps.'

'Shall I send your woman?'

'No need.'

As soon as they were alone she began to settle down.

His face had once been older than his years, so he had grown into his looks. The frown had stayed; the deep wrinkles on the forehead; the steadiness of his eyes when he looked at her.

Caenis felt fragile as a lovelorn girl. To find him here, in her house, plunged her into fluttering formality. 'Consul! My word what an honour. What can we do for you?'

Vespasian hated her when she was arch. 'Do you mind?' he felt obliged to enquire. 'Should I have made an appointment? *Do* you mind?'

Without thinking she replied sourly, 'Apparently not!'

They were talking in odd jerks. He seemed very quiet. He looked as if he had forgotten how to smile. She felt awkward. A different kind of woman would retreat behind her embroidery, but Caenis had never been one for handicrafts; as a slave she had had no time and as a freedwoman in the early days no money for the silk.

Despite all he had become, Vespasian was at a loss in this situation. She watched him run his hand over his hair – what was left of it – and though he was far from vain, she could see he wished at this moment that he had not lost quite so much. It was a strangely unsettling gesture. 'I still have your money,' he reminded her, for something to say. 'Need it?'

He had been here no time at all before managing to arouse her indignation: 'That's for my old age, Titus – I don't, thanks; not yet!'

The fact that she had automatically called him by his personal name disturbed them both, yet he was laughing a little when he replied, 'No. You look glowing.'

'The nap, dear!' Caenis snapped. They were already recovering their way of speaking to each other. 'And a sensible diet. Lots of fruit. In fact, almost too much to get through –'

'I'm sorry. Still repaying my debts . . . You can always hurl it after me when you send me out through your door with your foot in the small of my back.' He was testing her out. Caenis said nothing. 'Friends with me?' he cajoled her softly.

They were absolute strangers, Caenis thought bleakly; yet for the sake of the past she nodded, staring into her lap.

Vespasian stood up. It seemed premature; Caenis experienced a thread of disappointment. Still, ex-consuls were much in demand when they visited Rome from the country.

They knew they had failed to make real contact. They both realised this visit had been an error on his part. No point prolonging it.

'Thank you for seeing me.'

'My pleasure, lord.'

241

Not until she had risen too and was walking across the room to escort him to the door in her old way, did Vespasian diffidently come to the point: 'There's music this afternoon in the theatre. I've found out about it. It's a water-organ – some new-fangled machine Nero's discovered. Might be interesting . . . Were you intending to go?'

I don't want to! Caenis thought.

I don't blame you! answered Vespasian with his eyes. 'Afterwards,' he stated aloud, when she did not reply, 'I am invited to dinner at my cousin's house – bringing the guest of my choice.'

Caenis guessed that his family were worried about him. A widower, especially one in charge of two young boys, was easy game for well-meaning ladies who wanted to flap. He must be hating it. In fact, he seemed so subdued she was tempted to worry about his welfare herself. By now they were standing so near to one another that he was able to lift her hand in his, lightly by the fingers as if he were afraid he might offend her. With an effort he asked, 'Will I be stepping on anybody's toes if I ask you to go with me?'

He thought he had trapped her with his long, evaluating stare. Her fingers were still balanced on his, held by the faint pressure of his great thumb. Caenis realised just how badly she wanted to go. She reached a rapid, defiant decision: 'I should like that. Thank you.'

Amazed, the Hero of Britain cleared his throat. A hint of anxiety tightened the corners of his eyes. 'And will I?'

'Will you what?' demanded Caenis, whipping back her hand.

'Will I be stepping –'

'Mind your own business,' she said, and stalked ahead of him out of the room.

In the hall the steward Aglaus was hovering. Caenis spoke to him calmly. 'Aglaus, I shall be going out this afternoon.' She laid her hand for a moment on Vespasian's togaed arm as he followed her. 'This gentleman is someone I have known for a long time. If ever he comes here he is to be received as a friend of the house. Mind you –' she lifted her hand again – 'he's the type who turns up for one or two meals, kicks the cat, spanks the kitchen maids, then disappears again for twenty years.'

Being rude was a mistake. Caenis saw it at once; perhaps they both did. For one thing, the steward decided there was something going on. Nobody wanted that.

Aglaus noticed that the Hero of Britain faintly smiled. It was not, therefore, an irreversible error. The fact that Caenis was standing up to Vespasian only made both of them look forward to their outing even more.

The water-organ was amazing. It was played with skill by a lacquered young lady, though anyone could tell that the Emperor was already planning to make this spectacular toy his own speciality. As far as Caenis could judge from her place in the upper gallery it was a gigantic set of panpipes, partly brass and partly reed, worked by a large beam-lever that forced air into a water box; under pressure it found its way to the pipe chamber and thence to the pipes, released into them by slides which the musician operated. It was the most complicated instrument she had ever seen and versatile too, though she was uncertain whether she found the thing musical.

When she left, Vespasian was waiting for her, attended by six bearers and his personal two-seater sedan chair. 'You're the musician. Tell me what I am supposed to think of that contraption.' He said this straight-faced; whether he was serious Caenis no longer knew him well enough to tell.

'Very sonorous!' she exclaimed. 'I could see it was keeping you awake.'

The dignified person who passed for Flavius Vespasianus nowadays gave her an unexpectedly melting smile.

Dinner at his cousin's was pleasant; she was glad she had gone, for it clearly relieved Vespasian's anxious relations to see him bring someone, whoever it was. Caenis knew how to behave gracefully. Vespasian made her feel at ease, though was never so fussy it troubled her. Once, when somebody asked after his son Titus, he answered and then shared with Caenis a look which for all the wrong reasons attracted notice from the others present. Caenis could not detect whether people realised he had known her in the past.

One thing that startled her was the difference between dining out in the old days with Vespasian the struggling young senator, and accompanying him now. Nowadays the consular Vespasian automatically took the place of honour next to his host in the central position. Moreover, the free couch beside him was immediately given to his guest: whoever she was.

It was a relaxed, respectable party that broke up at an early hour, without excessive drinking. Vespasian then took her home. In the chair he sat opposite. Although they were both content with their evening, neither spoke. It was dark enough for Caenis to watch him, well aware that he was watching her; it was too dark to have to meet his eye.

At her house he ordered the bearers to wait while he himself carried a torch to light her to the door. He rapped on the fat dolphin knocker then stayed until her porter came.

'Thank you, Caenis. I enjoyed tonight.'

She was aching for him to touch her; it was quite ridiculous.

'Yes. Thank you.'

Her door was open. The porter had stepped back out of sight. He was normally inquisitive, so Caenis guessed that Aglaus had been lecturing the staff.

'Your door's open,' said Vespasian, without moving from the spot. There was a fractional pause. 'Good night, Caenis.'

Great gods, the man had no idea how to provide gossip for her servants. Nor – though they must be obvious – did he understand the feelings of the lady of the house. The man had no manners. The man had no sense.

'Titus.' She walked past him, inclining her head politely, no more.

The porter hesitated, then closed the heavy door. As he was bolting it Caenis told him everyone could go to bed; she would not need her girl. Unusually brisk, her footsteps crossed the hall and strode down the corridor to her room.

Really, she did not know why she was annoyed.

'Damn!' Caenis said to herself. 'Damn! Damn him! Damn!'

She had closed her bedroom door quietly enough, rather than have it known throughout the house how she felt; then to relieve her tension she flung open the shutters so all the turmoil of Rome at night flooded the room: the clatter of delivery carts barging one another at the Porta Nomentana, their drovers' barracking at traffic jams, the roar of activity from the Praetorian Camp, then from within the city the shouts, the whoops, the occasional screams, the rancid laughter, the wild soaring of solitary song as a man painless with wine leaned against a wall and admonished the stars.

Dressing to go out had taken her longer than usual – even though Caenis was impatient of fiddling and liked to follow a steady routine. Now preparing for sleep took no time at all. Her elegant white and gold gown was already over the back of a chair; she felt spitefully glad she had decided against a brighter colour, which she knew Vespasian would prefer. She poured water for herself, one-handedly scrubbing the cosmetics from her face with a sponge. There came a succession of angry sounds at the snapping down of hairpins and brooches, then her bangle clanged on the shelf. The decorative hairstyle that had taken Chloe an hour to create took Caenis two minutes to unwind before she was bending forward to comb the tangled mass with brisk swishing strokes. She stopped muttering, but amongst all the noise that she had introduced she failed to notice the distant knocking then a low murmur of voices. In her room after more vicious combing, she straightened with a great sweep of hair, then one earring chinked.

Aglaus knocked quickly and entered at once, carefully closing the door. Caenis did not encourage anyone to come into her room without permission; something had occurred. 'Excuse me, madam; your friend's popped back –'

She understood his haste, and the low voice. Then Vespasian himself opened the door.

Aglaus was shocked. 'Oh! Sir! I know there are special rules for heroes, but the lady's in her bedroom in her vest!'

She was perfectly decent, in a good under-tunic from neck to floor, yet she felt deeply embarrassed. Vespasian quickly brushed courtesies aside. 'Sorry, Caenis. Something I meant to say.' Somewhere, perhaps in her own hall, he had shed the heavy folds of his toga. It made him look much more comfortable: the country boy with brown arms and his tunic slouched over his belt.

Aglaus was an excellent steward. He had a fine ear, or eye, or whatever it took, for dealing with visitors just as his lady required. His problems started when Caenis herself did not know what she wanted to do. Scooping up her trail of discarded shoes, shawl, belt, he crossed swiftly and forced the shutters closed, snuffing the outside noise. It gave her time to think. 'I'll ask one of the girls –'

Caenis found she was furious, though not with him. 'Don't bother. Thanks, Aglaus.'

'Right. Well! As things seem to be so informal I expect you can let the gent out for yourself.'

'I expect I can,' Caenis agreed grimly. 'Good night, Aglaus.'

He stomped off in a huff.

Then once again they were alone. Because she was so flustered, Caenis began speaking too rapidly: 'Vespasian, I never was a proud girl, but I should not from choice receive you in my slippers with my face-paint all scrubbed off!'

He stayed where he was in the centre of the room.

'Luckily I had not yet put my teeth away in their silver box and my wig on its stand –' She wished she had not said that, for it made her self-conscious about having her hair loose. She was too old; it looked foolish. It was her own hair really; they were indeed her own teeth. He might not recognise the joke.

She turned away to replace the comb on her dressing-shelf, only to hear him approach. She spun back, but it was worse; he had come right behind her so she turned almost into his arms. Drawing an agitated breath she stepped away, but was stopped by the shelf behind her. A warm tremor shimmered over her skin.

'You've still got one earring –' Vespasian offered simply, beginning to reach for it.

'I can manage!' She wrenched it off and hurled it to join its fellow with another skedaddling chink. He had lost her

246

goodwill. She wanted him to go.

'Calm down,' he appealed, though a gleam in his eyes said frankly that she would not be Caenis unless she were pointlessly ranting, most of the time. He was not the least put out by it. 'What's the matter?'

Caenis sighed; she heard Vespasian grunt; they both relaxed. 'What did you come to say?' she asked in a quieter tone.

In his aimless, curious way he picked up her bangle. 'Did I give you this?'

'You did.' She was terse with irritation; their two names were still engraved clear enough inside.

'Sweet of you to look it out.'

'I wear it every day. It's good gold and I'm fond of it.'

He put it down. 'It's very plain. Would you like a better one?'

'No.'

Now he was at the earrings. 'Who gave you those?'

'Marius.'

For a moment he needed to think who Marius was; she enjoyed that. He dropped the earrings quickly into a box where they did not belong. Tetchily Caenis moved them out of the box to a tray. On reflection she remembered that these – gold acorns dangling from rectangles of green glass that could almost pass for emeralds – were a present from Veronica. She decided not to correct herself.

For the first time their eyes really met. She and Vespasian had never been shy with one another; they were shy now.

'I'm frightened to touch you,' he admitted, very close and quiet. Frightened or not, she found he was looping up a strand of her hair on one finger to watch the light shimmer along it.

Caenis tossed her head to pull free, but she replied sensibly enough, 'I'm not used to you any more; you're not used to me.'

He shrugged. 'I'm just the same.'

He was so close that Caenis could see the intentions forming in his face; instinctively she put her hands on his shoulders as if to keep him at a distance. His face set.

247

'You are the Hero of Britain!' she scoffed. Conscience dissolved her. She was at least old enough now to ask directly for what she wanted. She intended him to know it was her choice. Her voice dropped. 'Would that Hero accept a kiss from an admirer?'

Vespasian frowned, evaluating the change in her mood.

Without waiting she leant forward and kissed him – a mere brush of the lips like a moth landing on a sleeper's face in the night. It was really to see what he would do. He closed his eyes briefly, but otherwise hardly moved.

The sensation of their kiss clung with alarming intensity even when she drew away. Vespasian prevented her moving again with one warm hand on her shoulder, his fingers catching in her hair. Caenis could hear the blood in her own veins. He looked desperately sad; at first she thought she had made a terrible mistake.

The mistake was in doubting him. Suddenly she could see how great his self-control had been. She glimpsed the moment when he broke. He began to draw close to kiss her conventionally, but it was too much for him. '*Oh lass!*'

Then her cheek banged against his as they hugged one another like people meeting on a quayside after a long separation in far distant countries, two people falling into one another's arms and holding each other tight as if they would never be able to let go.

After a while his breathing eased and she heard him whisper hoarsely, 'What can I say to you?'

Still locked in his embrace, never wanting it to end, Caenis closed her eyes. Buried in the braided edge on his tunic her face had crumpled. She would not let him see her misery, but he must know; he must be able to feel her shaking. 'I suppose the Hero of Britain has a great many women asking to go to bed with him?'

'Some.'

'And what about my old friend Vespasian?'

'Poor unimportant beggar – rather less!'

Caenis leant away so she could look at him. Her face was drawn. His too. 'Well, there's an offer here – if he wants it.'

She watched the shadows go out of his expression, to be

replaced by some tenderness that she could not bear to contemplate. He released her completely, with a small open-palmed gesture, but his hand found hers as at once they walked together to the bed.

XXXI

Caenis had begun to believe she could not do it.

Nothing was going to happen. The situation was too important, and she was still standing on her dignity. It was all going wrong. She felt lumpen like wood, an unresponsive trunk.

She had accepted it. She was content merely to be with him, content with whatever companionship there inevitably was, and yet despite herself she must have made some sound. Hearing her distress he stopped. 'Sorry.'

She realised he had been waiting for her. She kept perfectly still. He was not a man with whom she wanted to pretend.

Being careful to disturb nothing else, Vespasian stretched one arm to the small table at the side of the bed and gradually moved the tiny pottery lamp which gave the only light in the room. She realised, with misgivings, it was the lamp she hated, where a satyr and a faun were doing unspeakable things to each other around the air-hole and the wick. She was relieved he left it there.

In the slight increase of light, Vespasian brought his arm back and set his hand on her brow, shading her eyes while he searched for whatever she was thinking. He could not be sure whether, after all, he was entirely welcome. Caenis herself was experiencing belated doubt. Perhaps the truth was that even though she wanted him so badly she could not bear to admit how she felt. She must be still quarrelling with him for leaving her.

'Not doing very well, am I?'

Suddenly he was smiling. The intimate sunny grin he kept for his friends was inviting her to share his self-mockery, and she found it irresistible. She was already reabsorbing the familiar feel, the scent, the size, the warmth, the pleasure of him.

For Caenis he had always been a good-looking man. He had a wonderful face. The interplay of strain and amusement was fascinating; she could watch his concentration at work, then without warning he would brighten into a crackle of shared good humour. All the time those deep, steady eyes were seeking hers. He was a man of such passionate decency. It was impossible to deal with him in her normal mood of prickly resentment.

'It's me,' he told her softly. The tension went sliding from her. His straightforwardness reached out to her. 'You remember me.'

She remembered: her Sabine friend; the second half of her.

She felt her senses afloat at once, almost before he bent his head to kiss her and moved to start making love again. Her body began to answer his. When the moment came, they were together. When the moment came, it was with an intensity that seemed not to have diminished but increased with time, and experience, and their separate knowledge of triumph and loss.

Afterwards he stayed with her, in complete silence, for a long while. Even when he was compelled to move from her he would not speak. But he held her; he was still holding her when she plunged abruptly into sleep and when, many hours later, she awoke.

It was just before dawn. For a short period the hubbub around the city gate had faded as the carters and revellers dispersed to their beds, while the early morning streetsounds of bakers and labourers going to their work had yet to begin. Even the sick were sleeping now. In this silent room the lamp had long snuffed itself; there was the faintest shift in the dim quality of the natural light.

Only gradually did Caenis realise that she had woken more comfortable, warmer, more tranquilly rested than usual. Only slowly did she become aware that her pillow was Vespasian's firm chest and that she was trapped in utter security under the weight of his arm across her back and his hand at her breast. She lay motionless, but her eyelashes had been tickling his ribs; she felt his fingers intertwine in her hair, where it grew thickest at the back of her head, softening away any last shreds of tension from her neck. He was awake. He had been awake for perhaps an hour before.

'Titus; you're still here!'

'Mmm.'

He always woke in the early hours. At home he would rise and use this time to read or attend to his correspondence without interruptions while others slept. Here he had simply lain still, lost in thought, holding Caenis in his arms.

She snuggled closer but said dutifully, 'I shan't mind if you want to go.'

There was no change in the slow motion massaging the tendons of her neck. 'Wanted to say good morning to you first.'

Then she leant up on one elbow looking at him. 'Hello, Titus.'

'Hello, my lass.' In the grey light she could make out nothing of his face, but his voice was full of amusement. 'Oh, *Caenis*! . . . People will think we are mad.'

'People,' remarked Caenis tartly, 'don't think! Thank the gods none of them need know that you bought back my favours with a sack of Sabine apples and half a crate of plums.'

'If they find out your weakness, you could be swamped under punnets of soft fruit . . .' Vespasian sounded unusually dreamy. 'Rome soaking up raspberry juice like a must-cake pudding. Trolleyloads of apricots blocking the Sacred Way. Quagmires of quinces, pears piled like the Pannonian Alps – mmm!' He stopped speculating to allow Caenis to kiss him quiet. 'Blackberries – mmm! Mulberries – *mm-mmm!*'

She was still fretting about his public life. 'Do you want me to get up with you, Titus?'

His sudden roll caught her unawares as he swept her back against the pillows full length, lying above her in his most sensual embrace. 'I said,' he said, 'I wanted to say good morning to you first.'

Then Caenis stopped worrying about his waiting secretary at home; she recognised from his wicked tone that he

252

intended far more than a mere verbal greeting. She stopped worrying about anything, as Vespasian began once again to touch her where she needed to be touched and hold her as she wanted to be held. This time there was no difficulty. He knew as Caenis knew herself that he was, and that he would always be, welcome.

The next time she woke he was no longer with her, but her body and all her spirit sang with the joy of his having been there.

XXXII

The noise from the Praetorian Camp was now quite loud even though the whole house was orientated towards its inner courtyards. Light increased the disturbance, as somebody unkind unfastened a shutter. 'Morning, madam. Rise and shine!'

Caenis groaned. 'No, thanks. Good morning, Aglaus. I shall just lie here, oozing goodwill —'

Her steward frankly whistled. 'Goodwill! Things must be worse than I thought.' It was the first time Aglaus had been so curious about a guest that he wanted to greet the lady of the house first himself.

'Was somebody up to see to my friend?'

'Naturally. I keep an eye on Heroes in case they pinch the silver. Breakfast out in the peristyle; his suggestion. What an amazing man! I gather we'll be seeing him again.'

'I should think we may,' Caenis conceded cautiously. Swathed in crumpled counterpane she sat up.

'Every five minutes, no doubt!' Aglaus quipped freely. 'You don't want the breadrolls to go hard; I'll send you a girl.'

The colonnade outside her dining room surrounded a very small courtyard garden that for most of the day lay in heavy shadow, a place of wet, dank greens and elongated spindles of unhealthy creeper which was sad, though first thing in the morning it was streaming with sunlight. Caenis rarely ate breakfast so she was surprised today to find that her steward had laid a refectory table with a minor banquet of newly baked bread, cold meat and cheese. A banquet for two. There were also three lopsided carnations in a vase.

Caenis, who did not enjoy cheekiness so early in the day, bellowed, '*Aglaus!*' before she noticed somebody sitting on a stool.

A burly figure had his feet in a shrub-pot, while he corrected a dictation tablet with a stylus. When she appeared, he tucked the stylus behind his ear and grinned at her. There was no sign of his secretary, though the man had obviously been here to bring the Flavian correspondence. Vespasian was scribbling away as if her garden was his normal morning workplace. Her Sabine friend was surprisingly well organised.

Aglaus poked his head out of a window, answering her yell. 'Leave us in peace, Aglaus,' Caenis countermanded herself placidly. The steward smirked at Vespasian – they were already allies – and duly obeyed. 'Titus.'

'Expected, surely?' Vespasian teased.

'Well, tomorrow perhaps,' Caenis tried to appear cool. 'Tonight even, if you're desperately keen – or just desperate. Hardly for breakfast.'

Vespasian left his work on the stool and took his place on a wooden bench at the table. 'Mind?' She joined him, sitting alongside, saying nothing. 'Looks good. Plotted it with your man. Notice the ample supply of cold meat.'

She had noticed.

They began to eat, Vespasian enjoying himself, Caenis more reluctant. Above them her pet finch chortled in the sunlight in a fine wire cage.

'Well?' she demanded. Vespasian served to her cheese which she did not want; she ate it anyway in case he had paid for this spread himself.

'Told you; something I wanted to say.'

Caenis laughed. 'I rather assumed you had done that.'

'Sidetracked, lady!' Grinning, he licked his fingers, which were sticky with honey from the rim of his cup, then reached out to lay his hand over hers, winsome with memories of last night. She waited. No one ever rushed him. He resumed his meal. 'Does your birdie get the crumbs?'

'If you like.'

Vespasian stood up and fed the finch. He chirped back at it for a while, as Caenis went on chewing; she was hungrier than she had thought. Before he sat down again he came closer and kissed her, once, on the cheek, leaning round her from behind. 'Hello again.'

He returned to his place, checked himself, walked back, thoughtfully kissed her other cheek like a man making everything equal, then smoothed up the hair on the nape of her neck where it was turned over and pinned; automatically she bent her head under his hand so he was able to kiss her lightly all round from just beside one earlobe to the other. Caenis quivered at his enjoyment. Still teasing, he sat down again with a relaxed sigh. 'Well! This is exceptionally pleasant.'

She could no longer bear the suspense. 'Flavius Vespasianus, you have suborned both my steward and my singing bird; this is obviously part of some scheme. Are you asking me to become your mistress again? I can tell you want a favour; you always did feed me first.'

He laughed. 'Blunt, bold, and up to a point astute!'

It seemed to Caenis that the subject had been fairly thoroughly agreed the night before, and the morning after too. 'Oh love; not after twenty years?' she mocked gently. 'The same woman! What is this – sheer laziness, or reluctance to reinvest?'

Vespasian grunted. He was neither offended nor impressed by her frankness. 'Set in my ways. And I chose you to last.'

'Well, I'm no spring chicken nowadays. You chose me when the hen-run was sprightlier.'

He grinned wickedly. 'Spring chickens are very bland to mature taste. For an old broiler you can hold your own – I'm a grandfather myself.'

'Your daughter died; I'm sorry. Were you very fond of her?'

'Fond of them all. Even Domitian, though he's a bit of a brat. Needs careful handling. And he's on his own a lot. I tend to forget there are more than ten years between him and Titus: separate generations; can't expect them to be as close as Sabinus and me.'

It struck Caenis, even then, before she realised just how close young Titus and his father were, that if the elder son kept his reputation for charm and talent, the younger one would spend all his childhood trying to catch up with an impossible goal. Titus was the type to attract a great deal of

256

attention. As an ex-slave she knew about running life's races from behind.

She felt this conversation was straying from its intended path, though she was still puzzled what it was really supposed to be about. She covered what was left of the food with napkins, then turned her back against the table, lifting her face to the sun.

'How is your brother?'

'Same as ever.'

'Just back from abroad?'

'Offered the city prefecture . . . When he was still in Moesia I wrote to him that I intended seeing you. He said –'

'What?'

'He didn't think I should rely on getting anything to eat!'

Caenis was about to chortle, but something in Vespasian's face stopped the laughter in her throat. The brothers must have been discussing more than food.

'Caenis. Caenis, I have done my duty. Good family man, two healthy sons, decent husband – duty done.'

For no obvious reason she was shivering.

'There were women?' she asked drily. 'Well; I know there were. There is the famous story of the one who squeezed four thousand sesterces out of you.'

Veronica had told her: some floozie declared she was in love with him, persuaded Vespasian into bed, and wheedled the money from him when she left. The story had whistled round Rome not because of that, but because word got out too that when his hard-tried accountant asked ruefully how to show the loss in his ledger, his master had retorted 'Jot it down under "Canoodling for Vespasian"!' Since Romans kept their accounts as documents open for public inspection, this bold move meant more heartache for a self-respecting ledger-man.

Vespasian looked up cheerfully. 'I keep being told that story. I can't even remember what she was like.'

They were both thinking of the money Caenis had lent him. She wondered how *that* showed in the ledger. She damned him without malice: 'I suppose you thought she was worth it!'

'Suppose I did!' he admitted, unabashed. 'Must have been unusually flush with cash at the time. Anyway,' he went on, his tone jarring as it sometimes did, 'you were no Vestal Virgin. What about that nasty piece of work Anicius who used to boast he slept with you?'

'*Boasted*, did he?' Startled, Caenis braved it out.

'Who wouldn't, my darling?' Vespasian caressed her quietly. She caught her breath. 'All right,' he said. 'There were some women. None of them was important. Not like you. You always were. I hope you knew that – I hope you still know it, lass.' She stared at the table. 'You know perfectly well,' he insisted, 'that was why I never tried to come.'

'Perhaps,' she muttered, more subdued than usual. Whatever became of them now, she would never be easy mentioning those years they had spent apart.

It was then that Vespasian proved he was a most amazing man. He waited until she looked up again, then began what was to be the strangest interview of her life.

'Live with me, Caenis,' he urged her quietly.

Not all the training in the Palace school could have prepared her for that. Caenis felt her jaw sag. '*Live with you?*' She was flabbergasted. 'Live with you *where?*'

Much as she knew him, he astonished her. 'In my house.' It was unbelievable.

The man sat, amidst the ruins of their al fresco breakfast – as he would sit, if she did live with him, every day – gazing at her as peacefully as if he had just asked her to read out the election results from the *Gazette*. They were sharing a table of the most casual kind. He must know she was happy. She had asked him for nothing. Yet he chose to offer this. 'That was what I wanted to say.' He was perfectly serious.

Caenis sat in silence while the world rocked, and every assumption on which she had built her bitter life was smashed. Caenis believed: it was impossible to win; it was impossible ever to regain what you had lost; life was unequal; affection was temporary; men took; men left and did not return; women lost, grieved, longed, made do with diminishing faith and fading strength . . .

With his astounding demand Vespasian had disproved it all.

'Oh you can't!' she managed at last to gasp. 'A senator and Consul – set up house with a freedwoman; not even one of his own? Oh Titus! Why not just marry again? Take a discreet mistress? Me if you want; you must know that I would –'

He was expecting this shocked protest from her. He stayed immobile, saying calmly, 'Caenis, we were strong-minded enough to follow the rules; we are strong-minded enough to break them. I am asking for you.'

'*What* are you asking?'

'Plain enough: live with me. Share my life; share yours with me.'

For a moment she could not bear to let him see her face.

When she dropped her hands, Caenis started briskly to return their relationship to a normal course: 'This is unnecessary. I would be quite content to have some regular arrangement. You don't need to cause social apoplexy. There are women a man sleeps with casually, and women he takes solemnly to wife; there is no middle way. It's not respectable. It's against the law –'

'It is not. It's against the law to marry you. If I could – I will tell you this now – I would have done it years ago. Now, the snobs won't particularly like it, but I have performed my obligations; I can choose. "Somebody to bully and a half-decent companion for your old age." You said it. Caenis, please: have me.'

She tried one last feeble protest: 'What about your family?'

'Ah yes; the family!' In that deliberate way he had thought it all through. 'Well, Titus is clean and well-tempered around the house, though he does practise the harp sometimes; Domitian is obstreperous and he's going to need attention. Sabinus seems grumpy but he's easily led. His wife thinks you are wonderful; always did. You will be one of the family – that is what I intend – so you won't expect good manners. You, however, may be your vinegary self in return. You will have to be in charge. My role as head of the household will be to disappear to the Senate whenever

259

there's a row: you'll have to cope all by yourself, of course. Normal home life with an antique hero – no money, no slaves, dismal food, poor conversation and endless bickering. I expect you to be a drudge, a nurse, an entertainer, a very sharp accountant and a provider of much physical comfort for me . . . I have every confidence in you, Caenis.'

Caenis wondered whether this speech, which was not obviously preplanned or overrehearsed, rated applause. She sighed, feeling helpless.

His voice fell to that low, benevolent tone that churned her stomach. 'Do you want a promise about how much you mean to me, and what I'll do for you?'

'Don't be disgusting; we're better friends than that!'

He laughed happily.

There was sunshine on her face, birdsong overhead. Someone in the house had begun to rattle a broom around the dining room in the normal daily routine. She rubbed her temples with both hands.

Vespasian offered wryly, 'I hope the unusual request speaks for itself.'

'Oh it does! You have spotted I come with a set of silver knives and the best steward in Rome –'

'It's your wonderful knives I want, of course! Are there matching salad-servers too? . . . Will you take me on then?'

'You and I?'

'You and I. I knew a girl once, Caenis – odd little scrap, fierce as a lion, didn't care who she was rude to, nice girl, very good in bed, a true friend – who said: life would be what we made it for ourselves.'

For the first time since he fed the finch he got to his feet and came to her, holding out his hands. Caenis was trembling. He always knew how to reduce her to rubble, then say exactly the right thing. 'Oh I have missed you!' declared Vespasian in a low voice; she was lost.

With her hands twined in his but still seated, Caenis spoke, once, what sooner or later she would have to say. Better now, than in some unrelated quarrel afterwards. 'I have lived the best years of my life, and lived them without you.'

260

He did not flinch. 'Agreed.'

'I built my own life.'

'Yes.'

He drew her to her feet. Coming to him, Caenis said, 'I missed you too. I missed you more than you or anybody else will ever understand. I have to tell you this. For the sake of what I have been, what I endured, what I have done. This has to be acknowledged between us now.'

Gravely he let her speak; probably he did not fear anything she might say because he knew she would always be just. He did not even agitate for her answer. Perhaps he knew what it would be. Then because even now Caenis could not bear to let him see her cry, she stayed silent for longer than she wanted. She had to struggle to control herself but in the end she managed in her calm, trained, competent voice: 'If it is what you want, yes I will come.'

His reaction was the last thing she expected: she saw suddenly, there were tears in his eyes.

'Titus? Oh *love*!'

He was smiling the small pale smile that she had seen once before when he left her, though only now with blinding recognition did she finally understand it. She saw him swallow as he recovered himself. 'Sentimental old beggar. Excuse me; I really didn't think you would.'

Faced with an emergency, Caenis was at once herself: 'Frankly, if I thought that you felt sure of me, I don't suppose I would agree.'

Then as he laughed once more in that delighted way, she remembered. It was Crete all over again. In public life the next step after consul was a provincial governorship.

'You are due for a province. Agrippina can't debar you for ever. You will be going abroad!' Life never changed.

Last time she had been fending him off; then they were so young they had years heaped like treasures in spoilheaps ahead of them. This time she was in his arms; he knew exactly how she felt. This time she could let herself feel his devotion to her – and to let him go now would be unbearable.

Titus Flavius Vespasianus muttered a country curse. 'I seem to have explained myself badly; or perhaps my assumptions were impertinent. When I asked you to live with me what I meant was that barring riot or rebellion, where I go I hope you will come too.'

Caenis could hardly believe it. 'One day you will be governor of Africa; and I –'

'You will be the governor's lady,' he said. 'Of course!'

XXXIII

Sometimes the most major events take place so quietly. Caenis was to live with Vespasian: it was as simple as that.

There were one or two riffles. There was a brief moment of tension the first time she went to Reate. She had been introduced to the servants, who seemed if anything more docile and pleased to see her than the high-handed experts with whom Aglaus had peopled her own home. In the house she had spotted the marks of long-term financial tension: not quite enough furniture, hangings pushed to last half a decade beyond their natural life, even items that were new all faintly drab as if years of having no money made it feel sinful to invest in anything that was genuinely attractive. Caenis did not mind. She was a woman who enjoyed tackling problems.

She had been sitting quietly with Vespasian. He was smiling at her. He tended to smile a great deal in private now; they were both as light-headed as rapturous young things. Then the door crashed open. (Caenis wondered how often the door hinges in Flavian homes had to be renewed.) The two boys, Titus and Domitian, burst into the room.

'*Aha!*' From what Vespasian had already told her Caenis knew enough to realise that the mere fact they were obviously conspiring boded badly.

Their heroic papa had started to look unusually diffident. 'Aha!' he retorted, with boisterous fatherly cheer. Then Titus strode across the floor in the full dignity of outraged seventeen, while Domitian ran alongside, a pugnacious six-year-old who was silently egging his elder brother on. It was Titus who had exclaimed. Domitian was running too fast to speak. 'Our noble papa – *and a lady friend!*'

It was plain that they knew her intended position. Vespasian must have made some formal announcement. They had discussed it hotly amongst themselves. They were bent on demanding that this situation be renegotiated on lines that better suited them. Boys do like to be respectable.

They had not until that moment known who their father's mistress was.

Caenis gracefully turned; her eyebrows arched in apparent mild surprise. Titus stopped. He clapped his hand to his head in frank and blissful amazement. He looked well. Better still, shining with delight. 'Oh, but you said you did not know him any more!'

'We renewed our acquaintance,' Caenis smiled. Titus was no longer any threat. He adored her. He always would.

'Come here!' said Vespasian cheerfully to the little one, pulling him into the security of that great arm. 'Now watch Titus realise that his old father has snaffled his special turtledove from under his nose.'

Since Titus was by now saying nothing Domitian, who was too young to be sensitive to immediate change, piped up aggressively, 'Is this to be my stepmother?' in tones of disgust.

Before Vespasian could speak, Caenis answered the child calmly, 'If you are thinking that you would not like it, Domitian, let me tell you at once, I should not like it either. No; I am not,' she assured him. 'So you don't have to hate me, and I shall not feel obliged to be wicked to you.'

The boy stared. They would never be friends, but he knew that temporarily at least Caenis had beaten him.

Vespasian, who evidently fell into the rough-and-tumble category of fathers, engaged Domitian in a minor bout of punch-bag scuffling. Whether this reassured anybody Caenis could not tell. Certainly Domitian himself wriggled under his father's arm as soon as he could escape, in order to demand of Titus, 'What shall we do?'

Pulling the stiff enraged figure from his father, Titus stooped down to fix his brother's eye. 'We are going to welcome this lady to our house.'

'You said –'

'It was a mistake.'

'Does that mean,' persisted Domitian, genuinely puzzled, 'we have to be polite?'

Titus gripped his brother by one tight fist. He walked the curly-headed tot, who looked much more appealing than he ever was, to where Caenis sat.

'Yes,' said Titus, before he gravely kissed her cheek and made Domitian do the same. 'It's a democratic vote: two to one against you in the other voting-urn – Father and me.'

'You *agree* with Papa? Why?'

'Little brother, she once saved my life.'

'Sweet, aren't they?' grinned their proud father.

Caenis pursed her mouth. 'Wonderful! And both so like their papa.'

There was comment on their relationship, at least initially. Veronica said, switching her opinion as sweetly illogical as ever, 'I saw it coming years ago. Now watch yourself, girl; at your time of life this could be an expensive mistake.'

'You have to admire him,' Caenis told her levelly.

'What – for taking his old mistress back? It stinks! I admire you, for accepting him.'

'It shows that I think he's worth it.'

'It shows he's a complete worm and you're a sucker. With no need to put himself out again, he gets himself a treasure – a good manager, clever and amusing, an armful any man would envy –'

'A canteen of cutlery, a good set of Greek bowls, cheap shorthand, and no risk any longer of having ragamuffin children.' Caenis spoke with a deliberate lightness which would prove to Veronica that she knew all the implications. Then, more benevolent than Veronica had ever seen her in thirty years, she handed her friend a small object which she took from a clip on her belt.

'Whatever's that?'

It was an old iron key. From a nation whose iron-masters and brass-founders were of the highest calibre, this was a pitiful specimen. It was two inches long, with a bent stem and missing one of its rusty teeth; it hung from a short piece of twisted leather thong that was greasy and blackened with age; an unsavoury toggle, possibly amber but probably some grimmer fossil, was knotted at the farther end.

265

Caenis explained: 'What you have in your hand is a symbolic gesture of the sentimental Sabine kind. I shall never be married with the witnesses and auguries, he won't take me in torchlight procession to his house, his servants will not greet me with fire and salt when I arrive. But there used to be a tradition – most people don't bother any more – that a Roman ceremonially handed the keys of his house to his bride as a sign that she was now in charge of his domestic affairs.'

'So?' demanded Veronica curiously, eyeing askance the grizzly little relic that still lay on her palm.

'That is the key to Vespasian's store-cupboard,' Caenis reported. Veronica hastily handed it back.

Their living together hardly merited public notice. Vespasian had been right. Because he had done all society required, society took a lenient view when he did that which – in theory – ought to be condemned. Besides, almost from the first day their partnership appeared to everyone as they saw it themselves: the inevitable way for Caenis and Vespasian to live. There was no fuss. There were few confrontations. Vespasian now held such a substantial reputation that an act of open eccentricity actually enhanced his position. Rome, which had bound itself in edicts and regulations, admired a man with the self-confidence to stand out for principles of his own in his personal affairs.

Vespasian was still living quietly in country retirement, which helped. He kept his house in Rome, since a consular senator had to appear from time to time, unless he wanted to be reprimanded by the Emperor – or worse. But he spent as much time as possible at Reate, and that suited everyone. His provincial appointment was continually deferred. Nobody told him that the delay was due to the enmity of Agrippina, but he drew the obvious conclusion. He had become more of an outsider than ever, not that he seemed to mind too much. He was still ambitious enough to want the post, but dreaded the expense of it.

The Emperor's mother had enjoyed a brief spell of unprecedented influence, but caused such outrage by her assumption of almost equal powers with Nero and her improper public appearances as his consort that a year after his accession Nero was able to insist that she withdrew from the main Palace complex and took up residence in the House of Livia. This freed Nero to indulge in artistic pursuits, sexual licence with male and female conquests, all-day banquets, gladiatorial shows, and a fairly humane political policy encouraged by his mentors, the philosopher Seneca and the Praetorian commander Burrus.

His alleged incest with Agrippina was long past. Eventually his irritation at her cloying mother-love and her dominating ambition reached the point where in the grand Claudian tradition he determined to be rid of her. Exile to a small island seemed insufficient; she had been exiled before, and proved she could survive and return worse than ever. At first he tormented her with lawsuits and encouraged her to take unwanted holidays. It took him four years of such scheming to work up the courage for a serious attack. Then while Agrippina was staying at Antonia's huge seaside villa at Bauli he managed to dispose of her – though not without a farcical series of failed attempts. He failed to poison her (she kept taking antidotes), or drown her (when her galley fell to pieces in the Bay of Naples she swam to safety), or to crush her under a collapsible ceiling (someone had warned her it was there). He stopped being subtle. He simply had her put to the sword: one more of Antonia's grandchildren violently destroyed. But the accusation of matricide was one Nero would find harder to shake off than he first realised.

Freed from Agrippina's jealousy, Vespasian began to spend more time in Rome again, and eventually – though not immediately – he was awarded his province. As Narcissus had long ago promised, he was to be governor of Africa.

'Of course you're heart-broken, Caenis,' Veronica consoled her. 'Still, you should get a nice rest from him while he trips off to the hot spots. Will he let you stay in his house while he's away?' She had phrased it tactfully, since she was well aware that the house Caenis owned herself was far more elegant and comfortable.

'I'm going to Africa with him.'

Even Veronica, who had seen a great deal of human nature

and of life, was nonplussed. 'Well! Make sure you keep your lease on your own house – and insist that miser pays your fare.'

'No need. As part of the governor's household, the travel pass for transporting me to Africa will be provided, with the customary bad grace, by the State Treasury. I count as one of the governor's travelling chests.'

'You really know how to make a fool of yourself for a man,' Veronica told her frankly.

By the time Caenis and Vespasian reached Africa their lives had grown into one another inextricably. Their domestic partnership was by then some years old and their relationship had assumed a solid permanence. They lived together, at the same pace, in the same style, sharing the same debates and humour, locked close in body and thought. They became a single unit, satisfied with one another and with life.

Of Vespasian's governorship in Africa three things were remembered afterwards: first, despite the opportunities for profit, Vespasian came home no richer than he went; in fact his credit was used up and he had been keeping his bank account buoyant by commercial flirtations, mostly involving wet fish. Second, it was grudgingly agreed that his term of office ran with dignity and justice. Third, the only sour incident recorded was when the people of Hadrumetum rioted and pelted him with turnips.

What went unrecorded – perhaps because though just it was not dignified – was how the Governor of Africa cursed the lively temperament of the people of Hadrumetum but managed to capture two of their turnips. He took them home to present to Caenis with his good-humoured grin. Caenis, straight-faced, had them made into soup, which the Governor ate with great gusto, particularly since he had not had to pay for it.

XXXIV

Nothing lasts.

They had enjoyed fourteen years under Claudius; then there were fourteen years of Nero to be endured. For most of that reign Caenis lived with Vespasian. Although in political terms the time seemed endless to those who did not court the Emperor's favour, for her it flew by.

They had achieved almost a decade of quiet domesticity, which was a long time. It was longer than most marriages survived before death or divorce intervened; it was much longer than many people even hoped to stick things out. Cautious as she was, she had begun to believe she could hope to end her days living like this.

Then, when Flavius Vespasianus was fifty-seven – late for any man to embark on a new phase in his life – he made the mistake of accompanying Nero on his fabled tour of Greece. It was a musical tour. Nero by then had ceased to heed his friends' warnings that stage and arena appearances, whether as a charioteer or a singer, would offend public opinion to a damaging degree. He now saw himself as an artiste; nobody dared to scoff at him openly, while the flatterers who surrounded him encouraged his flight from reality.

Vespasian was cultured. He always knew exactly what entertainment was available in Rome, because he liked Caenis to go. In his own house he had been observed to pause in the atrium for ten minutes at a time if he could hear someone singing, though that was because the person who sang in Vespasian's house was Caenis. He was not smitten with the sound of the lyre; in particular he hated it played badly. So going on an extended foreign tour with Nero was a mistake.

Titus came with them to Greece. By then Titus was twenty-six and *he* hated the tour with the frustration of a man who had a good ear, and who could himself play well, although unlike the Emperor he would not dream of performing upon a public stage.

Before they went to Africa, Titus had joined the army as a tribune in Germany. Vespasian long cherished a hope that his son would do his military service in Britain, best of all in the Second Augusta, his own legion, or at least the Ninth Hispana which was commanded by Petilius Cerialis who had been married to his daughter, Flavia. In the event they were all relieved Titus started in Germany instead. In Eastern Britain there had been a series of administrative atrocities, which Vespasian described in a short phrase that Caenis chose to interpret as a military term (he probably did learn it in the army but she guessed it was not a regular expression of command in line of march). Eventually the Queen of the Iceni, outraged by the dispossession of her chief tribesmen from their estates, her own disinheritance as her husband's heir, and the rape of her two teenaged daughters by a Roman finance officer's thugs, swept through the province in a ferocious rebellion. The scale and savagery were appalling. For a time it appeared Britain was completely lost. Three major towns were burnt to the ground, thousands of settlers lost their lives, and the Ninth Hispana were ambushed so disastrously that Cerialis and a few rags of cavalry only just escaped alive.

Titus subsequently did lead the German detachments sent to support the decimated British legions during the period of recovery. He became popular in Britain. He and his father exchanged an interesting series of letters on the subject of Empire and provincial government.

By the time they all went to Greece Titus had done a further stint as a quaestor and formally entered the Senate. He had been married twice, widowed once and once divorced; he had a baby daughter, Julia. He had been practising as a barrister, though more to make himself a name in Rome than because he was particularly eloquent. His brother, Domitian, was approaching sixteen; during their Greek trip he was left behind at school.

By this time Vespasian himself had become an elder statesman figure, respected for his military past though still disparaged for his unashamed country background. His brother, Sabinus, was regarded in Rome as the more substantial figure. Sabinus had been Governor of Moesia for seven years (though Moesia was not exactly the best-known province in the Empire) and had been Prefect of the City, a very significant post in Rome, to which he was now appointed for the second time. His wife had died. It was a source of regret to Caenis.

She and Vespasian still lived quietly. These were dark days, reminiscent of the brief dreadful reign of Caligula – but lasting much longer. Nero had begun well as a ruler, under the influence of Seneca and Burrus, though now he had murdered both. Seeking greater extravagance he had first attempted to strangle, then divorced, then executed his blameless young wife, Octavia. He married his fabulously beautiful mistress Poppaea, then kicked her to death, probably by accident, while she was pregnant.

'Sort of little mistake anyone could make!' Vespasian groaned. '*Whoops!* Careless bloody monster! Lass, was there ever a family so extravagant with other people's lives?'

There was worse to come. When Octavia's elder sister, Claudia Antonia, refused to take Poppaea's place as his wife, Nero accused her of rebellion and executed her too. In this way Caenis lost all those to whom she owed a duty as relations of her patroness, Antonia. The Flavians were now in every sense her family.

There was a terrible fire in Rome. Nero was blamed, though few dared breathe the accusation openly. Vespasian and Caenis had been away in the country; they returned to find that after six whole days and nights of conflagration the ancient heart of the city, including many sacred monuments, had been completely swept away while much elsewhere was seriously damaged. The first outbreak had raged from near the Circus Maximus around the Palatine and Caelian Hills, then a second conflagration began north of the Capitol. Shops, mansions, blocks of modest apartments and temples were destroyed, and part of the Palace too. Nothing remained there except rubble and ash. The fire had halted at the foot of the Esquiline. Vespasian's mansion on the

Quirinal was safe; so too the house that Caenis owned outside the Nomentana Gate.

'That place of yours could be a good investment with so many people homeless!' chortled Vespasian, apparently teasing.

Caenis only smiled. She never discussed with anybody what she would do – or not do – with her house. Vespasian might have asked her to sell it, but even when he himself was reduced to investing in contracts for the supply of Sabine mules in order to fund his public career, he never imposed on her.

Now she wondered if he was gazing at her with particular amusement, though it was hard to tell, for his face often lit sweetly when he stopped what he was doing to look up at her. It had become a habit; she thought nothing of it any more, merely accepted this as fortune's unexpected gift.

Depressed by the devastation in Rome, they went back to the country. So they missed, and were glad to miss, Nero's retaliation against the Christians whom he chose to blame for starting the fire. Sabinus, who was still City Prefect, saw it: the wholesale massacres in Nero's Circus on the Vatican Plain, the men and women torn apart by wild beasts, the human torches burning all night in the Palace Gardens. He heard the screams; he smelt the pitch and seared human flesh. He possessed the Flavian capacity for intense private feeling. He said little, but was deeply affected.

Nero's rebuilding of Rome typified the contradictions of his reign. The city itself was newly planned with its monuments restored, while new building regulations specified ways in which private householders must guard against fire. The measures were sensible. The new streetplans were elegant (though everyone hated them). Much of the cost was subsidised by the Emperor.

At the same time, this was Nero's opportunity to build the massive new palace complex which he called his Golden House. It enclosed whole farms, vineyards, and a monstrous lake – all in the centre of Rome. In fact the heart of the city was completely taken over by his new residence. The grounds contained a colonnade a third of a mile long. The

272

interior contained a revolving dining room, and other suites both private and public of breath-taking magnificence. The decor included some of the most exquisite painted frescos ever accomplished, with delicate trails of flowers, fauns, cherubs, swags and lattice-work, created with meticulous artistry in the freshest colours, and even executed on corridors so tall that it was impossible to pick out the fine detail with the naked eye. There were marble vestibules, ceilings of fretted ivory, lavish use of gold leaf, and incredible encrustations of jewels. Outside the opulent entrance the Forum was dominated by the Colossus, a gilded statue of the Emperor wearing a sunray crown, which was one hundred and twenty feet high.

The total cost of the Palace would be enormous; even more bitterly resented was the fact that to create this phenomenon Nero dispossessed many other landowners, who had already lost their property in the Fire; their anger contributed much to his downfall. When he had created his flagrant affront to the austere Roman tradition, he crowed that at last he could begin to live.

Vespasian said the good thing about the Golden House was that it was so amazing it took your mind off the appalling food and the length of the public dinners, some of which went on from noon to night. Also (said Caenis), it stopped you wondering what potions from the poisoner Lucusta the Emperor might have slipped into your drink.

This Emperor was not mad as Caligula had been mad. He was extravagant, vicious, self-obsessed, murderous and vain. But Nero was in command of his wits. Caenis judged him the worse for it: he lacked any excuse of delusion or dementia.

It was two years after the Fire that his interests in chariot-racing and public singing contests brought Nero to Greece. He was to maintain that only the Greeks appreciated his voice; that bore out many Romans' low opinion of the Greeks. After one abortive attempt to organise a visit, which he cancelled on some whim, he finally arrived to tour the main cities which sponsored musical events. In fact he also toured those whose contests were not due that year, compelling the festivals to be brought forward to accommodate his appearance whatever disruption it caused to the formal calendar.

By the time he came home he would have collected more than a thousand victory wreaths, including one for a chariot race in which he fell out and never even completed the course. Nero grew so adept at announcing his own victories that he even put himself down for the competition for heralds – which of course he also won. Greek judges demonstrated a keen understanding of imperial requirements. The Emperor was doing his best. He followed a rigorous professional training programme. He lay down with weights on his chest to strengthen his voice. He complied with every rule of etiquette, suffered agonies of stage fright and awaited the judges' verdicts with a solemnly bowed head even after it had become blatantly apparent what the verdict would always be.

Those who accompanied him entered the spirit too – if they wanted to avoid strict penalties. Everyone of consequence was expected to attend imperial recitals, and once they turned up they were forbidden to leave until the end. Spies were stationed to check not just who was there, but whether they appeared to be enjoying themselves. Caenis endured this better than most; apart from the fact she had a well-trained face, she chatted to the spies about their work. Others were not so adept at survival. Men were arrested climbing out of the stadium over the back wall. Women gave birth. People died; people *pretended* to have died in order to obtain the relief of being carried out.

It was, therefore, doubly unfortunate when a prominent member of the Emperor's own retinue displayed a clear reluctance to applaud. Sometimes at private functions he got up and left the room. Sometimes he never turned up in the first place. Even in Italy he had already been in trouble when he began to nod at one of Nero's earliest recitals and was only saved by a reprimand from a freedman who generously woke him up with a sharp prod.

But character will out. And at one of Nero's endlessly dreary public recitations in Greece Vespasian went soundly to sleep.

XXXV

Vespasian was dismissed from court. They had to flee to the hills. As Titus said later, it seemed a drastic way to work up a good suntan ready for the desert.

In fact the situation was desperately serious and Vespasian became unusually upset. In case he doubted what might happen, Nero had just recalled the great general Corbulo from Armenia, having him greeted the moment he landed in Greece with a suggestion that since he was about to be executed he might want to commit suicide. And that was the reward for too much success.

Faced with a harpist in a huff, Vespasian had tried to restrain himself, but after his disgrace there were splendid scenes outside the audience chamber, culminating with the overwrought Vespasian crying to a supercilious chamberlain, 'What can I do? Where shall I go?'

'Oh go to Hades!' responded the chamberlain. He was having a trying time arranging this tour without ludicrous ex-Consuls maddening the imperial musician with sheer bad manners.

Vespasian ruled out Hades; he decided on a family holiday, which he grumbled would be just as bad. Knowing that his unguarded drowsiness had this time placed him in danger of his life – and could have damaged his son too – he whisked Caenis and Titus to a remote mountain village. The village was, however, not so remote that he would be out of reach of the court if anybody wanted him back.

They had a wonderful holiday even though Vespasian was daily expecting Nero's order for him to commit suicide. Titus suffered the most and was given to outbursts of mild frustration at breakfast: 'Ah Greece! Its monuments are fabulous, but its mountain villages are pretty poky! You should have been there with him, Caenis. He never nods off if he

275

knows you're in the top tier keeping an eye on him. For one thing he keeps turning round to wink at you.'

Caenis listened for a moment to the clunk-clunking of the goat bells, the tireless cicadas, the sporadic whistling of shepherds in the distance and nearer at hand a few contented hens. 'Titus, I am a music-lover! It was a dangerous fiasco and I am not sure I could have kept my temper with anyone – including your fool of a papa. How fortunate that my uncharacteristic headache had compelled me to stay in my room.'

Titus grinned happily. 'Well, I knew he wasn't safe. I remember when I took up the harp myself he told me that from then on I was on my own in life – and by the way, I never want to see another little dish of hard green olives.'

'I've just served you some, my darling; eat them and be quiet. Vespasian, your son is teasing you.'

Vespasian, who was reading a letter, grunted.

Titus ventured, more cautiously, 'Father, I never really understood why you came on the concert tour. It was obviously an exercise in regal self-indulgence. We could have tossed dice on whether Nero offended you mortally, or you him.'

Vespasian sniffed this time.

'Playing his part in public life,' scoffed Caenis.

'By nodding off?' Titus guffawed. 'Well! I'm going for a walk. Yet again.' There was not much else to do.

'Give me a kiss then,' Caenis commanded.

Titus was on the point of leaving his couch, when there came a sudden commotion outside the dining room. Before anyone could move, through the doors from the terrace burst a terrified plough-ox that had broken its yoke and run amok. An aimless horn swept a table lamp to the ground with a sickening crash. Caenis, who was not keen on animals even in their proper place, stayed perfectly still. The ox dusted a shelf with the frowsty clump of its tail.

The room was small; the ox was huge. The servants who had been about to clear away breakfast all took to their heels. Caenis noticed even Titus swallowed. Vespasian looked over the top of his letter; the ox snorted then dribbled menacingly, as its frantic hooves scrabbled on the tiled floor.

'Hello, boy!' Vespasian greeted him. 'Lost your way?'

'Oh my love,' scolded Caenis, 'I wish you wouldn't invite your friends for breakfast.'

The ox took one step farther into the room; she picked up a spoon, the only implement to hand. She wondered if smacking it hard on the nose would make it go away. They could hear the approaching, panicky voices of the tillers of Greek fields who had lost their angry but valuable animal.

'Dear heart,' Caenis murmured seductively to Vespasian, 'do tell us what to do.'

'Trying to think of a plan,' he mused. 'Difficult logistics.'

'Well, you're the country boy!' Caenis snapped.

'The poor creature's frightened,' Titus sympathised.

'*I'm* frightened,' said Caenis, 'and I live here, so I take precedence! I'd like to go to my room and do a decent bit of sewing so perhaps one of you men could be masterful and sort out this incident.'

'I've never seen you do sewing,' Vespasian commented in wry surprise, then he continued talking amiably to the ox.

The tillers of Greek fields were peering in horror around the shattered doors. The ox filled the room. There was no space to turn it round. The tillers of fields plainly regretted having come to look.

'Shoo!' snarled Caenis crossly to the ox. 'Go home.'

Then the ox, charmed perhaps by the quality of Flavian repartee, suddenly advanced towards Vespasian, bowed its great head and sank to one knee as if it were very tired.

The chattering of the tillers of fields dropped to an awe-struck hum. Even Caenis and Titus looked impressed.

Titus said, 'You have to hand it to him. For the son of a tax-collector he knows how to bring a damn great beastie down at his feet!'

Removing an ox backwards from a small decorative room requires great skill. It was a skill which the owners of the runaway ox possessed only fragmentarily. The two Flavians provided a rope and offered them much sound advice based on military tactics and higher mathematics. By the time everyone had gone it was lunchtime and the room was wrecked.

Vespasian finally allowed himself to say, 'By the gods, I thought we came out of that rather well.'

Titus lay on his back on a bench. 'Something to write home to Domitian anyway. I think I might faint now if nobody minds.'

'Symbol of power, an ox, you know,' Vespasian winked, knowing Caenis would be annoyed.

'You are living in disgrace on a mountain top, eating fruit,' she quipped nastily. 'The only powerful thing round here is the smell of manure. Tell me, why is breakfast with the Flavians always so nerve-racking?'

Since the ox had gone home and she was still holding the spoon, she smacked Vespasian with the spoon instead.

Not long afterwards he was summoned back to the court. Knowing how Caenis felt about breakfast he waited to tell her until they were at lunch.

'I'm coming with you,' she said at once.

'No, you're not. If this means Nero has thought up a suitable way of executing a man who snores through his songs – slow torture by bagpipes, I dare say, or drowning in a water-organ – then I'll have to endure it – but no usurping Claudian with his brains in his backside is going to get his hands on my family!'

'In law I'm not your family,' Caenis commented quietly. Vespasian often swore though not so often in front of her because the Sabines were famously old-fashioned and in all cultures being old-fashioned means denying women any fun; but he said tersely, 'Sod the law.'

Caenis nonetheless went with him.

He was spared strangling with a lyre string.

They found themselves presented with a mansion in which to lodge; they were invited to dine with the Emperor; the chamberlain now greeted them with oozing respect. Vespasian was welcomed by Nero himself with flattery, good wishes, and every sign of amity. Vespasian had dreamt that his family would start to prosper from the day Nero lost a tooth; as they arrived they passed Nero's dentist with a molar on a little silver dish.

After dinner he was called into conference with the Emperor and his chief advisers, such as they nowadays were. When he emerged he had been offered a new post. He told Caenis at once what it was, and at once she understood what it must mean.

They returned to their donated villa in complete silence. Late as it was, Vespasian sent off a message to bring Titus as soon as possible. All the way home he had gripped her hand tightly in his.

They went into a room where they could sit. The house which Nero had placed at their disposal belonged to some wealthy old man who rarely visited. It was furnished in Roman fashion, but crammed with Greek artefacts. Every room was burdened with sideboards groaning under black-figure bowls and vases, bronzes, and pottery statuettes. There were carpets hung on the walls. Marble gods shared the dining room while the buffet table used at lunchtime was five hundred years old. It was like living in an art gallery. The very rugs flung over the ivory-legged couches were draped not for comfort but display. Caenis hated it.

Vespasian took a chair; she sat sideways on a couch. This reversal of the normal pattern was typical of the casual way they had always lived. One of their own slaves, sensing late-night discussion, poured them amber resinated wine, unasked. For a long time neither drank. Once they were alone Caenis wished Vespasian would come nearer but she realised that he wanted to be able to look at her. True to her old training her face gave little away.

There had been a serious rebellion in Judaea. Vespasian had been offered the province, plus control of a large army, with permission to take Titus on his staff. It was, as he admitted to Caenis at once, partly in recognition of his military talent but mainly because he was too obscure to pose any political threat if a major fighting force were entrusted to his command. The appointment would be for the usual period of three years.

Caenis tried to remember what she knew about Judaea. It was another restless province at the far end of the Empire, which Rome viewed with mixed intrigue and unease. Caligula had once caused a trauma when he devised a plan to destroy the Temple in Jerusalem – a plan fortunately never carried out. The ruling house was riven by domestic squabbles but had been drawn to Rome under Augustus. Caenis herself had known the late King, Herod Agrippa, a close friend of the Emperors Caligula and Claudius, who had helped persuade Claudius to take the throne. He had been brought up in the House of Livia by Antonia, who remained his friend and champion for life. Judaea was now ruled by his son, who had been placed in power by Claudius.

The recent troubles were the product of a rising mood of nationalism, aggravated by a series of Roman officials whose attitude had been unhelpful. Cestius Gallus, then Governor of Syria, had taken in troops to put down the unrest and been dramatically routed at considerable expense of equipment, the capture of an eagle and unacceptable loss of life. War was now inevitable. Nero feared that war in Judaea boded ill for the rest of the Empire; that was why he had humbled his musical pride. Having already executed the greatest soldier of their age, Domitius Corbulo, for being too successful, Nero realised that Vespasian was the only man he had left who would be capable of taking on the troubles in Judaea.

Caenis and Vespasian considered Nero's offer quietly. After a decade of sharing daily routines their patterns of thought were so similar, their sensitivity so acute, that it took few words to plunge into – and out of – what others might have made an endless debate.

Vespasian, his eyes never leaving her, offered fairly, 'If you want me to decline this, will you please say?'

'Do you want an excuse not to go?'

A ridiculous question, drily posed. At fifty-seven some men abandon enterprise; others are open to a new lease of life. Vespasian was eager. He wanted to show the establishment exactly what a plain man of good sense and real administrative calibre could do. He would rise to this opportunity perhaps even more strongly than he might have done in earlier days, for he was calmer and more confident.

'I can say I'm an old man.'

'You'll be lying then.'

'Caenis, I want to know what you think.' He paused. 'I can't take you, not into a battle zone.'

She had realised that. She had been thinking about it all the way home. 'No. It would be dangerous and pointless.'

'Quite. I wouldn't see you anyway. I'd have to lock you in some fortress miles from the fighting. You'd be bored and I'd be anxious. We could hardly ever meet.'

That he had even considered it was a graceful compliment. Caenis responded swiftly, 'I know. I'm not afraid to come with you –' He breathed with affectionate laughter, so she felt herself smile. 'But I'll stay in Rome. You need someone to look after things at home. You must go. Apart from the fact that you want it, I have,' she told him stiffly, 'given too much to your career to stop supporting you now.'

He did not immediately speak, then asked gruffly, 'Mind it?'

'Yes.'

'So do I. You know that, lass.'

Their eyes met, and held fast for a long time, though he made no move to approach her. She wanted to go to him, but was afraid her control would break. Tonight, for the first time, she no longer thought of herself as a girl. She felt the effect of every past year in her tired eyes, her lightening bones, her panic-stricken brain. Vespasian sat with her showing a grave concern that racked her more than indifference.

After a time they both slowly drank their wine. Caenis went to bed. He did not come to her. He recognised she would welcome time alone to adjust to her need to be brave. And already he had too much to think about. He could not spare himself to help her.

She saw little of Vespasian or Titus in the following days. They were working incessantly, commissioning their officers, studying maps, scouring the briefs and dispatches that poured in the moment their appointment was officially announced. Titus was to sail to Egypt to collect the Fifteenth Legion from Alexandria. Vespasian would travel overland after crossing the Hellespont, to make his first contact with the Governor of Syria.

Caenis was interested in the problem, and they made no attempt to shut her out. Yet Vespasian and Titus were forming a close association for an enterprise she would only be able to watch from the sidelines. Once they left Greece, theirs would be a life of action, immediacy and change. Caenis faced three years of suspense, hearing news selectively and long after the event. Once they did leave her she had decided to travel in Greece alone before returning to Italy; she had never been afraid of being by herself. That did not mean she was not lonely now. Even Vespasian's birthday passed with less than usual ceremony.

On the last night she sat with Vespasian and Titus until it grew dark, while they still worked. Then despairing of acknowledgement she went quietly to bed. She heard Titus go to his room, striding perhaps more noisily than usual. He called good night in a low voice as he passed her door.

The house that she hated grew silent.

Caenis was in bed. She had been trying to read, for she was unable to sleep, but the scroll now lay still half unrolled on a side table; Narcissus would have had something to say about that. The knock on her door was so gentle she was still wondering whether she had heard it when Vespasian came in.

'May I? Saw your light. I'm glad you're still awake.'

He came and sat on her bed. Shadows from the disturbed lamp raced for a time up the wall. He was weary, subdued, but obviously wanting to talk to her. 'All the work is done. I was determined to finish it so my mind was clear – did you think I had forgotten you?'

'No,' Caenis lied. Catching the dregs of her resentment, his eyes flickered momentarily. Her self-pity melted away at once.

Smiling, Vespasian told her, 'I've just had a novel experience – I've been given some fatherly advice by my son!'

Caenis was as fond of Titus as he of her; sensing they had quarrelled, she frowned. 'What was that?'

'He said I should put aside the planning and send for you to my room.' She stared down at her folded hands. 'Boy's a fool,' Vespasian commented. Besides an attractive tempera-ment, Titus had an enquiring mind, a phenomenal memory, less wit but probably more culture than his critical papa. He was loyal, generous, tactful and spirited – a delightful young man. And no fool.

Nor was his father.

'Antonia Caenis, I don't send for you; I never did and never will – you come of your own accord. You're not some girl to be called for in the afternoon, then used – and paid – and sent away again until the next gracious summons from the old man. Besides –' his voice dropped – 'he either has no imagination, or lacks the experience to know.' She looked up, her heart pattering. Vespasian seduced her with his eyes. 'It's so much more fun trying to persuade you to invite me to stay here with you!'

With a cry of relief, Caenis had already opened her arms.

They were both older, and so much slower, but some things were the better for that.

Afterwards they both lay awake the greater part of the night. The lights were out. They lay close, and still, neither wishing to disturb the other yet each aware from the steadi-ness of the other's embrace and occasional quiet movements that they were both awake. After many hours, when Caenis was easing the pressure on her arm, Vespasian finally spoke.

'Well, my lady!'

'Well, my general!'

His lips brushed her forehead as she gave him his new title. 'I'm coming back. Same as ever. Promise.'

She buried her face in the angle of his neck, her hand moving lightly over the familiar lines of his chest, his shoul-der, his strong upper arm. It was then he said, 'I never thanked you for the sausage; the one at the British parade.'

Caenis had forgotten all about that. 'Oh Titus! I was so glad I saw you that day.'

He remained silent for so long her heart raced with anxiety. 'That day was very odd, lass. I didn't seem to be myself.' He wrapped both arms around her, gripping her tight, then abruptly confessed, 'I wanted rather badly to come to you that night.'

Caenis felt she had intruded unintentionally on some private anguish.

He was determined to tell her: 'I actually walked out from the banquet on the Capitol and stood for a long time in a colonnade, willing myself to go back in. It would have been right,' he declared. 'Being with you; after the Triumph.'

Caenis made a low distressed sound, horrified to remember how at the time she had misinterpreted what he felt – and grateful that she had. To know this then would have been unbearable; it was difficult to tolerate even now. He released her a little, because he knew her so well that he realised even before she started to move that she wanted to kiss him.

So she did, trying to forget that he had made her want to weep.

When she was kissing him, she heard that soft groan of pleasure, no different now than when they were young. She supposed it might be flattery, but even if it were, the fact that he thought her worth flattering warmed her heart.

There was something about kissing Vespasian in the dark, when all the rest of the household thought them sensibly asleep. One thing led rather conveniently to another, one caress demanded more until, both laughing, they acknowledged what they both had been hoping from the start, as with every tenderness but yet the distinctly urgent passion of two people who were parting for a desperately long time, they moved closer than ever together and once again made love.

'This is perhaps not the moment to ask –'

'Lass, I am always free –' said Vespasian politely (though she was quite right; it was not an easy moment) – 'for a chat with you . . .'

'Whatever did you do with the sausage?'

'Ate it,' he responded, after a short pause. 'What did you expect?'

'*In the street*, lord?' Caenis demanded, as she had done once before.

And Vespasian answered, as he had done the first time, 'In the street!'

A four-baton general with full triumphal honours and the dignity of nearly sixty years: it seemed impossible that he would ever change.

PART SIX:
THE YEAR OF THE FOUR EMPERORS

When the Caesars were Nero, Galba, Otho, Vitellius
And their successor

XXXVI

Having wintered in Greece, Caénis spent the following spring by herself, travelling north through Dalmatia to Istria. When there seemed nothing to stay for, she returned to Rome.

During this time Vespasian reached Antioch, the chief city of the eastern Empire, where he made his first rendezvous with the new Governor of Syria, Licinius Mucianus (whom he described to Caenis as a bed-hopping wart posted here as an exile rather than a reward) and their ally, King Agrippa of Judaea (whom Vespasian crudely called a shifty bunch of ringlets on the make). He then marched his Fifth and Tenth Legions south to Ptolomaïs, which lay a short way north of Mount Carmel on the coast. There Titus joined him from Egypt with the Fifteenth. Campaigning began in Galilee, which had been heavily fortified by the rebels; after an easy assault on Gabara, Vespasian tackled Jotapata, a natural stronghold on a precipice where heavy numbers of enemy troops were dug in. He captured Jotapata in July.

He was a born soldier. More from what Titus told her than any indication Vespasian gave himself, Caenis knew that he possessed all the powers of analysis and organisation to bring off whatever was required. His talents flourished in the army, where no one cared who a man's ancestors had been provided he measured up to the current task. Set in charge of the brilliant Roman military machine, he was an ideal leader. Action fired him; he threw his energy and intelligence into the campaign, always accessible to the men, always aware of their mood. His down-to-earth character made him one of them; his competence made him a general they were proud of. It was already obvious how things in Palestine would go.

Caenis sailed to Italy. She travelled across country, pausing at Vespasian's Reate estate. It was on her return to his house in Rome that the notorious incident with Domitian occurred. He was eighteen now. Caenis sympathised with his grudge that his brother had been singled out for special advantage in Judaea; the natural close partnership between Vespasian and Titus had become impossible to conceal. Caenis and Domitian had never liked each other but she greeted him with more than usual kindness, turning her cheek as usual for his kiss. Domitian curtly offered his hand instead.

Caenis shook hands without a word. She never presumed to demand from other people the compliment Vespasian had chosen to give. She never complained. Yet it was noticed. Domitian would be condemned by the historians on her behalf.

By the end of his first year Vespasian had subdued most of Galilee. It was at Gamala, while the Romans were pressing a hard siege, that his enthusiasm carried him so far forward that he found himself trapped with only a handful of men at the centre of the citadel; they had to fight their way out backwards, inching step by step down to safety behind a wall of locked shields. Of course, by the time Caenis heard this it was old news, she realised that. 'Don't panic!' he wrote cheerfully. 'Eat a decent breakfast and *calm down*!' Caenis ate breakfast and half her lunch, then panicked and was sick. By now she had found out too about the arrow he had caught in his foot at Jotapata; this did not reassure her. He captured Gamala in October.

Vespasian retired for the winter with two legions, later travelling with Titus inland to Caesarea Philippi for three weeks of state banquets and thanksgiving sacrifice. Caenis was by then missing him dreadfully, for the dark days and bitter weather seemed to emphasise the quietness of their house in Rome and the coldness of her bed. Letters became infrequent due to the closed sea-crossing, though at least when they came there were sometimes more than one. Alone in Rome she received fewer social invitations, and lost interest in the theatre without his being there too. She wished she had known he would winter at Caesarea where the climate was pleasant at that time of year and King Agrippa – who had such close family ties to Antonia – was apparently being most hospitable. Despite the sensible discussion she had had with Vespasian in Greece, she would after all have gladly endured a summer on her own in Syria in return for spending time with him now. She wanted more than ever to be there.

It was only gradually that she realised Vespasian and Titus did not quite so badly need her. They were being entertained by King Agrippa in some style. Part of the entertainment comprised his radiant sister, Berenice.

Queen Berenice of Judaea was high-born, courageous, wealthy, and acknowledged throughout the Empire as the most beautiful woman of the age. She was forty, but at the height of her looks. Caenis must be nearly sixty, and had never been a beauty.

'Damn,' she accused her mirror mildly.

She trusted him; of course.

There seemed no alteration in the tone of Vespasian's letters. They had always been more anecdotal than sentimental. (He omitted anecdotes about Queen Berenice.) At the end he always mentioned that he missed Caenis; the statement became as regular as his official military stamp.

He used their correspondence like a man marshalling his thoughts. He summarised for her the strong Roman position in Galilee, and his proposals for taking Judaea, Idumaea, and Peraea next spring before the great effort that would be needed for the siege of Jerusalem; the capture of Jerusalem must be the crown of his campaign. When the Judaeans were not fighting Rome they were fighting one another; Vespasian wondered why the most inhospitable tracts of territory were so endlessly disputed. Perhaps while they were struggling against sun and wind, locusts and famine, it made small difference for the inhabitants to struggle against each other too. Dwellers in richer pastures found peace more convenient . . .

Suddenly once, as if it were by accident, he began a letter

291

'Oh Caenis, my dear love –' He had never done that before. In the rest of the letter he sounded wearier than usual, but that was no excuse. She knew then: nobody could ever be trusted.

'*Damn!*' exclaimed Caenis, not so mildly. She remembered Antonia saying that losing them to women never mattered; it was giving them up to politics that was final. Mark Antony's daughter should have known better, her freedwoman thought, envisioning another exceptional Roman general making a fool of himself with another ravishing foreign queen.

Caenis had intended to return a dignified answer, merely answering what he had asked her about events in Rome, in Gaul, in Spain. It was a complete mistake that she added at the end how keenly she was missing him, a plea which she in turn had always spared Vespasian. It was a mistake, but when she noticed she did not erase it. She felt he owed it to her to accept the truth for once, even though she understood – since she had always been a shrewd woman – that the moment was wrong and the declaration most likely to drive him away.

All his subsequent letters addressed her simply as Antonia Caenis, with the old-fashioned formality he normally used when he wrote. She noticed he was putting in more jokes. She could not decide whether that was good or not. She guessed it was guilt.

For anyone with an interest in political events whose attention was not dominated by the situation in Palestine, what happened that spring in Rome, in Gaul, in Spain, was fascinating. Nero's fourteen years had clearly reached their convulsive decline. After more than a century of Empire, and of executing their own kin, the Julio-Claudian family had thinned its own ranks to nothing. Nero's only child, a daughter, had died in infancy. There was no alternative heir. Rome hung on the brink of a climactic upheaval, into which this time the whole Empire would be drawn.

It was generally accepted that the lethargy and debauchery of the Senate, the private self-interest of the second-rank knights, the truculence of the mob, and a general decline in traditional values made a return to the Republic impossible. Perhaps the Empire was now too big. It needed an established administration, not subject to constant electoral change, while something in the current Roman character positively sought one guiding figurehead. It took little imagination to see that the next contest for the throne would involve more than murdering an ill-placed relative or suppressing an unwelcome will.

Vespasian suggested to Caenis that they should correspond in her old code. She found he had left the key for her, with one of his secretaries. That he had kept his copy for so many years was oddly reassuring. That he had left it ready merely seemed peculiar.

First there was a rebellion in Gaul. It was led by a man called Julius Vindex but put down by the Governor of Upper Germany who had at his disposal an armed frontier force. The worsening situation in Gaul, together with wild rumours circulating in Rome about Nero's Grecian tour, caused many frantic messages from Rome before the Emperor finally dragged himself back to Italy, showing off his trophies and his pretty Greek mantle spangled with golden stars.

Vindex was not in himself a major problem. His most daring personal offence in Nero's eyes, one which the Flavians adored, was that in an open dispatch to the Senate he had accused the Emperor of bad musicianship. But his revolt was important because it revealed widespread unrest in the provinces and heralded how the legions away on remote frontiers were about to take the issue of who governed them into their own hands. Any danger now lay not in the personal ambition of an individual general, as Rome had presumed from Julius Caesar on, but in the spirited resolution of the whole Roman army. The movement which first twitched in Gaul would flare throughout the Empire, gaining impetus in outposts as far flung as Moesia on the Black Sea, and Egypt, in Spain, in the Balkans, in Britain. The four legions in Syria and three more in Judaea would also be wanting their say. What this contest was to prove once and for all was that an acceptable emperor could be found outside the traditional Claudian family, that he could be created by the army, and created outside Rome.

Vindex rebelled in March. By April a far more significant candidate had arisen: Sulpicius Galba, one of the old breed of aristocrats. He first declared his support for Vindex against Nero but was subsequently hailed Emperor by his own troops in Spain, acquired the loyalty of the Praetorian Guards leaving Nero defenceless, then began a long, successful march to claim his position formally in Rome.

In May Caenis was called from her breakfast by an extraordinary incident. Nero was at the gates of Vespasian's house. He had arrived in the sacred chariot of Jupiter, which he had collected from the majestic Temple of Jove on the Capitol.

Nero's public response to the situation in the provinces had been merely to summon Rome's chief citizens to hear a demonstration of a new kind of water-organ with a lecture by himself about the various models, of which he was by this time an unrivalled connoisseur. (Caenis still did not like them.) Now his vain composure seemed to have cracked. Here he was, hair neatly ranged in a perfect double row of curls, looking as though he did not know what was expected of him next. Caenis had no idea either, though she supposed as a general's lady she must try to be polite.

Three-quarters asleep and halfway through her meal, she paused to collect herself. Aglaus whispered to her discreetly that Nero had been told in a dream the night before to bring the sacred chariot here. Caenis, who still wished breakfasting in Flavian houses could be less alarming, surveyed the Emperor dourly. He was thirty-one, and had the smell of a man who would not see thirty-two. As Antonia's great-grandson, this washed-out wreck could be viewed as her own patron; they both knew, she had never recognised that duty.

Ridiculously she remembered Vespasian's mild greeting to the unexpected ox: 'Hello, boy! Lost your way?'

'Welcome,' she managed instead. 'Dear me –' She was addressing the imperial charioteer as sweetly as she could at an hour of the morning when she was never at her best. 'The house of Flavius Vespasianus lacks adequate stabling for a vehicle so opulent as this! He will be so sorry he was not at home —' Nero was still looking uncertain. 'May I suggest, Caesar,' Caenis told him in a low confidential tone, 'a quick turn around the Circus Maximus then straight back up to the Temple and give thanks to Jove for the loan? Unless, that is, the gods inspire you otherwise!'

Rather to her surprise, Nero meekly acquiesced.

'I don't think,' she suggested cautiously to Aglaus, as they watched their visitor depart, 'we ought to excite sir with this nonsense.'

'Oh madam! It's just the sort of story sir would like!'

'Exactly,' said Caenis. 'He'll be sure it is a symbol; he'll keep worrying about what it could mean.'

By June Nero took fright at Galba's approach. He was in serious trouble; the Senate had declared him a public enemy. He fled to the suburban villa of his freedman Phaon where after some hesitation and some dramatic posturing he committed suicide just as the soldiers came galloping down the road to finish him. He begged his attendants not to let his body be mutilated after death, then one of his freedmen helped him stab himself in the throat. His funeral was arranged at the tomb of the Domitii on the Pincian Hill by Actë, the former slavegirl he had loved in his youth, who had stayed loyal to him through three wives and innumerable affairs: Actë, who had once been described to Caenis as a safe mistress for an emperor because she was a common girl who bore no grudges.

In Judaea the Emperor's death compelled Vespasian to halt his campaign while he waited for the new ruler to confirm or revoke his appointment as commander. Seizing advantage of the unexpected breathing space, a Jewish leader called Simon son of Gioras managed to overrun parts of Judaea and Idumaea which Vespasian had previously subdued, so all that was to do again: Vespasian grumbled irritably.

Galba took his time over reissuing Vespasian's command. Although they were both old soldiers, Galba was an inbred aristocrat, a homosexual, and a man who had governed

Tarraconensian Spain for eight years on the principle (which he openly admitted) of doing as little as possible so there was nothing for which he could be called to account. Galba and Vespasian lacked common ground. Indeed, Galba was the type of man Vespasian could hardly despise more. He made one or two bad moves. The worst, perhaps, was not giving the Governors of Syria and Judaea much more to keep them occupied.

The following year was what people were to call the Year of the Four Emperors.

XXXVII

Once, afterwards, Caenis overheard her freedman Aglaus giving his pet version of that tumultuous pageant of events on which so many historians would break so many pens. It was rather like the actor she had once seen mime a four-minute version of the *Aeneid*. It amazed an audience because it did seem so complete. It was magnificent. The outrageousness made her want to laugh and cry, but there was no time for either as well-known events whistled past in his brilliant quick-fire summary. The skill was that one recognised triumphantly all that was included – and forgot what had been left out.

Aglaus was talking to Julia, Titus' daughter. Julia was a vivid little soul, though Caenis preferred Vespasian's elder granddaughter, his daughter's orphan, Flavia. Flavia was a quieter, level-headed young girl, something of a favourite with Sabinus, to whose own grandson she was betrothed. Flavia would never seek a freedman's comments on the Year of the Four Emperors. She talked about it cautiously with Caenis, then in public she stayed silent. Of all his family it was Flavia who shared most acutely her grandfather's sense of morality and duty.

Not so the bubbling Julia. 'Tell me the story of the Year of the Four Emperors!'

'No; no; old history, child.'

'Oh, it's exciting; tell me!'

'Well . . . all right. I remember,' Aglaus began, 'the Year of the Four Emperors. I remember it for two reasons. One was that it never stopped being exciting. Also, it was that year my lady gave me my freedom. It seemed to me then, something had gone wrong. She had already told me she had put it in her will. So I imagined she must have fallen ill; some secret woman's business that she didn't want to mention – she was at that age; I kept an eye on her. The way she looked, I really

297

saw myself having to supervise the nurse and bury her . . . So; a freedman! I felt wonderful and terrible all at once.'

There was a shuffling as narrator and listener prepared to start.

'Go on; go on! Come to the year!'

'What a year! "The Year of the Four Emperors." Sounds quite organised. One after the other, nose to tail like elephants. No such luck. Utter confusion. Listen: Nero eventually topped himself in June the year before –'

'Do his eyes!'

Aglaus altered his voice to a thrill of horror: 'When the centurion rushed into Phaon's villa trying to capture him alive, Nero finally found courage to stab himself, crying, "What an artist perishes here!" He died with his eyes glazed, and boggling out of their sockets so that everyone present was horrified!'

Julia screamed happily. In his everyday voice Aglaus commented, 'So! Nero's last song; *enter Galba*. So old he's frightened he'll drop dead from sheer excitement; hastily names Calpurnius Piso as his successor: five days later, young Piso murdered; old Galba murdered; *enter Otho*. Otho is the poor dunce who had been married to Poppaea to cover up Nero's adultery, then packed off for ten years to govern Lusitania while Nero married her anyway: Lusitania is all right if you're *very* fond of sardines! Otho lasts from January to April. Next, Vitellius decides the legions in Germany need to stretch their legs. They start marching to Rome. We're off: civil war. Otho's nerve seems to crack. Keeps sending for his hairdresser to take his mind off things. Nice thatch; not much under it.'

Julia was giggling. Otho's thatch was a joke: it had been a clever wig.

'Vitellius smashes Otho's legions at Bedriacum. Otho decently tops himself; *enter Vitellius*.'

This was Aulus Vitellius, one of the sons of Lucius Vitellius who had once been a client of Antonia, the close friend and long-term supporter of Claudius, and once patron to Vespasian. But Aulus the son had other loyalties – primarily to himself.

'The German legions storm into Rome. Rome thinks it best to welcome them; they have a serious reputation. Vitellius sticks it from April to December – not bad for a loose type so drunk he can barely keep upright on the throne. And devious as they come. Your Great-uncle Sabinus would be alive today if that bastard Vitellius had accepted the thumbs down on 1 July. So what now? The legions in Moesia – *where the hell is Moesia?* we all wonder, except Sabinus, who once lived there – decide it's their turn to pick a Caesar. They beat up Vitellius' messengers, rip their flags, steal their money, then stick a pin in a list to decide whose name to attach under their silver eagles next. And who does Moesia choose? *We* know, Julia, don't we?'

Julia giggled hysterically.

Caenis had known as early as March. She anticipated what would happen exactly as Titus did. In many ways it was Titus himself who decided events.

They had been expecting Titus home; he was supposed to be coming to intercede with Galba about his father's still unconfirmed command. He never arrived. Caenis stood in the room that servants had opened and aired for him, with his letter in her hand, telling her so guardedly that he had decided not to come. Always polite, still he gave her no reason. She sensed it was one he could not yet formulate. She bent to smooth the coverlet on his newly made bed, while mentally she cancelled preparations and plans. As she listened to the silence, she realised that this was not simply a matter of disappointing the butcher and the fishmonger, of removing a pot of scillas from his window-ledge and piling his pillows back into the blanket-chest. A chill caught her, as she dreaded that because of what he was doing now Titus might never again be able to return to Rome.

He had actually sailed for home; that made it worse. His letter was written from Greece. When Galba had still not forwarded instructions to Judaea by March, with the campaign season at hand Vespasian had sent Titus back to Rome, to bend the knee in homage and ask formally for a new commission, releasing the Flavians to be up and at

299

Jerusalem as they wanted. That was all they wanted, whatever foolish rumours flew about it in Rome afterwards.

In fact by the time Titus put to sea, Galba was already two months dead. There had been trouble with the army, because he had promised them a bounty which it soon became clear he did not intend to pay. Detachments of soldiers, particularly those in Upper Germany who originally helped quell the Vindex rebellion, refused to take the New Year's Day oath of allegiance to a mean-handed Spanish appointee, and asked the Praetorian Guards to nominate another emperor who would be acceptable to all. Galba's adoption of Piso was intended to reassure them. Instead it antagonised Otho, who had been Galba's most significant supporter and who was not unnaturally expecting the privilege of imperial adoption himself. Hence Otho's bid. Hence Galba's murder. Hence young Titus Flavius Vespasianus, now abruptly yachting on a strange new tack in the eastern Mediterranean.

Titus had reached Greece when he met messengers bringing news of Galba's death. He should have continued his journey to salute Otho instead. His companion, King Agrippa, did indeed go on to Rome. Titus turned back alone. He visited Paphos. There stood a prophetic oracle, which he consulted at length. He spent a long time on his own, lost in thought. Then quite suddenly he sailed back to his father.

Nothing was said. But from that moment Caenis knew what was happening. Aglaus, who had been with her for nearly twenty years, saw the change in her face. It was, as he told Julia, enough to make him believe his mistress might be terminally ill.

There are two ways at least of being brave. In a sudden emergency, when the adrenalin floods, people act with courage because they have no time or no imagination to appreciate how much danger they are in. To have courage in a sudden crisis is comparatively easy. There are obvious and positive things to do. But to remain brave over a long period is a very different matter. To wait and to watch, for month after month, while inevitable tragedy stalks closer, that is the test. That exacts courage of a deliberate, self-wounding kind.

300

Life was hard. Caenis had always known it. Some people endure that certainty all their lives. If ever they dare think otherwise life restores their bitter understanding soon enough. Like her steward, Caenis would remember the Year of the Four Emperors. She would remember because it would be when her shared life with Flavius Vespasianus had to come to a swift, unplanned end.

She was not ill. Her freedman worked that out eventually. Some time at the beginning of that summer it struck Aglaus that the lifeless look on his lady's face was one which of course he recognised: it was the classic expression of an old, exhausted, badly beaten, dismally broken-down slave.

XXXVIII

Once Titus had sailed back to Syria there was never any question what he wanted his father to do.

He himself began working towards it immediately. Titus could always attract the friendship of the most unlikely men: so with adept diplomacy he persuaded Licinius Mucianus, the Syrian Governor, who was one of several statesmen who might himself have joined in the free-for-all, to set aside any jealousy he had felt towards Vespasian and abandon his own possible claim for power. The two provincial governors had previously loathed one another with cordial contempt; Titus brought them together. Mucianus joined Titus in urging Vespasian to act.

Spanish troops had made Galba. Otho was acclaimed by the Praetorian Guards. The German army raised Vitellius: now in Judaea the Fifth, Tenth and Fifteenth Legions sat in their camps deprived of action, all talking politics. Soldiers should never be allowed to do that. Yet Vespasian held his men in a firm discipline. He made no move; neither did they. Titus and Mucianus continued their private pressure for long hours in Vespasian's tent.

Otho's reign was so short, only four months, that Vespasian's views on him as a 'pea-brained Neronian pimp', which he wrote to Caenis, were soon redundant. When Aulus Vitellius pranced through Gaul to snatch the Empire like a bullying child with a coveted toy, Vespasian grew more angry. Both he and his campaign-hardened soldiers were seized with indignation. Vitellius in his youth had been one of the aristocratic boys who entertained Tiberius in debauchery on Capri. He had raced chariots with Caligula. He was a glutton. He was a drunkard. Now he was being carried towards Rome in extravagant triumph, crossing rivers in barges wreathed with garlands while a huge train of

302

hangers-on made merry at the expense of the populace, looting and terrorising the countryside. It accorded ill with the Sabine ideal of public service.

Even yet Vespasian did nothing. Having drawn up his three legions to take the oath of allegiance to their new Emperor Otho, four months later he drew them up again, himself expressionless, and made them take the oath to Vitellius. His behaviour on both occasions was exemplary. It was the soldiers, normally so boisterous at accessions, who when called upon to swear their allegiance just stood in their ranks in devastating silence. They stared at Vespasian; Vespasian stared back at them. Their mood was plain. Everyone present could see the commander in Judaea was genuinely moved.

Still he did nothing. He knew that to seize power was the first step only; holding it posed a very different task. He was instinctively modest. He listened to the appeals of his friends; he considered the risks. He remained withdrawn, watchful, apparently calm, although Titus knew, and Caenis could imagine, how the real state of his mind was highly active and alert. Many men know when to act; a few know when to wait. Vespasian let Otho and Vitellius fight it out among themselves.

Otho died well. Lurking in Brixellum he heard how, despite earlier successes and the ill-preparedness of the German troops, his own army had been crushed at Bedriacum. He took the brave decision not to expose his supporters to further bloodshed. After encouraging his staff and making arrangements for their escape, he burned his official correspondence, attended to his private affairs, then retired to his quarters. He drank a glass of cold water, tested the points of two daggers, placed one beneath his pillow and spent a last quiet night. At dawn he awoke and stabbed himself fatally once. He received an unpretentious funeral and a monument so modest it belied how far his reputation had been redeemed by his courageous death.

Vitellius stood mocking at Otho's simple monument; that summed up Vitellius.

It was in Moesia that three legions who had been hastening to Otho's support heard he was dead; heard that Vitellius was pronounced Emperor by the German legions; took against the Germans; took against Vitellius; and without anybody asking them for the favour, decided that Moesia would announce a candidate of its own. The theory was fine; they only had to choose their man.

The legions in Moesia, who happened to include the Third Gallica, a group of stout characters recently sent there from Syria, sat down sensibly with a list of all the Roman governors and senior ex-consuls who might be eligible for their support. One by one they crossed these off as unsuitable. At the end a single name remained. They held a democratic vote. The man's popularity was unanimously confirmed. The legions in Moesia methodically stripped their standards of the plaques that bore the dead Otho's name, then nailed up instead the title of the new Emperor they had chosen for themselves.

His name was:

VESPASIAN.

On 1 July Tiberius Alexander, the Prefect of Egypt, to whom Vespasian had written tentatively sounding out his views, made those views plain. Alexander was an equestrian who had risen to great position; he had started life as a freedman of Antonia's, so he had an inevitable loyalty to those who had enjoyed her patronage. Tiberius Alexander called upon his own legions to hail Vespasian as Emperor.

Meanwhile the legions in Moesia were persuading their neighbours in Pannonia to join their cause; their Pannonian neighbours encouraged the legions in Dalmatia to do the same. One by one provinces and kingdoms followed them – Asia, Achaea, Cappadocia and Galatia – until a complete crescent surrounding the far end of the Mediterranean had declared for the eastern Emperor. Spain was friendly to Vespasian; Britain too. On the morning of 3 July in Judaea Vespasian's own soldiers decided of their own accord to stop greeting him as governor. When he came out from his bedroom his bodyguard exchanged quick glances, saluted him,

'*Caesar!*' then defied him to put them all on a charge.

Vespasian spoke to them quietly, in his soldierly manner. The word spread: he had accepted the nomination. On the same day, without even waiting for Titus to return from a liaison trip to Syria, he received the oath of allegiance himself from his own delighted troops. It was reported to Caenis that Vespasian had looked pleased but bewildered.

In Rome, Vitellius censored any mention of Vespasian's name. It was pointless; everybody knew. There would be another civil war. If Vespasian lost it he, his two sons, probably his brother, and possibly even his brother's children too, would die. If he died, far away, Caenis would not even attend his funeral.

If he survived, it would be far worse for her.

She believed there was no better man in the Empire to undertake this role. She also knew there would be no question any longer that Vespasian could allow a freedwoman to share his life. Like Nero's Actë, as a common girl who bore no grudges she might be suitable to entertain him occasionally – but only within carefully defined sexual limits. The very qualities that had once brought him back to her, the decent temperament that made him ideal to govern, would inevitably take him from her now. Vespasian would behave as an emperor should. Their fine, equal partnership would be broken. She had received from fortune the greatest gift she could ever expect. She had enjoyed it for longer than a decade; now she had to give it back.

She said to Aglaus, when she granted him his freedom, 'I have decided it would be best if I moved back to my own house in the Via Nomentana. Perhaps you could mention it for me to the leaseholder.'

Aglaus knew she had continued to pay her ground rent all this time. He had organised it for her himself. It was supposed never to be mentioned, though Aglaus understood that Vespasian knew. Two men together, Vespasian and Aglaus had quietly agreed: independent that one. She did not trust her luck. She had had every faith in Vespasian, but none in life.

Aglaus was an excellent steward; he had paid her rent discreetly and refrained from teasing her. Caenis was therefore surprised, even though his new status as a free citizen allowed him greater frankness, when he replied bleakly, 'I think you'll want to explain that to the leaseholder yourself.'

Not for the first time that year, Caenis went cold.

Aglaus braced himself and told her: 'Well, it's not necessary, actually. The lease was acquired by someone else. Vespasian bought it, just before you went to Africa; that was one of the reasons he was so short of cash. He told me, and told me to explain it to you if anything ever happened to him – I don't think the present business was what he really had in mind! He rewrote his will at the same time to provide for you, but he wanted you to have something of your own in case anything went wrong. The estate is yours; it's been yours for years. He bought it, but the deeds are in your name.'

Caenis stared. For some reason she suddenly remembered Marius Pomponius Gallus, the man she was supposed to have married, who left her in his will (as Vespasian said at the time) little more than the price of a new hat.

'You had better tell me,' she commented coolly, 'exactly what you and that old miser have been doing with my rent.'

'Bank account in the Forum – also in your name – I can tell you the number: bit of capital for you, he said.' Aglaus smiled. Clearly he felt confident that he possessed legitimate orders from the master of their household. How like a man. 'It wasn't just that he thought he might die first. He told me you might one day get tired of him –'

'Hah!' retorted Caenis briskly.

Aglaus only smiled again. He looked tired; he was worried about her. 'He wanted you to be secure if you upped and left.' Well, she was doing that. There was an aching silence. 'May I ask you something, madam? Have you given me my freedom because you think my loyalty to Vespasian is greater than my loyalty to you?'

'No,' said Caenis.

She had done, of course. Because he was her gift from Narcissus, she had gone on keeping Aglaus long after she knew he deserved his release. Now with the world in tumult she did not blame him if he wanted to throw in his lot with the Emperor he admired; she had decided to allow him the

306

choice. Besides, she wanted to be free herself to act without pressure from his frank sarcasm and disapproving scowl.

'You and the new Emperor seem very close!'

He did look sheepish. With Aglaus this was a rare sight. But he said, speaking in a low voice with a steadiness he obviously copied from Vespasian, 'The new Emperor and I, madam, always had an interest in common.'

Caenis ignored that.

Perhaps for the first time she was acknowledging the change in their position. As his patron now, she sought his candid advice: 'Are you suggesting I am making a mistake?'

Her freedman's courage grew. 'No,' Aglaus replied quietly, for he knew better than anybody how high her standards were. 'You cannot be an embarrassment to him. We have both lived in that Palace. We know the filthy rules. There is no place for us now with Vespasian. You are right, madam; time to go home.'

Once again, therefore, Caenis was living on her own. At the time when she moved, no one looked askance. Rome was in chaos. There were soldiers everywhere, filling the camps, bunking down in the Porticos, cluttering up temple forecourts with bivouacs and braziers, billeting themselves willy-nilly on private citizens. Officers dashed about with unnecessary escorts, showing off. By day the streets were full of bored German and Gallic auxiliaries – shaggy lumps in animal skins, peering into shops, jostling passers-by, squabbling over prostitutes, and tripping over the kerbstones of the unfamiliar pavements. They swam in the river until they all caught fever and started an epidemic. Every night came sounds of looting. Soon all the best mansions were abandoned and boarded up. There were regular fires. Scarpering from the home of such a prominent man seemed a wise move. In fact Aglaus asked to come too.

Since she now understood that he thought he had a mission, Caenis did not forbid it. He was wrong, of course: Caenis would look after herself.

*

307

It took six months to conclude the civil war; six months of deprivation in the country and terror in Rome, to bring Vitellius within sight of abdication.

It was during that time Veronica became ill. She knew, as Caenis did, that she would die. Caenis went to see her.

'Well, Veronica: here's some lovely Sabine fruit!'

Pain was sculpted on every line of Veronica's once-exquisite face. Her bones stood; the flesh had started to shrink. She would not last until Vespasian reached Rome. Her beauty had become a ruin of its former self, clad in the remnants of her vitality like the soft muffling of lichen on fallen stones.

'Oh thanks! Good of you to come. Talk to me, Caenis. Make me laugh; make me angry; anything to make me forget! Tell me about that dangerous man of yours!'

Caenis had hoped to avoid a confrontation with Veronica. 'I'm a freedwoman,' she stated crisply. 'Vespasian was never mine.'

Veronica interpreted this in her own style. 'Hah! She's talking about the abundantly equipped Queen of Judaea.'

The beautiful Berenice had apparently made all speed to offer Vespasian her most generous support. Handy to own a fleet, Caenis thought. 'Leave it!' she warned.

Veronica scoffed. 'What, like some dead thing my cat has dropped between us on the tiles, which we pretend we haven't seen? Queen Berenice – the wonder of our age . . . Be wise; ignore it. May not even be true.' She changed her tone to a confidential mutter. 'Is he coming yet?'

Caenis resisted the request to be drawn into indiscretion. It was easy enough; she knew little. Vespasian rarely wrote to her now. His last brief colourless note merely told her he was well. He said he missed her; she doubted that. She had not replied.

She contented herself with what was, despite all the censorship, common knowledge. 'No. He's not coming. Generals we have never heard of, dear, are marching on Italy with legions who worship exotic gods from countries we can hardly find on the map.'

'So what's happening?'

'As far as I can understand it – there is no formal news from the east, but Sabinus lets me know what he can – the plan is that Vespasian will sail to Egypt to batten down the winter corn supply that's intended for Italy. Bread is running short already; the profiteers seem to have grasped the point with their usual smart business sense. A general called Antonius Primus is invading northern Italy with all the Balkan legions, while this person Mucianus has crossed the Hellespont and will turn up unexpectedly somewhere on the eastern coast. Primus is nicknamed Beaky and has some kind of criminal record though that did not deter Nero from giving him a legion, while Mucianus is a silky orator who sleeps with anything that moves, preferably male. Perhaps Vespasian hopes by contrast to appear immaculate.'

'Stodgy old bastard! I don't know how you put up with him.'

'Here as you know, Vitellius' rough-necks tear Rome apart and poor Sabinus, who has been elected Prefect of the City yet again, struggles to keep public order and loyally obey the man whom his own brother is opposing. Ludicrous! How wise of you, my darling, to keep indoors.'

Veronica had listened with half her attention. 'He'll do it, your man. I see that now. This was always what he was waiting for. It's wonderful.'

Caenis asked drily, 'Bit of a change of heart, dear?'

'I,' said Veronica proudly, 'am loyal to my Emperor!' Then she pleaded almost, for she knew perfectly well what attitude Caenis was bound to take: 'Oh I'm a drab hag deteriorating on a faded couch, with cold feet and a dying brain – but it warms me to think of you, a Caesar's darling! Caenis, you must do this. You owe it to all the girls in all the Palaces who sleep on flea-ridden pallets on stone ledges in cold cells, and who live by the hope that one day they will rise to a better place –'

Caenis could bear it no longer. Her own girlish dreams of breaking her shackles and stalking some throne room in a damask dress and a tasteless ruby coronet were long dead. All she wanted was to share her daily life with a man whose face brightened when he saw her. She finally told Veronica the truth. 'Pensioned off, dear.'

'Never!'

They began to argue, which was what Caenis had dreaded. 'Look, Veronica, he and I shared our lives on equal terms; for over ten years. Few wives are as close to their husbands as I was to him. How can I accept less?'

'He took you back.'

'He took me back while he was a private citizen.'

'Into his house.'

'But there's no place for me in his Palace.'

'Juno, Caenis; how can you be so stupid – how can you be so calm?'

'Realistic.'

'Mad.'

Caenis suddenly snapped. She cried out to her friend, whom she would probably not see in any lucid state again, as she had never allowed herself to do before: 'Oh I am not calm, girl! It's the bitterest of ironies and I am very angry! A freedwoman; oh Juno, Veronica, I would be better as his slave – then at least he could keep me where he lives without public offence. This is impossible. Once I did accept that I had lost him; I learnt to exist without him. I'm too old now to face all that anguish again. I'm too tired. I'm too frightened of what it will be like, never again having him there. I haven't any strength to deal with this.' Her voice dropped to an even more painful note. 'I hope he stays in the East; I hope he never comes. I tell you, I would sooner lose him to Queen Berenice, who married her uncle and sleeps with her brother, than have to see Vespasian in Rome as a stranger!'

Struggling to raise herself on one pitifully thin arm, Veronica complained in bewilderment, 'But he cares for you!'

'Of course he does!' Caenis bellowed. 'I know it; even he knows. He came back for me after half a lifetime. I was stout, and grey-haired, nasty-tempered and the wrong social class, but back he came. I cannot pretend any longer that the man did not care!'

'You were never stout,' murmured her loyal friend.

Caenis careered on heedlessly. 'So here I am, just where I

was thirty years ago; worse, because I actually know now how he cares! Yet I have to stand back again, knowing what it means. I have to watch his face – oh his poor sorry face – while that dear good man, the only straightforward honest man that I have ever met, tells me all over again that he must let me go!'

The silence rang through Veronica's house.

Caenis went home.

XXXIX

The last time Caenis saw Flavius Sabinus there was a violent rainstorm in the streets. It had been a terrible winter, with disastrous floods sweeping across the low ground on the Tiber's left bank. The Prefect of the City came wearily into her quiet room, where the rain could only just be heard outside the windows; she brought him at once to the intimate circle of a hot charcoal brazier to dry off and warm his ancient bones.

It was December in that eventful year. The week before, Caenis had lost a tooth; it was preoccupying her pathetically. As she huddled in a wrap Sabinus pulled back his cheek to show her a half-row of his own missing, so then they laughed and compared notes on the onset of pains, on the fading of appetites, on the lightness of sleep. Caenis flexed her finger knuckles where they were shiny and sore, probably not with chilblains as she pretended, but rheumatism.

'Came to see how you were, lass.' She was tired. She kept waking in the night from her dream about Britannicus and Titus. 'Domitian should be keeping an eye on you but he's far too busy seducing senators' wives.'

Vitellius had placed Domitian under house arrest, though he still managed to act the imperial lad-about-town. His father's rise had gone to Domitian's head, unlike Titus, who was by all accounts taking it sensibly. Titus was to take over as commander-in-chief in Judaea. He would be responsible for the siege of Jerusalem, though for the time being he remained in Alexandria with the Emperor. Domitian was stuck here with his fussy uncle Sabinus, and no real public role.

Vespasian had no intention of leaving Egypt yet, as far as anyone knew. In his absence his status in Rome steadily grew. News from Italy carried east, but during the winter Vitellius could obtain no intelligence the other way. The

312

silence enhanced Vespasian's mystique. Meanwhile the grain shortage was beginning to tell; when Vespasian came with the cornships he would be eagerly welcomed by a starving populace.

The armed struggle that had occupied the previous six months was best not remembered. Rome's casual attitude to dispatching other races was matched by a poignant reverence for the shedding of its own citizens' blood. For legion to fight legion, brother to die at brother's hand, racked Italy and the city both.

'I've been thinking about you,' Caenis told Sabinus. 'Your position as City Prefect must be dreadful.'

It was Rome that wanted Sabinus to continue in his post; for Rome he felt obliged to do it. Sabinus was held in great reverence, greater than his brother if the truth were told. His first stint of governing the city had been three years; now he had done it for another eight.

'Well. Exciting times!'

In his way he glossed over the problem. He remained a gentle, pleasant, well-respected, well-intentioned man, who was desperately trying to reconcile Vitellius to the inevitable without further bloodshed or disruption in the capital. 'I do my best.' He stared into the brazier, holding out his hands to the warmth. The red glow gleamed on his troubled face. Any frown, like his restrained smile, brought out a momentary likeness to his famous brother.

'You do wonders. But, Sabinus!'

For an instant Caenis had glimpsed that he was an old man carried on by an outgrown reputation, an old man rightly afraid he was at the verge of losing his grip.

'I know. They listen to me, Caenis; well, I hope they do.'

They did – so far.

Rain lashed the small windowpanes in long, beaded diagonal streaks. They talked for a time about the news that was filtering through, particularly about the sack of Cremona. In a display of spectacular generalship, Vespasian's man Antonius Primus had crossed the Pannonian Alps, established his headquarters at Verona, then defeated a large Vitellian army at Bedriacum, the scene of their own victory over Otho; the price was a disastrous siege of Cremona nearby, culminating in an immense fire.

'Is it all true?' Caenis requested. 'Tell me it's not.'

'Afraid so. Packed for the annual fair. Irresistible. The burning was not ordered by Antonius – I have his word. It began during the siege. He could not be expected to restrain forty thousand men who had just defeated the famous legions from Germany and saw the nearby city as their personal prize.'

Caenis was angry. 'Murder and rape; rape and murder. Old men and children torn from hand to hand, mocked and assaulted; women and boys violated; four days of carnage. Everything plundered; looters even stealing from themselves. Then the whole city burnt! Not a building left standing – just one solitary temple, outside the city walls.'

Sabinus looked uneasy. 'Civil war; it's brutal and bitter.'

'This is what Vespasian has done.'

As her passion crackled Vespasian's brother reprimanded her briskly, 'No; no! What he will stop, lass. Vitellius is so unpopular that if my brother did not make this claim against him someone else would. You know that. The Empire is sadly adrift. Vespasian is the best man; you must agree. There is more chance of a lasting peace at the end of this with Vespasian and his sons –'

Caenis had relaxed fairly early in the speech, but Sabinus had always talked too much. 'Well, then. What happens now, Sabinus?'

'Our troops rest, celebrate the Saturnalia, then march on Rome. I'm talking to Vitellius constantly; he assures me he is ready to abdicate.'

'Do you believe him?'

In his innocence Sabinus was shocked that she asked. 'Must do!'

She did not wish to dishearten him; he was a good man. 'Well done then. So . . . the Emperor Vespasian!' Her tone softened. They had come, they both realised, to the point of his call. 'Flavius Sabinus, don't be embarrassed. I understand what must be done. I have been your brother's best supporter all these years; should I offend against his reputation now? You know why I moved back here to my own house.'

'You are a good friend to the Flavians.'

He felt awkward. They both knew what his brave, clear-principled wife would have said about this.

Caenis reassured him gently, 'The Flavians were good friends to me.'

So he understood; his brother's mistress would do whatever had to be done. Caenis, the ex-secretary, would behave as she had been trained, with discretion and self-effacement. She would do it, moreover, despite anything his brother himself might say.

Flavius Sabinus leant back his head and sighed. 'This is very sad.' Caenis said nothing. 'Very sad,' he repeated sombrely.

He meant it. But for him, as for anyone who cared what happened to Rome, the important thing was a satisfactory resolution to the confusion, culminating in the best man taking charge. It was time to end Claudian vulgarity and scandal, time for Flavian discipline, hard work, and dedication to the public good. Time for Vespasian to be respectable again.

So although Flavius Sabinus honestly felt that what must happen to Caenis was tragic, though he liked her, and his late wife had liked her even more, he felt she had had a good run. His sadness was the type which must be dealt with staunchly then put aside.

'I have suggested,' he told her kindly, 'that if you feel uncomfortable in Rome, you might be allowed to live on our grandmother's estate at Cosa.'

Caenis drew a sharp breath. 'And what does Caesar say to that?'

Sabinus shifted with embarrassment. 'No answer yet.'

Conflicting emotions battered her. 'It is his favourite place!' she protested at last.

Vespasian's brother, who had known her as long as Vespasian himself, looked at her with a trace of the Flavian sentiment. They were poor, but they paid their debts. She would be provided for with decent courtesy. And Cosa was a good long way away. 'Well. Think about it. I feel sure he

315

will offer, if that is what you would like. Of course, you are quite right about the place. But you,' acknowledged the Prefect of the City unexpectedly, 'have always been my brother's favourite person.'

He was remembering the day when they discovered her, a scrawny fractious solitary girl amidst all those incongruous perfume flasks and jars. He was trying not to remember the look he had seen that day upon Vespasian's face.

In the last days of Vitellius, Flavius Sabinus continually attempted to bring about a peaceful resolution to the conflict before Vespasian's two triumphant generals reached Rome.

Antonius Primus had encountered the last remnants of the Vitellian field army without bloodshed. They met at Narnia, sixty miles north of Rome. Caenis knew Narnia; though it was on a different highway, it lay only twenty miles from Reate. The Vitellians had marched down through the Umbrian Hills to meet Primus with standards aloft and banners fluttering – but they kept their swords sheathed. They paraded through the Narnia Gap right to the point where Primus had drawn up his own men in closed ranks and full battledress on either side of the road to Rome. In silence the Flavian army parted, then simply closed around the Vitellians until the two groups stood amalgamated into one. In many ways it was the most moving sight of the entire war.

Now Primus was waiting for Mucianus, who had been held up by a Dacian rebellion at their backs, to join him at Ocriculum. They were just forty-five miles, say two days' standard march, from Rome. Rome lay two days away from being sacked by Roman troops. After the destruction of Cremona, the point was not lost.

Vitellius at last agreed to abdicate. He left the Palace and made a suitable speech of renunciation in the Forum. Friends gathered at the house of Flavius Sabinus to congratulate him on the skill with which he had resolved the situation. It was all over – apparently.

However, while attempting to leave the Palatine, Vitellius found all the roads blocked with barricades. Not knowing what else to do, he returned to the Palace. His supporters rallied to him in the night. Rumours of the change quickly spread. As Prefect of the City, Sabinus gave an order confining all troops to barracks; the order was widely ignored. Aware that Mucianus and Primus were so near, he then assembled his family, including his nephew Domitian, and seized Capitol Hill intending to make a stand until the Flavian generals arrived.

The Capitol, founded by the Roman Kings then completed under the free Republic, had stood throughout the centuries whatever else barbarians managed to assault. It had survived Rome's sack by marauding Gallic tribes. It had survived the invasion of Lars Porsenna in times so ancient no one was certain any longer whether they were history or myth. The citadel had been destroyed once by accident, but never in war. The Flavians seemed pretty safe.

It was the night of 18 December. It was raining again, all night. In the pitch black no one could tell friend from foe; watchwords went unrecognised or unheard. Even so the cordon flung around the citadel by Vitellius was so loose that messages from Sabinus passed in and out easily. But then next day Vitellian soldiers attacked on two sides; some climbed the Hundred Steps from the Clivus Capitolinus, others broke in on the opposite side by way of the Gemonian Steps. What had seemed casual now became desperate. Sabinus' men tore the roof-tiles from the temples to hurl down on the attackers' heads and rooted up the statues to form frantic barriers at the gates. At some point during the confusion one side or the other started a fire which raged through the houses on the lower slopes, then while all Rome watched in horror the flames leapt uphill towards the Temple of Jupiter.

The temple was the site for Rome's most solemn religious ceremonies. Here the Senate convened their first meeting of every year. From this temple the statues of Jupiter, Juno and Minerva were carried down into the city and paraded during festivals. To this temple victorious generals brought home their trophies. It was packed with dedicated treasure. The roof was covered with tiles of gilded bronze, the doors were plated with gold, and the peristyle was hung with solemn edicts engraved on ancient bronze plaques. The temple had symbolised Rome's destiny for hundreds of years. It had given poets their famous epithet for the Golden Capitol. It was the heart of the Empire. The Temple of Jupiter on Capitol Hill in Rome was the centre of the civilised world. On 19 December in the Year of the Four Emperors the Temple of Jupiter burnt to the ground.

Many Flavian supporters were killed. Domitian hid in a caretaker's house then disguised himself as an acolyte of the priests of Isis and escaped across the Tiber. The mother of one of his schoolfriends sheltered him, luckily outwitting his pursuers when they came to her house. Sabinus surrendered. He was dragged in chains before Vitellius. Vitellius came out on to the Palace steps apparently prepared to be lenient, but the mob screamed for blood. Sabinus was stabbed to death, his head sliced off, and his body cast on to the Gemonian Steps.

He had been placed in an impossible position, trying to negotiate with a slippery agent in an ungrateful city. Tragically, he misjudged both. The truest man in Rome, to Rome gave him a traitor's death.

Horrified, the army of Antonius Primus stirred. Without waiting any longer for Mucianus to join them they forged straight down the Via Flaminia. They sped the full distance to Rome in a single day. Ambassadors from Vitellius and the Senate were roughly handled, though a deputation of Vestal Virgins was received courteously enough. The remaining Vitellians had no intention of giving way. So three columns of Flavian troops invaded the city. They entered by the Via Flaminia, along the banks of the Tiber, and through the Colline Gate on the Via Salaria – only a few yards from Caenis' house. While citizens sat out on their balconies like spectators at a triumph, cheering first one group then the other, the two forces rampaged through the streets. The Flavians won – just. Vitellius was hauled from his hiding-place in a janitor's kennel, beaten to death, then his body too deposited upon the Gemonian Steps where Flavius Sabinus had been flung the day before. Vespasian's senior general,

Licinius Mucianus, arrived in the nick of time to prevent Primus' men from looting the city. Rome shuddered, and was finally still.

Domitian emerged from hiding and appeared to the victorious Flavian troops; they hailed him Caesar; they carried him in triumph to his father's house. On the whole Caenis felt glad she was no longer there when the exultant youth arrived.

Flavius Sabinus was awarded a state funeral.

Caenis wrote to Vespasian about his brother. She warned him of the shock which the destruction of the temple had caused in Rome. She reassured him that his younger son was safe. It was 30 December – Titus' birthday; she sent Titus her love. She gave them both her honest good wishes for the Flavian dynasty.

Then, with immense care, Caenis wrote to Vespasian alone.

> I have believed since the day I met you that you possessed a great destiny. I cannot wish you – or Rome – any less. I have come with you as far as I may. You must realise I shall never in the future cause you to regret the respect and devotion you showed me in the past. We are, as you once observed, strong-minded enough to follow the rules. You know my heart; you always knew. Together or separate, my love for you will never change.
>
> Perhaps you were right when you said once that we should not have given love to one another, but oh dearest of men, I am so glad that we did!

Even now, Caenis never felt entirely easy writing letters for herself. Still the regular whisper of her pen across the papyrus carried the resonance of a long-mastered craft, so she worked on to the end with the discipline of which she had always been so proud. In the way of a neat secretary she cleaned the spare ink from the split nib before she laid down her pen.

Twelve hundred miles away in Alexandria the newest Emperor of Rome was entertaining the ambassadors of King Vologaeses of the Parthians. For half a century the Parthians had been Rome's most dedicated enemies. Now the Parthians and this strong new Emperor were at peace. King Vologaeses had offered Vespasian forty thousand Parthian archers – an offer which he was gracefully able to refuse. In Alexandria it was a good moment. They held a lively Egyptian feast to celebrate.

Nobody noticed when amongst all the racket the Emperor paused in sudden deep stillness, as if he had heard somebody calling him.

XL

Vespasian released the cornships ahead of him in February next year, as soon as they could sail. He himself waited in Alexandria until the better weather was assured. Embassies of senators and knights frightened themselves and were seasick dashing across the Mediterranean under dark skies to court his goodwill. He received them gravely. They were impressed. They were particularly impressed to find him entertaining the fearful Parthians.

Titus returned to Judaea in April. He was Titus Caesar now. The freedman Narcissus had, after all, cultivated his dynasty. Sometimes Caenis wondered whether Narcissus had realised all along: so like the old schemer to have a second plan ready in case the first one failed.

Vespasian had shown Titus the letter from Caenis. He knew how his son would react. He explained to Titus briefly certain social facts of life. Titus said nothing. Neither of them wrote to her. Titus could not bear to. As for his father, he growled that taming an ox by telepathy was easy; women were best handled where you had space to get a rope around their horns.

Titus retorted grimly, 'Well – *you're the country boy!*'

There was unrest in Africa, which had no time for Vespasian; Africa was still in a sense bombarding him with turnips. There was an outbreak of piracy on the Black Sea which one of his lieutenants sailed to put down. There was civil war in north Britain. There was an extremely serious revolt in Germany, cleared up with good luck and some dash by Vespasian's relative Petilius Cerialis. Though they passed like a dream for Caenis, these were major events which occupied much of Vespasian's attention.

Domitian, whom she never saw nowadays, had acted as his father's representative in Rome. He made a commendable speech to the Senate, though then found himself struggling to take precedence over Mucianus who actually held the formal powers of deputy. At first Domitian conducted himself with distinction, though he overstepped the mark during the German revolt when he tried to coerce Cerialis into a conspiracy – whether against his father or his brother was typically unclear. Cerialis ignored it. Domitian was downgraded. He made himself a patron of the arts instead, a much more suitable way for an Emperor's younger son to waste his time. Vespasian was furious with his political manoeuvres, though Titus – more loyal to his brother than Domitian would ever be in return – interceded on his behalf with his usual diplomacy. Mollified, Vespasian embarked for home.

By then the Senate had awarded him in a pack all of the honours and titles which previous Emperors had assembled one by one. At this point Vespasian did not request and was not awarded a Triumph; there was an ancient rule that such honours were reserved for conquest over external enemies, not for shedding Roman blood. There would be one. There would be a Triumph for Jerusalem; that was understood. It would be awarded to Vespasian and Titus together – Titus who had worked so hard and with such grace to bring his father to the throne, and who would share the burdens of office with him from the start.

So Vespasian was coming.

Waiting for him to arrive, Rome could hardly bear the suspense. In the end crowds flocked out, some journeying many miles to meet him as he travelled up from the south. Behind them, the city lay strangely quiet. Every town on the way erupted when he arrived. In the country whole families lined his route to applaud. Even before they saw him they knew a chapter had closed. Once he appeared, they were surprised to find how good-natured the man was. People supposed becoming Emperor had changed him for the better. Caenis had always told him: people had no sense.

When Vespasian entered Rome the entire city was smothered under garlands and shimmering with incense. Caenis let all her household go to watch him arrive. She stayed at home. There was no longer Veronica to hire a balcony. Besides, any woman in the crowd who hurled her lunch at the Emperor would be strung up on a scaffold by the Praetorian Guard. Aglaus, loyal to the last, kept Caenis company. They could hear the noise in the distance throughout most of the day. Being near the Praetorian Camp made it worse. There was tremendous activity.

She knew Aglaus was frightened of what she would do. Caenis merely spring-cleaned her house.

Towards the end of the afternoon the inevitable equerry turned up. Vespasian had always been considerate. Caenis had understood there would have to be one brief skirmish: the kind gesture of recognition on his part; the formal resignation on hers.

The equerry, poor dog, was the man who had once in Greece advised the disgraced Vespasian to go to Hades. Aglaus enjoyed himself for some time over that; she could hear it going on through a half-open door.

'Must have been a sticky moment when he turned up in his nice new purple toga! What did he say to you?'

'I asked him what he wanted me to do; he said, "Oh go to Hades!" – and he grinned.'

'Neat! You'll learn to enjoy that grin. But you're working for him?'

'So far. Today he is refusing to settle new arrangements. Caused a bit of an upset, you can imagine. All those Greek eels with their neat lists hoping to wind their way into his good opinion; every one of them has been put off. They were jumpy anyway about letting Domitian take over the Palace – there's a strong indication already that papa has torn a strip off his young lordship . . . Only thing Vespasian *has* done is cancel the procedure for searching visitors; quite a few Praetorian palpitations at that! He says he wants to consult someone about the rest.' Aglaus laughed bitterly, knowing whom Vespasian used to consult on domestic matters. The equerry became more businesslike. 'Right. This won't do – better lead me to Antonia Caenis.'

'Just Caenis.'

The repartee over, Aglaus was at his most unhelpful now. Caenis smiled over the change in his tone as he erected his fences. No one would get past him.

'He wants her,' prompted the equerry.

'I shall tell her.'

'I must see her.'

'She won't see you. Listen; we expected this. You are to say: "Antonia's freedwoman thanks the Emperor for remembering her, but she is not free to come."'

The equerry was none too keen on reporting this rhetoric to a twelve-lictor general with a tricky reputation. 'I can't say that!'

'You must. So long as you don't ask him for money he doesn't bite. By the way, regarding money – you always do have to ask him, and when you do he always bites. As for this, tell him straight out – then stand back a bit just in case.'

'Oh she can't!'

'Yes she can.'

'Extraordinary woman!'

Aglaus said, 'He's an extraordinary man.'

Then it was over.

Her freedman left her a short time to compose herself, then stumped in. 'You all right?' She nodded but did not speak. 'Want anything?'

'Leave me alone.'

'Yes, madam!' He waited.

'What is it, Aglaus?'

'If you don't need me, I'll go out for a walk. As there's nothing going on here would you object if later I invited round one of my friends?'

'Do what you like,' replied Caenis drably.

She was well aware that as her slave Aglaus had felt free to consort in her kitchen with every kind of unsavoury customer. There had never been any disturbances so she had never pulled him up. He spared her the trouble of being asked for permission. Then when she gave him his freedom he had married with a promptness that informed her it was an established relationship; three children appeared overnight. She had told him she was annoyed because if she had known they existed she could have been spoiling them.

Now Caenis barked at him tetchily, 'Just do what you like.

Rome has a new emperor and its citizens can play all night.'

He returned her sourness with a short puff of laugher. 'Fun, isn't it, madam?' Later he went off, with a distinct pang of uncertainty leaving her alone in the empty house.

He was quite right: there was something Caenis intended to do.

Once all was silent Caenis rose and walked stiffly to her room. She had always hated fuss, but there was a routine she sometimes followed so for perhaps an hour she attended to her person as thoroughly as she had previously attacked her home. Even Veronica might have approved.

Her house had its own water supply, so from head to foot she washed off the grime of her day's labour. She bathed twice; Veronica had always held a theory that the first time only moved the dirt about. Slowly, thinking of Veronica, Caenis oiled her still-elastic skin. Years of sitting properly and standing well, combined with regular swimming, had preserved her figure and fine carriage. Her life had turned out much less hard than she had once imagined it must. There had been decent food, rest, time and money enough to nourish both body and soul. She had lived simply from choice but there was always rose-water and almond oil, then later perfumes and unguents that were more exotic, more expensive, more silky to apply, more agreeable and subtle to wear. She used them now, enjoying the tonic of massaged limbs, a face that felt groomed but not sticky or rigid with paint, manicured hands, clean-scented hair.

In other ways, even better ways, life had been generous. She had known contentment and a quiet mind. Whatever happened to her now, never again would she feel that tearing sense of unfulfilment she had struggled against as a young girl. She was born a slave; she won herself the rank of a Roman citizen. She had belonged to a family. Not as a slave; not as a freedwoman: in her own right she had become a Flavian.

From her fastidious wardrobe she chose a light formal gown that always made her feel graceful, which she fastened on the shoulders with two British blue-stone brooches. No

325

other jewellery . . . none at all. She held her gold bangle in her hand.

She walked back to the room where Aglaus had left her; on his eventual return he would look for her there. She sat down. It was rather like preparing to take Antonia's dictation. She cleared her mind of all thought and all pain, all prospects of the future, all yearning for the past.

She felt like Cleopatra, bereft of her Mark Antony; Caenis, who herself bore Mark Antony's name, waiting like Cleopatra for the last exulting Roman to stride into her palace and confront her. Cleopatra, robed in a blue that was clearer and deeper than gentians: Cleopatra, defeated, on the day that she died.

XLI

Rome: city of light.

Aglaus had found his friend on the Palatine. Now they were striding down from the old administrative Palace, across the eastern end of the Forum, and towards the Quirinal. They walked swiftly, for the city was humming and this was not an occasion for a quiet evening stroll. By now there were few people about. Some took no notice of the two men; others looked after them thoughtfully, as they disappeared unobtrusively, heading for the Viminal Gate.

At the Forum they had paused. They had come on to the Via Sacra just by the round Temple of Vesta with its little pointed roof and distinctive latticework. Looking to their left down the long southern edge of the Forum, past the Julian courthouse and the massive portico of the Temple of Saturn, they could see at the far end the Tabularium, solid as a harbour wall around the base of the Capitol. Above it, the brow of the hill stood shockingly altered. Gone was the glittering roof of the Temple of Jupiter; gone the Temple itself. All the buildings which clothed the lower flanks of the hill were blackened; some leaned dangerously, others were reduced to occasional half-walls upthrust in stark jags to the evening sky. To the far right beside the prison, deserted and deceptively bathed in sunlight, lay the Gemonian Steps where the bodies of dead traitors were flung.

Without a word they moved on.

It was the time of the evening that took the breath away. As the dusk fell, there was always this magical moment in Rome when the tufa blocks of the buildings and the pavements seemed to reflect their own glow, exuding an aureole of mellow golden light, faintly tinged rose, as if that light had been held back like the day's warmth within the city's stones and now slowly released itself. The freedman with the blue chin smiled.

327

A city of statues. At every crossroad, on every level, before and beside every temple, clustering around every square: faces both men knew so well they normally hardly noticed them became suddenly vivid that evening. Some tranquil eyes stared out over their heads; others followed them. The gods, the generals, the Caesars – impassive noble faces in gilded marble and bronze, soon to be joined by Vespasian's wrinkled brow and blithe expression. Catching Aglaus' thought, his companion smiled faintly too. His expression was ironical.

A city of water. The fountains played only a little sluggishly as the pressure sank after an exceptional draught of millions of gallons had been sucked from the aqueducts into the bathhouses which took priority. Fountain-spray drifted across the deserted streets in a fine haze. Occasionally as they crossed a paved-in conduit they could hear the chuckling of the water that rushed so energetically from the baths towards the mighty caverns of the main sewers.

The Romans were in their houses. After the joyous excitement of their Emperor's long-awaited entry that afternoon, only their litter remained behind in the streets. They were at home, snatching at food, loudly comparing notes on what they had managed to see. Later that night every one of them was to sit down by voting tribe and district to a thanksgiving banquet, the whole city feasting like a big cheerful family presided over by their fatherly Emperor.

Once the Emperor was known to be in residence, the city had relaxed. He would be living, since it existed, in Nero's dreadful Golden House: its hated entrance was opposite them now, studded with gemstones and glittering gold, its approach from the Forum surrounded by a triple colonnade. Nearby stood the mighty bronze Colossus: Nero in a radiate crown, dominating the skyline from every direction.

Something would have to be done about all that, Vespasian had already decreed. The extensive grounds of the Golden House must be restored as soon as possible to public use. For the rest, perhaps the best thing would be to pull it all down, fill in that vast lake, then build over the crater something for all Rome: some wonder to unite the city and excite the world . . . He and Titus could always live in the old Palace of Tiberius and Caligula. That place of tall cold corridors, rarely used staterooms, abandoned offices. And pantries.

He had asked after Caenis. He had been told what she had said.

At the Golden House, after his baggage was brought in, the Emperor had made a personal sacrifice to his household gods. 'Who arranged for my *lares* to be here?'

Standing beside him his teenaged granddaughter Flavia raged through her teeth, '*Who do you think?*'

Caenis.

Afterwards Flavia Domitilla interviewed her grandfather just long enough to accept the present he had brought her, then to inform him that in the matter of Caenis he was an unprincipled pig. The Emperor Vespasian would be famous for allowing people to be frank. 'Thanks for the opinion!' growled her grandfather to Flavia. 'Come and give me a kiss.'

'No,' said Flavia. He looked at her with mooning eyes. She knew what Caenis would say. So Flavia, who was fiercely fond of her grandpapa, gave him a pecky kiss.

Shaken, the Emperor requested a bedroom – not too fancy and nothing Nero had ever used – where before the banquet that evening he could give his elderly bones a quiet lie down. Someone with no sense asked if they should organise a girl for him. He stared.

Then the Emperor said, no thanks; he had always preferred to organise his own.

Aglaus and his friend had reached the Porta Nomentana. They walked more quickly, for here people were standing about looking curious. The Via Nomentana, home to a famous female resident, had been expecting something better than one seedy chamberlain today. In a small crowd outside the Gate there was an air of disappointment, mingled with lingering hope. Aglaus saluted those who greeted him. He seemed harassed and unfriendly. His companion, modestly smothered in an old mulberry-coloured cloak with

329

its clasp hanging off by a thread, looked endearingly shy. Behind them a dog barked, then when Aglaus spun angrily it scampered away.

Aglaus banged on the door, but although the parade was over the porter had not returned. He swore briefly, then scrambled to fetch out his own keys. He swiftly unlocked the formidable ironmongery, talking now all the time. He was beginning to feel nervous. The dead silence of the deserted house gave him an unexpected chill.

'Come in. Mind how you step. There may still be water about. You must be entering the cleanest house in Rome; try not to slip over on the tiles. Let me relieve you of that terrible cloak. Today all Rome took to the streets, but in this house we polished up our door-furniture and washed our frescos down. All Rome troops off to cheer, but our lady tucks her skirt in her belt and scrubs out the latrine. We, sir, have rearranged our sideboards, swept our steps, and poked out the nasty desiccated things that were lying in dark crevices under the beds . . .'

He lowered his voice as they crossed the atrium.

He went first. That way Caenis would have her moment of warning, his companion a moment of grace, and Aglaus his moment of fun.

'Madam?'

He opened the door to its widest extent. Amidst the quiet barley and buttermilk tones of her house, blazed one bright nub of brilliant sapphire blue. Caenis sat upright in a chair opposite the door. She was holding her plain gold bangle between her two hands in her lap. She looked as if she had a headache. Her eyes were closed. She was completely still. Someone drew a scorching breath.

At an involuntary movement, light shivered amongst the delicate scrolls of embroidery at the neck of her vivid blue robe. To have supposed her anything other than fiercely alive was to misunderstand her completely. She seemed pale, but neat, alert, ready to be marvellously truculent.

'Madam, I'd like to introduce my friend.'

She opened her eyes. She looked up. She scowled. Aglaus swallowed. The man behind him frowned.

Caenis assumed the restrained expression of a first-class secretary to whom an ill-timed request had just been made to give priority to an illegible draft many pages long. But before she could say anything, her freedman announced with a clarity that proved he had been practising: 'Antonia Caenis – here is Titus Flavius Vespasianus, Conqueror of Britain and Hero of Judaea; *Vespasianus Caesar Augustus – Consul, Chief Priest, father of his country and Emperor of Rome!*'

Her Sabine friend. She had expected him, of course.

XLII

'Hello, Caenis.'

Unsmiling, his dark gaze absorbed her.

'*Hail Caesar!*' Caenis retorted, trying not to let it sound like an insult. He received it quietly enough. After a year of Egyptian flummery, presumably he was used to it.

Caenis saw Aglaus nervously shift his weight.

'Don't worry,' Vespasian reassured him, without moving. 'The first thing she ever said to me was, "Skip over the Styx!"' From the front he was completely bald. Still, his character would always come from that light in his eyes and the handsome muscles of his face. 'As you see, I'm still here.'

'And how long,' murmured Aglaus, newly suave, 'will your Caesarship be staying?'

His Caesarship pronounced ominously: 'As long as it takes.'

Aglaus went straight out and closed the door.

'Don't get up,' he said as he paced farther in. 'I'm sick of people bobbing about.'

She did not get up. 'What are you doing here?'

He was taking off his shoes. Slowly he went to a couch. 'What are *you* doing here?'

'I live here.'

'You live with me.'

'I can't come.'

'I've come to fetch you.'

'I won't let you.'

'Overruled. Privilege of my rank!'

'Not in my house.'

'All right.' Vespasian eased himself on to the couch where he reclined on his elbow. 'I've brought nothing to eat since you'll be coming to dinner. Titus sent some Persian slippers; your freedman has those in case you decide to wear them

332

tonight. When you come you'll find a great bale of Tyrian silk, some crystal from Ptolomaïs, and one or two decent books I found for you in Alexandria. Plus – if you want it – a ravenous appetite for taking you to bed.'

Their eyes locked for an interesting moment.

'You don't want it,' he observed, testing her. She did. He knew she did.

He could not waste time. The Praetorians would soon come crawling through the city nosing after their lost charge before they became a laughing stock. He had stolen his last stroll as a private citizen. Emperors could never slope off by themselves.

'Now! Is this about Berenice? Want me to explain?'

Caenis was torn between relief, pride, and sheer nastiness. 'No thanks; I am expertly briefed: *At Caesarea Philippi after reducing Jotapata, Vespasian was entertained by King Agrippa – and his sister.* High standards of entertainment at Caesarea Philippi! If you must tangle with a slut, dear, it may as well be one crusted with emeralds and decently crowned. They tell me she's forty but ravishing.'

He actually laughed. It was a soft, engaging laugh, with her and not against her. 'Oh she's a lovely girl!' he exclaimed laconically.

Caenis became furiously sarcastic: 'And Titus admires her too? What a positive sense of family she has! . . . I'm sorry.' She hated to quarrel.

'Fair enough.' So did he.

'Oh you're so understanding I could spit!'

Suddenly Caenis found she did not care about Berenice. Titus was supposed to be seriously in love with the woman; best leave it at that. There would be enough to do trying to ensure that that damned romantic Titus was not too badly hurt.

Of course, worrying about the Emperor's son was not for her.

She was squinting at Vespasian's feet. Everyone knew he had stopped an arrow at the seige of Jotapata. There had been so much blood and pain he had fainted, then the army panicked until Titus galloped up distraught, thinking him dead. Now Vespasian raised one foot quietly so she could inspect the healed scar. She realised it was unlikely Queen Berenice had been able to conduct two separate conversations with him at the same time. He was a very private man.

He was staring at her. Caenis glared back. He was vividly tanned. He was covered with purple – gaudy folds of the stuff drooping almost to the floor – and so stiff with padded gold she could hardly take it in. Embroidered acanthus leaves writhed about his neck. Her familiar friend had become something abominable. Thank the gods he had left his wreath behind; she could not have stomached the sight of him ceremonially crowned.

Yet he looked utterly right. He was matter-of-fact in his new splendour, slightly rumpled after a long day, and ignoring the effect he must know all that colour and bullion braid would make. This was the man for Rome. Rome looked to this man, and his gifted sons, for common sense and stability. Rome would not be disappointed: a quiet life with high taxes, business moving in the lawcourts and smart new civic buildings. Order in the provinces and fine wares in the marketplace. Oratory valued, but philosophy too dangerous: old-fashioned public service virtues. Music and the arts modestly encouraged. Plenty of work for schoolteachers, accountants and engineers. Decent statues set up in safe clean streets to an amiable emperor whose way of life would be notorious only for its simplicity.

None of the Caesars had ever kept a concubine. Yet after the antics of the Claudians, would anybody notice? Would anybody care?

They were silent together, as only friends can be. The longer he stayed with her the more difficult parting would be, yet Caenis felt calmed by his presence in a way she had not dared to expect. It was impossible to pretend to feel hostility. Between them lay too great a legacy of frankness in the past.

Vespasian was remembering that astrologer at the Theatre of Balbus who said her face could never be upon the coinage. On the obverse the old man, grinning with embarrassment; flip over – only some suitable religious scene: Mars perhaps, or Fortune. He needed a great coin issue; soon have to decide its design.

Not Caenis; no. Thinking of all the prinked madams who did make it through the mint – Messalina with corrugated rolls of hair all across her great fat head, or starched Livia with her long nose and that wild squint, or worst, Agrippina – he was glad. Caenis would never belong in that mad company. Besides, no dye-cutter could catch her character. And he would not like to see her debased, reduced, diminished to some staring nag in an improbable coiffure: Caenis slipping through the filthy fingers of fishmongers and fornicators; Caenis dropped down drains at all the outposts of the Empire; Caenis cemented under the footings of every barracks and basilica.

Yet the man in the booth had known it; she was his life's true reverse.

'So much to tell you!' His voice was soft. Spotting her stiff look, he added wryly, 'And no doubt one or two points of order you intend putting to me.'

Certainly: Cremona; the Flavian generals; Domitian; Sabinus; whatever Vespasian could have imagined he was doing when he let himself be lured into faith-healing at Alexandria . . . Caenis said none of it. For one thing, he knew. For another, he probably agreed with her.

'I'm a republican,' she told him.

'Every Caesar should keep one,' he returned patiently.

'I shall always say what I think.'

'Wonderful –' He moved abruptly. 'Look at me, Caenis! Just look, will you? Well?'

'What?' She pretended she could not fathom him. She noticed there were laughter lines, seamed white by the desert sun, at the corners of his eyes. 'What?' she demanded again gruffly, though she knew.

'Look here! This man collapsed on your couch is Vespasian – older, balder, paunchier, a little more scratchy and a great deal more slow. Tired out with grief and sick of Eastern food, yet your man . . . Why won't you come?' he asked, and his tone dropped.

'You would be disgraced –'

'You're worth it.'

'Oh stop staring!'

'Stop ranting! I'm just looking at you. Such a relief to be in the same room again. See you. Hear your voice . . . To wonder which of us will win.'

'You're enjoying this.'

'Of course. Been longing for a wrangle with you.' Caenis was blindingly tired. She knew he could see it. He was offering to let her bury her weariness in him. 'Your house was always so wonderfully peaceful, lass . . . You look all in; have you had anything to eat today?'

'No.'

He was reaching for the handbell but she stopped him with a violent shake of her head. He gave her a look that said she would dine decently tonight if he had to grip her jaws and post in the food like feeding medicine to a sick dog. Caenis stared down at the floor. When she looked up again Vespasian mouthed her a kiss like some liquid-eyed lad lounging on the steps of a temple annoying female passers-by. She could not help it; she blushed.

'You had better go,' she told him. 'The banquet.'

He shrugged. He stopped flirting and became more businesslike. 'Entirely up to you. If you don't want to go, we'll just have a quiet night in. I don't mind. Might as well enjoy my position. Entire city reclines at table formally, only to be told: the Emperor is having a bite of supper at home instead. Don't suppose they'll mind either, so long as they all get a nice slice of goose in sesame sauce and a pomegranate to take home.'

He was being ridiculous. Caenis ignored him.

He waited a short time then tried again. 'Caenis; don't renege. I never asked you, "Live with me just until something better crops up."'

'No. No; you were always generous to me. Don't worry; I won't grizzle or throw vases or make you watch me cry –'

'No,' he answered bleakly. 'I remember that. But don't you know, your stricken face haunted me for twenty years?'

Caenis thought she knew. 'I forgot to say,' she murmured, soothing him because he was upset, 'you may of course keep

336

my set of silver knives.'

'Oh thanks! Those were all I was worrying about.' She saw him sigh slightly, still in a low mood. She gazed at him with smiling eyes until she knew he had rallied because he exclaimed, with one of his surges of energy, 'Caenis, stop clinging to your rock like a stubborn winkle! Lass, you have your fixed view of what you are allowed – not much. An emperor invites you to dinner with all Rome, and you have to prove that you're still down-to-earth by cleaning out the lavatory yourself!'

'I keep a tidy house,' she muttered defiantly.

'You'll keep a tidy palace.'

'After four emperors in eighteen months I dread to think what's clogging up the drains.'

'Don't bring it to show me, that's all I ask –' He leant towards her more urgently since she had hinted at the possibility she might be there. 'I want you to come – you must come!'

'The Emperor commands!'

'Don't be ridiculous; I was always polite to you.'

Caenis was running out of strength.

She took a deep breath. She told him bluntly she did not want to lurk at his Palace in some dark nook across a cold corridor, the sorry embarrassment from his past that he was too kind-hearted to shed. This dramatic declaration which she had been practising in her head for a year now rang less nobly than she had always hoped.

Vespasian had been listening noncommittally but he became more agitated suddenly. 'Oh I know all *that*! I've known you a long time.' He shifted like some restless lion before the opening of the amphitheatre cages. 'How do you intend I shall manage?' he mocked curtly. 'Take on some slovenly cow who lies in bed with a couple of charioteers all day, then spends her nights watching tragic actors guzzling off my best plate and vomiting in the fountains afterwards? A prudish stick whose interest in politics means murdering me? Some wondrous little teenager with big breasts and melting eyes who'll present me rather unexpectedly with twins? Or maybe those pimps in charge of the Emperor's pins and pots that I seem to have inherited can fix me a new girl every day, every hour if the correspondence can spare me and my stamina holds out. What a glorious position for a man to be in. I can have any woman that I want in the world; I can have them all!'

With this final explosion of satire, he collapsed. He was himself. 'It won't do. I'm a plain man; Rome must take me as I am.' His eyes softened; Caenis closed hers, set-faced. She heard him laughing. 'I remember you looking just like that one night, standing in the street – we had nowhere else to go – raving that you *liked* me; all the time you were absolutely terrified I was going to jump on you and rape you against a house-wall – and to tell the truth, I wanted you so badly I was terrified I would!'

'I was just a slave; why didn't you?' Caenis asked coldly.

'Same reason you were saying no.' Their eyes met. 'Forget the rules,' he said. 'We share our lives; we are a partnership; that is our way.'

Caenis protested hoarsely, 'Oh Vespasian, you *cannot*!'

The Emperor adopted the formal air of a man who was about to make a speech. 'Lady, there are only two things that I cannot do. You are a freedwoman; I am not allowed to marry you. Nor, therefore, can I make you an empress. You may never be Caenis Augusta; when we're dead you will not be invited by the Senate to join me as a god: neither of us takes *that* seriously – nor, I suspect, do the gods! But you were born in that Palace a slave; you shall rule it. You who were once Caesar's possession shall live equal to a Caesar of your own. I can give you no titles but while I live, Antonia Caenis, Caenis my darling, you shall have the state, the place, the position, the respect . . . No dark nooks in corridors. Our terms were to go side by side.'

It was a good speech. Caenis replied from a gentle heart, 'We never had terms. You and I never sank to that. You and I managed with trust, decency, fondness for each other's quaint ways – and in a real crisis the fact, O my Caesar, that you owed me ten thousand sesterces!'

Unintentionally she had reminded him. At once he rose and came a little way towards her. He pegged something solemnly under a lamp, then whistled quietly. 'Don't argue. That's my banker's draft for you. No more votes for you to buy. I need four hundred million sesterces to put the Empire back on its feet but that can be arranged without your nest-egg now!'

Caenis was curious to know how a man who never managed to make any money for himself planned to find four hundred million sesterces for the State. His eyes gleamed, longing to explain. Vespasian's father was a tax collector; Rome had forgotten that.

'You and I are square, lass. I pay my debts and I don't forget. Caenis, you have such faith in the public man: trust the private man too.'

She did. They were one. They laughed at the same things, grew angry at the same time, scoffed at hypocrisy in the same tone of voice. They were comfortable together; they were close. Their daily lives ran at the same pace. After four years away, the world and their own lives in upheaval, he had walked through that door – and really, neither of them needed to say anything at all.

She sat riveted by the banker's draft. The fact that Flavius Vespasianus owed her money had always been her lifeline; it kept one notional tie between them whatever else occurred. They did not need it any longer.

A yard away, he was waiting. The room had become very quiet.

'Caenis, you daft old woman, be gracious to a poor old man.'

'Is it what you really want?'

'Yes. Oh yes!'

'Why?'

'You know very well why.' He seemed to have been saying that to her for years. Her chin lifted, telling him so. When for once he decided to explain, it was without fuss or drama: 'I love you. I always did. I always will.'

Caenis could not answer him.

It seemed to Vespasian there was something wrong with her face. Her mouth had set in an odd line; her eyes were squeezed too tightly closed. It was so strange he felt tem-

339

porarily crippled by doubt. Caenis held out her hand to him, helpless to reassure him any other way. He had never seen her cry before.

In amazement he flung open his arms. 'Oh my poor lass!' The first sob, restricted for so long, hurt her throat. She was on her feet. With one stride he clamped her in a great, comforting imperial embrace. 'Come here; come here to me –' He was wresting his bangle from her hand to slide it back over her wrist into its proper place. That she had taken it off must have been bothering him ever since he came in. '*Oh Caenis, my dear love!*'

He meant it. He had meant it all along. She bruised her forehead on the padded bosses of his rich embroidery.

People had come. Outside the door there were the restless shuffles and chinks of the Emperor's retinue filling her hall, parking their spears against her furniture and crowding down her passageways . . . the floors hardly dry and big men in gigantic boots trampling all over them. Vespasian ignored it. They could hear Aglaus in ecstatic form, giving the Palace rankers a good ear-bashing. Twelve lictors leant on their axes and wilted before his scintillating sarcasm. Praetorian Guards braced themselves for backchat while their centurion of the day felt the perspiration running helplessly between the cheek-guard of his helmet and his rigid jaw. Litter-bearers were wetting themselves with worry out on the public road; secretaries flexed their note tablets; a chamberlain with high blood pressure prepared to expire against the old fern tub on the step. The Emperor's chief wardrobe master had brought – upon a tiny crimson cushion with four slithery silken tassels – the Emperor's missing wreath.

'There,' chortled Vespasian, aware of it all and yet oblivious. 'Oh love; if it's all too much for you, however do you imagine that I feel? Blow your nose on the purple; never mind if the dye runs. You cry. Cry on the most important shoulder in the world; snuffle all over the silly gold braid.'

'The wretched stuff will go green –' She knew about imperial embroidery.

She raised her damp face. The man she had loved all her

life sniffed slightly himself just before he grinned. He was just the same. 'Look – we'll have to go now.'

Caenis was still crying.

'That's settled then. So are you ever,' enquired Vespasian curiously, 'going to condescend to kiss the Emperor of Rome?'

She stopped crying. She wished she had thought of it before. 'Titus,' she said, as if she had just remembered to welcome him home. 'Titus – oh Titus, I'm so glad to see you!'

She waited until he had finished drying her face on the rather prickly edge of the imperial gown. It took some time because Vespasian was a soldier, so he carried out practical tasks with textbook thoroughness. Of all the luxuries she would be able to command, none would equal the careful attentions of those big familiar hands.

Then Caenis kissed the Emperor. She kissed him as fiercely as she had kissed him once before, intending the man to realise *exactly* how she felt. Enjoying it immensely, he allowed her to finish then this time kissed her back, with a tenderness that balanced her defiance and a glint in his eye that promised more to come. For a moment they stood locked together, sharing their own deep companionship and peace.

'There's no winner,' Caenis told him.

He laughed. 'No contest! You always were a challenge; that was understood. Now come home to your palace, lass, and dine in state with me!'

From the day Caenis met him, she had known what he might be. 'You will be Caesar. And I –'

He gave her a tolerant look. 'You will be Caesar's lady,' said the Emperor Vespasian.

HISTORICAL FOOTNOTE

The political events in this story are true.

Vespasian ruled the Empire for ten years. He died of natural causes and was succeeded by each of his sons in turn. Although Domitian became a tyrant who was murdered by members of his own household, the Flavian dynasty had long before then re-established peace and prosperity, making possible the Golden Age of the Second Century when the Roman Empire's political and cultural achievements were to reach their height.

Caenis lived with the Emperor for the rest of her life.

THE POWER OF READING

Visit the Random House website and get connected with information on all our books and authors

EXTRACTS from our recently published books and selected backlist titles

COMPETITIONS AND PRIZE DRAWS Win signed books, audiobooks and more

AUTHOR EVENTS Find out which of our authors are on tour and where you can meet them

LATEST NEWS on bestsellers, awards and new publications

MINISITES with exclusive special features dedicated to our authors and their titles

READING GROUPS Reading guides, special features and all the information you need for your reading group

LISTEN to extracts from the latest audiobook publications

WATCH video clips of interviews and readings with our authors

RANDOM HOUSE INFORMATION including advice for writers, job vacancies and all your general queries answered

Come home to Random House

www.randomhouse.co.uk